Praise for
Mortal Love

"*Mortal Love* is at once a painting in prose, an investigation into artistic obsession, and a re-evaluation. . . . Negotiates cleverly between its twentieth-century and Victorian time frames, embroiling us in a rich stew of lost artworks, the folklore behind them, and (merely glimpsed) the reality behind that folklore. . . . All these conspire to give *Mortal Love* a satisfying, story-rich texture. . . . Ambitious and richly imagined . . . offers its readers the satisfactions of a detective thriller. Here, however, the mystery goes deeper than murder. Nothing, Hand convinces us, is quite as mysterious as art." —*Washington Post Book World*

"A literary page-turner . . . deeply pleasurable. . . . Hand ambitiously (and deftly) explores the complex connection between art and madness, sex and death, love and mortality. . . . Hand's lushly worded tale is consistently gripping. . . . *Mortal Love* inhabits a world between reason and insanity—it's a delightful waking dream." —*People* magazine (four stars)

"A brilliant novel like Elizabeth Hand's recent *Mortal Love* deserves all the readers it can get." —Michael Durda, *Washington Post Book World*

"Superb. . . . Hand does a marvelous job of making the ineffable tangible, lacing her tale with references to the work of artists ranging from Algernon Swinburne to Kurt Cobain and capturing the intense emotions of her characters in exquisitely sculpted prose. . . . With its authentic period detail and tantalizing spirit of mystery, this timeless tale of desire and passion should reach many readers."

—*Publishers Weekly* (starred review)

"The novel succeeds as both a thriller and a meditation on the mysterious nature of inspiration." —*Village Voice*

"An original work of considerable sensuous force . . . great fun, in an impressive synthesis of bygone times and forgotten lore."

—*Kirkus Reviews* (starred review)

"*Mortal Love* is bewitching, sexy, creepy, and, under all, dazzlingly romantic. . . . You can read *Mortal Love* to delve into its layers of meaning, and relationship to folklore and creativity, and history of what-have-you, if you are stuffy. Or you can just grab on to the greenness of it, swing through time and across landscape, and watch what Hand and her red-haired madwoman are really up to." —*Detroit Free Press*

"One of the most sheerly impressive, not to mention overwhelmingly beautiful, books I have read in a long time. . . . Quite clearly, it is the product of an exceptionally gifted writer using her mind and heart to blast through every limitation or restriction or sense of caution that she ever had, writing as if to create her own life. I think she has written the best book of her generation." —Peter Straub

"Elizabeth Hand combines wonderful eloquence and historical imagination with an immediate access to the primal sources of story: longing and dread. Wholly different from the common run of fiction that touches on her themes, *Mortal Love* provides all the shuddery pleasures as well. Don't turn the pages too fast—if you can help it." —John Crowley

"A wonderfully Gothic atmosphere, with lush visual imagery and rich poetic language." —*Library Journal*

"Elizabeth Hand is a writer whose vision, and whose writing into that extraordinary vision of hers, is exceptional. With *Mortal Love* she proves herself, in a fictional moment for all of us to savor and be smitten by, a writer who's gone beyond, into somewhere wonderful. Read this."

—Bradford Morrow

Annie Higbee/Imageveright

About the Author

A *New York Times* notable and multiple award-winning author, ELIZABETH HAND has written seven novels, including the cult classic *Waking the Moon*, and short-story collections. She is a longtime contributor to numerous publications, including *Washington Post Book World* and the *Village Voice Literary Supplement*. She and her two children divide their time between the coast of Maine and North London.

ALSO BY ELIZABETH HAND

Mortal Love

Elizabeth Hand

HARPER
PERENNIAL

HARPER ● PERENNIAL

FIRST HARPER PERENNIAL EDITION PUBLISHED 2005.

Designed by Nicola Ferguson

The Library of Congress has catalogued the hardcover edition as follows:

Hand, Elizabeth.
    Mortal love : a novel / Elizabeth Hand.—1st ed.
      p. cm.
    ISBN 0-06-105170-5
    1. Creation (Literary, artistic, etc.)—Fiction.   2. London (England)—Fiction.
3. New York (N.Y.)—Fiction.   4. Artists—Fiction.   I. Title.

PS3558.A4619M67 2004
813'.54—dc22

                              2003062398

ISBN-10: 0-06-075534-2 (pbk.)
ISBN-13: 978-0-06-075534-8 (pbk.)

05 06 07 08 09 ❖/RRD 10 9 8 7 6 5 4 3 2 1

"If we shadows have offended,
Think but this, and all is mended,
That you have but slumber'd here
While these visions did appear."

As fire burns the leaf
and out of the green appears
the vein in the center line
and the legend veins under there,

So, the world happens twice—
once what we see it as;
second it legends itself
deep, the way it is.

—*William Stafford,* "Bi-Focal"

During the night, if another world enters the one in which
we ordinarily live, we call it a dream. When it enters in
daylight, we often call it illness.

—*Robert Shuman*

Painters are apt to end pessimists.

—*Hope Mirrlees,* Lud-in-the-Mist

Contents

Contents

Acknowledgments

I thank the Maine Arts Commission and the National Endowment for the Arts for a grant that helped make this work possible.

Eternal gratitude to my agent, Martha Millard, still sole proprietor of the world's only full-service literary agency. My heartfelt thanks to my editor, Diana Gill, and to Jennifer Brehl, both of Morrow; and to my former editor, Caitlin Blasdell, who read the earliest draft of this manuscript.

During the last five years, a number of people read various versions of this book, under its various titles, and offered suggestions to improve it. I owe a profound debt to Peter Straub, John Clute, Bob Morales, Paul Witcover, Bill Sheehan, Eddie O'Brien, Ellen Datlow, Christopher Schelling, and especially John Crowley.

My friend Ben Smith offered help and encouragement in a dark time. He didn't live to see this book completed, but I wouldn't have finished it without him.

Judith Clute offered round-the-clock assistance with fact checking on London. Mike Harrison helped me with the proper terminology to describe the Cornish cliffs near Tintagel. Judith Beale offered a portal into Highbury Fields, Anne Wittman one into Muswell Hill. My love and thanks to them, and to my other friends and extended family in North London, for sharing their time and knowledge with me. Most of all, my love and gratitude to John Clute, my compass in Camden Town, North Penwith, and beyond.

Mortal Love is an imaginary tree with roots in the real world. There is a seemingly infinite amount of information in written and illustrative form relating to the members of the Pre-Raphaelite Brotherhood and their circle. Whenever possible, I drew on primary sources and contemporary accounts, including Georgiana Burne-Jones's *Memorials of Edward Burne-Jones,* Algernon Swinburne's collected letters, *The Home Life of Swinburne* by Clara Watts-Dunton, and the correspondence of John and Effie Ruskin and J. E. Millais compiled in Mary Lutyens's *Millais and the Ruskins,* among many others. Gay Daly's *Pre-Raphaelites in Love* and the work of Jan Marsh, including *Pre-Raphaelite Women,* provided invaluable insights into the distaff side of the PRB. John M. MacGregor's *The Discovery of the Art of the Insane* opened a window for me many years ago, as has his subsequent work on visionary artists. For information on nineteenth-century madhouses in the United Kingdom, I have drawn from the work of Janet Oppenheimer, Ellen Dwyer, Andrew Scull, and W. F. Bynum, among others. For more information about the Victorian fascination with fairies, I recommend Carole G. Silver's *Strange and Secret Peoples* and *Victorian Fairy Painting,* the catalog of a 1999 show at the Royal Academy. For biographical details of the great fairy painter Richard Dadd, I am indebted to Patricia Allderidge's *The Late Richard Dadd* and *Richard Dadd: The Rock and Castle of Seclusion,* by David Greysmith. Richard M. Dorson's *The British Folklorists: A History* is an interesting account of various folklorists, including Lady Wilde and Andrew Lang.

The tale of Queen Herla ("The dog has not jumped down yet") is adapted from "Queen Herla," derived from Walter Map's *De Nugis Curialium,* and recorded by Katherine Briggs in volume 1 of *A Dictionary of British Folk-Tales.* There are several versions of the Wooing of Etain, including one recorded by Lady Gregory and another by Lady Wilde.

Excerpts from "Kyng Orfew" are from the version in *The Breton Lays in Middle English,* edited by Thomas C. Rumble. Any errors or omissions are strictly my own and will be corrected in future editions.

For more information, visit my website, Winterlong: www.elizabeth hand.com.

Part One

The Green Girl

———◇———

In 1839 there was published a Method of Designating Colors as a
solution of the problem proposed by the first chairman of the
Inter-Society Color Council, E. N. Gathercoal, who said,
"A means of designating colors . . . is desired; such designation
to be sufficiently standardized as to be acceptable and usable by
Science, sufficiently broad to be appreciated and used by Science,
Art, and Industry, and sufficiently commonplace to be understood,
at least in a general way, by the whole public."

Under proper conditions the color names agree well with
common usage. Use of other light sources will yield object
colors not correctly described by these names.
—*The Inter-Society Color Council Method of Designating Colors*

CHAPTER ONE

Lost on Both Sides

T**he letter was written in German.** Learmont recognized the hand as that of Dr. Hoffmann, head physician at the mental hospital in Frankfurt—his friend and colleague, a man who had played host to him three decades earlier, in 1842. Since then their friendship had been maintained exclusively through correspondence, despite Hoffmann's written adjurations that Learmont was always welcome at his home, and that Hoffmann's wife, Therese, wished to be remembered to him with all good grace, and (more recently) that the three Hoffmann children were now no longer children but themselves nearly as old as the two physicians had been when first they met.

We would not recognize each other now, Thomas my friend, read Learmont. *I pray that Time has been gentler to you than it has been to those poor souls in my care.*

Learmont lifted his head to gaze out the window of the inn where he was staying, near Wallingham in Northumberland. Sleet spattered the stony path that traversed a long incline toward the moors, all but invisible behind a shifting veil of gray and white. *We would not recognize each other now.* Thomas Learmont thought wryly that quite the opposite was true: Hoffmann would have no trouble at all recognizing his old friend, because in thirty years Learmont had aged not a whit. With a sigh he glanced back down at the letter.

It is a distressing topic I now wish to draw to your attention, dear Thomas, and a puzzling one. I know that you recall many years hence asking me to inform you if ever one of my female patients should exhibit certain traits, of which you have long made practice of examining and treating. My own hospital continues to deal first and foremost with children and young persons whose infirmities cause them great turmoil as they forge their ways into respectability. So it was these five months past that a young woman was commended into my care by an acquaintance who requested that I not question him as to his relationship with her. I think you will understand my meaning here. My friend is a composer, promising though not well known, and this woman had sought him out after hearing a recital of his music at a small party. She gave her name as Isolde, but my friend said this was a romantic affectation, that as a child she had seen the modern opera performed—a wicked parental betrayal if true!—and that her Christian name was Marta.

She had no family in Frankfurt. She told me first that she had been abandoned by a married lover (as indeed she had) but at other times suggested that she had in fact abandoned her own husband. She certainly suffered from *dementia praecox* and seemed to be arrested in that state between maidenhood and womanhood, when girls are most at risk of falling prey to their latent impulses.

She displayed clear signs of inversion; sometimes her facial appearance seemed quite frankly masculine, a puzzling anomaly for which I could find no explanation. Her behavior toward me was wanton, and I administered hydrotherapy hoping to cure it. It was during this treatment that her behavior grew markedly more extreme, and put me in mind of writing to you.

She did not resist her hours in the bathing-closet, nor did she indicate in any way that she noticed when the temperature of the shower-hoses changed, from frigid to hot. Rather, she *spoke* to the water, and when I began to make note of her conversation, it grew clear that she imagined herself to be an Undine. As in the verses—*Know you the Nixies, so strange and so fair? Black their eyes and green their hair . . .*

Learmont felt a familiar pounding in his chest, the taste of green apple on his tongue, the sound of wind in the leaves.

Again, I must point to the danger that the fantasias of Opera sometimes present to the female temperament! Her ravings indicated that she alternately viewed me as her husband, her lover, and her gaoler: not uncommon when dealing with such women *in extremis*. On the fourth day, her behavior in the bathing-closet became so extreme that I was forced to administer a sedative.

Learmont hurriedly turned to the last page.

. . . continued to administer the sedative cure. This arrested her behavior, but she grew increasingly listless.

I had begun an earlier draft of this letter to you, Thomas, in hopes of enlisting your opinion and perhaps your services, when very early yesterday morning the matron woke me in my bed at home, screaming that the hospital was ablaze. With all haste I returned, to find that the building—thank God!—was not ablaze, but only a single room. This was the cell to which Marta had been appointed.

And in which, alas, she perished! And not alone, for in the room I discovered the charred corpse of another patient. The night matron insisted there had been no candle or lantern left in the room and that the man must have brought one with him.

I spent many hours sifting through the remains, but of the

girl found nothing except her shoes. I have yet to learn whether a key was stolen by the man with her or if the girl herself somehow granted him entry. He was a harmless fellow, given to fanciful writings which I enjoyed, and sadly his stories all seem to have perished with him, as I found no sign of his papers in his cell.

Marta's fate serves to illustrate too clearly the fury which base passion arouses in the female, if untempered by mother-love or the steadying embrace of a husband. Reimerich Kinder-lieb might have found some grim humor in her fate, but I do not! My friend's grief was well salted with guilt when I brought the news to him. I could give him nothing but the poor girl's shoes and a box of ashes which he has pledged to throw into the river.

So, my old friend, I deeply regret that I could not share this opportunity for you to expand upon your studies of female alienism, and perhaps effect a cure. I hope my failure will not hinder you from calling me Friend, who has remained one for these thirty years, though at much distance. I continue to read with great interest the articles you have sent me from your London Folk-Lore Society, though I translate them slowly and with I am sure some amusing results. I pray that God keep you in His grace, and that before we are both given to Him we may one day raise voices in laughter together, as we did so long ago.

Ever Yours Sincerely,
Heinrich Hoffmann

Learmont set the pages aside. His hand shook as he wiped the corner of his eye.

Gone again.

As a boy he had been entrusted with a young brachet while his father and the other men went hunting. Thomas had taken the dog to the top of a hill overlooking the river. The dog was untrained, so restive it seemed in danger of choking itself upon its leather leash as it yanked the boy through stands of alder and gorse. He had begged for the chance to go with his father, just as he had begged for the dog.

But by the end of several hours, he hated the animal, a loathing mixed with pity, that it should be so stupid, and helpless, and utterly dependent upon a hapless, exhausted boy. He remembered standing atop the hill, the brachet wheezing and making a horrible gargling sound as it strained at the lead, while the summer sun slid down to meet the river below. When he finally opened his fingers and let go the lead, the dog shot off, yelping joyfully. And Learmont felt a sickly exultation, knowing that he had been the cause of its torment as well as of its release, knowing he would be punished when his father returned—the brachet would, no doubt, tangle itself upon an overhanging limb and die.

He ran down the hill in pursuit, but it was too late, the brachet's yelps were lost in the twilight sounds of water gurgling, wood doves calling, the distant music of hounds and men. He had found an oak near the river's edge and thrown himself on the moss beneath to await his father's return.

Now, at the inn, Learmont felt the same way: feverish, his blood roiling. He thought of poor Hoffmann holding a pair of smoking shoes and laughed out loud, then reached for the shears in his back trouser pocket.

You are very young, the woman by the river had said to him. He had fallen asleep, and for a moment thought she was his mother, before remembering that his mother was dead. *You are very young,* she said again, wonderingly, then knelt to lay her head in his lap, undoing his breeches with long thin fingers.

Gone gone, he thought, and savagely began to cut Hoffmann's letters to shreds. A tallow candle guttered in a tin holder at his elbow; when the desk was littered with strips of paper, he began to feed them, in twos and threes, to the flame.

He had come to Wallingham to see another acquaintance, the poet Swinburne, but Swinburne, too, was gone, to London. Ashes settled in drifts upon the desk; Learmont swept his hand across the surface, scattering them. He lifted one hand and held it above the candle, then slowly lowered it until the flame seared his palm. He held it there, his arm rigid and the smell of singed meat filling the chamber. Finally he gave a small gasp and let his arm fall heavily to the table. The flame flickered but did not go out: a bead of translucent fat trickled from the candle to the tabletop. Learmont turned his hand back and forth, gently tugging at the sleeve of his cotton shirt to reveal an arm latticed with older scars, red and pale blue, ice white, petal-shaped scars like the one that bloomed upon his palm and others that formed the fan-shaped imprints of a hand.

He would find her. He would go to London and seek her there, question his associates at the Folk-Lore Society and the Metropolitan Lunacy Commission.

No sooner had the thought come to him than he knew she would go there, too; though she would take care to avoid Bethlem Hospital. She would seek out Swinburne or someone like him; pounce on him like an owl upon a vole, then spread her wings looking for other prey. She would travel more swiftly than Learmont, and she would travel unknown: he must leave immediately.

Learmont lowered his head and licked his palm, the skin fiery beneath his tongue. Then he retrieved his long-handled shears and slipped them into his trouser pocket, gathered his few things, and went to arrange for a coach.

Several weeks passed. Now it was December, and the nights seemed endless, especially in North London. On a narrow street, the poet Swinburne stood, swaying slightly with drink and excitement.

" 'Red, red blude,' " he sang aloud, and laughed. He had just come from a gathering of the Cannibal Club at Bartolini's, where they had raised a toast to Burton, exiled to Trieste, and Swinburne had to hold his nose to keep from expiring in laughter at a rude joke played upon their waiter. After the meal he had wanted to walk, alone—he loved walking—and so he'd wandered for hours until he made his way here, through the warren of streets that separated Islington's army of black-clad clerks from their places of employment in the City.

As he walked the poet talked to himself. " 'There's nothing foul that we commit/But what we write and what we shit./There's nothing reeks that can't be shunt/Between the arsehole and the cunt./There's nothing . . .' "

The clerks had with the evening dispersed, to bleak terraces asquall with infants and the unceasing gravel cough of London's poor. The yellow-green night haze bore the charnel stink of the great river, two miles southward. From Highbury Fields came the sound of the steam fair's carousel and the cries of children. Swinburne walked and talked, arms swinging wildly, making queer pinwheeling pirouettes into the street at the approach of another pedestrian and giving a shrill paroquet squawk of dismay or amusement. Now and then he would produce a silver flask of brandy—a legacy of Burton's—and open it to wave beneath his nostrils, as though it were a nosegay that might drive away the pervasive stink of frying fish. Then he would drink, and weave on through the shadows of the long winter dusk.

He was a small man, his elfin face and ginger hair already graying from drink; so small that one might almost mistake him for a foot soldier in the legion of women—laundresses, prostitutes, children—who made a Sunday of Mondays, giving themselves over to such drunken excess that more than once he had to step over a figure sprawled insensible across the path, her face smeared with filth and her petticoats smelling of vomit and semen.

" '. . . nothing fair lies in the muck/That we won't meet, then mount and fuck. . . .' "

He giggled, his laughter rising to a shriek as he saw ahead of him a signpost swinging in front of a corner gin mill. The carved plank showed the image of two hands, each holding a glass, and below them a font of white spume.

THE EVERLASTING ARMS
St. Drustan's Well

"Saints bugger me, bugger me," Swinburne sang, then stopped.

Beneath the sign stood a woman. She wore a heavy wool mantle over a stiff black silk dress, good fabric though frayed; a housekeeper's garb. She had neither bonnet nor kerchief; her graying hair was tightly pulled back above a high smooth forehead. As Swinburne approached, she did not look away but lifted her head to meet his gaze.

"Medusa!" shrieked Swinburne, and clapped his hands against his cheeks. "Swine swan! Such a thing, poor thing!"

Her lower jaw was gone, eaten away so that a spur of soft-looking black bone remained, like a bit of charred wood. But her eyes were sly and mocking, a pellucid blue in the thin light cast by the window of the Everlasting Arms, and her voice was sweet and coaxing.

"My mistress said I should meet you here, sir."

"Mistress! Monstrous!" Swinburne pulled his cloak tight, peering at her. "Phossy jaw? Poor Flossie."

His hand reached for a coin to give her—he was a kind man, especially in his cups—but the woman shook her head, sliding forward to grasp his wrist. The poet snatched away his hand. The woman laughed.

"No money, sir—just follow me—"

Her hands slipped back beneath her cloak; he noted that she did not wear gloves, but not that her fingernails had the deep-blue glow of a lit gas mantle.

"Follow you?" he asked.

"Yes." She tilted her head so that he had a clear view of her ruined face. Swinburne swallowed, thinking of the pain she must endure, felt a flicker of desire, and without a word nodded. The woman stepped into the street. With a quick look over her shoulder, she fled down an alley, so narrow the protruding gables of the structures fronting it met and blotted out what remained of twilight.

Swinburne followed, the sound of her feet echoing before him. The alley twisted and twisted; with each turn it grew narrower, darker. The cobblestones gave way to gravel, then packed earth, and finally a mire of mud and dead grass that stank of the boghouse. He was in a tunnel now, a channel through which the New River had once flowed in wooden pipes, supported by an aqueduct that had long since decayed to skeletal timbers and disintegrating mats of weeds. A few feet ahead of him, the woman halted.

"I'll tell her you've come," she said, then turned and disappeared into a shadowy recess.

"Bumstick!" The poet flailed at the air, cursing and laughing. "Phossy's made a fool of me! Come back, dear—"

He was reaching for his brandy flask when he heard a rustling in the darkness.

"I know the way," said a soft voice.

The poet looked up. In the middle of the passage stood a man holding a lantern. "Swinburne," the man said. "I am Jacobus Candell. We have met before, do you recall? Three years ago, an afternoon at my patron, Dr. Langley's. You spoke of swimming in the sea at Padwithiel and nearly drowning."

Swinburne grinned in delight. "Yes, of course! And you are acquainted with Burton—surely he has arranged this! He—"

"No. *She* has arranged it."

The man smiled. His overcoat was dirty and opened to reveal an artist's smock beneath, smeared with flecks of eggshell, strings of dried paint, leaf mold. "I know the way. I will be your guide. I have come a great distance to find you."

Swinburne took a sip of brandy. "Then I am indebted to you, sir. I had understood that you were with your patron, Langley. That you were in Egypt. The Tombs of Sestris . . ."

The painter stepped toward him. The lantern's glow touched his face: a round, pleasant face, bearded and with wide, pale-blue eyes above a rosy mouth. He was not more than thirty-three or -four, roughly the same age as Swinburne.

"I have just arrived!" Candell gave a small gasping laugh and began to talk excitedly, as though picking up a conversation they had left off an hour ago. "I have come to show you! The tombs were nothing, Egypt is nothing—you will see as I did, the world is beneath us! A tunnel. A—"

He gestured at the passage, mouth working as though he could not recall a word or name. "Her aperture. The mound."

Swinburne giggled. Candell smiled slowly, a smile of great sweetness, then gently touched the poet's arm. "Such things as I saw. . . . We spent another week in Alexandria, because Langley wanted to be certain that I had enough time to record his travels properly. There the light is so rich that beggars promise to sell you a quantity of sun for a single mejidy! I paid them, and see, see . . ."

He held out a filthy hand. "It dazzles you," the painter whispered, fingers spreading as though he freed a captive sparrow. "But you must accustom your eyes to brilliance, else you will go blind at what we are to see."

Swinburne let his head fall back so that he could stare into the vaulted darkness overhead. "I see nothing."

"You will!" insisted Candell. "Wonder. Worship."

He began to walk away from Swinburne, deeper into the tunnel. "Oh, wonderful. Such brilliance. You will see, we will all see."

"He knows the way!" the poet exclaimed. He began to run after the painter. "Wait, wait—"

Candell grinned broadly. "Green!" he shouted, his hands outstretched before him as he ran. "Green!"

Swinburne struggled to catch up with him. They were deep beneath the city now. Around them, half seen, were ruins of Londinium. A temple, a brothel, huge polished stones. "He will show us marvels," Swinburne whispered, squeezing his hands together in anticipation.

"Verdetta, vetiver, woodbine," said Candell, and groaned. "I *will* see," he said and, snatching at the air, crushed something between his fingers.

Before them the passage narrowed, ending in an earthen wall. Candell's lantern bobbed as he stooped, then crawled through an opening.

"Oh, glorious lumen. I see light," said Swinburne, hastening after him. "A crack, a crack!"

He wriggled through the gap, and stood.

They were in a large room or cavern with a rough convex ceiling, composed of stone and mortar. Threads of vegetation protruded from between the stones overhead; as Swinburne began to walk around, small things burst and belched beneath his shoes, tiny conical caps of mushrooms, fleshy green earth tongues, red-tipped fungi that exploded with a scent of apples and kelp. There were heaps of very old brick, marbled with a soft bloom of turquoise mold. The air was sweet with a strange pervasive smell of apples, as though they stood inside an orchard within sight of the sea.

"What is this place?" murmured Swinburne.

Here and there odd relics could be glimpsed amid the detritus of rock and broken mortar: long, slender, smooth green stones shaped by hand, but for what purpose? Bronze arrowheads, lapis lazuli beads, lozenges of variscite no bigger than a pinkie nail. There were piles of ammonites, jet-black, malachite; a few were studded with gems like glittering barnacles.

"What is this place?" repeated Swinburne. "Why, *I* certainly don't know! Candell?"

"Oh, but see." At the far side of the chamber, the painter knelt, his back to the poet. As Swinburne turned to look at him, he realized that the light that suffused the chamber did not come from Candell's lantern at all.

His lantern had gone out.

"*Wonder!*" shouted Candell. His head was lowered, his hands pressed against the stone wall as though forcing it apart. "*Open!*"

Swinburne crept up behind him, twittering with laughter. "Tuppenny peep! Let me by—"

He squatted next to Candell, heedless of the damp on his bespoke trousers, and elbowed the painter aside. "Take your turn, gents, take your—"

He fell silent.

In the wall before them was a vertical opening as long as a man's hand and no wider than a finger. Radiance seeped from the crack, emerald green flaring into a white brighter than the sun. Swinburne shaded his eyes. Candell leaned back on his haunches and stared at the opening, his tongue caught between parted lips.

"Let me see," whispered Swinburne. He pushed Candell away and pressed his face to the stone. "Let me—"

It was as though someone had given him a lens that could miraculously illuminate the sea. Within a green world, prismatic things flickered and flew and spun: rubescent, azure, luminous yellow, the pulsing indigo of a heart's hidden valves. All were so brilliant he could see nothing clearly, yet he sensed—no, he *knew*—that behind the wall was another world: he could hear it, cries like seabirds, a rhythmic roar of waves. He could smell it, too, an odor so fragrant and rich his mouth filled with sweet liquid. His eyes stung; he blinked back tears, pressed his face against the stone with tongue extended, trying to steal some sweetness from the rock.

The painter just laughed and knelt beside him, knocking his forehead against the stone. When the crack closed, they never knew; only knew that the green world was gone and they had been left here, on the wrong side of the dark.

"Wonder," Candell gasped, licking his dry lips. "See."

"Cunt!" cried Swinburne; and, arms flailing with excitement, he staggered back to the world above.

CHAPTER TWO

The Trees of the Garden

There are no secrets on an island; only ways of hiding what went
wrong. That's what Red always told me, anyway. From his boathouse he watched the lobster boats chugging out across Man-
drascora Reach, watched the mail boat come and go, watched the
summer people arrive first of June and leave right after Labor Day. Red
knew who'd be living on food stamps and government cheese that winter and who'd be buying that new SnoCat, whose kids had to go live
with relatives on the mainland after DHS made a home visit.

"There's only one island, really," Red said. "One island, one story,
told over and over again. You just got to figure out where you fit into it."

Red wasn't a Maine native. He was from away, one of those unreconstructed old hippies who washed up here in the early seventies, one
of the ones who stayed long enough to see a sort of reverse evolution at
work, as the rednecks and hippies who once despised each other
passed through an uneasy truce until now, thirty-odd years and another
century later, they'd become almost indistinguishable—same hair
pulled into graying ponytails, same beat-up old pickups and bashed-in
Saabs, same homegrown seeds carefully culled and saved from one year
to the next to be planted out back with the potatoes and peas on
Mother's Day.

Red never told me where he lived before Aranbega. He didn't look like the island people, who tend to be small and dark, wiry as wild grapevines, their offspring sour and hardy as wild grapes. Red was tall and thin and fair, with coppery hair and eyes the same shade as Aranbega's legendary fringed gentians; you could pick him out at Town Meeting like a cranberry in a bowl of raisins. The oddest thing about him was his fingernails, which were a strange sheeny blue. Stain from the dyes and wood preservatives he used, he explained. In all the years I knew him, the color never faded. I just figured it was another weird thing about the island.

Because when you're visiting for a month or two in summer, or into the lingering fall, Aranbega seems like a hallucinogenic dream of heaven: sky so blue it burns your eyes, fir-bound hills and pink granite cliffs overgrown with lupines and fireweed, the smell of balsam and the sea strong enough to disturb your sleep.

But then the fog comes in, and you're sitting on a rock for a week. Worse, you decide to winter over and see how the natives do it: get back to that simpler, purer lifestyle, haul your own wood and have your own generator shipped over from the mainland, with plenty of candles and canned goods just in case . . .

And reality kicks you in the jaw. You get burned for the firewood, two short cords of birch and green ash instead of seasoned oak and beech. Your neighbor's jacking deer; when he leaves the carcass on your land, the coyotes come and eat your cat. Out on Green Lake, some guy is doing wheelies on the ice in his pickup; the truck goes through and no, the body's never found and no, the DEA won't be there before June, and yes, the leaking gasoline is probably not real good for the water quality. A fifteen-year-old blows his head off with a shotgun in the living room of his stepfather's single-wide. The local constabulary is the same guy who runs the general store and delivers the mail; he also takes care of the summer people's empty mansions and plows your drive, when it gets plowed. If he's busy, you're snowbound.

He's always busy.

See, I'm a Comstock; so I know something about the island, too. If you skirt the southwestern end of Aranbega, past the harbor with its congeries of pleasure boats and working craft, and continue to putter along the coast, eventually you'll see a ragged cuff of boulders and granite cliffs spiked with black firs and driftwood. There aren't any houses here—it's too exposed, the rock face impenetrable until you round the long, narrow spit of Knight's Head and get your first sight of the Maidencliff, a sheer granite crag crisscrossed with fissures so it looks like a giant chessboard. The Maidencliff stretches from the island's highest point, four hundred feet above the North Atlantic, down into a roiling chasm that the locals called "the thunderhole." When I was six, my older brother, Simon, pointed out to me the wreckage of a Coast Guard cutter that had gone down there in a storm forty years before.

"*That's* what comes of messing around with boats," he said.

This is where, in 1893, my grandfather Radborne decided to build his great folly Goldengrove, with the apocalyptic crash of waves echoing from the thunderhole and the cliff face crumbling slowly into the sea. He was thirty-three years old, flush with the success of *Johnny Appleseed* and *Babe Ballads,* his wallet fattened still more by an unexpected legacy from an obscure English painter who had died in an insane asylum and, inexplicably, left a small fortune to Radborne. That year my grandfather married a girl almost twenty years younger than he was, a fey Brookline nymph named Honoria Sweet. She died in childbirth along with Radborne's infant son; he remarried eighteen months later, but this bride, too, died of puerperal fever with her child.

To assuage his grief, Radborne threw himself into designing additions to his already vast house: bays and turrets, outthrust porches and stairways that led nowhere, windows opening onto empty airshafts. Last and most useless of all, he constructed a wooden stairway that descended the cliff face and ended in a wooden platform that stretched out above the thunderhole. The sets of stair risers were held against the ledge by a series of iron rebars bored into the granite, but the entire cantilevered platform was more a test of faith than engineering.

A man died building that stairway. When I saw it for the first time, more than three-quarters of a century later, it had disintegrated into an Escher nightmare of twisted iron and exploded Catherine wheels of rotten wood that dangled from the cliff, splotched with black fungus and flaming-orange *Xanthoria* lichen.

"Manderley on bad acid," Red used to call it. He was an old drug-dealing friend of Simon's who became Goldengrove's caretaker by default. He was also the closest thing I ever had to a father. I never knew either of my parents. Simon told me that I turned up one day like those babies left on church steps in old movies, although the truth, or what was passed on as truth, was more complicated. Our father was a failed painter who spent his early years trying to replicate his own father's success, before giving up and devoting the rest of his life to drink. He married and divorced three times. Simon—my half brother, really—came from the last of these unions. No one seemed to know or care who my own mother was, although my father dutifully adopted me and changed his will to provide for me.

Good thing, too, since he disappeared a few months after my arrival, when his sloop went down the thunderhole during a Labor Day squall. His body was never recovered, though pieces of the sloop continued to wash up onto Knight's Head for years afterward—mangled spars, a piece of decking covered with thousands of bright-green crabs.

By that time Simon was himself old enough to be my father: twenty-three, in his second year at Georgetown Law School, and utterly disinclined to have anything to do with me. So responsibility for me fell to Red, who by then was living in the boathouse at Goldengrove, keeping an eye on things while supporting himself doing custom carpentry. I grew up among the odds and ends of a woodworker's shop, breathing sawdust, scarring myself from chisels—and Red's absentminded habit of leaving burning cigarettes in peculiar places—sleeping in a futon bundled into a dinghy up on blocks. Summers we'd move up into Goldengrove, with its bizarre gallery of paintings by my late grandfather, keeping the place warm for Simon until he came to visit, usually with a dozen or so friends in tow.

An idyllic childhood, and like all idylls doomed to end. The summer I was nine, Simon's entourage included a rather sweet pedophile, a Harvard classics professor named Harvey Icht, who never laid a hand on me but did encourage me to strike Alice Liddell–ish poses on the gravel beach while he took photographs. This resulted in an alarming discovery for Harvey and worse consequences for me, after Harvey burst into the room where my brother was sleeping and announced that I was not a girl.

"Of course he's not a girl." Simon sat up, annoyed, and tossed me a T-shirt. "For Christ's sake, Val, put something on before you freeze."

"But . . ." Harvey stared, stricken, at my long black hair and cherubic face. "Look at her. Him. And her name. I thought—"

"Valentine *is* a boy's name," I shouted, throwing the T-shirt at him. "You asshole pervert."

"Hey, Val," Red said mildly from the doorway. "Harvey's not an asshole. C'mon, let's get something to eat."

After that, Simon arranged for me to go to school; boarding first at St. Anselm's in D.C., where Simon had his practice, and then at Andover. By the time I was thirteen, there was no doubt that I was a boy, tall and gangly and green-eyed, with unruly black hair, features too large for my face, and my father's penchant for booze and women.

The one constant in my life remained Goldengrove. It was the kind of house that looks supernaturally beautiful in the period photographs you saw in the biography of my grandfather Radborne—sky always a blinding, washed-out white, the house not the malign black it actually was but that soft silver-nitrite color you want to swallow, like mercury.

In real life Goldengrove was creepy as shit, especially the yews that shadowed the house's entrance like thunderheads. My grandfather had planted them over a century before. He loved to paint trees, and he had a knack for growing real ones that looked positively demonic. The gardens were filled with them: melancholy crabapples, wind-savaged poplars, stands of birches cancerous with peeling bark.

None were as disturbing as the yews, great tortured-looking trees with red berries that glistened like eyes and blackish needles thatched with spiderwebs. Their branches blocked the sun from my bedroom and knocked ceaselessly against the glass if there was the slightest wind at night. I used to beg Red to cut them down. But he couldn't do that without permission from Simon, and my brother refused.

"Bad for the real estate values, kid. You can always move into another room."

But somehow I couldn't move into another room. I tried, and lay awake at night listening for trees that weren't there. So I moved back into the room above the front entrance. To protect myself from the yews, I took to drawing them. Red was always good about finding me lost hoards of Radborne's pastels and inks and dried-up oils to use. I became hypnotized by my own pictures, and my grandfather's.

There weren't many of these left at Goldengrove. By the time my father was born, the years of Radborne Comstock's lucrative commissions were long past. Books with pictures were just for children now. The public appetite for wonder and exoticism was sated by the likes of Douglas Fairbanks and Ivor Novello, Theda Bara and Pola Negri.

And so Radborne turned to painting fairy tales. Not for any publisher that I could ever discover, either. I always suspected he just made up the stories himself, stray sentences or characters that served as lightning rods for his weird talent. When I was at Goldengrove, all of the earlier, really famous works were long gone. Johnny Appleseed and Paul Bunyan, Beatrice and Benedick and Prospero from *The Boys' Own Shakespeare*—all had been sold by Simon to pay the mounting tax bills and support his cocaine habit. I knew them only from visits to the National Gallery or reprints of Radborne's classic editions for Stonebridge Press. All that remained at Goldengrove were his disturbing last works.

In his final years, my grandfather's style grew increasingly inward. From what I read about him in the books and tattered magazines Red assembled for me as a sort of Comstock archive, he was utterly indifferent to the great modernist trends of the late nineteenth and early twentieth centuries. Impressionism, cubism, fauvism—all passed him by. And yet in the isolation and encroaching madness of these last years, he began to create things that were truly new and strange. His work began to implode; without commissions or a story to follow, he had no creative compass, nothing to keep him from wandering deeper and deeper into his own nightmarish visions. When I was a kid, Red gave me a book that contained images of Louis Wain's schizophrenic fractal cats. I recognized in them the pattern that my grandfather's late painting followed, nearly photorealistic detail giving way to fancy and, in the end, ferociously fragmented, almost purely geometric images, like the endlessly replicating honeycombs traced across your eyelids during an acid trip.

These were the paintings on Goldengrove's fourth floor: extravagantly detailed canvases filled with trees whose trunks sprouted nests of bees with men's faces, armies of insects, women who rode dogs big as horses. Each canvas was framed with the acorn-and-twig designs that Radborne himself made from autumn gleanings and birds' eggs, the husks of dragonflies and hawkmoths, sea glass and dried fungi. Each bore a small brass plaque stating its title.

ESELT EISPLAYS HER HAIR TO THE FLEEING CHILDREN
A PERSISTENT SUITOR'S RUIN

HALBOL THE BOLD

WITHIN THE WHEEL, AN EYE

RAPTURE OF THE QUEEN UPON DISCOVERING HIS SHOE

THERE THE SLEIGH BEGGAY STAYED THE NIGHT,

   AND IN THE DAWN FED

I was six when I discovered them. Red was taken up with the reno-vation of a custom Hinkley for a Boston stockbroker. He had the blue-prints laid out on the kitchen table in Goldengrove, the only room in the mansion where you could rely on sunlight. I'd spilled something on the blueprints, which made Red swear for about five minutes without stop-ping. When he finally caught his breath, he gave me a peanut butter sandwich and my lumpy toy dog and pushed me into the living room.

"Go play for half an hour, okay? And stay out of trouble."

The first floor was dark, but light spilled down the stairway from the upper stories. I started climbing the steps, passing from rooms I recognized to rooms I didn't, until finally I reached the fourth floor.

It was bright up there, and cool. A not-unpleasant air of neglect hung about the corridor, and the house's pervasive smell of turpentine and oils. Drifts of dead insects covered the windowsills. I started walk-ing, sandwich in one hand and dog in the other. I remember stopping in astonishment in front of a closed door. There was a piece of jewelry stuck on it, a gold-and-silver dragonfly with wings of silvered crystal. I tried to pick it up, and the dragonfly skimmed from my fingers, disap-pearing down the corridor toward a window.

I chased after it, but I wasn't fast enough: the dragonfly was gone. When I stopped, I saw that what was before me was not a window but a painting. I stared at it, sucking on my stuffed dog's nose.

It was a painting of a woman. She had very long red-brown hair falling across her face. She seemed to be asleep, but not in bed: she was lying on top of a mossy rock, which I thought was strange if she was supposed to be sleeping. What was stranger was that she was naked.

And strangest of all was that a man, or a sort of man, was kneeling between her legs, grasping each of her calves and pulling them apart so that he could peer between them.

The picture was hung too high for me to get a clear look at what the man was staring at. So I put down my dog and ran through the hall, opening doors until I found a room with a footstool in it. I dragged this back and clambered onto it to examine the picture more closely.

The man had horns on his head, flat curling horns, almost hidden within his shiny black hair. The horns reminded me of seashells I found sometimes on the gravel beach. Once Red had shown me a very, very old one, hard as a rock, older than the dinosaurs, he said: an ammonite.

The man's horns were like that. He had long, slanting eyes and a very red tongue, like a bloodworm. As I stared, I began to get a jittery feeling in my stomach. I brought my face very close to the painting, until I, too, could see what was inside the sleeping woman.

Silvery green spilled from the cleft between her legs. At first I thought it was fog. But it wasn't fog; it was light falling from a tiny lantern, held by a tiny man. He stood in the recess between the woman's legs as though he were guarding a door, and as I squinted I saw that it *was* a door—a tunnel, opening in the mossy cleft and leading . . .

Where? I wasn't sure, but I was almost certain that I could see other figures, if I squinted just right and looked past the lantern bearer. An entire crowd of them, some tiny and others not small at all, giants they would be if only I could see them clearly. My heart began to race; I thought I might throw up.

Because there were still more figures in the painting, hidden in the trees and leaves: all watching, all staring at the sleeper and the peeking man—but also, I realized, staring at *me*, Valentine, the peeking boy.

"Remember me," said a woman's voice. She said a word then that I did not recognize; yet it was somehow familiar to me, and I knew it was not just a word but a name. Her voice came again, a whisper, but when I whirled to look, no one was there.

"Red!" I shouted. I jumped from the footstool and ran toward the staircase. *"Red—"*

That was when I remembered my toy dog. I looked back and saw it lying near the wall. Something hovered in the air above it. A dark fluttery thing like a leaf or petal; as I stared, it floated down to land upon the dog's matted head. With a scream I raced down the steps, shrieking until I found Red in the kitchen.

"You know you should never go upstairs alone," was all he said. In fact he had never told me any such thing. "You know that."

He didn't ask what had frightened me, and he didn't seem surprised that I was scared out of my wits. If anything he seemed pleased, even relieved. He made me another sandwich and retrieved my toy dog, and we returned to the boathouse.

I began drawing all the time. Red started by buying me coloring books and crayons and cheap drawing paper, but after a very short while, it became clear that my talents were precocious, and we began raiding my grandfather's studio for still more pens and ink and color pencils. When I filled one sketchbook, we'd rifle Radborne's bureaus and closets for another.

It was years before it dawned on me that some of those pigments had been manufactured a century before. The dozens of empty sketchbooks we found were of similar vintage, their covers faded but the pages inside unblemished. One November day Red went up to Goldengrove and dragged Radborne's ancient drafting table to the boathouse. It was immense, custom made of mahogany with walnut inlays, and engraved with the initials JC. I always assumed they represented some other unknown ancestor who'd also been a painter.

All through the long island winters, I'd sit there with the woodstove burning, drawing while Red worked on bookshelves and cabinets and masts. The floor was covered with curls of pine shavings and balled-up papers. Red made me a special stool so that I could reach the drafting table.

"There you go." He eyed me approvingly, his beard flecked with sawdust and cigarette ash. "You look like a real apprentice now."

Day after day, year after year, I drew trees: labyrinthine trees that metastasized into vast yew cities, with ladders and ropes linking one level to another and long-eyed people rustling in the shadows. By the time I was eleven, the yew cities metastasized into the land that I named Ealwearld. I drew maps that formed the outlines of oaks and tamaracks, and detailed genealogies of the trees' denizens, who fought wars over fruit and walnuts and lobsters, carved spears and longbows from yew wood, distilled poisons from monkshood and skullcap.

Ealwearld was not a happy place. Its human-size inhabitants ate so much that there was never enough food for the smaller long-eyed warriors in the trees, whose nocturnal depredations upon their rivals involved blinding them with the stingers of wasps and yellow jackets or tying them by the hair to iron bedsteads and leaving them to starve. I'd go up to the fourth floor and look at my grandfather's paintings, sometimes incorporating his characters into my notebooks.

But then I slammed into puberty like a brick wall, and Ealwearld changed. Radborne's painting of the sleeping woman especially fascinated me, and gradually my imaginary land became her: a woman who was a vast tree, with boles for breasts and leaves for eyes and a mouth that opened into another, hidden country where even stranger creatures lived. I drew her obsessively, masturbating over the images when I was done. My childhood stories of Ealwearld became a chronicle of the woman, who had herself become a labyrinth. I hid these notebooks beneath a loose shelf in my room at Goldengrove. Eventually there were nine of them. I called the woman, and her chronicle, Vernoraxia. When I was fourteen, I saw her.

*   *   *

I was home from Andover for Halloween. Red drove down and brought me back to the island for the weekend. Halloween was the closest my family—if you could call my brother and Red and me a family—ever came to celebrating a holiday together. For as long as I could remember, Simon had hosted a party on Halloween night. His friends from the city and D.C. would come up several days beforehand, taking over Goldengrove's spare rooms and studios; Red would fire up the propane lanterns and gas refrigerator, fill the fireplaces with applewood and oak, arrange to ferry any latecomers from the mainland, and invite all those island friends who were wintering over. It was the only time I ever felt as though I occupied the same world as my brother did, or his friends.

The day of the party was crazy, as always. Simon made multiple trips to the island general store and the harbor to get supplies. My brother's friends pillaged Goldengrove's closets and my grandfather's studio for costumes, trading makeup and wigs and drugs in the corridors, shrieking and blasting old Roxy Music albums on the ancient cabinet hi-fi. Radborne had kept two quartersawn oak wardrobes in his studio, filled with antiquated clothing that he used in his paintings—Revolutionary and Civil War uniforms, Edwardian gowns, Johnny Appleseed's ragged trews, medieval-style tunics that had graced models for Robin Hood and Maid Marian, Benedick and Beatrice, Tristan and Iseult.

But by the time I rolled out of bed late that afternoon and found my way to the second-floor studio, all of the good stuff was gone. A torn satin doublet lay on the floor, surrounded by green glass beads sprung from a broken necklace. On the windowsill was a bottle of Jack Daniel's, nearly half full. I took a long pull from this, then started looking for a costume.

It was slim pickings. One wardrobe was completely empty. Alongside the other, T-shirts and flimsy dresses were heaped like rummage-sale leftovers: nothing but crap. I kicked them aside, yanked open the door to see if there was anything left. Torn stockings dangled from a wire coat hanger like a snake's shed skin; on another, wooden hanger hung an old-fashioned woolen jacket. I pulled it out: dark burgundy, smelling of camphor and some kind of fruity perfume. It had glass buttons and enough detailing around the collar that I figured it must have cost a lot of money, once upon a time.

It was big, too big I thought at first. But I'd grown since last summer, shooting up nearly five inches, so I was now over six feet, though it would be another few years before I stopped growing. When I pulled the jacket on, I was surprised at how well it fit; and when I examined myself in the mirror, I was surprised at how good I looked. I pushed my lank hair back from my face and stared at myself unsmiling: a tall, slightly gawky kid.

Yet not even so gawky anymore: I could see that, and I'd heard it, from girls (and some boys) at school. I lit a cigarette, sat on the windowsill, and drank most of the rest of the Jack Daniel's.

By now I had a pretty good buzz on. Outside, it was already dark, not twilight or sunset but that terrible full dark that falls like a fire curtain onto the islands in late fall. From downstairs echoed my brother's idea of party music—Thomas Dolby, show tunes, Bryan Ferry crooning "Both Ends Burning." I stared beyond the scrim of yews, the trees so black they were like rents in the sky.

"You don't fucking scare me," I said, and stumbled into the hall.

There was no electricity at Goldengrove. Red had lit one of the gas mantles on the second-floor landing, and it sent a thin yellow gleam through the corridor. At the top of the steps, I recognized one of Simon's lawyer friends, despite his face's being hidden behind a rubber Ronald Reagan mask. A guy I hated, drinking a cup of tea between tokes on a joint. Before he could see me, I turned and staggered back down the hall. There was another set of stairs at the other end, a servant's passage that led to the kitchen, and I hurried toward it.

That was when I saw her. Standing in the doorway to one of those empty rooms where Simon's friends were camping out: a woman nearly as tall as I was, taller even, wearing chunky lace-up Frye boots and some kind of long hippie dress. She was swaying back and forth, her hands catching the gaslight in a weird way so that her fingers had a gray-blue glow to them. I usually avoided my brother's friends, but something in the way she was moving, the way she was watching me without seeming to look at me, made me stop.

It was her: the woman in the painting. Her long red-brown hair covering half her face, her eyes shining out green, then gold, then green again.

Green again.

I stopped, staring. Somewhere in the room behind her, something moved, small footsteps on a bare wooden floor.

"Is—is that a dog?" I said.

She stepped into the hallway. On the wall a mirror flickered—I thought it was a mirror—a figure moving, a dark, slow rush like water flowing across the wallpaper. Her hand moved to take my chin, tilting my head back so that I was staring directly into her eyes, splintered with gaslight, shining yellow gold then green, always green.

"You are very young," she whispered. Her eyes grew unfocused; her breath upon my face was warm and smelled of cider. "So young, too young."

I gazed at her wide-eyed, unable to move, unable to do anything until she began to tug off my jacket and let it slip to the floor between us. Her head tipped so that she was staring at me sideways; she began to move her hand through the air slowly, up and down, so that the light from the gas lamp flickered strobe-wise across my vision, slats of yellow light between fingers like cracked blue slates.

"Shadows," she whispered. She looked and sounded like someone hypnotized. "See?"

Then her mouth touched mine, and I grabbed her, pushing her onto the floor and gasping as she pulled up my T-shirt, then unzipped my jeans and tugged them down. I thought of nothing, not discovery nor who she was, nothing but how she smelled, of apples and smoke, and how she felt under me, solid and liquid, moving and still. I fucked her, and it felt like hours, but it was only minutes, a minute, before I came, the same song from downstairs just winding to an end, the dog just completing its circuit of the room, the woman crying out but not in pleasure, even I knew that, but in disappointment and what sounded like despair.

"What?" I gasped, pushing myself up on my hands to stare down at her. "What, what is it?"

She was gone. On the floor beneath me lay someone else, someone I knew, a model named Maddy who was a sometime girl of Simon's. Eyes blue not green, hennaed hair, breath a bitter exhalation of meth and gin. She stared at me, then smiled crookedly, wriggling to pull down her dress.

"It's okay, sweetie," she said. "You're just young, that happens. . . ."

I pulled away, staggering to my feet and yanking my pants up, bashing against the wall as I rushed to leave. There was no sign of my woolen jacket. Something fell to the floor, not a mirror but a drawing, its frame shattering and a spray of glass momentarily igniting the air.

"Aww," said Maddy. "Look, it broke."

I fled down the steps and through the crowd gathered in the kitchen, heedless of who I ran into, and out into the garden. The last thing I remember of that night is Red staring at me from the kitchen window, his hands blue-white against the panes, and, from somewhere in the woods nearby, the four high, swooping notes of a barred owl's call.

* * *

Next summer my brother found the drawings. He was back at Golden-grove with his usual cohort of cocaine lawyers and stockbrokers and junkie models. Maddy was there, too. I did everything I could to avoid her, but she only smiled and treated me the same sweet, clueless way she treated everyone else. It was Maddy who discovered the stash of books in my bedroom.

"What the fuck is this?" my brother demanded as I walked into the living room.

I'd been gone all day. Simon and his friends were sitting around blank-eyed, surrounded by drifts of cigarette butts and glassine en-velopes. Empty bottles were everywhere. Someone had been cutting lines atop one of Radborne's glass-framed drawings. A halfhearted ren-ovation was in progress, with stacks of two-by-fours and plywood piled by the door. Scattered among the building materials were my sketch-books.

"What?" I stared at the room like it was an accident site. One of my maps lay on the floor, its corners weighted down with champagne bot-tles. Another was resting on the fireplace mantel. "Simon . . . ?"

I turned to him helplessly. I felt as though someone had drilled a hole in my head and all the blood was leaking out.

"This shit—you're really crazy, you know that, Val?"

My brother held up an open sketchbook. There was Vernoraxia, her hands pulling her knees apart so that you could see the army issuing from between her legs, women riding greyhounds, men whose heads were on backward. A tiny woman brandished a pair of old-fashioned scissors like a sword.

"Leave him alone, Simon." Maddy sat on the floor, her head bent over another of my sketchbooks. "I think these are so cool. . . ."

Simon started to laugh. "I think he's a fucking fruitcake."

I attacked him with a two-by-four, smashing him on the head, then turning blindly on his friends. It took four of them to subdue me. Someone ran for the constable; someone else raced down to the boathouse and got Red. My brother was medevacked to Rockland, where he was treated for a concussion and released the next day.

Somehow Red arranged for me not to be arrested. Instead I was shipped off to the adolescent unit at McLean in Boston. The new generation of psychotropic drugs weren't yet in use; I was put on a regimen of MAO inhibitors and lithium and released in time to return to Andover in the fall. The medication seemed to cure me of wanting to kill my brother. It also killed my obsessive need to draw. Without ever stating it out loud, I knew that I had lost the one genuine gift I had, the thing that made me feel that I deserved to be alive.

I was kept under a psychiatrist's care for years after that. As new drugs were developed, more sophisticated diagnostic tools, the exact nature of my illness was determined—a seasonal bipolar disorder, spiking in early spring and late autumn; not an uncommon pattern, I was told. Mood stabilizers kept me from hypomania in spring; higher doses of antidepressants muted the devastating onset of winter, when a veil would be torn from the world, and I sensed—imagined that I sensed— the real world beyond and felt things trembling behind my eyes like splinters of lightning seeking ground. The converse happened in late April, when the flickers of new green in Goldengrove's birch trees darted and swam around me as though seeking to pierce my skin. It was during these months that Simon and my doctors reminded me constantly not to vary my medication.

And, in what always felt like the most terrible betrayal, Red agreed with them.

"Maybe someday, Val," he'd say when I'd rage about it, home for a week or a month from school and, later, just home. Adrift. "When you're older, maybe. But not now."

Of course that went against everything the doctors ever told me: I could never go off medication. It was a life sentence. I was imprisoned.

Years passed. My meds were adjusted again and again. Some springs I went off them, and Red would somehow find me, raving and raging on the streets of D.C. or New York, London or San Francisco, and bring me back to Goldengrove. Once I was arrested in a bar in rural South Carolina and sentenced to three months in jail for aggravated mayhem, after I almost killed a man with a pool cue. Once I nearly killed myself after a Halloween binge in New Orleans. Always Red would rescue me.

I avoided thinking about drawing, or my stories about Vernoraxia, the way you avoid thinking about your own death. The last time I saw Goldengrove, the yew trees were gone, their yellow stumps raw and oozing clear, pinkish sap. Some more years passed, and it was another century. I was thirty years old, skating on the last remnants of the Comstock family fortune, designing sets for fringe theaters in New York and London. I had a few lovers, no real friends, an expensive motorcycle, no fixed address. I never knew what happened to my notebooks.

Part Two

London Boys

To London he always returned with the tremulous eagerness of a
lover who has been separated a long time from his mistress. . . .
—*Lawrence Durrell*, Mountolive

CHAPTER THREE

Love Disguised as Reason

Daniel was staying in Camden Town, directly across from a block of steel-meshed storefronts, tiny shops selling cheap leather goods, ersatz SM gear, London Underground postcards, and T-shirts squalling MIND THE GAP. Each morning beneath his window, a trio of middle-aged unreconstructed punks emerged from the tube station to set up a boom box that blared an endless loop of "Anarchy in the UK" and "Pretty Vacant"; they sold Official Classic Punk T-shirts (ALL MOD CONS; OH BONDAGE UP YOURS) and did a brisk business posing for tourists before quitting work around lunchtime. Daniel imagined they then got back on the train and returned to nice little flats in Swiss Cottage and Shepherd's Bush, where they changed from their greasy leathers into Tommy Hilfiger khakis and polo shirts, picked up their children, and prepared wholesome vegan dinners for their wives. He wondered sometimes if they would permit him to join their T-shirt cooperative: he was the roughly the same age—forty-four—and, with a bit of work, his own unruly blond curls could be teased into a facsimile of Scary Hair. Then at least he'd feel that he was doing something constructive with his time in London, rather than losing another day to the increasing despair that met him when he faced his computer screen.

His e-mails from colleagues back in the *Washington Horizon*'s newsroom were fondly envious and teasing, variations on SEE WHAT YOU'RE MISSING? or HOW'S THE GREAT AMERICAN NOVEL COMING? Of course he wasn't actually writing a novel (technically he wasn't actually writing anything), but An Exploration of Mythic Love. Or, as he had outlined in the proposal he'd given his agent,

> Prizewinning critic Daniel Rowlands, who has discoursed on topics as diverse as "The Eternal in the Everyday" and "K Street Courtesans," now brings his trademark wit and literary bravura to *Mortal Love,* an exploration of one of the great romantic myths of all time: the ancient and enduring legend of Tristan and Iseult. Drawing on a wealth of material, from Celtic mythology and Denis de Rougemont's classic *Love in the Western World* to Wagnerian opera and contemporary musical treatments like Nick Hayward's *Black Sails,* Rowlands's exploration of timeless love promises to be one of the major literary events of our era.
>
> Rowlands studied comparative literature at Williams College and holds an M.A. in medieval romance literature from Yale University. For the last fourteen years . . .

Unfortunately, creating a Major Literary Event of this or any other era relied rather heavily upon one's ability to write, something Daniel had done very little of since arriving in London two months ago. Not that he wasn't working. He'd done the usual, filing reports on the London Scene and an interview with this month's Brightest Young Thing, the obligatory pieces on disgruntled members of the Booker short list and the differences between American and British literati (the latter smoked like chimneys and had few qualms about getting shitfaced at afternoon book launches; they were also more likely to have in fact read something in the last week).

As for Tristan and Iseult?

Well, Daniel had visited the Tate a number of times to look at Millais's *Ophelia* and various other works with Arthurian themes. And he had spent a good bit of time and a large amount of money buying expensive art books at the Waterstone's down the street. But mostly he had wandered the city by himself, or in the company of his friend Nick Hayward. It was Nick's flat that Daniel was staying in, Nick having decamped to his girlfriend's flat in Highbury Fields.

And it was Nick whom Daniel awaited this morning, in the narrow passage just off Camden High Street. Daniel could remember when the open-air market occupied every square inch of Inverness Street. Now fewer than a dozen greengrocers set up there, with barrows full of oranges and figs from Israel, greengage plums, grapes so round and golden they looked like champagne bubbles in an old Merrie Melodies cartoon. He was standing in front of these, marveling at how huge the grapes were—the size of Ping-Pong balls—and how they glowed in the damp morning air alongside a crimson pyramid of pomegranates.

"No, no, no!" came a voice at his elbow.

> "*—We must not buy their fruits:*
> *Who knows upon what soil they feed*
> *Their hungry thirsty roots?*"

Daniel turned, smiling. "Good morning, Nick."

"A few of these pips and you'll be spending your weekends in hell." Nick picked up a pomegranate, casting a sideways glance at the woman behind the barrow. "Lucy, dear—how much?"

"Fifty p," she said, already reaching for the fruit. "How many, love?"

"Well?" Nick cocked an eye at Daniel: a bird-bright brown eye with a strange yellow sheen to it. "What do you think? Breakfast at Camden Kitchen, lunch with Hades?"

Daniel laughed. "Oh, why not?"

Nick picked up another pomegranate and handed it to the woman, who wrapped each one in violet paper, then dropped them in a small paper bag. "One pound, love, thank you," she sang, turning to another customer.

At Camden Kitchen Nick produced a pocketknife. "Now then, let's see what's inside," he said. Carefully he peeled back the violet tissue paper, then cut the crimson globe in two. "Why, it looks exactly like—a pomegranate!"

Daniel took his half and spooned a handful of jeweled seeds into his palm. He chewed a few thoughtfully, announced, "I don't think you're supposed to eat them with coffee," and put the spent seeds into an ashtray.

They had breakfast, bangers and mash and baked tomatoes for Nick, a feta cheese and olive quiche for Daniel. Afterward Nick had a pint; Daniel drank a glass of sparkling water and tried a few more pomegranate seeds. "They sort of grow on you," he said.

"Careful they don't grow *in* you." Nick speared the last nubbin of sausage with his pocketknife and ate it slowly. On the other side of the table, his friend opened a notebook and looked mournfully at a page filled with his own neat, square handwriting.

Here in this island we arriv'd and here
Have I, thy schoolmaster, made thee more profit
Than other princes can, that have more time . . .

Daniel was gangly and rather dewy-looking, with an aureole of dark-blond hair, large moist eyes the color of new tin, a wide wry mouth. He fancied himself a cynic in the mode of Hamlet, or perhaps Benedick; in truth he most resembled Viola, a yearning heart hidden behind a wardrobe carefully selected to disguise. Since coming to London, he'd forsaken his customary striped button-down shirts and corduroys and Harris tweeds for paisley Henleys and loose linen trousers, a vintage brown leather RAF jacket, and heavy felt clogs; his sole concession to his former self was a pair of fabulously expensive prescription glasses with frames of certified farm-raised tortoiseshell. The dandyish, souk-colored clothes suited him: not world-weary journalist but knight errant, wide-eyed, slightly stupefied in the dazzling sunlight of an older world.

Nick was the Anti-Daniel. Small and spare and dark, his upturned topaz eyes forever taking in something that Daniel could not quite see—something that Daniel was pretty certain he didn't *want* to see. Nick wore his gray hair in a long, tight braid, his beard trimmed to a sharp point, heavy gold bangles in his ears, his fingers callused and blackened from decades of handling his guitar. Thirty years of high living in London hadn't softened his Midlands accent or the raw class rage that had rung through the songs he'd played in the last quarter of the last century, starting with covers of "Hard Times" and "John Barleycorn" that he'd scored into the heart of folk clubs like Covent Garden's Middle Earth and Dingwalls here in Camden Town. *Human Bomb* had been the name of his first solo album; the tag stuck, and he refused to give it up, even during these gun-shy years of the new millennium. He was ten years older than Daniel, his gaunt face walnut brown, seamed from laughter and the harsh blaze of spotlights; even on the streets of North London, he moved foxlike, stalking the edges of a stage no one else knew was there.

"Ah," he said, and pointed the blade of his pocketknife at Daniel. "I nearly forgot—Sira told me I must ask you to dinner tonight. We have a friend she wants you to meet; she's staying with us while she visits from the West Country. You'll love her," he added, lowering his voice conspiratorially. "She's a former mental patient."

Daniel scowled. The inamorata who had helped clarify his decision to take a leave of absence from the *Horizon* had left him for her psychopharmacologist at the Haseltine Clinic, a man who quoted Rumi and had recently taken up quilling. "Excuse me. Did something happen to my brain while I wasn't looking?"

"Oh, please. You Yanks are so trusting. So trust me. Come to dinner, say sevenish, and make Sira a happy lass."

"Her place?"

"Unless you feel like cooking dinner at mine. Oh, and bring champagne—"

"Champagne?"

"*Expensive* champagne." Nick slipped from his chair, winking at the waitress as he slid a couple of ten-pound notes onto her tray. "Didn't I tell you? This is a champers gel. None of your nasty Old World claret for her."

"But that's the only reason I'm in London," Daniel said grumpily. "I came here for the Old World."

"You were misinformed." Nick wriggled his hands like a conjurer and moved swiftly through the restaurant and out onto the sidewalk, where he made a show of withdrawing a pair of sleek, scarlet-lensed sunglasses and fitting them onto his nose. He gave Daniel a mocking nod and began to walk backward into the crowd. "Seven o'clock, Danny-o . . ."

"How can he *do* that?" Daniel asked in a beleaguered tone. Beside him a woman carrying a baby stopped and looked where he was pointing.

"Do what?" she demanded, clutching the baby to her breast. "There's no one there!"

With a furious glare, she turned and strode down the High Street.

Sira's flat was on a tiny street in Islington, the last in a terrace of Regency-era town houses overlooking Highbury Fields. The yellow-brick buildings had wide sills painted white and window boxes filled with masses of begonias, their petals glossy as new satin. The town houses shared a sweeping view of Highbury Fields, a wide green swath bordered by plane trees; there were lime trees behind Sira's house, and in front an old wrought-iron fence marked where the narrow road turned into a pedestrian way. It was the most pastoral residential neighborhood Daniel had ever seen in London; he could easily imagine sheep and cattle grazing there, as they had done a century before, or performers setting up Punch-and-Judy shows, which still happened sometimes on the weekend.

He arrived promptly at seven. Sira opened the door, exclaiming, *"Daniel!"* and throwing her hands up in such delighted surprise that for a moment he was uncertain that he had, in fact, been invited.

But no: that was just Sira's way. "Daniel, dear, come in, come *in!"* she cried, kissing his cheek. "Nick's just opened a bottle of wine. He's out on the deck."

She grasped his hand, rather tightly, Daniel thought, and led him through the hall, past a pair of bikes and Nick's in-line skates and up the twisting stairway. "I am so glad you came, Daniel. Nick's invited a . . . a friend," she said, and gave him a look that might have been either relief or alarm. "She's between flats, so she's storing some things here. She takes up a bit of psychic space as well," she added. "Like Nick."

Daniel smiled, making sure the champagne was tucked safely under his arm. He thought of Nick and Sira as being like those magically paired demons and angels that appear in movies, egging the hero on to certain doom (Nick) or salvation (Sira). She was a barrister who had met Nick twenty years before; since then, their relationship had withstood tours, a paternity suit, canceled album contracts, failed musical technologies, and a half-dozen record companies. Sira claimed this was because they had always kept separate flats, migrating between them like swallows. She was Nick's height, bone thin, her silver hair cut so close to her skull you could see the indigo veins beneath, like a faint tribal tattoo. When she opened the door, a burst of scented steam rolled into the corridor, lemon and coriander and cumin.

"Nick!" she called as she drew Daniel through the living room and out a pair of open French doors onto the deck. "Daniel's here!"

"Hello, Daniel." Nick sat at a round café table, arranging olive pits into a pyramid. "Can I get you some wine?"

"Sure. But I thought you said your friend likes champagne."

Sira frowned. "You mean Larkin?"

"Your houseguest. Nick says she drinks nothing but Dom Pérignon."

"From a shoe," Nick added.

"Nick." Sira turned to him. "What are you up to? I don't think Larkin's supposed to drink," she explained to Daniel, who was still holding out the Veuve Clicquot. "She's on medication, and Nick knows it. I don't know why he would tell you otherwise," she said, and, taking the champagne bottle, went back inside.

Daniel turned to Nick. "You prick. Why—"

"Pay no attention to her. I know all, Danny-o." Nick smiled and patted the chair beside him. "Never doubt me, Dan. Never doubt me."

Daniel sat, swiveling to look out onto an expanse of lawn green as a grass snake. An asphalt path etched its way through it before ending in front of a small gated enclosure, the local Two O'Clock Club. There were no children or beleaguered mothers there now; the ice cream stall was shuttered, the overflowing rubbish tip had been emptied. He sighed, turned, and stared to where the westering sun had turned the City's shining caverns into a glittering dream of the Future, while behind it the immense blue-and-gold Mongolfier balloon moored at Vauxhall made its strange stately ascent every half hour. Gazing at this incongruous vista, his face bathed in syrupy light and mouth slightly open, Daniel looked even more daft than usual.

"Look," said Nick to a pigeon on the railing. "I bet he's humming 'Waterloo Sunset.'"

Daniel grinned sheepishly. "Actually, 'Shangri-la.'"

It was the truth. He'd been coming to London for over twenty years, and he still saw it through the scrim of songs he'd grown up with: Terry and Julie crossing Waterloo Bridge, feckless women moving from

St. John's Wood to Knightsbridge and Stepney and Berkeley Mews, Muswell Hillbillies and London Boys. This city was a place his senses recalled more keenly than his conscious mind; with each return it seeped back into him, its ashy smell and dreamy crepuscular light, rain-swept limbs and crowds pouring from the Underground, Cockney back-chatter and the sibilant greeting of the grocer across the street.

"'Sa fine day, Mester Roolands, 'sa fine day. . . ."

"Well, cheers," said Nick, handing him a wineglass. Daniel raised it to the leafy canopy, smiling, as Sira stepped back onto the deck with a platter of olives and bread and pale cheese wrapped in what looked like goldenrod.

"Daniel—eat, please. I'm so sorry, dinner won't be ready for a bit."

Daniel gulped his wine and stood. "Umm, I need to find the loo first—"

"Use the guest toilet, Daniel," said Sira as Nick speared a haunch of bread with his pocketknife. "All the way up, on the fourth floor—the other one's not working right."

"Gotcha."

He'd never been on the fourth floor. He didn't even know the place *had* a fourth floor, but he dutifully followed the narrow twisting stairs from the cheery first-floor landing to the second (half-open bedroom door, suggestive scatterings of torn lace and leaves and candle-wax on the Baluchi carpets) and the third, until finally he came to a landing that Nick and Sira, slight as they were, would have had difficulty occupying at the same time. Daniel pressed one palm against the wall. The space was so small he couldn't extend his arms outright: where the hell would you put a bathroom?

But there *was* a room, behind a heavy brocaded curtain. He pulled the curtain aside, expecting to find one of those tiny head-knocking lavatories the English liked to torture themselves with.

"Wow," he breathed.

Before him a tiny bedroom had been fitted into the eaves. The slanted ceiling held etched-glass windows of amber, emerald, scarlet. The sills were carved with honeybees and octagons, the Turkish carpet patterned with stylized wasps and ants. A carved cupboard bed had been built into one wall; opposite it was a matching wardrobe. Beside the wardrobe hung another length of brocade. This was pushed to one side, so that he could glimpse an ancient water closet, its porcelain reservoir suspended from the ceiling and a length of silver chain hanging above the wooden commode.

"Holy cow," said Daniel. "George Meredith pissed here."

He could stand upright only in the very center of the room, where the roof peaked; inside the loo he had to stoop uncomfortably in front of the toilet. Still, this gave him a good view of the porcelain tank, which depicted the crystal domes and spires of Alexandria Palace in full Dying Empire mode. When he pulled the chain, the explosive roar of water rushing through the exposed pipes deafened him, and he backed out quickly, tripping on something.

"What the hell?"

It was a shoe. A woman's shoe. A very expensive woman's shoe, to judge by the minimalist curve of black leather affixed to a deceptively fragile-seeming spindle of polished chromium. He picked it up and studied it—where exactly did the foot go?—then turned to find someplace to put it.

The wardrobe? Its wooden door was slightly ajar, a fragment of velvet wedged in a corner. He tugged at the handle, and with a faint thump the door opened. Daniel whistled softly.

It was like Aladdin's cave. Or Madonna's. On one side hung floor-length dresses of burned velvet and satin and pale gray eelskin, black lace sheaths fringed with feathers or sewn with scales, shimmering peignoirs so fine they looked as though they would melt on the tongue. There was a gown made entirely of orange cock-of-the-rock plumage and another of hummingbird feathers woven into what looked like a spiderweb dewed with seed pearls. The other side of the wardrobe held shelves overflowing with knickers, brassieres, tap pants, merry widows, corsets and corselets, camisoles and stockings of gold mesh, sleek leather gloves and lacy fingertip sleeves liberated from ball gowns. At the very bottom, nestled among fluid coils of apricot satin and a marten stole, lay a single shoe: the mate of the one he held.

Daniel stared at it all in amazement. Who on earth could it belong to? Sira? He felt himself flush, imagining her in that or *that* or . . . well, any of it. He glanced cautiously over his shoulder, then leaned forward, burying his face in the voluptuous mass hanging in the wardrobe. He had a flash of that primal sexual rush he'd experienced as a child, opening his mother's lingerie drawer and sinking his arms up to the elbows in silk stockings and garter belts.

Of course his mother hadn't owned a moleskin brassiere with the fur on the inside. And nothing his mother owned had ever smelled like this—opium and new leather and beeswax, musk and sea wrack. He pushed aside several gowns, curious to see just how much space there was inside.

It seemed immense. The stained-glass windows sent a cathedral glow over everything; he could make out more shelves at the very back, and what looked like a heap of glass globes on the floor. Their curves shone with glints of deep red and purple and blue, and for some reason these fascinated him even more than the confectionery clothing. He glanced back again, then took a step inside.

For a moment he stood, one foot upraised, waiting to see if it would hold his weight. But the wardrobe must have been made of solid oak: he heard nary a creak as he took another step, bending his head as hangers and trailing sleeves grasped at him. He made sure the door behind him stayed open—he'd read the right sort of children's books—and was just reaching for one of the shining glass balls when he heard someone coming up the stairs to the landing outside.

"Oh, fuck," he breathed. He turned, peach-scented folds of chiffon falling across his face. If it was Sira, she'd think he was some sort of furtive fetishist, which would only puzzle her: why hadn't he ever mentioned it? If it was Nick . . .

He sucked in his breath: if it was Nick, Daniel would have to leave the country. For an instant he stood there, still hidden by scores of gowns, wondering how to explain—

And then it came to him. He wouldn't explain: he'd just pop out of the closet, shouting Boo!, and pretend he'd been hiding there as a joke. Sira would be annoyed, Nick would think he was an idiot, but he could live with that. A shadow flickered along the landing; Daniel let his breath out, steadying himself as best he could as he waited. . . .

But it wasn't Sira or Nick. It was a woman he had never seen before. Tall and powerfully built, her long legs encased in black jeans and a pair of worn magenta cowboy boots with python inlays. She wore a tunic of indigo velvet, embroidered with silver filigree, and heavy silver bracelets set with turquoise and jade and carnelian. Her hair was chestnut-colored, unraveling from a loose French braid, her neck long but not slender: a neck like a pillar; Daniel had never seen a neck like that on a woman. She had a chiseled, big-featured face—square cheekbones, heavy, nearly black eyebrows; wide, red-lipped mouth—a face that should have looked masculine but instead asserted itself as a kind of beauty Daniel knew only from paintings. Not modern paintings, either: he thought of Mischa or Jane Burden or Lizzie Siddal: women who were too big for their world, women who could be captured only by scaling them down to fit inside a wood-and-canvas keep.

She strode into the tiny room, her boots thumping upon the carpet, glanced around quickly before heading for the bed. Daniel felt sick but couldn't avoid angling his head slightly so that he could keep her in his sight. Was she going to get undressed? His hands had gone cold; he knew he should do something, shout or cough or laugh nervously, reveal himself *this instant,* before anything worse could happen, before she pulled the tunic over her head, or lay down to take a nap, or *stepped back over to the wardrobe to change her clothes.* . . .

Instead she stooped and sat on—within—the cupboard bed. He could see her profile against its oak panels, and for the first time realized that, like the carpet and windowsills, the bed was carved with insect wings interlocked in a repeating pattern. The woman sat, her long legs tucked beneath her. As he watched, she bent forward, held one hand beneath her mouth, and made a retching sound. Daniel grimaced as she gagged, then spat something into her palm, something small and round and glistening. She drew her hand close to her face, frowning as she examined the tiny object. She dried it on her sleeve, pinched it between two fingers, and held it up, staring at it fixedly. Finally she leaned forward, placed it on the pillow, and climbed out of the bed.

For a moment she stood there, as though she were trying to remember something. Daniel's entire body ached. His hands had gone numb, and his legs: any second now he'd be overcome by a spasm of pain or fear or pure mortification.

But before he could move, the woman was gone, striding out the door as quickly as she'd arrived. Daniel listened until her footsteps died into silence, and then he stumbled from the wardrobe. His heart pounded; he could feel the blood pumping hot back into his hands as he turned and shoved the wardrobe door shut, pushing at the coils of silk and velvet trying to escape. Two long strides brought him to the door, poised to race silently downstairs. But then he stopped.

What had been in her mouth?

He listened for sounds from downstairs. Silence. Before he could think better of it, he turned, hurried to the cupboard bed, and bent over the pillow.

He'd thought it might hold a tooth, even had the mad thought that the woman was a smuggler, one of Nick's old wild friends, coughing up nuggets of heroin in the spare room, uncut emeralds, teardrops of Baltic amber. But it was none of these.

Nestled within the pale green pillowcase was an acorn. Daniel stared at it, frowning.

An *acorn?* He hesitated, then picked it up: smaller than the bole of his thumb, its smooth curves burnished to a soft fawn color, with a ring of pale furze covering the crown. It had no cap. He touched its point, which was surprisingly sharp, and a pinprick of blood appeared on his finger. He rolled the acorn between thumb and forefinger, sniffed it, but could smell nothing.

Just an acorn, then; nothing remarkable about it at all. He stood for another moment holding it before his face. Almost without thinking he touched his tongue to it, a cool satin bead without taste, and rubbed it against his lower lip. He held it out once more, gazing at it perplexedly, then shoved it into his pocket and made his way back downstairs.

Nick was on the deck, leaning against the rail and talking in a low voice, his hands moving suggestively. Beside him stood the woman. She was laughing; her hair had come undone to fall around her shoulders, and a yellow leaf was caught in the loose curls. Sira stood alone on the other side of the deck, watching them as she absently folded and unfolded a linen napkin. When she saw Daniel, she gave him a tight little smile.

"Ah. You're back," she said. She smoothed the napkin and set it on the table. "I've got to see to dinner. You can keep an eye on them."

"What?" said Daniel, but Sira was already gone.

"Here he is!" cried Nick. "I thought you'd fallen in."

"Sorry," said Daniel. He crossed to the table and picked up his wineglass, trying not to stare at the woman. In the honeyed sunset light, she looked less imposing than she had upstairs, the harsh lines of her face softened and her hair a warmer color, chestnut tinged with auburn and glints of gold. But all Daniel could really fix on were her eyes. An astonishing deep pure green, like a marble held up to the sun, they seemed oddly unfocused, her gaze abstracted, like that of a nocturnal creature unaccustomed to the sun, or some marine animal dragged onto dry ground.

"Hello," she said, smiling. "Nick was telling me you're a famous American writer."

"He says that about everyone. Nick refuses to know anyone who's not famous. It's one of the perks of being a musical legend."

Her dark eyebrows rose. "Are you?"

"A legend? No. I'm not even mildly famous."

"Totally unknown," agreed Nick.

"My name is Daniel Rowlands," said Daniel.

"Larkin Meade." Her hand closed around his: he had the sudden dreadful thought that he still held the acorn, she would know. . . .

"I've just been hearing about you—from Sira," she added, "not bad old Nick. You're doing a sabbatical here? That must be brilliant."

Daniel smiled glumly. "I'm not really a writer. I'm a journalist. I'm supposed to be writing a book, but I've never written a book before."

"Just these little bits of paper that get published—you know, like fortunes," said Nick. "Or horoscopes."

Larkin looked at Daniel. "Really? You're an astrologer?"

"No. But it's a concept." Daniel finished his wine, let Nick take the glass and refill it. He was starting to feel drunk, flushed and slightly giddy—*happy* drunk, which he hadn't been in . . . well, ages. "Let's see, a Rowlands horoscope—'You will be sexually unfulfilled, and your children will despise you. Yet long life will be yours.'"

"Miserable long life," Larkin corrected him.

"You're a writer, too?" asked Daniel. "Or musician?"

She laughed. "Me? No. I wish I were. I've always wanted to do something like that. Paint or write. Compose music. Something creative. I play at it a bit, but . . ."

Her voice trailed off. She lifted her head to stare at him, her expression distant, almost pained. Daniel waited for her to continue. Instead Nick broke in, his voice brash and annoying as a boy's.

"That's what she always says! But then she just goes on as before, swooping through the garden, leaving a trail of broken hearts. And she doesn't even have the grace to be ashamed of it!" He headed back into the house. "Mind her little claws, Danny boy!"

Daniel winced and cradled his glass against his chest. Larkin turned to plant her elbows on the rail and gazed down at the Two O'Clock Club. A strand of hair had caught at the corner of her mouth; he wanted to reach and brush it aside, he wanted to ask about what Nick had said—could she really be a mental patient?—but before he could do either, she turned back to him.

"What's your novel about? If it's not rude to ask."

"Well, it's not a novel." He stepped beside her, looking down at that mass of unruly hair, her leaf-colored eyes. "It's a . . . well, a sort of study—not an academic study, a popular one, at least it's supposed to be popular—a history of romantic love. The Tristan and Iseult mythos."

"You mean Wagner?"

"No. I mean, Wagner's in there, of course. But I'm trying to trace all the versions of the story, not just the famous ones—Gottfried and Malory, Béroul—track them all, see if I can find a single primary source, then come back around again and do the Victorians—Swinburne and Arnold, the Pre-Raphaelites—then the twentieth and twenty-first centuries so we can see what *we've* done with it."

"It's a bit ambitious." She laughed, but not mockingly. "I think you're brave to try it."

"Not really. There's a whole cottage industry in this stuff. Especially the Victorians. Little books for Valentine's Day, upmarket romance novels."

"So how will yours be different?"

"I guess I'll just have to bring a certain level of literary distinction to it," he said, and laughed. "Without sacrificing the populist touch. Show how much we have in common with our Victorian forebears."

"You believe you understand them?"

"Sure. Add or subtract a few revolutions in scientific thinking and abstract art, and we could all be sitting here together right now, being insulted by Nick Hayward." He grinned, but Larkin shook her head. "What, you don't think so?"

"No. A few of them would feel and think the way you do, but . . ." She lifted her head to gaze at the City's distant towers. "You forget. Some of them actually believed in what they wrote and painted about."

"Meaning I'm a crass twenty-first-century cynic cashing in on their idealism?"

"Meaning maybe they weren't being idealists at all. Maybe the world was different then."

"Of course it was different. But that's the whole point—it's never different *enough*." Daniel stared past her, his expression hardening. "We think things change, that they get better—but the truth is, nothing ever changes all that much. Except maybe for the worst."

"You *are* a crass twenty-first-century cynic," said Larkin, and turned. "Ah, here's Sira with dinner."

They ate at the table outside, the long twilight brightened by candles that Sira set along the rail. Everyone but Larkin drank Daniel's champagne, though she clapped in delight as the cork flew overhead. Nick seemed more brooding than usual, staring at Daniel as though he were someone unknown who'd dropped in by mistake; he hardly spoke at all. Daniel, meanwhile, sat beside Larkin, grinning so broadly he felt somewhat embarrassed, as though he were an impostor, playing someone who was cheerful and confident and good with women.

And yet he *was* good with women, he thought, finishing another glass of champagne. Or . . . well, at least he had his moments; he'd be very interested in reviving some of them with this Larkin here, now.

He found himself watching her avidly. He didn't normally go for dark-haired women, or women so flamboyant. Those Early Anita Pallenberg clothes, that old velvet tunic and Tony Lama boots; her mass of serpentine hair; her strong, rather masculine features and those strange green eyes; not to mention that business with the acorn.

He couldn't keep his eyes off her. When Sira finally stood and started clearing the table, he began to relax, certain that Nick would follow.

But Nick didn't go. Instead he moved his chair beside Larkin. "Well, lass," he said, and flashed her a smile so false that Daniel scowled. "Why don't you step inside with Sira and leave us gents to have our brandy and cigars."

Daniel's scowl deepened. Before he could retort, Sira's voice came from the kitchen. "Nick! Leave them and come in here, please!"

Nick swore softly, and Daniel was surprised to see his friend staring at him with an expression that, in anyone else, would have betokened genuine concern. It only made Daniel more suspicious. "Yes, Nick," he said. "Go help Sira. Where's your manners?"

Nick started to say something but stopped. He pushed his chair back and headed for the door. With a last glance at Daniel he went inside.

Daniel sighed with relief. Larkin smiled, swiveling her chair to face him; her knees touched his, and he felt strangely exultant, that he had been chosen over Nick.

"Well," she said, her eyes narrowing. "Tristan. Have you ever seen the Burne-Jones drawings?"

He shrugged. "Just prints of watercolors based on his Oxford panels."

"So you've never heard of any others he did?"

"Well, the stained-glass designs for Morris's company. Is that what you mean?"

"No."

"Believe me, I've looked at them all, and I couldn't find anything unusual that dealt specifically with Tristan and Iseult. There's that one

Morris painting, and the Beardsley *Morte D'arthur*," he said, ticking them off on his fingers, "one or two minor Rossettis, and a whole bunch of off-brand Pre-Raphaelites. I don't find any of them very interesting, except maybe the Beardsley. And Jean Belville's drawing—it's kind of different. But all that other PRB stuff's just been overexposed. Like I told you. I wanted to find something new, but . . ."

He opened his hands. "Nada. It's all been done."

Larkin picked up his champagne glass, refilled it, and handed it to him. "These pictures are different."

"How?" He raised his glass, then drank. "What do you know?"

"Well, for starters, hardly anyone has seen them. They're studies, not actual finished paintings," she said. "A series of studies—three of them. You're familiar with *Pygmalion and Galatea*? Burne-Jones did two versions of that story, an early one commissioned by the Cassavetti family and another series in 1878. These are similar."

"Cassavetti? Wasn't that—"

"Yes. Maria Cassavetti became Maria Zambaco, the model for all the famous Burne-Joneses. They were talented, those girls. Her cousin Marie Spartali painted a Tristan—"

Daniel felt a flicker of excitement. "And Maria Zambaco modeled for this Iseult?"

Larkin shook her head. "Ned had broken with her by then. He treated her quite badly, you know. He thought she was something she wasn't. When he finally admitted the truth to himself, he left her. The drawings date from after their affair was over, the early 1880s."

"Where are they kept?"

"A place called Paynim House."

"A gallery?"

"A private club. At least it was, a hundred years ago. It's in private hands now. And it's not open to the public. But . . ."

Larkin leaned toward him. He could smell her hair: a woodsy scent, crushed bracken and a sharper underlying smell like green apples.

". . . I know how to get in. There's not much there, some odd-ments. A small painting by Jacobus Candell. Do you know him?'"

Daniel was so entranced that it was a moment before he realized that this demanded a reply. "Uh, no," he stammered. "Another Tristan?"

"Nothing that normal. Candell's a bit of a loony," she confided, and laughed. "But he knew all those people—Swinburne and Burne-Jones and Rossetti, and—"

"Knew them until he was locked away," broke in Nick. He stood in the doorway, staring at them; Daniel wondered how long he'd been there. "I'm surprised you've never heard of him, Daniel. He's just your sort of person."

"Obscure literary figure?"

"Homicidal maniac." Nick slipped back beside Larkin. "Hasn't he bored you to tears yet, Lark? Has he started quoting Bulwer-Lytton on Gottfried of Strasbourg?"

"Oh, shut up, Nick." Larkin turned her electric eyes on Daniel, who hoped the candles wouldn't reveal his blush. "Nick's just jealous. It's a *brilliant* idea. Sexy, too—"

Nick hooted. Larkin ignored him.

"So it's to be an illustrated book, Daniel?"

He shook his head. "Well, that's the problem. I want images, but not the same old stuff. There's supposedly some remnant of the frescoes Rossetti and Burne-Jones and Morris did at Oxford, Iseult embroidering the black sails—"

"Doesn't exist," said Nick. "I know, because I wanted it as cover art for *Black Sails*."

"But it *did* exist." Behind them Sira appeared, holding a tray of steaming demitasse cups. "I remember hearing about it when I was at Oxford. They hadn't prepared the surface properly, only whitewashed the brick, and the paint wouldn't hold. The frescoes fell to bits and faded away. You can barely make out where they were in the gallery above Oxford Union Debating Chamber, just a few vague patches. Oh, dear, I forgot the milk!"

She bustled back inside. "A lesson for us there," said Nick. "Always do your prep work."

Daniel looked at Larkin. She smiled at him; he smiled back, rapturously, and Nick kicked him under the table.

"Excuse me." Larkin stood, resting her hand on Daniel's shoulder. "I've forgotten something upstairs."

As she left, Daniel felt a wave of vertigo. *The acorn.* He slid his hand into his pocket, and yes, it was still there. His fingers closed around it; he thought of tossing it over the railing, had begun to turn when Nick grabbed his arm.

"Danny." Daniel froze, certain that somehow Nick knew what he was up to. "Danny, listen—don't."

His mouth went dry. "Don't what?"

"Don't fall for her. Don't fall for it."

Daniel's hand relaxed. The acorn slid into his pocket as he stared belligerently at his friend. "What're you talking about?"

"Her. Larkin. Don't fall for it, lad. It's a trap. It's just beauty, Danny, and you're above all that."

"The hell I am," said Daniel. "You were the one wanted me to meet her. She's . . . interesting. Intense."

"That's—"

"Nick!" called Sira. "Phone!"

"Don't move," warned Nick. "Stay right there. Don't touch her."

Nick stalked inside. Sira passed him in the doorway and slipped back into her chair.

"It's the manager at Dingwall's," she told Daniel apologetically. "This midsummer concert they're trying to set up. He won't be long."

Daniel waved magnanimously. "Sure, sure. So . . ." He flashed her his most sincere Professional Journalist's smile. "Tell me about Larkin."

"There's not a lot to tell. I mean, from my perspective."

"I thought you were good friends?"

She laughed. "With Larkin Meade? Not likely! I hardly know her." She glanced at the door, then lowered her voice. "She and Nick were involved, ages ago. It was awful. But you knew that, right?"

Daniel tried not to look taken aback. "Oh, sure, sure."

"She really did a number on him. That was when we first met, Nick and me. He was a mess. He looked so bad, I thought he was a junkie. Didn't want anything to do with him. He was drinking himself to death, not eating—he weighed less than I did, which is saying something. One of his friends, Robert Lord—I knew Rob from school; he was just starting to do bookings back then—he introduced us, thought I'd be a good influence on Nick."

"Which you were."

"Which I am. Robert told me Nick had gone 'round the twist over this girl he'd gotten messed up with—a photographer's model, one of those David Bailey birds. There was a rumor she'd been Leonard Cohen's girlfriend, so of course everyone wanted a piece of her. Rob said she absolutely cut a swath through their crowd—all these young lads, you know, folkies making the scene down at Covent Garden who were used to passing girls 'round like cigarettes. Only, this one girl just *wasted* them—Rob said she was worse than heroin. She had a different name then—you know, one of those silly sixties things, Liberty Belle, Susie Goldenrod, something like that."

"Susie Goldenrod?"

"Well, no, not really. But something awful. I know, hard to believe, isn't it? Our Nick falling for that. He was just a lad."

"What about her? She must've been, what? Twelve?"

"Oh, no. She's the same age as you, I think."

"Just taking the same drugs as Dick Clark." Daniel craned his neck to peer into the flat, but Nick was still safely on the phone. There was no sign of Larkin. "So Nick took up with this groupie, and . . . ?"

"I don't think she was a groupie. I think she might have played something, the psalter maybe? Something twee like that. Rob wanted to ban her from the club, but the lads—and the girls, too—they still couldn't stay away from her. When I met Nick, he and Larkin had just split up. He was completely mad, told me he was in love with this girl who'd tried to kill herself. Which I thought was strange, because from what Rob told me, *she* left Nick, not the other way 'round.

"As a matter of fact," she went on, "after a while someone told Nick she actually *was* dead. That's when we first moved in together. But then someone else told him no, he'd seen her somewhere—Turkey, maybe? Anyway, Nick heard she was still alive, and that almost ended it be-tween us. It really made me hate him."

She turned to stare at the row of candles on the porch rail.

"I never knew any of this," Daniel said. "I mean, you always seem so forgiving of him."

Sira gave him a rueful smile. "I was—I *am*. But this was different. I truly thought he was going to go mad. He got so ill he had to go into hospital for several days. I think—no, I *know*—he had somehow man-aged to see her again. He'd gone off alone to Budapest for a weekend, and when he returned, he was so sick I thought he'd die. Fever. And these . . . scars."

She fell silent, gazing into the darkness beyond the porch. From the other side of Highbury Fields came the sound of a car alarm. Daniel stared at her. After a moment he gently asked, "How could you let her come here, then?"

"I don't know." Sira sighed, running a hand across her cropped scalp. "It's been such a long time, and I suppose I wanted to make sure that the fire'd gone out, you know? And it's what I've always done with Nick's girls—befriend them, try to make it like family. I guess I was mostly curious, to see what she was really like. And, well, she seems perfectly all right, doesn't she? She's attractive, but she doesn't quite seem like the sort you'd kill yourself over. Does she?"

Daniel smiled wryly. "Probably not. How long ago was all this?"

"The first time was, what—thirty years ago? 1973; so yes, more than thirty years. The time in Budapest was about ten years after that—'82, I think."

"How long were they together? The first time, I mean."

"Well, that's the other odd thing. Even before we met, I knew Nick's music. All his best songs came from then—they were *all* about her. And the way he talked about her, I always assumed they must have been together for ages. But it was just a little while."

"How little?"

"A week, maybe. Nick told me once it was less than that."

"A *week?* Jeez, I've had hangovers that lasted longer than that!"

"I know—it sounds funny, doesn't it? But you know, Daniel, if you'd seen him then, you wouldn't laugh. He looked like death. He looked like someone who'd have looked *better* dead."

"What about her now?" Through the open door, he could see Nick pacing back and forth in the hall. "Nick said something about her being mentally ill."

"I don't really know anything about that. I suppose she can't have been all that together if she tried to kill herself. He did tell me once—this was when he was in hospital, so I took it with a grain of salt—he told me then that he thought she was delusional, or had some kind of personality disorder. Which was why she would use a different name—although he lied to me about that, too. He said the woman he'd seen in Budapest was named Durene, but later he told me it was really Larkin. So who knows? Anyway, Nick says she's fine now, she's taking medicine, and she's not supposed to drink. But that's pretty common, isn't it? She appears sane enough to me."

"Me, too," Daniel said. "And we all did some fucked-up stuff back then, right?"

Sira smiled sadly. "Right."

He wanted to feel relieved. Instead he had an unpleasant sense that he was fooling himself about this woman. But even that was absurd—he didn't know Larkin well enough to have any sense of her whatsoever. He began to shake his head impatiently, when a sound from the next room made him look up. Larkin was heading toward the porch, while behind her, Nick scowled at the phone, then with a rude gesture hung up.

"It's a bit later than I thought." Larkin stopped in the doorway, smiling down at Daniel. "I think I'll be heading back now."

"Really? Wait, hold on, I'll walk out with you."

Quickly Daniel scrambled to his feet, nearly forgetting Sira beside him. "Oh—Sira, thanks, that was great."

She looked at him, amused. "Right. Here's Nick."

"Well, we got the Wednesday night," he said. "But not without a fight. What, going already, Danny?" He looked from Daniel to Larkin. "But the night is still young!"

"I've got work to do. Someone from *TimeOut*'s interviewing me in the morning." Daniel said. "But thanks."

"*TimeOut*? Must be a slow news week." Nick stared at Larkin. For a moment it looked as though he'd move toward her; instead he abruptly turned to go inside. "Well, I will leave you two to discuss your minor Victorian artists. Fucking bourgeois wallpaper."

"Nick, no one but you wants Chris Mars wallpaper," Daniel shouted after him, then turned to Larkin. The two of them left the flat, calling good-byes to Nick and Sira as the door clanged shut behind them.

They made their way down the sidewalk. The broad expanse of Highbury Fields had a sickly orange glow from the streetlights. A small white dog minced across the grass, foxlike, its brushy tail held high and its pointed ears erect as its owner sat on a bench and watched.

"Look," said Larkin, pointing. "It's stalking something."

The man on the bench whistled; the dog leaped into the air, its tail a white pinwheel, then darted across the lawn. Daniel glanced back at Sira's place. He had a sudden nagging sense that he had forgotten something, but what? When he turned back, both dog and owner were gone. Larkin stood waiting for him against the iron fence.

"Ready?" she asked.

They walked slowly, heading in the general direction of the Underground and saying nothing. Daniel shivered; the unease that had touched him briefly in Sira's flat grew more pronounced. He glanced at Larkin. She appeared lost in thought, her hands in her pockets, a tangle of dark hair obscuring her eyes.

When they reached the corner, she stopped. Above them loomed an old-fashioned street lamp. Brown moths spiraled in a frenzied orbit around its egg-shaped lobe. Larkin stared at the insects, then cocked her head so that one acid-green eye shone from beneath her hair.

"Can I give you a lift?" She pointed to the car parked beside the curb, a red-and-white Mini not much bigger than a bathtub. "Or did you drive?"

"I took the tube. Sure, I'd love a ride—but where're you going? I'm in Camden Town."

"I know. Nick's place. That's not far—come on, get in."

She unlocked the car. "I've never been in a Mini before," Daniel said, stooping to peek in the tiny window. "I don't think I can fit."

"Sure you can." She opened the passenger door and performed an intricate series of adjustments to the seat. "There. *Lots* of room."

They drove off. Daniel had to slump with his knees almost touching his nose and one arm dangling out the window; this gave him a child's-eye view of the streets outside, as well as an intimate perspective on Larkin's left elbow. They circled Highbury Fields and headed toward Camden Town, passing Indian take-aways and a desolate stretch of sad-looking shops and shabby Irish pubs. He shifted so that his head was cradled against the door, and gazed at Larkin.

"So is that your real name? Larkin?"

"My real name?" She smiled and steered the car down a cobble-stone alley. "I suppose it's real."

"I mean, were you christened with it?"

"No, I wasn't christened with it."

"Were you *born* with it? I mean, did your mother quote Philip Larkin's poems when you were a little girl?"

"No." Her expression grew wary. "I chose it for myself. I've done that several times now."

"Changed your name?"

"Why not? I mean, look at you—'Daniel Rowlands.' Wouldn't you like to change *your* name?"

"To what?" He tried to angle his knee more comfortably beneath the dashboard. "No. My name is branded. And I'm not a rock band— people read my column; they don't want to see Daniel Rowlands one week and Grope Swansong the next. And I happen to like my name. But you just change yours whenever you want? Very interesting. You're not a spy, are you?"

"A spy? I'd be a very bad one if I admitted it. No. I just liked Larkin. Some people call me Lark."

"Christ, that's *much* worse."

"Hush!" She slapped his thigh, and Daniel grinned. "Now, listen— would you like to see those studies I was telling you about? The Burne-Jones *Tristan and Iseult*?"

"Sure." He liked watching the glitter of light upon her face as they darted in and out of traffic, trucks and double-decker buses suddenly looming above them like ocean liners. Even pedestrians seemed huge beside the Mini. "Can you give me directions?"

"I'll take you there. Are you busy tomorrow?"

"Larkin, I'm on sabbatical. I'm never busy. But aren't you? Don't you have a job, or an important list of new potential names to consider?"

"I told you, I don't work."

"You must do something," he said, then blushed. *Back off*, he thought.

"Arcana imperii," retorted Larkin. "It's a secret." She frowned, peering out at the bright rush of Camden High Street, minicabs and motorcycles, the tube station like an afterthought shoved in among storefronts with cartoonish bas-reliefs protruding from their upper stories: Doc Martens as big as a man, a Brobdingnagian corset speared by an immense pair of scissors. Without warning, the Mini lurched into a space in front of Nick's maisonette. Daniel's head banged against the front seat as Larkin announced, "I'll pick you up tomorrow at nine."

Daniel rubbed his head and stared at her, not wanting to leave. He waited for her to say more, then suddenly remembered his interview. He groaned. "Tomorrow morning?"

"This offer will not be repeated."

"Yes, yes!" Fuck the interview: he began to pry the door open. "Can I buy you breakfast?"

"At nine o'clock? I'd have starved by then."

"Lunch?"

"We'll see." She turned and smiled at him. "Daniel."

He went cold. In the car was a smear of silvery green where Larkin was, where Larkin had been: a nimbus that cohered into a blinding jab of light, emerald-colored. He gasped. His fingers clutching at the door handle were wet, and the door handle was wriggling; it was *gone,* like a minnow sliding from a cupped hand. He closed his eyes, sick and shivering, felt something small and smooth pressed against his lower lip. With an effort he blinked—

—and there was only Larkin, if that was really her name, a woman with strands of gray in her chestnut hair and fine lines drawn down the side of her mouth, wearing faded clothes and silver bracelets set with lapis lazuli and variscite, a woman leaning over the stick shift to touch her finger to his lip.

"Good night," was all she said.

And yet, and yet. He was outside the car now, stumbling to his feet with his upraised hand mirroring hers as she pulled the door shut, then turned from him and wheeled the Mini back into traffic. And yet she had eyes of a color he had never seen, moss green, acid green, apple green; and she had never really told him who she was or what she did.

And the acorn . . .

He reached into his pocket, pulled it out, and held it up to the streetlight.

"Shit," he whispered.

Thrusting from a crack in the acorn was a tiny root—bright red, pomegranate red—curling like an inchworm. A minute droplet of clear fluid clung to the root's tip. Daniel stared at it, bemused, then, with a half smile, stuck out his tongue and touched it. The fluid had no taste, but when he swallowed, a bitter warmth spread across the back of his tongue.

"Huh," he said. He lifted his hand to throw the acorn into Inverness Street—and stopped.

There was a sound, a prolonged sibilant sigh. His hand remained half raised before him. Something moved against his cheek; he brushed a strand of hair from the corner of his mouth.

"What is it?" he said aloud.

There was no one there. He stood alone in front of Nick's flat, the summer air tainted with the smell of rotting greengages and cabbage leaves strewn along the curb. He turned to gaze back at the High Street, half expecting to see Larkin there, laughing at him from inside her Mini.

But no. There was nothing save the night's traffic, a group of teenagers drinking in the abandoned stretch of market across the road. Daniel shoved the acorn into his pocket and trudged toward the door. Upstairs in Nick's maisonette, the phone begin to ring.

"Damn it," muttered Daniel.

He fumbled for his keys, opened the door, and ran upstairs, grabbing the phone just as the answering machine kicked in.

"*. . . reached Nick Hayward at 0207 . . .*"

"Hello?" he gasped. He had a quick exuberant thought that it would be Larkin. "I'm here—"

"Is that Daniel?"

"Nick." Daniel swore and sank into a chair. "Christ, I nearly killed myself—"

"Just wanted to make sure you got home all right."

"What are you talking about? Of course I'm home. I answered the fucking telephone!"

"Alone?"

Stony silence as Daniel glared at the kitchen table, the tumble of his own papers and a few loose music sheets, Nick's unanswered mail. He could hear reedy music on the other end, then Nick drawing a deep breath.

"Listen, Daniel. *La belle dame sans merci*—did she ask you out or anything?"

"What are you talking about? Larkin? Are you nuts?"

"You're right." Nick laughed. "I must be nuts. She'd never ask you out."

"I meant, why the hell should you care? And yes, of course she did. Tomorrow."

"Don't go."

"Don't go? *You* were the one introduced us!"

"I've changed my mind. Bad idea. She's not your type. It'll end in tears. Trust me."

"Nick." Daniel fought to keep his voice even. "She's taking me to see those paintings she was telling me about. The Burne-Jones studies for Tristan. It's for my fucking *book*, Nick—remember? I'm writing a book?"

"I'm starting to think that was a bad idea, too. Listen—remember that Cramps song? 'What's inside a girl? Somebody told me it's a whole other world—' "

"Good-bye, Nick."

"Can't I talk you out of this?"

"No."

"She'll just use you, Danny—trust me, I know."

"I've never trusted you in my life, Hayward. Why would I start now?"

Nick's voice edged higher, pleading. "Danny, listen! I introduced you because . . . well, because I knew she'd like you. You're her type."

"I thought *you* were her type," Daniel said coldly. "That's what Sira told me."

"I know. Sira said she spoke to you." Nick sighed. "Look, Danny—I know what you're thinking, and it's not that. I'm not jealous. Or I'm not *only* jealous. I'll say this: I did think that if the two of you hooked up, I'd get to see more of her. That she'd be around.

"But now . . . well, it was a mistake. Larkin can be dangerous. She *is* dangerous. It always starts like this—she doesn't remember, is what it is. She's not looking at you. She thinks you're someone else. Something else."

"I thought she thinks *she's* someone else," Daniel retorted. "Or is that another of your pathological fictions? I'm seeing her tomorrow. It's not a big deal."

"You're the one who's shouting."

This was true. So Daniel said nothing: just sat, furious, and refused to give Nick the satisfaction of hanging up on him. Nick remained silent. Finally he said, "All right, Danny. You win. Can I come with you tomorrow?"

"*No!*"

"Then promise me this, Danny—go see a movie or something. The Tate Modern, that's a good idea! But for God's sake don't have dinner with her, Daniel. Or lunch. Don't eat anything. Just promise me th—"

Daniel hung up and stood, feeling wide awake now and quite cheerful. He turned and gazed at the orchestrated chaos that was Nick's home: old pine and oak furniture from the West Country, old guitars, old gold records encased in Plexiglas frames. The World War I campaign desk where Nick did most of his writing. Notebooks, boxes of CDs, the original artwork for *Black Water White Rock* and *Sleeping with the Heroine*. Floor-to-ceiling bookshelves crammed with collections of folklore and folk song, odd photographs and scribbled drawings, yellowing science-fiction paperbacks and books by the depressive women writers Nick favored—Jean Rhys, Laura Riding, Jane Bowles.

"Ha, ha," said Daniel.

He had completely forgotten about the acorn. He wandered over to the bookshelves, picked up a photograph of himself and Nick, taken shortly after they'd first met. Daniel looked sweet-faced and about fifteen years old; he'd very recently graduated from the Columbia School of Journalism and was still flushed with delight over getting a job at the *Horizon* covering pop music. Nick was grinning lewdly and brandishing a joint the size of a zucchini; he had just finished a gig at the Bayou, the *Sleeping with the Heroine* tour. With his unkempt hair, Nepalese tunic, and knee-high suede boots, he looked very much the madman bard of the younger Daniel's imaginings. Behind the two of them, you could just make out the nightclub's brick façade and neon sign and the blurred shape of someone slipping through the door—a woman dressed like Nick in haute Celtic Twilight gear, head half turned toward the camera, her face indistinguishable from the smoke billowing from Nick's joint. Daniel turned the picture over, to read his own scrawl on the back.

Remember me when this you see!
April 29 '78

A softly amazed smile flickered across his face.

April 29. That was today.

For just an instant, he looked almost exactly like the boy in the photograph. Then he replaced it on the shelf, shaking his head.

Remember me. Back then he'd thought Nick Hayward was something close to divine. He'd even written an article to that effect for *Cream. Hayward plays an autoharp strung with his own sinews and broken bones, ragged fragments of love affairs gone bad and the metallic taste of too many mornings when the coke supply's run dry.*

Daniel grimaced. He knew now that was all crap. Songwriting was work, just like writing was work. If Nick still thought otherwise, that was just self-indulgence.

And jealousy, too—what the fuck was Hayward doing, telling him not to see that woman? Daniel's grimace turned to a scowl. He ran his hand along the shelf and yanked out a book at random, opened it, and read.

> *To bring the dead to life*
> *Is no great magic.*
> *Few are wholly dead:*
> *Blow on a dead man's embers*
> *And a live flame will start.*

He threw the book onto the floor and stalked to the window overlooking the High Street. This whole fucking sabbatical had been a misguided attempt at blowing on ashes, to move on to the next level, leaving his comfortable aerie above Connecticut Avenue, surrounded by his Bukowski first editions and vinyl picture disks, signed Caponigro photographs and Cremaster 3 screensaver.

But Daniel had no clear idea what the next level was supposed to *be*. In his wildest dreams, he doubted that a pop-culture study of Tristan and Iseult was enough to garner him a MacArthur Grant, or even a good review in the *Sunday Times*. And yet he knew he'd spend the rest of his life thinking he was a failure if he didn't strive for *something* more, even if he didn't know what that something was.

He stared down at Camden High Street, the insectile throngs clad in black and neon microfiber, mobile-phone antennae bristling as the crowd repeatedly coalesced, then dispersed, seeming to heed the dense interior static of a hive mind. A Humvee, a rare sight in the U.K., was parked in front of the Electric Ballroom, its black windows hiding whoever was inside—drug dealer, DJ, office drone. A girl wearing glass stiletto heels and a hat made of a satellite dish hawked glow necklaces and Dasani by the tube entrance while the shoe store across the street played a trip-hop cover of "She's Going Bald." From the guest room came the soft voice of Daniel's computer, reminding him of the morning's interview, and an answering chime from one of Nick's Palm-Pilots.

He was living in the future he'd so gleefully projected twenty-five years before in one of his first columns for the *Horizon,* and he was bored stiff.

"Your dream of safety has disappeared," Nick had remarked dryly when Daniel announced he was coming to stay in Camden Town, and yet everything around him now seemed nothing *but* a dream of safety. The Web had become a vast electrical cocoon, and he was trapped inside. He pulled the curtains shut, went into the guest room, checked his e-mail, and went to bed.

He couldn't sleep. His thoughts flashed relentlessly between Larkin and Nick, lit by memory of that strange green light he'd seen, or thought he'd seen, in Larkin's car. No, not light exactly, but not darkness or shadow either: "absence" was the word that came to him. He wished now that he hadn't hung up on Nick, wished he'd listened to whatever ridiculous reason his friend had cooked up to excuse his behavior.

La belle dame sans merci.

Should he have agreed to let Nick tag along with him in the morning? *She thinks you're someone else.*

But who was she? He remembered her eyes, a tendril of dark hair pulled taut against her cheek. Should he call Nick after all?

He yawned: nah. His anxiety burned off like ash. In the morning he would not recall it. He pulled the covers over his head, adjusted his earplugs so as to drown out the trippy thrum of the High Street, and at long last fell asleep.

Larkin buzzed herself in next morning. "I've got a key," she shouted through the intercom. "Don't come down."

He met her on the stairs, Daniel shrugging into his leather bomber jacket, Larkin shaking out an umbrella.

"It's really pissing out there." She tossed her head, droplets of rain flying from her hair, then glanced dubiously at his trendy clogs. "Are you sure you're ready? Don't you want a hat? I'm double-parked."

"Yes. No. Let's go."

He ran after her into the street, folding himself in half to scrunch inside the Mini. Music blasted from the speakers, the title song from *Sleeping with the Heroine*. Without thinking, he turned it off as Larkin slid into the driver's seat. The car lurched forward, and Daniel knocked his head against the side window.

"Ow!" He turned to Larkin, rubbing his temple. "How long have you known Nick?"

She switched the music back on. "This was a good album. I've known Nick forever."

"How long is forever?"

"Ages. Nick and I have a history, if that's what you mean." She glanced at him, her eyes guileless. "Is it?"

He nodded. "And . . . ?"

"I was fascinated by what he did. I've never been able to understand how it happens—writing songs. It seems . . ."

She shook her head. Her expression became implacable. "It's something I wish I could do. I wanted to help him with his work."

"Really?" Daniel had once seen Nick kick a fan who'd offered him a suggestion on the chord changes in "White Rock." Nick had mellowed since then, but not much. "How?"

"Folk-song stuff. I gave him some ballads back when he was with Dark Diamond."

"Oh, so *you're* to blame for 'Starry Skies and Long Good-byes.' "

"I thought Nick was your best friend."

"Tragically, he is."

"Then why do you give him such a hard time?"

"Do I?" Daniel thought about this, then shrugged. "I guess because things just always seem to come so easy to him."

"Easy? I don't think it's easy to do what he does."

"Yeah? Well, he should try meeting a deadline."

"I thought you were on sabbatical now—no deadlines!" Larkin gave him a disconcerting smile. "Doing what you've always wanted to do . . . that's what Nick said anyway."

"Nick doesn't know shit. Is this place in Soho, or what?"

"Bloomsbury. Hang on—"

The car veered into a side street so narrow it was practically a sidewalk. Daniel braced himself against the dashboard as they wound through alleys and cobblestone drives and past the ruins of an abandoned council estate, its shattered windows opening onto corridors where he glimpsed figures moving slowly toward each other, then away again, as though performing some grotesque gavotte; past trash tips and the backs of restaurants smelling of fenugreek and sour steam, emerging at last into a brick courtyard surrounded by heaps of rubble and a series of grim attached houses dating to the early 1800s. Rain sluiced around piles of broken brick and mortar, pooling in cloudy white puddles scummed with a livid chemical green. One building stood apart from the rest, a solitary relic of a slightly later era; it looked dazed and out of place, its mid-Victorian architecture a form of overdressing for its sentence in this bleak place. As the Mini pulled up beside its doorway, a rat humped from the shadows and began to swim across the poisonous green pool.

Daniel turned to Larkin. "So this is where Fagin lives now, eh?"

She shut off the motor and peered out. "Over there's Woburn Street. This is Saracen Court. And *that's* where we're going."

She pointed to the door of the solitary building. It was painted dark red, the color of raw liver. Above it was a stone lintel carved with the words PAYNIM HOUSE 1857. "Daniel? There's no point waiting for this to let up. . . ."

She jumped out and ran for the door. Daniel sat for another minute, staring gloomily at the rain, before unfolding himself from the Mini. He had just closed the car door when he heard a voice cry out, high and desperate.

"Marianne?"

Daniel turned, hunching his shoulders against the rain, and saw a girl staggering to her feet beside a pile of rubble. Young, maybe seventeen or eighteen, wearing flared jeans and platform trainers, her filthy blond dreadlocks matted against her skull. She was emaciated, her face bright red. "Marianne!" she shouted.

Daniel looked at Larkin. She paid the girl no attention whatsoever; just struggled to get a key into the door.

"Marianne!"

The girl began to stumble across the courtyard. Daniel turned and ran to Larkin. "Hey—look, maybe this isn't such a great place—"

"Come on, come on," Larkin muttered, then cried in triumph as the door swung open. She slipped inside, Daniel at her heels. He looked back to see the girl still racing toward them. The door slammed closed; there was a crescendo of sobs and curses, then weeping. Daniel stepped quickly into the center of the room.

It had a high-ceilinged foyer, flooded with aquamarine light from skylights of opalescent glass, their copper muntins green with age.

There was a green marble floor whorled with dust and dead leaves, plaster walls verdigrised with rot, an oak taboret supporting a vase of dead parchment-colored roses. On the wall behind the taboret hung a tarnished plaque.

Greater Outer London Folk-Lore Study Society
Established October 1857
Fas est et ab hoste doceri

"Oh!" Larkin cried softly. She stooped to pick up something on the floor. A leaf, Daniel thought at first; but then she straightened and held it out to him. He cupped his hands to receive it.

A moth. "Is it alive?" he asked.

"Not anymore."

It had blade-shaped wings, dusky blue-green; a crimson-furred thorax; faceted green eyes. Gently he touched its thorax, soft as down, then drew his hand to his face, sniffing tentatively. "That's weird. It smells like—apples?" He looked at Larkin. "Where did it come from?"

"From away." She took it from him, walked over to the vase, and nestled the moth within the dead roses. There were others, green moths like handfuls of leaves scattered among the flowers. "They come here by mistake, they get trapped, and then they can't get out. I wish I could help them," she added, and gave him a stricken look.

"Well, gee. I'm really sorry it's dead. Was it—are they—rare?"

"Oh, no. They used to be very common."

She turned and tugged off her anorak, draping it over the edge of the taboret. She was wearing the same clothes as last night, only with a long black scarf looped around her neck. She shook her head vigorously, and her thick hair sprang out, the way a fern straightens after a heavy rain. Daniel took off his leather jacket and set it on the floor beside the taboret, glanced again at the brass plaque on the wall behind it.

"That's kind of weird," he said, frowning as he tried to recall his altar-boy Latin. " 'It is fair to obtain knowledge, even from the enemy.' Sort of an extreme motto for a folklore society."

Larkin shrugged. "Oh, back then people believed there was a system for understanding everything—they just could never agree what the system *was*. These people thought it was folklore."

"Fairy tales?"

"No. More like folk memories. They were scientific, in their own way—they had a sort of Darwinian approach, always looking for a single source for their stories."

"Well, that's what I'm doing."

"Yes." The rain-washed light gave her skin a foxglove shimmer that made her green eyes glow spectrally. "That's why I thought you'd like coming here. Everything is upstairs, just mind your head."

She turned, indicating he should follow her into a corridor, immediately ducked through a low doorway, and began to climb a narrow flight of steps.

"So is that what you are?" said Daniel. "A folklorist?"

"No." She pushed open a door and walked into a small room, wood-paneled and dim, its single round window overlooking the courtyard. There was no furniture save a plain wooden map chest. "I told you, Daniel. I'm not anything."

She looked at him with that strange covert gaze, as though she were peering at him through a gap in a curtain, then knelt beside the map chest and began tugging at its bottom drawer. "Damn, it's *always* stuck."

Rain slashed at the window. The air around them felt chill and close; it smelled of dust and old books, though there were no books that Daniel could see, nothing but the wooden chest. He watched, silent, as Larkin struggled with the drawer; he fought the urge to step closer, to kneel beside her and feel his own hands on the worn drawer pulls, the dusty wooden floor beneath his knees and this woman beside him.

"Oh, come on, please, please . . ." she muttered.

He felt a tremor of excitement, but not at the thought of seeing the sketches. A dreamy anticipation, like opening night of his high school play, when he suddenly stepped out onto the stage and discovered that he did, after all, know his lines, knew where to stand and when to move, knew everyone around him, all those half-shadowed figures he'd never really paid attention to before—he knew them all, knew their names and what they would say next, what they would do, just as he somehow knew the woman right beside him . . .

. . . and he *was* beside her, kneeling, his hands on the map chest. Gently he worked his fingers into the crack above the bottom drawer, prying the drawer loose, and yes, he felt it give slightly, just enough to slide free. Larkin tipped her head to look at Daniel, unsmiling, then bowed so that her hair hid her face from him. With great care she began to withdraw a large portfolio of thick caramel-colored leather pebbled with age, its clasps intricate as the fittings on a corset, and set it upon her knees.

"Thank you," she said softly.

His hands were no longer on the wooden chest but grasping her shoulders. He lowered his face to meet hers, but she was already there, her lips slightly rough and the tip of her tongue tasting of fruit and burned sugar. He kissed her, could feel nothing but her mouth; his hands slipped through folds of cloth then seemed to slide into empty air. When he opened his eyes, she was staring at him bewildered, as though she had just awakened in a strange place.

"Daniel," she said. Her eyes widened: he could see her pupils contract, then expand until they filled each iris, like a time-lapse film of a blossoming flower. "Daniel."

The breath caught in his throat: *she saw him.* He drew back, resting his hand upon the map chest to steady himself, and looked at her without speaking: a word would freeze the moment, make it inescapable. He almost saw what would happen next, he almost knew the right thing to say if he were to speak; he had to speak—

"I—should we look at them here?" he stammered.

Larkin flushed, then quickly looked down. Daniel grew hot with embarrassment and frustration.

"Yes," she said, stumbling to her feet. "Yes, just set them on top of the map chest."

His hand shot out to steady her. She flinched, and he moved away. She was intent upon the portfolio now, undoing the clasps and gingerly spreading the boards atop the chest.

"Here," she breathed, lifting and setting aside first one, then a second and third sheet of protective onionskin. "Here they are. Aren't they beautiful?"

He stood beside her, surprised at how small the drawings were—scarcely bigger than a sheet of letterhead—and meticulously worked in pencil and charcoal and ink. All showed the same two figures, a man and woman. The few clothes they wore were rendered as stylized medieval garb. Tiny precise lettering identified each drawing.

HOW THEY WERE ENCHANTED

HOW THEY WERE DISCOVERED

HOW SIR TRISTRAM WAS RECOGNIZED BY A BRACHET

"Yes. Yes, they are," he murmured. He glanced at Larkin and smiled in pure delight. "Really, *really* beautiful."

Daniel moved to the other side of the chest, angling until he clearly discerned where the artist had sketched then rubbed out earlier lines, ghostly figures in attendance upon the lovers. In the air above them, Daniel traced a near-invisible arm, entwined bodies, a curl of ivy that echoed a dog's tail. When he turned to Larkin, his eyes were shining.

"I see what you mean!" he said. "They're not like his paintings at all. I mean, these are amazingly . . ."

He hesitated.

"Explicit?" suggested Larkin.

Daniel laughed. "That's one way of putting it," he said, and set the pictures side by side atop the chest.

Enchantment. Discovery. Recognition.

He stared at them, brow furrowed. The style was familiar, that immediately recognizable Burne-Jones synthesis of medieval and romantic imagery, strong elegant lines and soft-eyed models. Yet there was nothing merely pretty about these images. It wasn't just that the figures were nearly naked and anatomically correct or that they were conjoined in conspicuously erotic, even brutal poses—their enchantment was not symbolized by a cup, the one who discovered them appeared neither surprised or dismayed, the brachet was not a dog but something else, something that made Daniel look away. To be sure, these details contributed to their strangeness. But it was more than the contrast between the familiar illustrative style and its unexpected deployment, the shock of sex where one expected sunflowers.

Rather, as Daniel stared, each drawing seemed to crystallize the most powerful desire and yearning that he had ever experienced—desire that he realized suddenly had never been fulfilled, yearning that whelmed him like the memory of a dream he had till this moment forgotten, a dream that overshadowed his waking life so that it was unbearable to think that he was not sleeping now—and it was this distillation of longing and ecstatic despair that took his breath away.

Beside him Larkin bent to peruse the third drawing: Recognition. "Of course, he did produce some intensely erotic work," she said. "They all did. You forget that. You're so used to thinking of all those Victorians as being sexually repressed or frigid or—"

She looked at Daniel and smiled. "Well, all that sort of thing. Maybe it's too much like imagining your parents having sex on the kitchen table."

"Please." Daniel pointed a chiding finger at her. "But—come on! You have to admit, there's something extreme about this stuff. I mean, *that—*"

He pointed at the thing that wasn't a brachet, then averted his eyes.

"How have they been kept secret all this time? Why haven't I heard of them or seen them?"

"Ned said they were never to be seen."

"But why? He did all those paintings of Maria Zambaco—they were shown in his lifetime. And these . . . well, yes, they're explicit for their time, but their time was a hundred and twenty years ago! How could anyone prevent these pictures from being shown *now*?"

"Well, no one really knows they're here."

"Do you mean they're stolen?"

"No," said Larkin. A flare of black in her green eyes. "I mean they're not supposed to be anywhere. Georgie Burne-Jones ordered them to be destroyed after her husband's death, but . . . someone got hold of them and brought them here. They're a secret. That's why they've never been reproduced, and there's no mention of them except in a few contemporary accounts from his friends."

"I can't possibly be the first—you said researchers come to see them."

"No. That's not what I said."

Daniel stared across the room. The porthole window was a bleary eye opening onto a blur of silver-green; he could hear the muted roar of a sanitation truck making its rounds. What had become of the girl screaming "Marianne"? He stepped over to the window but saw nothing but the courtyard's enclosed wasteland, the Mini a red island surrounded by black water.

"Was it the model, then?" He turned back to Larkin. "His wife was afraid of another affair?"

"Yes. She was afraid she'd lose him forever. She almost did."

Daniel returned to stare at the woman in the drawings. Very tall, full-breasted, with long dark hair and a piquant face at odds with that columnar neck. He didn't speak his thought: that she looked like the woman beside him. "Who is she?"

"Her name was Evienne Upstone. She found him after he broke

with Maria Zambaco. He was . . . vulnerable, and that made him very beautiful to her."

"When did he do these? Are they dated?"

"This one"—she pointed at *How They Were Discovered*—"there's a letter Burne-Jones wrote to Rossetti a few months before Rossetti died—this would have been the winter of '81. He refers to a painting with that title. The painting was never found, just this study. I think his wife destroyed it. In the letter Burne-Jones says that he has 'seen once more the girl in the well.'"

"And she was . . . ?"

Larkin hesitated. "No one really knows. But his wife, Georgie, refers to a dream he had. . . ."

She crouched in front of the chest and tugged at another drawer. This one opened easily. It was filled with books—old books, though he recognized a battered copy of *The Helga Pictures*—as well as sheets of drafting paper covered with penciled scrawls, several videotapes, and a bundle of dirty brown yarn wrapped around a stick. Larkin withdrew a volume with gilt letters on the spine: *Memorials of Edward Burne-Jones*. She thumbed through the pages, finally stopping to read aloud.

"One of Edward's dreams remains in a letter about 'a shadowy girl who was by a well in that mournful twilight that is the sky of our dreams. "Now listen to the noise of my heart," she said, and dropped a vast stone into the well—which boomed and boomed until it grew to a roar unbearable, and I awoke.'"

Daniel made a face. "Well, at least he felt guilty about screwing around on his wife."

"He wasn't feeling guilty about Maria Zambaco."

"Really?" Daniel raised an eyebrow. "Who was he feeling guilty about?"

"I don't believe that he was feeling guilty at all. I think the dream meant something else. It—she—was something else."

Daniel said nothing. *She's a former mental patient.* He thought of Robert Lowell imagining himself to be the king of Scotland and becoming obsessed with hammers, screwdrivers, bushels of nails, and baling wire, all because T. S. Eliot once admitted a fondness for hardware stores; he thought of Nick trying to warn him last night, and of the *TimeOut* interview he'd blown off this morning.

"I don't get it," he said at last. "Burne-Jones dreamed this person, and then he found someone who looked like her to pose for his painting?"

"No." Larkin shook her head adamantly. "He did see someone."

Daniel started to laugh. "I'm sorry," he said. "I haven't kept up with that kind of stuff since I was an undergrad. It's—"

"Enough." She held out her hand for the book and returned it to the drawer, then set about replacing the studies of Tristran and Iseult in their portfolio. "We should leave soon if we're going to have lunch. Would you like to see the Candell painting before we go?"

"Sure."

He followed her back into the hall. "It's in here," she said, and opened the door to a tiny room that must have been a linen closet, pervaded by a faint smell of starch. Light seeped from a clerestory window; dark bands ran across walls where there had once been shelves. Beneath the high window hung a small oval painting. Daniel's gangly frame filled the room as he stepped inside to peer at the canvas.

"It's so small!" he said.

"Most people need a magnifying lens to see it properly. But it would be lost in a bigger room, so I keep it here."

"It's yours?"

She smiled. "A gift of the artist."

The little oval was so crowded with tiny figures he couldn't determine what, if anything, was its subject—it made his head hurt just to try. He crouched to squint at lettering in the lower curve of the canvas: THE DOG HAS NOT JUMPED DOWN YET.

He frowned: he couldn't find a dog within that throng of minute people and fanciful vegetation. "'The dog has not jumped down yet.' Does that mean something?"

"It's from a story. 'King Orfeo.'"

"Don't know it. Orfeo, like Orpheus?"

"I suppose." She was staring at the picture with a sad, puzzled expression. "People come up with strange things to explain what they don't comprehend."

"Like . . . ?"

"Like the dead," she said. "I can never understand how it works. You yearn for them, you miss them, they're gone, and no matter how long you look, you can never find them again. But you desire them. You grieve. It's very beautiful." She turned away, her long hair falling across her face as she stepped back through the door into the hallway. "And this—"

She lifted her hand to a window, twisting her hand back and forth so that light filtered between her fingers, turning them from white to black, white to black. "Shadows. Chiaroscuro. It's so beautiful! But confusing."

Daniel stared at her blankly, then followed her down the hall. "Well, I guess I won't argue with that."

Abruptly she turned to face him. "Are you hungry? Because I'm famished."

"Oh. Well. Gee." He tallied two columns in his head:

1. Go to lunch   **2. Leave now**
   Eat
   Drink
   Listen to more stories about English art figures
   Have sex with beautiful though disturbed woman

"Um, well, I . . ."

"There's a brasserie near here. The food's brilliant."

She smiled, and he found himself staring right into those green-glass eyes, wondering what it would be like to touch her cheek, there, and if the strange periwinkle shimmer stopped with her face or—

"Sure! I mean, yes, I'm hungry." He cocked his thumb at the door. "Thanks for showing me the painting by Jack the Ripper."

Larkin laughed. "Cobus Candell. As far as I know, he wasn't anywhere as prolific as Jack the Ripper. But you never can tell."

"You never can tell," Daniel agreed, grinning, and followed her back downstairs.

They walked to the restaurant. There was no sign of the girl who'd been in the courtyard. The rain had stopped. High above them pale sky gleamed, and a chill breeze stirred puddles in the street.

"Boy, I'd never be able to find my way back from here," Daniel said, pulling his leather jacket tight around him. "I bet your restaurant isn't in *TimeOut.*"

"You lose," said Larkin, disappearing behind a corner.

"Hey, wait—!"

He stumbled after her, trying to grasp her arm. She only laughed, shaking her head so that hair blurred into shadow and her face seemed to float before him. "I'm fine, really. But it's a good thing we're early. They get packed at lunchtime."

She turned and swept through the door. Her hair whipped back into his face, smelling sweetly of green apples. He reached for her collar, felt her hand pressing his. Then she was gone ahead of him, inside.

Daniel blinked as he tried to adjust to the darkness. The dining tables were stainless steel; what he could glimpse of the kitchen seemed as floodlit as a hospital operating room. The overall effect was of dining in an underground abattoir. Still, it smelled great—roasting garlic, fresh bread, anisette. And the clientele looked expensive, thin men and thinner women in black, waving mobile phones and cigarettes.

They sat. A waiter appeared to hand them menus. "I'll have the sweetbreads," Larkin announced without looking at hers. "And wine— do you want wine, Daniel?"

"Wine? It's barely eleven."

He almost said, *And you're not supposed to drink.* Instead he did a quick survey and yes, in front of every diner there was either a wine bottle or a cocktail glass. *There'll always be an England,* thought Daniel.

For a moment he considered his responsibilities. The right thing would be *not* to drink, for her sake. And since when did he drink at lunchtime anyway? Not since he used to hang out with Nick, twenty years ago. . . .

Bad idea, he decided as the waiter handed him the wine list. Still, when in Londinium . . .

He ordered a bottle of claret and garlic steak. When the wine arrived, he toasted Larkin, who had settled contentedly back into her chair. "Now will you please tell me the name of this temple of fine dining?"

"Café Chouette. It's a very louche place," Larkin said. "That's why I thought you'd enjoy it."

"It seems very louche indeed," he said, flattered. "Do they serve absinthe? I've never tried it."

"After lunch. Look, here's our food."

Larkin glanced at the platter of sweetbreads steaming before her, then watched expectantly until Daniel lifted knife and fork. She looked like a cat waiting to be fed. He smiled, making a show of cutting his meat and tasting it.

"Mmmm-mmm, good."

Only then did she attend to her own food.

"So," said Daniel, "how did you get a key to that place?"

"Paynim House? Someone gave it to me."

"People seem to give you things a lot."

"They do, don't they?" She took a sip of wine. "I'm fascinated by how it works. Art. Making things. I want to understand it, become—"

"Become part of the process?" Daniel shook his head. "Uh-uh. I think a work of art is what the artist intended it to be. Period. You and me, we contribute nothing to the process."

"We contribute *something*. If you're looking at a nude by Lucian Freud, you'll see a different painting than I will, because you're a man. And we both might see a different painting if we knew that the nude woman was not just a model but his lover. His muse. Like all those Rossettis where Lizzie Siddal was the model, and Jane Morris—"

"That's not being part of the process. That's getting a vicarious kick out of knowing the painter was sleeping with his models."

"It's more than that," said Larkin. "I think the muse brings something real to the work. Something numinous."

Daniel snorted. "That's ridiculous. What about Picasso? He slept with thousands of women—were they all numinous?"

"Picasso is sui generis. Someone like that doesn't need to derive power."

"Interesting theory: the muse as alternate energy source." Daniel turned his attention back to his plate. "Anyway, Nick's right, those Pre-Raphaelites, even the best ones—they're all second-tier artists. If that."

"I'm not interested in how important they are. It's their energy—where does that come from? I don't understand it at all."

Daniel reached to touch her wrist. "Larkin, I can help you here. There is nothing, *nothing* to understand. It's a job, just like my going home and writing a column is a job, just like anything's a job. There is no mystery to it at all."

"There is to me."

He shook his head. "I'm sorry, Larkin, but I just don't buy it. All that White Goddess stuff—" He stopped.

"What?" said Larkin.

"Nothing. I suddenly remembered—last night, I was fooling around with one of Nick's books, flipping through it at random. There was a poem by him. Graves."

"Which one?"

"I don't remember. Something about blowing on ashes."

"Divination by books."

"Hey, I'm a critic, it's what I do. But I'll tell you, since you're talking about muses—*The White Goddess*? Half of it Graves made up, and the other half he got from crackpots who'd made it up before him. He's been totally discredited."

"Just because someone makes something up doesn't mean it's not real."

Leave now, Daniel thought, but didn't move. Larkin pushed her plate aside, her face thoughtful.

"Do you know Radborne Comstock's work?"

"Sure. When I was in college, every girl I ever slept with had a Radborne Comstock poster above her bed. That or a Maxfield Parrish girl in a swing."

"He did a Tristan painting, too. He had his first commissions here in London."

A waiter took their plates and the empty wine bottle. Daniel briefly considered ordering another, but before he could, Larkin cocked a finger at another waiter.

"Hugh," she said. "Could we please have *l'absinthe*?"

"Of course," he said.

Larkin smiled at Daniel. "You Americans. So innocent. Imagine, never having tasted absinthe."

"I thought it was illegal. Or poisonous."

"Americans think everything is illegal or poisonous."

"Then how come all those guys got so messed up by it? Verlaine and the rest?"

"The grape crop failed in France, and everyone who was used to drinking wine started drinking absinthe instead. Only it was about seventy percent alcohol, instead of fifteen, and they were still drinking it from the same-size glasses. Now, if you wanted to, Daniel, you could order a cocktail here identical to one drunk back at Café du Rat Mort. La Momisette, 'the little mummy'—absinthe and orgeat on ice."

"Orgeat?"

"Almonds and orange-flower water. Don't they drink that in your newsroom?"

"Not often enough." He leaned across the table. "So. Are you married? Or . . . ?"

She stared at her empty wineglass.

"I was," she said at last. "I suppose that's what you'd call it. A long time ago."

"What happened?"

"I'm not sure," she said. "I don't really recall it that well. I think we quarreled."

"Over what?"

She looked at him, confused. "I don't remember. I can never remember. Is it important?"

Daniel shook his head. "Not at all," he said softly.

The waiter returned, bearing a tray with two tall glasses filled with ice, a silver sugar bowl and tongs, a perforated silver trowel. Last of all he set down a bottle of green liquid so brilliant it appeared radioactive.

"*La fée verte,*" he said with a flourish. "Shall I do the honors?"

Larkin smiled. "Thank you, I'll take care of it."

She placed one of the glasses before Daniel, laid the silver trowel on top, then arranged sugar cubes into a pyramid on the trowel. Daniel watched, mesmerized.

"That's amazing. Can you bend spoons, too?"

"Now, watch—"

She picked up the decanter and poured a ribbon of green liquid over the sugar. The pyramid dissolved like a sand castle beneath a wave. The absinthe dripped through the perforated trowel into the glass. When it struck the ice, all seemed to explode into a cloud of green and white.

"Wow." Daniel watched wide-eyed as she did the same thing to her own glass. "That's the difference between American and English public schools. I chugged beer, and you learned how to do *that*."

Larkin lifted her glass. "To the Old World."

Daniel picked up his absinthe, inhaling the sharp anise scent and an unfamiliar bitter smell: wormwood.

"To the Old World," he said, and drew the glass to his lips. "Here goes nothing."

"Here goes nothing," agreed Larkin, and they both drank.

CHAPTER FOUR

Chill October
Radborne Comstock, 1883

But Muses resemble those women who creep out at night and
give themselves to unknown sailors and return to talk of Chinese porcelain—
porcelain is best made, a Japanese critic has said, where the conditions of life are hard—
or of the Ninth Symphony—virginity renews itself like the moon—except that the Muses
sometimes form in these low haunts their most lasting attachments.
—*William Butler Yeats*

He was twenty-three, tall and already stooped from hunching over his sketchbook, with the stunned and slightly wearying expression of an American visiting Europe for the very first time. His father's death the previous spring had left him with a small inheritance: the house where he had grown up in Elmira, New York, which he had promptly sold to a young banker eager to install indoor plumbing and brand-new electroliers in the ramshackle structure. Augmented by what he had saved from his position at Garrison Asylum, there was enough money for a summer's lease on two rooms in a Mulberry Street tenement in Manhattan, painting lessons from the supercilious but brilliant Wilhelm van der Ven at his studio near Central Park, and, after a boyhood spent dreaming over the smudged etchings in the Elmira Library's tattered copies of *Punch,* enough cash to pay for passage to Bristol and thence by train to the city that had haunted him day and night, like one of the spidery figures in his own drawings.

London.

The city seemed far more dangerous than New York. Just a few days after he arrived, the *Evening News* headline declared

ANOTHER 2,000 ANARCHISTS RUMOURED IN LONDON
No End of Threat to Innocents in This Great Metropolis

The single cramped room Radborne had taken in the Grey Owl rooming house in Mint Street seemed itself quite suitable for habitation by an anarchist, albeit one with high tolerance for dirt, noise, and the smell of the black cigarillos smoked by Mrs. Beale, his widowed land-lady. Mrs. Beale, a russet-haired subscriber to the Fellowship of the New Life with a penchant for gin punch, had lent him a copy of a pamphlet by Mr. G. B. Shaw titled *The Difficulties of Anarchism.* But when Radborne found himself contemplating the widow's frankly inviting assessment of himself over the breakfast table, he declined her invitation to attend the Fabians' next meeting.

"Oh, that *is* a shame!" Mrs. Beale offered him more tea, which Radborne also declined. He had seen her drying last evening's leaves over the spirit lamp, to find their way back into the pot this morning. "We are to discuss Aspects of Spiritualism. And so this morning you will be . . . ?"

"I think I'll visit Kew Gardens." He ran a hand through his hair, which had gotten far too long and embarrassingly unkempt. At Mrs. Beale's admiring smile, he dropped his hand hastily back onto the table. "I would like to sketch some of the rare plants there."

"How pleasant, to be an artist! 'As happy as a bright sunflower!' But of course, you will be *drawing* the sunflowers," she added. "And not *being* one. Yours is not a vegetable love, I fear."

Radborne stared at her blankly. Mrs. Beale put a finger to her cheek in a frightening imitation of coquetry, then stood and swept up the platter holding the remains of breakfast. As she made her way back to the kitchen, she began to sing in a clear, girlish voice.

> *"If he's content with a vegetable love which would certainly not suit me,*
> *Why, what a most particularly pure young man this pure young man must be!"*

Radborne smiled wanly. *"Patience,"* he said, and sighed. In the week since he'd arrived, Mrs. Beale had insisted twenty or more times that he must see the play, at the newly opened Savoy.

"Electricity," she had confided. "It makes all the difference. You cannot imagine the miracle of seeing them perform by a thousand electric lights! It is magical, Mr. Comstock! *Magical.*"

Mrs. Beale had a friend who was a Savoyard, a young woman in the chorus who could almost certainly make special arrangements for Radborne to accompany Mrs. Beale to the stalls one evening. Afterward they could have a late supper, whiskey punch and oysters at Raoul's. But when Radborne inquired after the young friend, it quickly became apparent that this was the wrong line of questioning to pursue. The invitation was not repeated, though selections from the opera continued to pour from Mrs. Beale's throat.

He was initially embarrassed, and then secretly pleased, to realize that his landlady had taken him to be one of the very aesthetes that *Patience* parodied. His unruly hair, the result of poverty and not fashion; his unrefined American wardrobe; his sketchbook, of course—all impressed upon Mrs. Beale that he must be a genuine artist, not a "Chancery Lane young man," oh, no!

He was handsome enough that women winked at him in the street. He had his mother's pale Irish skin and rather fierce features: thick black hair sweeping across a high forehead, hazel eyes beneath black brows, jutting chin, high ruddy cheekbones (this from having to walk everywhere in the damnable cold), an angry set to his full mouth that kept it from prettiness. Since he'd come to London, his voice had grown hoarser, deeper than it had been at home. Here, breathing was like swallowing mouthfuls of sand; some nights he could actually feel the grit on his lips left by coal smoke and the dirt thrown up by passing coaches.

What disturbed him more was that twice he had been followed in the streets. Each time he was walking to Blackfriars Bridge when, from the corner of his eye, he saw a tall figure striding behind him. At first he ignored it, but his unease grew until he finally whirled, fist raised and mouth opened to shout.

But the figure was gone, lost behind heaps of rubble where a block of tenements was being torn down. Radborne had a fleeting impression of a tall, almost emaciated form, a sharp white face with long, uptilted eyes.

"Tinkers," Mrs. Beale pronounced when he mentioned his encounter. "Gypsies, street arabs. They're everywhere. Give 'im a penny. Or hit 'im with a rock."

Radborne wondered how this fit with Mrs. Beale's sympathies for the Fellowship of the New Life. "He was too quick," he said. "A half-starved wretch, too, that's what surprised me—that he was so quick."

"Hit 'im," Mrs. Beale repeated with a nod. "*That'll* slow 'im down."

Radborne said nothing. He recalled his Irish mother's warning him about tinkers—traveling people who stole children and cursed those who were not kind to them, people who shared peculiar gifts with those whom she called the Good Neighbors. He took to carrying a few extra pence when he went walking. He did not see the figure again.

Still, a vague disquiet accompanied him everywhere. He blamed the bad food and terrible air and general strangeness that surrounded him. And yet the unease was broken by surges of joy and exhilaration such as he had never known. He found himself laughing out loud at the wheeling of crows across the sky, laughing so hard that he had to lean against a lamppost to steady himself, until a bobby began to take notice and Radborne moved on, wiping the tears from his face. Another day the sound of a drunken man singing from a rooftop froze him in the street below.

> *"My darling, my darling, my darling young wife*
> *Where have you lain your head?*
> *I turned and beside me found only cold stone*
> *Cold stone where you'd lain in my bed. . . ."*

Radborne had looked up and seen a ragged silhouette waltzing behind a broken balustrade. Suddenly the man stopped, arms outstretched, and stared down at Radborne. His voice became a shout.

> *"In the gorse and the heath*
> *And dark places beneath*
> *You laid me to bed, my husband*
> *There to lie with stones and the sky*
> *In the dark, in the dark and the day."*

As Radborne gazed at him, an odd pulse began to pound behind his eyes. The wind made the man's faded blue work coat ripple up and down his arms; it seemed to have too many sleeves. He was like an insect pinned against the sky. When once again he opened his mouth to sing, vapor poured from it, and tiny black things. Radborne turned and fled, filled with a horror he could not explain or obviate.

He was neither young nor naive enough to believe that a great and terrible city would welcome him, a lanky young American with no connections and no money. But he had thought that, after all these years, he himself would embrace the city, recognize it, love it as he had never loved anything save the images he drew.

Instead London ravaged him. This morning, sitting alone at the breakfast table as Mrs. Beale trilled her last lines from *Patience* and began shouting orders at Kathleen in the kitchen, he could feel the day coming down on him like a fever. This wasn't entirely his fault: the Grey Owl stank of scorched ironing and gin and damp cocoa-matting carpet that never really dried. The furnishings were cheap attempts at luxury—rosewood chairs that creaked when he sat in them, a parlor carpet with a "House of Lords" pattern, piss-yellow on a dark-blue ground; the ubiquitous piano strewn with broadsides and sheet music. The dark curtains were drawn so that the Axminster carpets would not fade, and Radborne had to share the dank backyard washing house and water closet with the other renters.

But the Grey Owl cost only twenty shillings a week, including maid service. If Radborne paid for a month in advance (he did), this would be reduced to eighteen shillings. And Mrs. Beale had a covert arrangement with the cook at the nearby White Horse, another Mint Street rooming house that proudly advertised a library of over five hundred volumes. For an additional one penny a week, the White Horse's cook would let Radborne in through the scullery door to avail himself of such treats as the brand-new magazines, *Tit-Bits* and *People,* as well as popular novels and newspapers.

None of this really made him feel at home. He had not been expecting electric streetlights, which had come to Manhattan only the year before, but he had difficulty hiding the nausea he felt, assaulted by the stench of horse dung, of thousands of years of humanity squatting in the alleys to defecate, the sulfurous reek of the gas lamps, and the more malign odors that rose from ancient churchyards in the poorer quarters, where only a few years earlier the dead were still thrown into shallow graves and the air was colored a faint glowing green on damp afternoons. The open sewers had been cleaned nearly twenty years before, but in some places near the Thames—and Mint Street was one of them—the night-soil man could still be seen on his morning rounds, a sad-eyed draft horse dragging his reeking cart, while around them the crumbling brick buildings released ammonia fumes when it rained.

And it always seemed to rain.

Like now. In the kitchen Radborne could hear Mrs. Beale arguing with Kathleen, followed by an ominous silence, and then the even more ominous sound of his landlady returning to the dining table, humming "Quite Too Utterly Utter." Before she could capture him, he shoved his plate aside and hurried to the front door.

"Damn again."

Outside, all was swabbed in shades of taupe and pewter. Rain pelted down; the narrow cobblestone street was already ankle deep in mud and pus-colored water. Radborne stared out with a kind of desperation, as though plotting an escape such as his more ambitious charges at Garrison used to do. He had left his wooden color box beside the umbrella stand. If he went out, at least the color box would stay dry: he had taken the precaution of waterproofing it before he left New York.

But his raincoat had disappeared on the train from Bristol. It had been raining then, too, and a Gypsyish-looking boy had poked his head into Radborne's compartment several times, pretending to search for his sister. It was only after the train arrived in Paddington that Radborne had found his coat missing.

"Mr. Comstock. You're not going out again like that." He turned to see Mrs. Beale frowning at him. "Your last adventure . . ."

She wagged her finger at him coyly. A week earlier he had ventured to the Tate and returned in a downpour. "That is why my carpet never dries," she went on, stamping at an offending curl of cocoa matting and then looking at him sideways. "But see now! Mr. Balcombe has gone up to Cheltenham for three days, and *he* has left his overcoat!"

She pursed her mouth and crossed to the coat stand. "Now, he would not mind, I don't think, if a very nice young American made use of this. I don't think he would mind at all," she said, removing a black oilcloth ulster and holding it out with a flourish.

"Oh, no," Radborne said weakly, backing away. "Honest, I couldn't—"

"No honor among thieves!" warbled Mrs. Beale, winking. Radborne tried to determine if this was a joke, but she was already tugging the oilcloth over his shoulders and patting his cheek. "Looks very nice, very nice. 'And ev'ryone will say, As you walk your mystic way, Why, what a very cultivated kind of youth this kind of youth must be!'"

Radborne gave her a wan smile. "Well. I must hurry if I'm to catch my train."

He shoved his arms through the sleeves. A good three inches of wrist showed; when he glanced at himself in the mottled mirror across the hall, his reflection seemed more cottager than cultivated. But he only nodded and turned to go.

"Thank you." He ran a hand across the top of his head in lieu of doffing a hat. "I'll do my best to walk in a mystic way."

"Oh, you can't help it," bridled Mrs. Beale. "Such an attentive young man! Mind you come back to us! Oh, but wait—"

It seemed Mr. Balcombe had forgotten a tortoiseshell-handled umbrella, too. Mrs. Beale handed it to Radborne, who cast her one last sheepish grin and ducked through the door.

Outside, the rain had slackened. A small knot of children clad in tattered blue cambric shifts and trousers took this opportunity to race toward the entryway of the Ragged School next door. They ran shrieking and cursing around Radborne, and one of them yanked at his umbrella as he darted past.

"Won helpcha!" the boy shouted, pausing to kick a spume of filthy water onto Radborne's trousers. "Won helpcha!"

Radborne turned angrily. He was stopped by the sight of the

schoolteacher, a grim blade of a man who had materialized in the school's doorway. He held a cane, and as the children slowed to climb the steps, he lashed perfunctorily at their legs, as though striking the heads off flowers.

"Good Christ," muttered Radborne. Then, clutching color box and umbrella, he hurried in the direction of Blackfriars Bridge. To one side of the street loomed the ruins of the demolished Marshalsea Prison, piles of twisted iron, crushed brick, and knots of what looked like human hair. Even in the rain, the process continued, workers shouting as they trundled barrows back and forth, but whether they were erecting new buildings or dismantling older ones, Radborne could not guess.

He huddled deeper into Mr. Balcombe's ulster. He had little money for such luxuries as a hansom, let alone the train fare to Richmond and the entry fee for Kew Gardens, but the thought of another sunless day in the belly of Southwark, with Mrs. Beale's mutton stew congealing on the table and the Ragged School's master declaiming Deuteronomy to his charges at the top of his lungs, was unbearable.

He trudged on, hopping between the high curb and the scant shelter of tattered awnings. He looked hopefully for an omnibus, but none passed, just the usual carts bearing dead horses to the knackers and gray-faced women hurrying to market. Leggy michaelmas daisies the faded blue of old china straggled between the cobblestones; other than these, Radborne saw nothing green or alive.

"No vegetable love for me," he said, and laughed. "No mystic way for me."

Near Blackfriars Road a poster flapped bleakly in the chill wind off the Thames.

PHRENOLOGY

ARE WE ABOUT TO MARRY?

HAVE WE CHILDREN?

DR. JUDA TRENT

LECTURER & TEACHER OF PRACTICAL PHRENOLOGY

TERMS & TESTIMONIALS

A man, his hands swathed in bandages, stood beneath the poster's torn edge and stared at Radborne as he hurried across the street.

"Have we children?" the man shouted. Where his bandages had unraveled, Radborne could glimpse patches of bluish skin. *"Have we children?"*

Radborne bent his head and went on, the ulster plastered to his thighs. Ahead of him the arch of Blackfriars Bridge loomed across a sky pearly with the promise of weak sunlight. Suddenly he felt overheated. The collar of his wool jacket stuck to his neck; he felt a trickle of sweat in the hollow of his throat. The light was strange, at once watery and smoky, like gazing through the glass of a dirty vivarium. He tucked the umbrella tight beneath his armpit and shifted his color box so that it covered his breast, lifted his face to the sky, and stepped toward the curb.

Kings Road was crowded with carts and dray horses, hansoms, and four-wheelers. He looked for a omnibus that bore a placard for Paddington Station. Mrs. Beale had taught him how to summon them—one whistle for an omnibus, two for a hansom—but it seemed he would have to cross the bridge first. He stood on the curb, waiting for the traffic to ease. A sudden ray of sun fell sweet upon his face. A barrel organ played "Champagne Charlie," the organ grinder singing along in a wheezing tenor.

> *"Good for any game at night, my boys,—*
> *Yes, good for any game at night—"*

Within the stew of dirt and dung and coal smoke, Radborne could smell something faint but piercingly familiar: not the sewer reek of the Thames but the sharp clean odor of seawater, a scent that somehow had a sound: high-pitched, almost painful. As he inhaled, the sound became a spike of fire in his head. A shudder rent him, from the back of his throat down his spine; his eyes seemed to open wider than they ever had, as though something pushed its way free from his skull. He staggered to curb's edge, avoided falling into the street only because someone shouted at him from an oncoming cart.

"*'Ey now, watcher—!*"

With a grunt Radborne reared back but lost control of umbrella and color box. The first flew like a javelin into the street, fell before the cart's wooden wheels, and exploded into scissored black wings and broken spines. Radborne dropped into a half crouch, desperately grabbing at his color box before it, too, was destroyed.

He caught it mere inches above the filthy pavement, then collapsed onto his rump. For a moment he sat there, horses stomping past and cartwheels rumbling, their din growing to a hollow roar as they turned onto the bridge. The sun slipped behind a cloud as he stumbled to his feet again.

A woman was on the bridge. Directly across from him, separated by thirty feet and the seething throng of vehicles and foot traffic: as he stared, the sun broke through to cast a flood of pale light upon her. Her clothes were ragged—he had only a vague impression of soft grays and greens, a violent slash of cyan at her throat—and she stood with arms at her sides and the chalky flesh exposed, her sleeves pushed up like a fishmonger's. Her skin had the powdery gleam of limestone, and there were faint green shadows in the cleft of her throat and the hollows of her cheeks. Her eyes, too, were green, a dark, almost muddy color, but the irises were salted with amber, which gave them a strange glitter. He did not think how it was he could notice all this from such a distance, yet he did; her eyes and hair and skin pressed themselves upon him as though he were washed paper absorbing the touch of sable and ink.

She did not see him. She did not appear to see anyone, though her eyes moved restlessly, as if straining to find a point of light in a dark room. Her hands hung limp at her sides as the breeze lifted a strand of hair that gleamed like a dewed cobweb. The rest of her hair was plastered to her skull; a faint vapor hung about her shawl, smoke or mist, and a flicker as though she held a burning lucifer in one hand.

*"One night last week I went up in a balloon,
On a voyage of discovery to visit the Moon. . . ."*

Behind Radborne the organ grinder's voice rang out. He elbowed his way past Radborne to stand on the curb, blocking his view of the woman. Radborne blinked, startled. He swore, pushing the man aside, and jumped into the road. For an instant he saw her; then her face was obscured by a woman with a perambulator. From the corner of his eye, Radborne saw an omnibus approaching. Gripping his color box, he lunged into the middle of the street, heedless of a woman's shriek and the bellowed curses of the omnibus driver, the swelling notes of the hurdy gurdy and a child's laughter.

"Miss!"

Water and icy mud spattered him; someone might have thrown a stone. But he reached the other side and stood upon Blackfriars Bridge, a miniature city crowded with vendors and pedestrians, buses and wagons and cabs and dray horses, with ragged dogs skulking between lampposts and legs.

"Miss!" he cried again.

She was gone. Though, for all he knew, she might have been there still, hidden by the crowd or hiding in it. He looked for her despairingly, ignoring the curses thrown at him by drivers in the street.

"Sir—sir, your bus!"

He looked up to see a young workman in blue moleskin smock and trews stained black with dye. He was pointing at an omnibus wheeling onto the bridge. "I saw yer, nearly killed yerself—don't miss it, now!"

Radborne hesitated. He could see no sign of the woman: had she really been there? Quickly he scanned the bridge again, then heard someone shouting.

"Make up yer mind!"

A few feet away, the omnibus slowed to a crawl, its wheels rattling. The driver stuck his head through the open window and motioned angrily at Radborne.

"Go on, then!" the workman behind him urged. He stuck his fingers into his mouth and whistled once, piercingly. Radborne looked at him, cast a last desperate glance for the woman on the bridge, then sprinted toward the bus.

"Paddington Station?" he gasped as he clambered aboard. The driver nodded, and the bus lurched on its way.

He found a seat and sat alone, color box on his lap, staring out at the scrolls of advertisements on storefronts, walls, rumbling hansoms, and buses. He kept looking back into the street, in futile hope that he might see the woman again, but he knew that was absurd. He could not even say *why* she had compelled his attention. Something about the way her head tilted to the sky, her damp hair gleaming silvery-brown in the pale sun, the wash of light across her skin and the soft gray of her shawl against her white arms where they hung helplessly at her sides, the flashes of light in one hand where she must have clutched a sputtering match: all conspired to stir and inflame him, as a wayward snatch of music could, or the sight of a fox running across a field in daylight. When the bus grew mired in traffic, he pried open his color box and pulled out his sketchbook and a charcoal pencil, then began to draw, from memory, the woman on the bridge.

It was noon before he arrived at Kew Gardens. The quiet shock of finding himself in an unspoiled open space made Radborne feel that he had begun his journey in October but ended it in early spring. The sickening strangeness he had felt at Blackfriars Bridge had dissipated, exorcised by his sketches and the promise of sunlight. He paid his entrance fee, pocketing the change with his return ticket, and in a daze found his way into the Palm House.

High above him burned the glass dome, hung with sulfur-yellow gasoliers. Underfoot, fallen leaves rustled, crimson, viridian, purple, and gold. Radborne felt as though a hole had been bored into the middle of his forehead and all the colors of the sky poured inside. He was in a green, warm world that smelled like no other place he had ever been; he was in another country. He laughed, breathing air sweet and moist as tea cake, then began to follow the winding path through the forest of palmettos and ferns, past nurses with prams and benches where silent couples sat side by side, staring dreamily up into the dome's gold-green eye.

It was a long time before he gave any thought at all to painting. But after an hour, he finally found himself alone in a cul-de-sac. Here a small display table held bell jars, fern cases, vivariums, with neatly lettered signs.

FROG-BIT
CRISPED HART'S-TONGUE
MERROW'S SUNDEW
VERNAL STARWORT

Across from the table was a wrought-iron bench. Radborne sat here and wolfed down the sausage sandwich and ginger beer he'd purchased outside of Paddington.

Now, at last, he could work.

He opened his color box. Inside were his sketchbook, his drawing board, and a thick bundle of coarse drawing paper. He set the board on his lap, fastening a sheet of paper to it with pegs and then sharpening a pencil with his pocketknife. He selected two sticks of charcoal, friable and smelling faintly of the fire pit, rolled one between his fingers, and pensively rubbed his cheek, leaving a dark smudge.

"Well," he said.

He decided to sketch the sundew first. Radborne prided himself on his horticultural knowledge, honed by years of drawing the woods around Elmira. It was why he had fallen in love with the Pre-Raphaelites when he first saw their paintings reproduced in magazines: their loving and obsessive attention to the nearly invisible details of pistil and stamen, petal and leaf.

He had been utterly chastened when, a week before, he finally saw Millais's *Ophelia* at the Tate. That emerald glamour, the astonishing veracity of his bluebells and marshwort! Radborne had never come close to capturing anything like it—and "capture" is what it felt like, that sense of ravishing a live thing, then imprisoning it upon page or canvas.

He glared at the sundew in its globe. Then, gnawing the inside of his cheek, he began to draw.

He was not certain how much time had passed before he noticed he was no longer alone. As he reached for another pencil, he glanced up to see five men standing in a half-circle behind the display table. None was younger than late middle age. All were staring at him with an expression somewhere between curiosity and alarm.

"Ahem."

One man, taller than the rest and obviously in a position of authority, glared briefly at Radborne. Then he extended a pointer to indicate the sundew Radborne had been sketching.

"The one in the middle." The man tapped the glass globe so that it rang like a bell. "No, Horace, not that one—that is the *false* Merrow's sundew. The one in the middle with the overlapping stems—*that* is the true Merrow's sundew."

The others crowded around him—all save one. He continued to stare curiously at Radborne, finally stepped alongside the young man and peered down at his drawing board.

"Why, what a coincidence!" the man announced. "He's sketching it!"

Radborne frowned. "Excuse me," he said. "But—"

"Look here, Learmont!" the man called. "It's really very good!"

The tall man with the pointer ignored him, commanding, "Observe the way it seems to bleed when I touch it!" His voice was deep, with a faint burr. He stuck a finger into the vivarium and poked at the sundew. "And yet I would vouchsafe that there is not one among us who is, in fact, a maiden."

The interlopers snorted in amusement. When the tall man began to lift the vivarium globe, Radborne stood and called out angrily.

"Excuse me! I am working here! Would you mind replacing that and leaving me in peace?"

The men stared at him in astonishment. Then the tall man nodded and replaced the globe.

"I beg your pardon," he said. "I thought you were one of the staff."

"No." Radborne gestured at his drawing board. "I'm an illustrator. I'm making some sketches for a magazine in New York City."

"An American!" the tall man exclaimed as his companions scurried excitedly toward Radborne. "Drawing the Merrow's sundew? You are aware, then, that this plant has an unusually superstitious pedigree? In the West Country, they say it bleeds if a maiden's tears fall upon it."

Radborne forced a smile and tried to protect his color box from the jostling onlookers. "Because of the sap?"

"But the sap is not red—"

"No, of course not." Radborne moved his drawing board to safety, then edged past the others to join the tall man. "It's the way light hits it—see?"

Radborne peered into the globe, where a gnat hung above a beckoning green frond. "For some reason the refraction of light makes the sap glow red. I think it must attract insects to the plant. And then, of course, when they land on it, they're caught, and the plant devours them."

Excited murmurs from the men bent over Radborne's drawing board. The tall man glanced at them, then at Radborne. "You are observant, even for a painter," he said. "Have you studied botany?"

"Not really. I studied medicine at school. Anatomy. I have an amateur's interest, I suppose."

The man tapped a finger against his cheek. He was gaunt, with a long, narrow face, high forehead, pointed chin with no more beard than a boy's, and lank gray hair that hung to his shoulders. A youthful face, save for his sly restless eyes, large and slightly protuberant, the vivid blue of cheap glass jewelry. His eccentric clothes were dandyish and out of date: faded red trousers, tight-fitting blue waistcoat over a canary-yellow shirt, loose tie patterned with violets. "May I see your drawings?"

Radborne hesitated. Then, "Certainly," he said. He stepped back to retrieve his sketches, and handed them to the tall man. The man shuffled them between his long, slender fingers, grunting softly to himself.

"Hmm. Ha. Ha. *Ha*—" He lifted his head. "These are for your own amusement?"

"No. They're sketches for a story I'm illustrating. For *Leslie's*—it's an American magazine; I don't know if you've heard of it?"

"I regret to say I have not." The man smiled and extended his hand. "May I introduce myself? I am Thomas Learmont—Dr. Learmont— and these gentlemen are my fellow members of the Greater Outer London Folk-Lore Study Society."

Murmurs and genial nods from the other men, who were now drifting back to the display table. Dr. Learmont's hand closed around Radborne's. "And you are an illustrator? An artist? How very interesting. I must apologize for interrupting your work and thank you for your original observation about our little plant. Dr. Gill had suggested something similar, but he is merely a botanist and lacks, I think, your particular aesthetic insight."

Radborne smiled. "Radborne Comstock, pleased to meet you."

Dr. Learmont turned to gaze at the drawing board. "Are there other pictures? Might I look at them?"

"Be my guest," said Radborne as Dr. Learmont sidled over to the bench. "They're very rough."

As the others continued to discuss the sundew, Dr. Learmont perused Radborne's work. Not just the studies for "The Knight of the Garish Shield and the Cockatrice" and his drawings of the slums around Mint Street but the hasty sketches he had just done on the omnibus and the other, more fanciful drawings Radborne had never shown to anyone. He found himself oddly anxious to hear this stranger's opinion of them.

"Very interesting." Dr. Learmont stopped suddenly, staring at one of the drawings of the woman on the bridge. He looked at Radborne, his expression watchful, even wary. "You have a very good line, Mr. Comstock. And unusual subject matter."

He tapped a drawing of a man who had tree limbs instead of arms and bees flying from his eyes. "Let me ask you this, Mr. Comstock—would you by any chance be interested in attending our next regular meeting? That would be Monday week, at Paynim House in Bloomsbury."

"Oh—but I don't actually know anything about—"

"That doesn't matter. We're all amateurs of one sort or another, aren't we? I'm sure you'd find something of interest. Where is it you're staying?"

"In Southwark."

"Ah." Dr. Learmont gave Radborne an appraising look, taking in his frayed cuffs and worn shoes and unkempt hair. "It is a bit of a distance from Southwark. But there will be refreshments. And you will almost certainly meet a different sort of people than your neighbors."

Radborne flushed. "I don't think—" he said, but Dr. Learmont had already withdrawn a card and was scribbling out directions.

"It's not difficult to find. I gather you've not been here long?"

"A few weeks—"

"Well, we don't want to lose you just when we've found you." Dr. Learmont handed him the card. "There. Follow those directions, and tell the cab not to wait. We'll expect you Monday."

Before Radborne could protest further, Dr. Learmont had turned away. "Gentlemen!" he cried. "Time for our final statements!"

Radborne watched as the members the Greater Outer London Folk-Lore Study Society took their leave. Last of all went Dr. Learmont.

"I do desire we may be better strangers," the doctor said, and bowed. It was only when he turned to go that Radborne saw the pair of long-handled brass scissors protruding from the doctor's back trouser pocket, their narrow eyes winking at him as Learmont disappeared into the greenery.

The following Monday, Radborne made his way to Paynim House. Mr. Balcombe had returned and once more taken possession of his ulster (no mention was made of the missing umbrella), but by then Radborne had found a woolen coat at a stall in Petticoat Lane, dark crimson, with buttons that the rag seller assured him were real crystal. It was slightly moth-eaten, but the sleeves covered his bony wrists, and the pockets were deep enough to hold the apples that supplemented Mrs. Beale's mutton stew each day. He counted out a few shillings from his alarmingly diminished funds and prayed it would be enough to hire a cab—he had no idea which omnibus went to Bloomsbury.

He mitigated the expense by walking across Blackfriars Bridge. As he approached, the memory of the woman overcame him: her hair, the color of her eyes. He glanced around but felt such a pang at the thought of not seeing her that he forced himself to walk with his head bowed, ignoring the laughter of the motts who left a raw smell of unwashed crinolines as they passed.

On the other side of the river, he hired a cab. The driver looked askance when they reached the entrance to Paynim House. The building was not old, but its neighbors were in disrepair; Radborne could see figures standing in the shadows, see the flash of blue flame as matches were struck, and sniff an acrid odor of burning cloth.

"You're sure?" The driver chucked at his horse and glanced dubiously at Radborne. "It's the address you gave me, but it don't look right."

"Yes, thank you, this is it."

Radborne paid the driver, then stood in the dark courtyard. In the distance gaslights flickered through yellow fog, casting a dismal glow over Woburn Place. He peered at the terrace of buildings across from him, but the figures were gone. There was no sound save the diminishing echo of the departing cab. He took a deep breath and went inside.

He was met at the entry by Dr. Gill, who did not remember him but was disinclined to turn him away—the evening's lecture was already in progress, and he was obviously anxious to return.

"Mmm, yes, Dr. Learmont's guest, mmm. Come now, this way, this way. . . ."

Radborne followed him through to a central room where rows of chairs had been arranged to face a lectern. An elderly man stood there, rustling through a sheaf of long blue postal paper. Radborne found a seat in the back, although he could have sat anywhere—there were only a dozen people present, all clustered in the front row. He recognized all of the men from the Palm House at Kew. A solitary woman in a monstrous blue hat with a stuffed ibis on it was seated beside Dr. Learmont.

Radborne settled himself quietly, trying not to stare at a table set with tea caddy and a platter of cakes. The elderly lecturer, an amateur archaeologist employed by the Government Census on Hallucinations, was presenting a lengthy and apparently controversial exegesis of the Subboreal Problem at the First Maiden Castle in Dorset.

"... *we need not despair of the ultimate emergence of some insular equivalent of the old 'dry subboreal' ...*"

Radborne gave up pretending to comprehend any of it. But he enjoyed the heated commentary provided by the audience, especially the caustic comments offered by Dr. Learmont. When the lecture finally ended, there was a burst of enthusiastic applause, after which the other members of the Folk-Lore Society rose and, to a man (and woman), rushed to the food table. Radborne joined them, helping himself to a slice of treacle tart that looked much nicer than it tasted.

"Did you enjoy Mr. Trefoil's paper?"

Radborne looked up to see Dr. Learmont. He wore the same faded red trousers and brilliant blue waistcoat, augmented by a bottle-green jacket that hung to his knees.

"Very much," Radborne replied, dropping crumbs on the carpet as he shook Dr. Learmont's hand. "I only wish I knew more about the subject of subboreal excavation."

Dr. Learmont laughed. "I daresay you know more now than you ever thought you would."

"Well." Radborne smiled. "It might be useful someday,"

Dr. Learmont nodded, then glanced over his shoulder. Behind him a figure loomed, a mountain of red silk topped by a dead bird. "Ah! Lady Wilde. This is the young visitor from America I was telling you about."

Dr. Learmont stepped aside. Radborne hurriedly wiped his mouth. "Yes. Er—"

"Lady Wilde, Radborne Comstock," announced Learmont. "Mr. Comstock, this is Lady Wilde. One of our most esteemed members, from far greater Outer London."

"Ire!" shouted Lady Wilde. "Ire!"

Radborne flinched, then realized she was using the Gaelic, *Eire* for Ireland. "Oh—yes, of course," he said.

She stared at him fiercely: a woman tall as he was, towering over six feet in high-heeled boots. She wore a sweeping dress of crimson silk, tufted with black velvet tassels and with numerous onyx and ivory brooches pinned haphazardly across the bodice. Beneath the ibis-crowned hat, her hair was the color of a magpie's wing, blue-black and so heavily lacquered that the smell made Radborne slightly ill. She must have weighed nearly twenty stone, not fat but genuinely massive— broad-shouldered and with a wide, once-handsome face, now thickly dusted with pearly gray powder, deep-set brown eyes kohled cartoon-ishly black, her hands all but invisible beneath dozens of bone and ivory and tortoiseshell bracelets. When she took a step toward Rad-borne, she clattered like a wheelbarrow over cobblestones.

"Why, you are an American!" She had an aristocrat's orotund dic-tion, somewhat at odds with her Irish accent. "And yet I have never been to America. My son will be touring there later this year. He ex-pects to find the wilderness distracting. I would find it merely disagree-able. What do you think, Mr. Comstock?"

Radborne swallowed. "Well . . ."

"You have made a home there for many of my countrymen. And *women,*" she added.

Radborne raised his hands. "I wouldn't know, actually—I live in New York. Which, ah, is not much of a wilderness these days—

"—though as a matter of fact," he went on quickly, seeing Lady Wilde's eyes narrow, "I'm half Irish. My father was American, but my mother was from County Meath."

"Was she." Lady Wilde looked Radborne up and down. "Well. I find your Irish top quite as appealing as your American bottom."

Radborne turned bright red. Beside him Dr. Learmont laughed softly. Lady Wilde continued to gaze at the young man, then smiled to reveal uneven teeth. "So, Mr. Comstock. What is your particular interest in the the lore of our island?"

"I . . . well, I —"

"You have chosen a propitious time to visit. A few days from now is Samhain."

"Sow in?" Radborne looked puzzled. "Something about pigs?"

Lady Wilde laughed, the ibis on her hat trembling as with imminent flight. "No, no. Samhain, An t-Samhuinn. One of the two days when your mother's ancestors believed that the walls between the worlds fell down. I have been studying it for a book I hope to publish. *These* people"—she gestured disdainfully at the men chattering beside the remains of treacle tart—"*their* ancestors called it Blod-monath. Blood-month. They slaughtered their livestock then for the coming winter."

Radborne grinned. "So it did have something to do with pigs after all."

"Certainly not," snapped Lady Wilde. "'Samhain, when the summer goes to its rest.' It is a holy day for the country people; Puca Night, they call its eve. A dangerous time, Mr. Comstock, especially for handsome young men. Mind your manners if you meet new neighbors."

To his astonishment she winked at him, then turned, slow and grand as a schooner coming about, and crossed the room.

"Lady Wilde takes many masculine prerogatives," said Dr. Learmont sotto voce. "As does her son, I hear. Well, come along."

He grasped Radborne's shoulder and began to steer him away. "Who is her son?" Radborne asked.

"An affected young Irishman. But amusing. Lady Wilde arranged for him to speak to us last fall. He lectured movingly on the romantic possibilities of blue china." He gave Radborne a sideways look. "I did not know you were Irish."

"My mother—"

"A noble race ruined by poverty and drink. You are not to be ashamed. I mention it only because Lady Wilde is compiling a compendium of folklore of her country."

"So she said."

"She spends a good deal of time among her countrywomen, noting their stories and superstitions. I find her research extremely useful for my own work. There is another history told in those old tales. Ah, Esperanza—"

A few feet away, Lady Wilde had gone aground beside another table. "I was just telling Mr. Comstock of your work," said Learmont.

Lady Wilde looked at Radborne. "Are you a writer?"

"No—an artist. A painter."

"An artist?" Her eyes narrowed. "You have a muse, then?"

"A muse?" Radborne glanced at his host for assistance, but Dr. Learmont was busily inspecting a stack of pamphlets on the table. "Do you mean an artist's model?"

"I do not. I refer to your genius. If you do not have one, Mr. Comstock, you will fail. If you do find one, it will devour you. It will *destroy* you, but in that case we will have your paintings to remind us of you. In the event we want to be reminded."

She seemed to consider this extremely unlikely. Radborne stared at her, speechless. Finally, "Thank you very much," he said, and walked past her to the table.

There were no refreshments here, only back issues of the Folk-Lore Society's journal, along with assorted monographs, pamphlets, and cheaply bound books with titles like *English Antiquities: A Popular Guide* and *The Jappy System of Cork-Grip Exercises*. There was also a thicker, heavier volume, some sort of textbook. He picked it up and glanced inside.

PSYCHOMANCY
Further Inquiries into Some Elemental Conflicts, with Suggestions for Their Resolution
by B. Strout Warnick,
D.C.L. Oxford, LL.D, Glasgow, Ph.D. Univ. of the Archangels and St. John the Divine

Radborne feigned interest in the book, but it was difficult: he could feel Lady Wilde's gaze boring into him like a drill into a bad tooth. He cleared his throat, replaced the text, and hurried to the end of the table.

"Oh, look," he said hopefully. "Postal cards!"

But peculiar ones. Apart from a few images of Uffington and Stonehenge, the cards depicted burial mounds containing human remains, mostly the skeletons of infants. Radborne stared at a picture of two skeletons lying side by side, the little bones of their arms and hands entwined.

"The Green Children." Radborne jumped as Lady Wilde's voice boomed in his ear. "I can arrange for you to examine them, if you wish," she went on, tapping the card with a grimy fingernail. "The curator of the Raitling Museum is a dear friend of mine."

"Thank you—I mean, no thank you." Radborne hastily replaced the card. "I think . . . well—this one is more suitable as a souvenir."

He held up an image of Stonehenge. Lady Wilde glanced at it with disdain. "Shallow. The mystery of Stonehenge is shallow. But theirs"— she gestured at the card with the Green Children—"theirs is *deep*."

She turned and strode to where a man stood guard over a cash box. Radborne waited until she was a safe distance away, then picked up the card with the skeletons on it.

"Have you survived your siege by Lady Wilde?"

Radborne looked up. "Dr. Learmont! Yes—at least I think I have. She seems . . . possessed of her own opinions."

"Indeed she is. A very knowledgeable woman, our Speranza. A great believer in genius."

"Which she does not feel that I possess," said Radborne.

"Her argument would be that *it* must possess *you*," said Learmont. "But don't make the mistake of thinking her a mere bluestocking, Mr. Comstock. When I organized this society several years ago, I had hoped to entice many minds like Lady Wilde's, but our members, alas, are mostly dilettantes. She alone has helped me find some of the information I seek, and she has as well introduced me to some interesting and useful informants."

Dr. Learmont glanced at the postcard in Radborne's hand and smiled. "Now, if you will excuse me, I must congratulate Mr. Trefoil on his lecture. But if you are not busy afterward, Mr. Comstock, could I interest you in joining me for dinner at Bartolini's? I have several hours before my train departs for Padwithiel, and I would very much enjoy your company."

With a slight bow, he went off in search of Mr. Trefoil. Radborne paid for his postcards, made a final circuit of the room, and went to meet Dr. Learmont in the foyer. A large figure in a canary-yellow opera cape blocked his way.

"Mr. Comstock. I will leave you with one bit of advice."

Radborne smiled weakly. "Lady Wilde."

"This is the eve of St. Luke's Day. Do you know St. Luke?"

"Well, no, not—"

"The patron of artists. And physicians. And madmen." Lady Wilde adjusted the folds of her cape. "I do not adhere to the Church of Rome, of course. But her believers say that this is a lucky time, if you would seek one who would guide you through uncertain ways. And so I will give you a bit of advice. . . ."

She leaned toward him, exuding an oily musk of tuberose and camphor. "Anoint your stomach, breast, and lips with a powder of dried marigolds and wormwood, simmered in virgin honey and claret." She poked him, hard, in the navel and chest, then pressed her hand against his mouth. "Then repeat three times: 'St. Luke, St. Luke, be kind to me, In dreams let me my genius see.'"

Radborne tried not to gag at the reek of tuberose as Lady Wilde stared at him through kohl-rimmed eyes.

"Do you know, you may have it yet," she said. Without warning, she drew her mouth close to his and, before he could turn away, kissed him full on the lips.

"'Sweets so sweet they burn,'" she whispered.

Her mouth was gone, her hand. There was the feathery sound of her cape sliding across the doorsill, and Lady Wilde disappeared into the alley.

"Mr. Comstock? Are you unwell?"

Radborne pressed his palm against his forehead. He did indeed feel ill, but when Dr. Learmont's face loomed beside him, he only shook his head.

"No, thank you, I . . . I'm fine. And I'll be glad to join you. Lady Wilde was just sharing some bit of superstition with me."

"Ah, yes. Esperanza is a repository of such things. A *vast* repository." Dr. Learmont smiled. "Come now, Mr. Comstock. It's not far, but I've hired a cab. Leicester Square can be terribly congested. . . ."

The approach to Leicester Square proved Learmont correct, though Radborne noted that most of the congestion was caused by others like themselves, in hire cabs that crowded the streets and sidewalks. They passed Cavour and the Corner House, restaurants where Radborne would never have dreamed of dining—far too dear—and at last came to Bartolini's. Radborne dug into his pocket resignedly, seeing what little remained of his funds dispatched for this evening's pleasure. Dr. Learmont gestured at him with impatience.

"Please. You are my guest, Comstock. And we perhaps may come to an understanding before the night is through. This way!"

It was late enough that the restaurant was filled with noisy theater-goers recently released from *The Bells* and *The Cup* and *The Silver King*. Learmont, despite his odd attire, had managed to secure a table; indeed, he seemed to be recognized by the staff and several diners, who stood to grasp his hand eagerly as he bustled past them.

"Your Folk-Lore Society must have a great many members," said Radborne as they entered a small side room.

"Oh, they know little or nothing of that," said Learmont, laughing. "That is my avocation, not my profession— Oh, but see, here is dear Algernon! You've managed to escape and join us?"

Inside the private dining room stood a single table, and here sat a short, slight middle-aged man, staring gloomily at a glass of beer.

"Hello, Learmont," he said, but did not bother to stand. His child-like voice was so high-pitched that Radborne began to laugh, thinking this must be some shared joke. At the little man's disgusted expression, he stopped and looked down, abashed. This gave him an excellent view of the man's shoes, which were tiny and made of walnut-colored kid with pearl buttons.

"But it's *your* fault—I told him I wished to see you, and old Watts-Dunton thinks you're safe as houses, so . . ."

He lifted a hand delicate as a doll's and flapped it in front of his face. Wisps of long ginger-gray hair blew across his eyes. "Here I am. Do sit, Thomas. You give me a headache standing there."

"Of course. Thank you." Learmont sank into a chair and motioned Radborne to join them. "Algernon, may I introduce Radborne Comstock. He is a young artist visiting us from Manhattan. I hope to offer him some employment."

Radborne glanced at the doctor in surprise, but Learmont was busy summoning a waiter.

"Manhattan?" Algernon's watery green eyes brightened somewhat. "Do you know *The Beautiful Flagellants of New York*?"

"I beg your pardon?"

"Never mind." Algernon picked up his glass of beer, looked into it mournfully, and set it down again. "Do you know, there was the most adorable little babbie in the street as I came in—her ickle nursie had her out at this hour, can you imagine! The only shining star in all this firmament of fuckery and shit."

Radborne was unsure how to answer this. "A . . . baby?"

"A precious child. Nursie looked away to admire a young brute, and I boxed her ugly ears for it." He leaned across the table, poking Radborne with an elfin finger. "They steal babbies, you know."

"But not in Bartolini's," said Learmont as a decanter of claret was set before them. He filled two glasses, handed one to Radborne, then turned. "Your good health, Algernon."

"I only ever had bad health," said Algernon bitterly. "Once they stole that, there was nothing left."

"But you're looking so much better," said Learmont. "Admit it, Algernon!"

Algernon took his glass of beer and sipped from it. He shot Radborne a keen look. "Do not let him cure you, whatever the matter is. Do you know, I used to sit at this very table with Burton and Bradlaugh and Bendyshe, and we would devour *human flesh*."

"Don't be absurd, Algernon," said Learmont.

"Human flesh!" Algernon's fluting voice grew shrill. "Oh, Mr. Cuntstick, I was a far happier madman and cannibal—"

"Algernon—"

"Happy, and merry, and *bad!* 'And I would have given my soul for this, To burn for ever in burning hell.'"

Radborne watched in alarm as the little man got to his feet, raising his glass. "'Preserve us from our enemies,'" he recited,

"Thou who art lord of suns and skies
Whose food is human flesh in pies
  And blood in bowls!
Of thy sweet mercy damn their eyes
  And damn their souls!"

He took another sip of beer, grimaced, and sat down. "I despise beer," he said. "Watts-Dunton told me it made Tennyson great. I do believe it is what killed him."

"I didn't know Tennyson was dead," said Radborne. Algernon glared at him.

"Mr. Comstock," broke in Learmont. He lifted his glass. "May I welcome you to London!"

Radborne turned to him gratefully. "Thank you. To your health."

Learmont downed his glass, indicating that Radborne should do the same, then refilled both. He made no move to offer any to Algernon, who continued to stare unhappily at his beer. " 'Give a scholar wine,' " said Learmont, " 'going to his book, or being about to invent, it sets a new point on his wit, it glazeth it, it scowres it, it gives him acumen.' "

He nodded as a waiter arrived with plates. "Now, Mr. Comstock, we have *appointed* ourselves. But you must tell me—did you enjoy the lecture?"

"It was very interesting." Radborne smiled. He was relieved to see that the platters clearly held cold boiled beef and sprouts. "Though I was sorry not to hear you speak."

"Ah! But that is why I brought you here. I don't often have the opportunity to meet visitors from America. Do you know the West Country, Mr. Comstock? Padwithiel—where the train takes me—is on the northern Cornish coast. There is very little there at all, save my hospital."

"Your hospital?"

"Yes. My pursuits with the Folk-Lore Society are for my own

amusement and enlightenment. Not my occupation. I am Physician in Charge of the Sarsinmoor Benevolent Asylum."

"An asylum? You mean a convalescent hospital?"

"I do not. My hospital serves those whose derangements have made it impossible for them to live elsewhere. I make few claims to effect any cure."

Algernon gave a shriek of disdain, which Learmont ignored.

"But . . . this is extraordinary!" Radborne shook his head. "My last position back in the States was in an asylum—Garrison, in New York State."

"Was it indeed?" said Learmont.

"Yes, my very situation. It was a hospital for the insane. I had studied medicine, you see, but I was not very happy with it—"

"Who would be?" cried Algernon.

"—because what I've always wanted to do, really, is paint."

Dr. Learmont nodded. "How long were you employed, then?"

"Thirteen months. My father was an assistant physician. Not at Garrison, but in Elmira. That's in New York State, where I grew up. I attended university near there as well. After I graduated, my father arranged for me to take a position at Garrison, as staff editor of the patient magazine. *The Prism*, it's called."

"An admirable effort," said Learmont. "But you were not happy studying medicine?"

Radborne stared into his glass. "No. I'm a painter. My studies included medical procedures and anatomical illustration, but I made my intent clear to my father many years ago."

"That you would paint."

"That I would paint. I took the position at Garrison with the understanding that I would work there for two years and earn enough money to pay for individual painting lessons—"

"Which you accomplished."

Radborne flushed. "Well, in a manner of speaking. My father died unexpectedly and left me a small inheritance. My mother died when I was very young. I arranged for the sale of the house in Elmira, and that made it possible for me to go to New York City this past spring. I studied with a Dutch painter. Wilhelm van der Ven—"

"Van der Ven?" Dr. Learmont lifted an eyebrow. "You must have talent, then."

Radborne looked surprised. "You know him?"

"Not personally. I am familiar with his work. *The Flight into Egypt,* in particular, is a very fine painting. Was he a good teacher?"

"Extremely good—and generous. He was kind enough to secure me a position as illustrator for *Leslie's* magazine. And he arranged introductions for me here in London, and helped arrange my travel accommodations as well. It has been a dream of mine, to visit London—"

"And one which proved impossible to achieve while your father lived."

"No! That isn't—"

"Oh, leave him be, Thomas," said Algernon irritably. "God knows he's *cleaner* than most of them ever are at his age. I had rather wanted to have a blancmange than this mess of beef. Where is that waiter?"

His limpid green eyes fixed on a hapless figure on the far side of the room. "May I inquire as to a blancmange?" Algernon cried in a high, braying voice. *"May I?"*

Radborne cringed, but Dr. Learmont only placed a hand on Algernon's waving arm. "Please—I will speak to the chef," he said, and, excusing himself, headed for the maître d'hôtel. Algernon waited until he was out of sight, then leaned across the table to grab Radborne's hand.

"You're not to go with him," he said in a low, warning voice. "Promise me! You *won't* go."

Radborne stared at the wild-eyed little man, his graying hair awry and his face flushed with emotion. "I beg your pardon? Go where?"

"To his asylum." Algernon shook his head violently. "It will be your ruin, Mr. Cornstick—"

"*Comstock.*"

"Mr. Comstock. Do you fancy yourself an artist? He ruins artists— do you know how? By flattering them, by claiming to save them from their diseased minds. By *collecting* them, as though you were a scrap of canvas or a page torn from a book. Do you value your soul, sir?"

"Not especially."

"Oh, you are young and a fool!" Algernon snatched his hand back. "I trusted him once—we all did."

"Who?" demanded Radborne. "Dr. Learmont? I hardly know him, but he seems perfectly agreeable."

"Do not trust him! He is corruption and deception masquerading as a rational mind. A panderer and a jailer!"

His voice dropped; his little hands clenched, and he slammed them on the table so that the wineglasses danced. "And yet you do not believe me. That is no surprise: I heeded none of the warnings that I received, and were it not for the love of my dear friend Watts-Dunton—my *savior*—I would be lost as well. You doubt me?"

"I have no idea what you refer to!"

"No? Ask Lizzie, breathing worms and darkness!" he hissed. "Ask Gabriel! He is quite mad now and sees no one—he will be dead within the year."

Radborne sat up. "Do you mean Rossetti? The painter?"

"Ah! He speaks!" squealed Algernon, his face violet with anger. "Yes, I mean Rossetti! And Ned, and Ruskin—all of 'em! He lures them to his lair and shows them Beauty, and She devours them—but, oh, how they love to burn! How we all loved to burn. . . ."

Radborne took a long draft from his wine. "Do you know Lady Wilde?" he asked, refilling his glass.

Algernon licked his lips. "A terrifying woman. Her son is a poetaster."

"I met her earlier this evening, with Dr. Learmont. She also spoke to me of burning: pretending to be a sibyl, I supposed. *She* didn't warn me of Dr. Learmont."

"She's a fool and does not know his nature. Her son, now—a tadpole poet, but very ambitious. He will be destroyed by her."

"By his mother?"

Algernon fixed him with a cold beryl eye. "Don't *you* be a fool, Mr. Comstock. Arrogance becomes you, but not idiocy. Lady Wilde dabbles in witchery like the rest of 'em. Lang and his cronies—they would make a science of stories, but Learmont has no interest in science: he is a lover who has lost the thing he loves. He pursues one who spurned him, even though it means his death. 'Yet there are worse things waiting for men than death.'"

His mouth curved slightly in a smile. "How old are you, Mr. Comstock?"

"Twenty-three."

"Twenty-three. When I was twenty-three, I had already been Beauty's slave for years. It was the happiest time of my life."

He picked up his glass and raised it toward Radborne. "To your destruction," he said.

"My destruction," echoed Radborne. He finished his claret. Algernon replaced his own glass untouched. "Well, you're a cheerful sibyl at least."

"Am I?" Algernon smiled sadly. "I do not feel so cheerful these days. I sensed that Beauty was leaving me, and, not wishing to be a spurned lover, I departed first." He stared at Radborne, then past him toward the door. His wistful expression faded. "Look, I've no time for you, young man, and no business either. But."

He leaned forward, grasping Radborne's wrists with thin fingers. Radborne glanced back to see Dr. Learmont talking to a man wearing the restaurant's blue-and-black livery. As the doctor turned, the bright flicker of shears flashed from beneath his jacket. Algernon's voice dropped to a whisper.

"Mr. Comstock. You are a painter, not a poet: so were many of my dearest friends in their youth. I have no use for them now. Our history is one of disappointment and betrayal. Yet you remind me of them—you so clearly have bad fortune on your side.

"And," Algernon added, "you are tall and handsome. And arrogant. A stunner," he said, and giggled mirthlessly. "I will give you some advice.

"Do not go with Learmont. He said he is offering you employment? Refuse him! If it means you starve in the streets or end up in the workhouse, refuse him! But—if you find yourself unable to escape him, be very wary of any woman in his care."

"Women? Do you mean patients—lunatics?"

"Yes. He has theories about the birth of Art: they involve entrapment and madness and—"

Behind them a figure loomed. Dr. Learmont smiled down at Algernon as though he were a beloved if troublesome child.

"Algernon, have you been egging on Mr. Comstock?" He pointed at Radborne's empty wineglass and the empty decanter beside it.

Algernon sniffed. "You know that I despise claret."

"I'm glad to hear it!" Learmont clapped his hands together, then turned to indicate the man waiting by the door. "The maître d'hôtel has just informed me that Watts-Dunton has sent a driver for you, Algernon. All the way from Putney. I think we should not keep him waiting any longer."

Algernon stared at the tablecloth, defeated, then glanced at Radborne. The little man's green eyes were weary and bloodshot, his face lined and sad. After a moment he nodded, pushed his chair back, and shuffled to his feet.

"Mr. Comstock." He made a mocking half bow, his unruly hair falling across his face. "I hope your visit to London will be a happy one."

Radborne smiled. "Thank you."

"Happy, because happiness is anathema to art, and I wonder if you know what it means to be an artist. But if you truly wish to pursue painting, why, then, I wish you misery and madness and an early death. Good night, Mr. Comstock."

Radborne watched him go. "What a weird little gentleman," he said.

Learmont took his seat. "You know Swinburne's work, then?"

"Swinburne!" Radborne sat up, appalled. "*That* was Swinburne?"

"Of course. Who did you think he was?"

"Why . . . I had no idea! You never told me his name!" Radborne swiveled to see if he could get a final view of the departing poet. "Of course I know him! His books—a college friend gave me the loan of *Laus Veneris*. What a remarkable work! I regret to say I never returned it." Radborne laughed. "He looks so old. Was he a patient of yours?"

"No. Though he was indeed in danger of dying of his strange obsessions and drunkenness. Much to my regret, he avoided any sort of treatment with me, but this Watts-Dunton took him under his care, moved him to the wilderness of Putney, and . . ."

He made an odd gesture, half dismissal and half regret. "He is as you see him: one whom the gods have abandoned."

Radborne felt a shiver pass through him. For a few minutes he said nothing, poking at his plate while his companion stared at the ceiling. Finally Dr. Learmont glanced at his pocketwatch, then beckoned for the waiter.

"Well, I fear the time has come to begin my long journey westward. If you are in no hurry, Mr. Comstock, why don't you accompany me to Paddington, and then I will have the cab bring you back to Southwark."

Radborne began to protest, but Learmont was already on his feet. "As I mentioned, Mr. Comstock, I wish to discuss a matter of possible employment—my original intent in asking you to dine with me, before we encountered dear Algernon. Now, if you please . . ."

It was well after midnight when Radborne at last stumbled from the cab and upstairs into bed, his giddiness and exhilaration replaced by a pounding headache. When he finally came down to breakfast in the morning, Mrs. Beale greeted him coolly, though Mr. Balcombe gave him a knowing (and sympathetic) look as he spooned his oatmeal porridge.

"Mr. Comstock," Mrs. Beale announced when Mr. Balcombe had gone upstairs, "if you are going to keep midnight hours, and company, I must suggest you take rooms elsewhere. There are gentlemen's coffee rooms and accommodations at the Old Gander. No doubt your stimulating companions can make other recommendations for you as well."

As it turned out, this was not necessary. Late that morning an envelope arrived.

Mr. Radborne Comstock

c/o The Grey Owl

Mint Street, The Borough

Mrs. Beale cast such a malevolent eye upon the letter that Radborne fled outside and down the street, to read it beneath the flapping wing of Dr. Trent's testimonials.

. . . most propitious that we met. I have for some time sought to engage a Painter, a Young Man of good health and respectable talents, to serve as companion to one of my patients. Himself an artist of formerly great repute, this Person for the last decade has suffered most tragically from deliriums initiated by his travel to climates unfit for an Englishman. I will not repeat here the details of his sad history, which have at any rate been recorded by the Press. I do feel compelled to inform you that the incident which precipitated said person's being placed in my care was Murder, the victim a young woman engaged as the artist's model, herself prone to deliriums. I am in a position to remunerate you, if not with extravagance, still to a degree which I hope you may find generous, and which I gather may be welcome to you in consideration of your present situation. . . .

Radborne couldn't recall mentioning his constrained circumstances to Learmont, but then he supposed that one would not have to be a Physician in Charge, or even a Renowned Phrenologist, to take the measure of a secondhand greatcoat and paint stains on a best shirt. For some minutes he stood in the chill noonday sun, watching vans rattling toward warehouses and observing the flight of a single rook as it circled around and around the black spire of Southwark Cathedral. He read the letter one more time, folded it, and replaced it in the envelope. Then, his headache starting to recede, he hurried back to Mrs. Beale's to post his reply. The next morning he was on his way to Cornwall.

CHAPTER FIVE

The Eve of St. Agnes

Take; I have seen the branches of Broceliande . . .
yet the wood in the wild west of the shapes and names

probes everywhere through the frontier of head and hand;
everywhere the light through the great leaves is blown
on your substantial flesh, and everywhere your glory frames.
—*Charles Williams, "Bors to Elayne: The Fish of Broceliande"*

Daniel *was no stranger to intoxicants.* Psilocybin, cocaine, methamphetamine, LSD, opium, Ecstasy: in the name of Art, and, occasionally, Love, he'd tried all of them, even once watching in rapt horror as a junkie girlfriend injected brown liquid into his own green-sick vein. His subsequent physical and psychic nausea was enough to flense the last bit of curiosity from him regarding altered states of consciousness. He now reserved sensual experimentation for California wines, occasionally investigating some outré Web site recommended by Nick and inevitably regretting the experience.

So he was completely unprepared for what happened to the world after three absinthes with Larkin in the Café Chouette.

"Is it always like this?" He was sprawled across the table, arms draped around her, his face buried in her hair as though it were a mass of flowers. "Like, uh . . ."

He attempted a meaningful gesture, falling from his chair in the process. Larkin caught him, laughing, and Daniel stared at her imploringly as she helped him back into his seat.

"I think traditionally it's the woman who gets potted and falls down." She swiped the hair from her eyes and smiled. "But apart from that? Yes, I think it is always like this. It's why all those poets and painters went mad."

"And me? Will I go mad?"

"After three drinks? Highly doubtful. Especially for a journalist. I'd think your resistance would be fairly high."

"I knew it." He grasped her hand, so tightly his fingers tingled. "The first moment I saw you, I *just knew*."

"Did you? What did you know?"

"Well . . ."

He opened his mouth but suddenly found that he had no idea what he was talking about. He could not, in fact, think of anything at all: couldn't even look at anything save the woman beside him.

"Just . . . *you,*" he said helplessly. Around him the room had contracted to two points of yellow light centered in her bottle-green eyes. "You. Who . . . are . . . you?"

He leaned toward her, and she took his face in her hands. Her fingers were so hot he flinched. When her mouth touched his, he resisted, but only for an instant. Then he felt as though his entire body were somehow being remade beneath her touch, her limbs flashing heat so intense he gasped, the skin burned from him so that his ribs scored her breasts and his skull her cheek, his hair tangling hers in tendrils of ash and flame and his fingers blue fire flickering across her face.

"Walk with me," she whispered, and of course he could not.

But of course he did. Because where was he but in a bar in Bloomsbury of a late afternoon, the maître d' bowing slightly as he let them pass, a flushed, drunk man in youngish middle age with his arms around a tall woman—russet-haired, strong-featured, green-eyed—whose age was impossible to guess.

"Where are we going?" he asked when he was finally able to talk again. "Not that it matters. And who paid the check?"

"I did.

"You may thank me later," she added, with a look that nearly sent Daniel walking straight into a lamppost.

"Oh. Well, sure." He paused, zipping his bomber jacket and watching Larkin as she strode on, oblivious of puddles underfoot and the drizzle silvering her hair. Above them the narrow band of sky had brightened from gray to the lustrous green of seaglass. He put a hand to the lamppost to steady himself and glanced at his watch, dreamily registering that it was almost four-thirty. He laughed: a three-absinthe lunch!

It had been years since he'd gotten drunk during working hours. Storefronts looked glazed, like the sugared windows of a gingerbread house, and yellow mist rose from the pavement. A sweet summery smell floated above the reek of diesel exhaust. Beneath his hand the lamppost felt charged with heat.

The air breathes upon us here most sweetly, thought Daniel. *How lush and lusty the grass looks! How green!*

From somewhere high overhead, a bell pealed softly, as though the diminishing rain had a sound. Daniel stared at the sky, waiting, but nothing revealed itself.

Only when he glanced down again, a large black cab was driving past him, very slowly, just inches from the curb. He saw his own face reflected in the rain-flecked window, and behind it another face.

The cab stopped to idle at the curb. As Daniel stared, the window rolled down. A long-fingered hand extended a sunflower to him—a woman's hand, he thought at first, though the nails were very dirty. He squinted, trying to get a better look at whoever it was inside the taxi, could barely glimpse a thin figure wearing a mustard-colored zoot suit over a V-neck sweater: short scruffy blond hair, downy mustache, slightly upturned pale-blue eyes, vulpine grin.

" 'Be not afeard, the isle is full of noises.' " The voice was hoarse and reedy: not a man's voice at all. Daniel gaped as the figure lifted a hand in farewell and the window slid shut. The cab rolled forward. Daniel ran into the road behind it, watched it turn onto Woburn Street and disappear.

"What the fuck . . . ?" He stared at the sunflower, its bloom the size of his hand, looked up to see Larkin waiting for him halfway down the street.

"You coming?" she shouted.

He ran to catch up with her.

"Look!" He handed her the flower. "Someone in a big black cab just gave me this."

"She must've liked your looks."

"I don't think it *was* a woman. She had a mustache."

Larkin laughed. "A drag king! And she gave you this?" She tapped him on the chin with the sunflower. "In Whitechapel that'd mean you were betrothed."

"Really?"

"Of course not." She took his hand. "I could tell you anything and you'd believe it."

"Absolutely." He pulled her to him. "You know, I think I'm going nuts. 'Cause I was just standing there, thinking of a line from *The Tempest*—and I swear to God that cab appeared and—"

"Be careful—you almost walked right into that one, too!" She steered him away from another lamppost. "You Yanks can't hold your liquor, that's all."

It was a few minutes' walk back to Paynim House, winding through the alleys around Woburn Street and jumping over channels of rainwater surging alongside the curbs. In the side street, someone had pried loose several manhole covers, and the bright yellow warning cones set beside them had been blown onto the sidewalks.

"Watch it, Daniel!"

Gouts of steam rose from an open manhole, freeing a lost childhood memory: downtown Manhattan, the burned-cloth scent of roasting chestnuts and the roast-chestnut man himself, singing in a cracked Irish tenor. "'My darling, my darling, my darling young one . . .'"

"An old man died here last spring," said Larkin. "Fell right in and broke his neck."

"Jesus." Daniel stopped and stared at the hole. A rusted ladder protruded from it. Balanced on the pile of rubble was the manhole cover. Raised letters marched across its center: ELF KING.

"Elf King?" said Daniel.

He stooped to examine it. Filth and rust covered the heavy metal disk like lichen, but he could see the faint outlines of other letters, nearly worn away.

SELF-LOCKING, it read.

Daniel traced the words with his finger. "Hey, Lark! Look at this!"

"I know. You'd be amazed what you see, once you start looking."

She glanced at Paynim House. "Listen, why don't you just wait here? I'll only be a minute."

She ran toward the front door and went inside. Daniel waved his sunflower forlornly, then looked around at the desolate courtyard, pools of standing water, disintegrating newsprint, a crow picking at an orange peel. There were no television aerials or satellite dishes, no lights burning in any of the surrounding buildings. Except for the parked Mini, the place probably looked much as it had a hundred years ago.

The thought made Daniel feel isolated and anxious, and with the first dank stirrings of a hangover. The odd brilliance that colored everything since he'd left the Café Chouette clung to the courtyard as well, though here it had a harsh metallic glare that made his eyes ache.

Still, it was only a few minutes before the door opened again and Larkin stepped back out. She headed toward the car, looking at Daniel. "You coming?"

He took a deep breath. "Sure," he said, and hurried to join her.

She was bending to unlock the car. As she straightened, her hair fell across her face. Without thinking, he reached to draw it back.

"Wait," he said. He felt that if he didn't touch her, he would faint, that the cobblestones would shift beneath his feet and he'd be gone, like that, into the earth. "Please . . ."

She stared at him, one hand still upon the car door, and he could not bear her gaze, he could not bear that she should see him like this, nothing but raw yearning. His face dipped to hers, and he pulled her to him, the folds of her scarf falling away as he kissed her. Pale green light exploded behind his eyes, heat and the pressure of her mouth on his, her coat falling open and his hands on her shoulders. There was a smell of green apple and fresh sap. He moaned and drew back, his desire so strong it was like a sickness, like a poison; the sunflower fell between them, its stem broken. He gasped, blinking.

"I . . . I'm sorry," he said. "God, I . . ."

She shook her head. Her face was flushed, and there was a speck on her chin, a feathered frond of moss. She flicked back a strand of her hair, then glanced at the ground where the sunflower lay, its dark-green eye gazing back from within a fringe of gold and black.

"No," she said, and lifted her head to stare at Daniel. "I wanted it. I wanted you."

He shuddered, fighting to keep from grabbing her, from coming right there, fully clothed, as a woman he hardly knew pressed her hand upon his chest.

"We should go." She let her hand trail upward to cover his mouth. He kissed her fingers: earth and sweetbreads, bitter wormwood. "We should go now."

She stooped and retrieved the sunflower, then got into the car.

Daniel slid in beside her, still trembling, and they drove away from Paynim House.

The juddering stop-and-start of London rush-hour traffic went a long way toward purging Daniel of sickening desire. Now he just felt sick. Leaning out the window didn't help much; the Mini afforded a dizzying view of the passing cars and buses. It also put Daniel in direct contact with an endless spume of exhaust. He finally settled on slumping in a miserable heap in the passenger seat, waiting for his hangover to pass.

"Would you mind if we made a stop first?"

Daniel glanced up to see Larkin looking far too cheerful for someone stuck in a roundabout near Charing Cross. "Stop?" he asked weakly.

"Yes. Well, two stops. I almost forgot. I have this reception to attend. A going-away sort of thing. You can come," she added. "It won't take long. You might find it interesting—artists and collectors."

Daniel frowned, rubbing his unshaven chin. "I'm not really dressed for an artistic reception."

"That's why I thought we'd stop by Sira's first—"

Daniel groaned. "No! *Please!*"

"They're letting me keep my clothes there. My place is so small. This way I can change and you can borrow something of Nick's."

"Nick is ten inches shorter than I am."

"Then you can borrow something of mine. Look, we're almost there!"

They weren't. When they finally did arrive, it was past six. Neither Nick nor Sira was home, but Larkin had a key; she opened the door and ran upstairs. Daniel followed grumpily, stopping in the kitchen to pour himself some fizzy water, then searching the cupboards for something to help his headache.

"Maybe this isn't such a good idea," he said. There was no ibuprofen in sight, so he settled for eating most of a jar of lime pickle. By the time Larkin came back downstairs, he'd broken a sweat and was feeling much better.

"Daniel? What do you think?"

He set the empty pickle jar in the sink, turned and whistled. "You look fantastic. Did you borrow that from the V&A?"

She flashed him a smile, tossing an armful of clothing onto the sofa. She was wearing a long, clinging dress of midnight-blue velvet, low-cut and long-waisted, with a necklace of jet beads and gold dragonflies gleaming against her pale skin. Daniel looked in dismay at his own clothes: loose black linen trousers, white cambric shirt, no belt, no tie. He said, "I'm not worthy."

"He's an art collector, Daniel. Everyone will think you're somebody."

"I *am* somebody," he protested. "But not when I'm not dressed like a yoga instructor."

"Then don't worry. Or here, wait—"

She turned to the heap of clothes on the sofa, sorting through them until she held up some sort of jacket. "Try this."

"Jesus, Larkin, is it a costume party?"

He tugged it on: a long jacket of very fine soft wool, so dark a red it was nearly black, with crystal buttons and deep slash pockets lined with white satin. It was old and worn but fit him beautifully. He smoothed the cloth, grinning despite himself, then looked at Larkin. "Well? Do I pass?"

"It's gorgeous. *You're* gorgeous. Look."

She turned him around to face the full-length ormolu mirror in Sira's living room. Daniel winced. "I look like I've just come from the Council of Elrond."

"You look great." She glanced to where the sunflower lay on a table. "Here."

She broke off what remained of the stem and tucked the flower into his lapel. "There: perfect. Come on, now, or we'll be late."

They went back outside. Once more he folded himself into the Mini, and it began the circuit around Highbury Fields. The April sky had deepened to violet. On the grass, members of a local rugby team were playing, their briefcases and backpacks scattered beneath a plane tree; lovers lay with arms entwined, oblivious of dogs pulling at leashes and the cries of children from the playground. To Daniel it was almost unbearably beautiful—glimpsed through a small, grimy windscreen and immediately consigned to that pastel-tinted province of memory it shared with its fellow prisoners of Time: the sound of an unseen bell chiming one Christmas Eve, he and Nick Hayward drunk and laughing themselves speechless on the Mall, the full moon gazing upon Middlesex Beach like a placid eye.

And now this, the car wheeling into Holloway Road with the April night just starting to bloom all around them. He sighed luxuriously, his hangover forgotten, and shoved his hands into the pockets of his dress jacket. His fingers closed around something familiar: another acorn.

He glanced furtively at Larkin, let the acorn slip back into the pocket's folds.

"So. Where, exactly, is whatever it is we're going to be late for?" he said.

"In Chelsea—Cheyne Walk. Right next to where Rossetti lived. It's a going-away party for Russell Learmont."

"Is he an artist?"

"No. He's the CEO of Winsoame Pharmaceuticals."

"Winsoame? As in Eli Lilly, Pfizer, and Winsoame? The people who invented Exultan?"

"That's right. Russell has this absolutely brilliant place, you'll see. He's retiring, sailing his yacht off to America in a few days. He's buying an island in New England. He's an interesting person."

"I'd think retiring with a trillion dollars from the world's biggest pharmaceutical concern would make him extremely interesting."

"No, really—he collects art brut. What do Americans call it—outsider art?"

"I gave up on art brut after seeing that cow cut in half at the Tate."

"That wasn't art brut."

"I hope not. My butcher can do better installations than that."

"Well, we don't have to stay long, just say hello, good-bye, and bon voyage. Russell has something of mine that I must get back before he leaves."

"Well, I just hope they don't throw me out into the street."

Daniel glanced at the rearview mirror. His gray eyes were slightly bloodshot, but the pale stubble on his face gave it more definition, so that he seemed at once younger and more world-weary, worthy of his glamorously shabby dress coat, his sunflower, and the woman beside him.

"This is all so strange," he said. "I mean, meeting you and just taking off like this. Getting drunk in the middle of the day. Wearing someone else's clothes. It's not what I usually do. With women, I mean."

"What do you usually do with them?"

"Not enough," he said, and laughed. "But really, don't you think it's funny—sort of a weird coincidence?"

"I don't believe in coincidence. Or maybe I define coincidence differently than you do."

"How do *you* define it?"

"By what the word actually means. To 'coincide' means for one thing to occupy the exact same place and time as another. There's a Latin term—*incidere*—to fall into or come into something unexpectedly. Oh, damn, I missed the turn."

It was another half hour before they found a place to park on the busy street alongside the Thames Embankment and made their way to Cheyne Walk. Neat redbrick houses and terraces that had once been bohemian digs now were the trophy homes of Sainsbury heirs and Sloane Rangers.

"That's Rossetti's house," said Larkin, pointing at an expansive building with bright white trim and tidy topiaries. "Back in the seventies John Paul Getty lived there and trashed it, but it's been fixed up quite nicely now. You're still not allowed to have peacocks, though."

"Peacocks?"

"Rossetti's animals made such a mess and so much noise that the landlord put a clause in the deed that no one was allowed to keep peacocks here, in perpetuity."

Daniel smiled, but Larkin seemed subdued.

"You look pale," he said. "You sure you want to do this?"

She looked up at him. The April twilight gave her eyes a strange cast, the way a violet's tracery of veins shows both green and purple.

"I'm fine." She lay her hand upon his cheek. "And I'll be better later. I promise."

They reached Learmont's house. The plangent strains of a string quartet echoed from windows open to the street. Larkin rapped upon the door, and it swung open. A man in black tie looked at them courteously but without warmth until she flashed a large black envelope.

"Please come in," he said, and beckoned them inside.

It was a vast, sparely furnished house—high walls painted white, arched doorways opening onto long bright passages that reminded Daniel of hospital corridors. Everywhere were paintings, of every imaginable size and shape, their frames made of gilt and plain wood, scrap metal and Popsicle sticks and aluminum foil. There were peculiar sculptures—huge cocoonlike masses of wool and twine, tree trunks carved in shapes that were not quite human—vitrines and Plexiglas cases displaying homemade books and tapestries composed of fur and wax and human hair. Daniel tried to keep up with Larkin as she strode ahead of him through a crowd of people evenly divided between those dressed in evening clothes and those who seemed to have wandered in from one of the bondage shops in Camden Town.

"Larkin!" Daniel called as she disappeared down a hallway. "Larkin, wait—"

Too late. Daniel looked around at the press of faces burnished by wealth and booze: a woman in a flamingo-pink feather sheath, another wearing black trousers and halter top and, God help her, a gold monocle. Two middle-aged men whom Daniel recognized from last week's *News of the World;* several buff and silent fellows in black tie and cordless headsets who must be Learmont's security staff.

And, preening by itself in the middle of the wide formal center stairway, a live peacock, its tail extended to form a rainbow-eyed fan nearly four feet across.

"Jesus Christ," said Daniel, and hurried to find the bar.

There was no absinthe being served at the party, so Daniel contented himself with two glasses of peaty-tasting scotch poured by a man who looked like his last job had involved standing very still at Madame Tussaud's. Daniel accepted a third glass, then wandered around vainly searching for Larkin. There was the usual blue scrawl of cigarette smoke, the usual desultory conversation elevated, for American ears at least, by elongated Oxbridge delivery.

". . . got another seven in stock from the Singapore venture—"

". . . a *boy.* Told him he'd be better off with a Cairn terrier."

". . . no option. Then next you know, *pfff!* she's lying on the floor, and I still have the wire in my hand. . . ."

". . . tell them I don't give a fuck if it is breach of contract. Make more money selling my stuff on the Internet now anyway."

Daniel felt a shiver of apprehension. He turned to see Nick Hayward pointing his pocketknife at a very large, well-dressed man. When the man noticed Daniel watching, he grabbed him by the arm and pulled him over.

"You two must meet," he said. "Please excuse me, but there's my mother now," he added, and fled.

"Hallo, Daniel." Nick turned and prodded him with the knife, which had a bit of sausage stuck to its tip. He was dressed as usual in black jeans and a stained khaki anorak, heavy gold hoops in his ears. "Hungry? I brought this, food here's terrible. Look at all these walking skeletons. Fucking charnel house of Prada."

"What are you doing here?" demanded Daniel.

"What am I doing here? *I* was invited." Nick surveyed Daniel's jacket and sunflower curiously. "Whatever are you wearing? You look like Mott the Hoople."

"Shut up. Have you seen Larkin?"

"Larkin." Nick's expression clouded. He ate the nub end of sausage, closed the knife and slid it into a pocket, then took Daniel by the elbow and pulled him to an empty corner. "Larkin is precisely why I'm here. Look, Danny, I know you have limited patience with me these days—"

"I have *none,*" Daniel snapped. "Just tell me if you've seen her, since I don't know a single goddamn person here—"

"You wound me, Danny."

"—and I feel a little out of place."

"Don't worry, you're with me. Come on."

Nick spun and began walking quickly up the broad stairway. As he passed the peacock, his foot shot out to kick it. In a frenzy of shrieks and iridescent feathers, the bird sailed off above the crowd.

"I've always wanted to do that," he said as Daniel ran up behind him.

Daniel glanced back at the bird sympathetically. "Who is this Learmont guy anyway?"

"Russell Learmont? Why, he's the man who sold the world." Nick stooped to grab a stray peacock feather and stuck it into his braid. "I suppose the short answer would be that he's a collector."

"Of outsider art."

"Of whatever he fucking wants."

"What's the long answer?"

"That's what I'm taking you to find out, Danny."

They reached the second floor. There were more paintings here, but no people. Nick hurried across the landing into a large living room, empty save for several wing chairs arranged before a cold fireplace and a dog dozing on the Ashtaban carpet. "Art collector, that's what he'd tell you. He's a dangerous brute."

"Meaning he's a good CEO." Daniel reached down to stroke the dog's ears. It was a Border collie, its muzzle gray with age, its piebald coat black and white; when it looked up, he was startled by its eyes, one champagne gold, the other a blanched blue that was almost white. "Nice doggy. Nice weird doggy."

He glanced up to see Nick pulling first one and then a second pocket door from the wall, sealing off the room. "Should you be doing that?" said Daniel. "This isn't your house."

"I'll do whatever I fucking please. Piss on the carpet if I choose. And no, I don't mean he's a good CEO." Nick flicked a disdainful finger at Daniel's dress jacket. "I mean that had better be a lead-lined bit of business you're wearing, if you mean to keep your balls intact."

"You're a lunatic, Nick. I'm out of here."

"You can't do that. You've only just arrived," someone said in a hoarse voice. A slim figure was extracting itself from one of the wing chairs, a boy wearing a neo-retro polyester zoot suit a shade darker than his blond hair.

"We haven't met." The figure extended a hand with very dirty fingernails. "Although I see you're wearing my token. Juda Trent."

It was not a boy but a young woman. The down on her upper lip was mostly a trick of the light: when she tilted her head back, it faded into her skin. The blunt fingernails weren't dirty either, but painted metallic blue. She had an open, freckled face and wore no makeup; the roots of her bright hair were dark brown, and her eyes were icy blue.

"Juda," repeated Daniel, dazed. "I'm Daniel Rowlands."

Juda smiled, and once more Daniel was staring at a man maybe ten years younger than himself, but then she leaned forward to take his hand, and he caught a flash of small freckled breasts beneath her V-neck sweater.

"*Dr.* Juda Trent," said Nick. "Juda is a Jungian psychiatrist, as well as the World's Foremost Authority on ancient pagan survivals in the modern world, north of Finsbury Park."

"Please. Call me Juda." She withdrew her hand, uptilted eyes mocking. "I saw you this afternoon by the café. And now we meet. What a coincidence."

"Yes." Daniel glanced helplessly at Nick, who had settled into a chair and was fanning himself with the peacock feather. "You gave me the sunflower."

"I did." Juda reached to adjust it in his lapel. "Now, in the language of flowers, a sunflower means 'adoration,' or alternately 'love above one's station.' It looks quite nice on you."

"You're a psychiatrist?"

"I am." Juda picked up a leather briefcase. "Although I don't practice much analysis anymore. Mostly research now," and she handed him a business card.

JUDA TRENT. Ph.D., D.D., F.R.

0 207 484-9999   psychopomp@demon.co.uk

"Psychopomp?" Daniel laughed and put the card into his pocket.

"My clinical work involved people with terminal diseases—cancer mostly, and AIDS. This was before the drug cocktails became available."

"Sounds challenging."

"It was." Juda sank into a chair and lit a cigarette. The Border collie stood and pattered over to Daniel's feet, gave a loud sigh, and sat. "Exhausting. But extremely interesting. You spend a lot of time, going back and forth with dying people."

Daniel thought that such journeys were usually one way but said nothing. Juda Trent continued to stare at him, smoking.

Finally she spoke. "Anyhow, good to meet you, Daniel. Your friend's told me a bit about you." She glanced at Nick, then gestured at the door. "That locked?"

Nick nodded. "Yeah. And Fancy there will keep an ear out. Won't you, boy?" he added, clucking softly at the dog. The Border collie looked up, feathered tail giving a halfhearted wave, then laid its grizzled muzzle on Daniel's foot.

"Locked?" Daniel looked around. "What . . . ?"

Without warning, Juda jumped from her seat and strode over to him. She took his chin in her hand and tilted his head back, staring intently at his face. Daniel was too stunned to speak. After a moment she dropped her hand and turned to Nick.

"It's not him," she said.

Daniel whirled: he couldn't tell if Nick looked disappointed or relieved. "Hayward, what the fuck is going on?"

Juda put a hand on his shoulder. "Daniel. Please don't—"

He pushed her away and stormed toward the door, but as he did, Fancy whined. Daniel glanced down at the dog's imploring eyes and groaned.

"God! If I leave, you'll probably kill it, right? Okay—you both have one minute."

He stood, arms crossed, and looked balefully from one to the other as Fancy walked over to lie at his feet once more. Nick glanced at Juda Trent and shrugged.

"The dog does like him," he said.

"Thirty seconds," snapped Daniel.

"All right." Juda tossed her cigarette into the fireplace. "You've met Larkin?"

"*He* introduced us." Daniel shot Nick a venomous look. "Is that what this is, Hayward? Some screwed-up intervention so I don't go out with one of your old girlfriends? Christ, how does Sira put up with you?"

"Stop," said Juda. "Larkin is someone *I* look after. Or try to anyway. Larkin is . . ." She hesitated.

"What?" demanded Daniel. "What's wrong with her?"

"Wrong with her? Nothing. Who told you that?"

"Well, for starters, Mr. Hayward here said she's a mental patient."

"*Former* mental patient," said Nick.

"She's not crazy," Juda said emphatically. "She has . . . well, let's call them boundary issues. Does she seem dangerous to you, Daniel?"

"Of course not. I mean, I don't think so. But how would I know? We just met."

"Have you slept with her?"

Daniel flushed. "Look, I don't know where you're going with this, *Dr.* Trent, but frankly it's none of your business."

"Because she is very dangerous, Daniel." said Juda. "To you and—"

"If she's not supposed to be here," Daniel broke in, "if she's going to get into trouble for being here, or hurt someone, hurt herself—why aren't you helping her, instead of giving me a hard time?"

Juda stooped to pat Fancy's worn head. "That's what I'm trying to do. But there's not much time."

In his chair Nick slouched, until all Daniel could see was the warning glitter of his eyes. "Do you remember, Danny," Nick asked, "how we used to wish the world was a more interesting place? Or no—wait."

He looked at the ceiling. As if on cue, music seeped down from an upper room: a thin, hollow-sounding recording of the "Liebestod." "Let me rephrase that. Do you remember when the world *was* a more interesting place?"

"What do you mean?"

"That night in D.C., after the Glass show at that place—what do you call it, the one with the big columns?"

"The Old Pension Building."

"Right." For a minute Nick sat, brooding. "But you remember it, right? How we felt?"

"Jesus, Nick, we were tripping our tits off! I almost got canned 'cause I missed my deadline."

"That's not when I mean. I mean *after*—after the acid wore off, before the sun came up, when we were walking down by that canal there in Georgetown. It was so fucking beautiful. This time of year, too. I said it was like Regents Canal. . . ."

"No." Daniel looked up sharply. "You said it was *exactly* like the Regents Canal. And for a minute . . ."

The room was still. Overhead the "Liebestod" had stopped. Daniel could hear mumbling voices, a man's bellicose laughter. He stared at Juda, and then at Nick.

"For a minute they were the same place," Daniel said. "They . . ."

He stopped, recalling his conversation with Larkin. "They coincided."

Silence, except for Fancy 's wheezing breath. In his chair Nick was curled like a great amber-eyed cat, watching.

"That's right." Juda touched the sunflower at Daniel's throat, ran a finger along his collarbone. He shivered. "It happens, Daniel. And when it does . . ."

Her finger moved into the hollow of his throat. "It's very dangerous. People get trapped. They can't get out. They can't get back."

"Back? Back *where?*" Daniel shook his head. "Explain to me again exactly what kind of psychiatrist you are?"

He looked at Nick. "Look, I have to get back. I have work to do. And since this all seems like some kind of sick setup by you and your friends, you can tell Larkin that I've gone home."

"Danny," said Nick, "I would be very surprised if you could leave her. Larkin is a remarkable girl. The sort with hooks and talons."

Daniel ignored him. But when he reached the wall, he stopped. Pain lanced him: a blade of longing, and he knew whose name was on it.

Larkin.

"No." He shut his eyes. *Oh, no. Not this, not her, no.* Like an after-image of the sun against his eyelids, he saw an acorn, felt its smooth skin pressed against his lower lip, and recalled Nick's mocking words:

> *We must not buy their fruits:*
> *Who knows upon what soil they feed*
> *Their hungry thirsty roots?*

Someone spoke aloud. " 'We daren't go a-hunting for fear of little men.' "

It was Juda Trent.

The hairs on his arms rose. He reached for the door, was arrested by the crackle of flame and something that blurred his vision: a bright arabesque coiling and uncoiling in the air before him. He cringed, watched in horror as the shining arabesque became a rainbow-finned tail. The pressure on his mouth exploded into the taste of burned fish and honey. He felt a jolting sensation, as of a train jerking to a halt, and flailed at the air for safety.

"See or shut your eyes," commanded Juda.

He saw.

Around him the room shuddered, the way the image thrown by a jammed projector shifts, then changes. Then the room was gone. In front of him, a fire burned; he could feel the heat, near scorching, of something in his hands. He looked down and saw that he was holding a blackened iron pot with something cooking inside it: a whole fish.

"Fuck—"

Gasping in pain and amazement, he dropped the pot, snatching his hand back to suck his singed fingers. With a cry someone caught the pot before it struck the ground, but not before the fish, flipping this way and that within, lifted its head and, gazing at Daniel, smiled.

"Now you know," it said in Nick's voice.

Daniel fell to his knees, retching; the oily taste of salmon clung to his lips. Once again the world around him lurched and juddered forward. He braced himself against the ground, his nausea overwhelmed by terror. When he looked up again, the fire was gone, and the fish.

He was back in the brightly colored attic room at Highbury Fields. Before him stood a woman, Larkin, he thought, but younger and more beautiful—terrifyingly so, like a glowing figure in a stained-glass window that had stepped from its leaded frame. As he stared, she drew her hand to her lips, opening her mouth to disgorge a jewel. Its radiance hurt his eyes. The woman stared at it unblinking, then turned and held it up to him.

"Look."

He saw then that the gem was not perfect but marred by two flaws: a black imploded star and a jagged line of yellow-green, like sun blazing on a lake.

"They think it must be emended." As she spoke, her lips did not move. *"They do not see that it is whole as it is."*

She opened her hand as though to let the gem drop. But it did not fall. Instead it hung suspended in the room before him, spinning and flickering, until in a sudden burst it exploded. Where it had been there was now a shining sphere no larger than a hazelnut, yet with every stone, every stream, every blade of grass inside it revealed to him as though beneath a microscope.

Daniel was inside that world; he knew that as simply as if he had awakened in his own apartment. But this wasn't his apartment. It wasn't anyplace he had ever been, or seen, or even imagined.

To either side of him rose the horizon, twin lines of jagged hills surrounding a wide green country under a viridian sky. Beyond the hills he glimpsed malachite seas, an emerald whirlpool like a fallen nebula, jade pools that reflected a starless firmament. There were no shadows. Everything shone with the blinding radiance of midday sun on desert sand. He stared in amazement, his breath coming too fast.

"Green," he whispered. His fear returned, a smaller wave; he swallowed and tasted sweetness in the air. Like green apples, or the quickening smell of a spring marsh, at once honeyed and choked with decay.

With that sweetness the world behind his eyes smashed open. He saw Larkin as he had first seen her—laughing on the terrace at Sira's flat, then bent over her hoarded drawings, her mouth almost touching his and her eyes half closed. He blinked and looked around wildly.

And yes, on the rim of the green country stood a figure with the sea behind her, her naked form blazing green as the sea was green, the hills, the starless sky.

"Larkin!"

She was too far away. "Larkin!" Daniel cried again, and began to run toward her. "Larkin!"

She turned, and he saw something beside her—a rent in the horizon. The rent wavered, shifting up and down like a flame, grew darker, then flared into an emerald spire, whirling in slow eddies. Before he could blink, both figures disappeared.

"Larkin!"

He stopped, panting. In the distance were nothing but willow-green cliffs falling to the sea and a sky the color of absinthe.

Absence.

He had scarcely thought the word when the green country faded. Color drained from it like water from a cracked bowl. A warm breath came into his ear: *See or close your eyes.*

"No—"

He tried to cry aloud but could not. Neither could he flee: he was as immovable as the hills. Which he saw now were not hills at all but something else, two endless and opposing lines of figures. One line was formed of men and women, dressed in every kind of clothing—suits and gowns and tunics, robes and trousers and even pelts. Some of them were naked. They had presence, but, gazing at them, Daniel knew they had no real power. They were an irruption upon the green world, as he was.

It was the others who terrified him.

They were nothing but light, an awful confusion of refracted rays, green blue gold, dazzling and horrible. The light had a sound, a deafening retort like an electrical discharge. Daniel doubled over, sickened. Yet almost immediately his nausea passed. The wordless song grew more refined—he could discern notes within it, a rising and falling scale that echoed inside him. The bones of his hands quivered; he could feel his skull's plates grinding together like teeth.

Unmaking, Daniel thought. *It is unmaking me.*

Yet as he felt himself splintering into motes of light and heat, another sound echoed across the plain. A word, a command. He could not then or later determine what the command was, but that did not matter as much as that it *was* a word. Like the music, the word went on and on, and Daniel was held within its sound—within both sounds, suspended as the jeweled world had been suspended, his Being momentarily the focus of two great wills. It was a dreadful immurement: eternity without light or thought or reason, the annihilating weight of those opposed powers pressing upon him until Daniel himself was nearly extinguished. They did not perceive him at all; he was nothing but a space between, to be crushed and erased in eternal mindless striving.

The voice cried out again. This time Daniel understood its meaning: *No more.* The roar of conflict faded. Light jabbed at his closed eyelids; he opened them to see a cold fireplace with three empty chairs before it. Sweet liquid filled his mouth as he drew a hand to his face. Somewhere within the house, a woman's clear laughter echoed. There was the sound of a bell tolling and another sound, strange to hear indoors—birdsong, the *cheet cheet cheet* of a wren.

"Daniel. Daniel, do you hear me?"

With an effort he turned and saw Juda Trent's hand extended to him. The steel-blue sheen of her fingernails seeped toward her knuckles. He stared at her, uncomprehending, then at Nick beside her with the dog Fancy at his feet.

"No." Daniel choked on the word. "No."

He lunged for the door. Before he could reach it, Nick grabbed him from behind, yanking Daniel's arm behind his back.

"Oh, fuck," Daniel breathed. From the corner of his eye, he saw Nick withdraw his pocketknife, then felt its cold edge against his windpipe.

"You can't go, Danny." He spoke calmly. "I'm sorry. You have to stay now."

Daniel held his breath. The blade scraped against his Adam's apple.

"Don't go," whispered Nick. His gaze flickered from topaz to green. "Don't leave me."

Daniel waited a heartbeat, felt the hand holding the knife relax. He shook himself free, pushing Nick away.

"All right." He pointed at Nick, his hand shaking. "Just . . . tell me . . ."

"It's her." Nick looked down at the knife in his hand, then at Daniel. His eyes were wide and helpless. "Larkin. Do you remember, Danny? Did you see? Look at this."

He threw off his anorak and yanked up the T-shirt he wore beneath. "See, Danny? Do you see?"

Daniel sucked his breath in. Nick's chest was mapped with scars, whorls and streaks of red and white and blue-green. Some were edged with pinkish lappets like fringed petals; a few were deep enough to thrust a finger inside. Daniel stared, repulsed not just by Nick's ravaged torso but by the patterns of the scars themselves, which seemed to shift and dart like specks of light behind his eyelids.

They meant something.

He looked away, but the lines floated across his vision, tangled roots or branches, dendrites, rivers, roads. That scorched, sweet taste came again, a wash of spectral green across his vision.

"Nicky," he said. "Nicky, don't."

"Nick," said Juda. "*Nick.* Stop."

He looked from her to Daniel; a grin spread across his face. He held up his pocketknife. With one sure stroke, he drew the blade across the back of his wrist, took the knife into his left hand and scored the other wrist, then raised both hands so Daniel saw the blood welling, then running in thin black lines down his arms.

"She wrote on me," said Nick. "Like that."

Juda grabbed the knife from him, snapped the blade back into place, and tossed it on the floor. "Don't make it worse," she hissed.

Nick picked up the knife, got his anorak and pulled it back on. Drops of blood stained the rug at his feet as he began to laugh. "Worse? It can get worse?"

"It's not him. It will never be him," said Juda, and her voice rose with desperation. "Not ever, and the time is leaving us, and there's nothing else I can do—*nothing,*" she cried, her hand slashing at the air. "Fancy!"

The dog scrambled to its feet. Juda stalked to the wall, pulled the pocket doors open, and hurried downstairs, the dog at her heels. Daniel stared after her, stunned. When Nick began to laugh, Daniel turned to him, his face white. "You think this is a fucking joke, Hayward? What, did you drug me?"

"A drug, Danny? When's the last time a drug did that for you? Open your eyes, Daniel! You're in it now with all the rest of us—in for a penny, in for a pound."

Daniel fought to keep his voice steady "Look, Nick, if this really is about her—if Larkin really does have a problem—"

"Larkin doesn't *have* a problem—Larkin *is* a problem. Come on, Danny—a girl like that. Why would she bother with you? Why would she bother with *either* of us? Even me, Danny—even me! Think about this. You met her, when? Six, seven o'clock yesterday evening? What've the last twenty-four hours been like for you, Danny?"

"Pretty weird."

"Yeah? Well, it's going to get worse. Do you remember what you saw a few minutes ago?"

"You cutting your wrists with a Swiss army knife?"

"I mean, what you saw when Juda told you to *see*."

Daniel frowned. Of course he did—that shattering moment when he'd seen . . . *something* . . .

. . . but whatever it was already had started to fade, one of those luminous dreams you're certain you'll never forget, that disappear within minutes of waking.

"Sort of," he said. "Something about a fish?"

Nick moved forward and pressed a finger to his lower lip. Daniel's mouth filled with the taste of scorched fish and burned honey.

Not just his mouth. His entire sensorium was flooded—burning leaves, green sap, wormwood, a blinding aureole of emerald light, the taste of anisette and salt and—

"Stop!" he cried. "God, *stop* it!"

Daniel clutched at his head as Nick stepped back. "What *is* it?" Daniel looked at him desperately. "How are you doing that?"

"I'm not. She is. Larkin."

"But . . . how?"

"I don't know." Nick's entire body sagged. He thrust his hands into his pockets; suddenly he looked small and old. "Or . . . well, everything I think might explain it is just too crazy."

"What about Juda? How do you know her?"

"She found me. Tracked me down, years ago. After Larkin left me." He lifted his face and gazed at Daniel, his eyes wild and desolate.

"She said the same thing about me, Juda did. *It's not him.* What she did to you, Danny—she did that to me, too. Twenty years ago.

"And now that's what the world is like for me, Dan. Every waking hour. Every fucking moment."

Before Daniel could reply, a voice called from the stairs. "Daniel? Daniel, you up there?"

Daniel's face brightened. "Larkin!"

Nick pulled up the hood of his anorak. "I can't stay," he said in a low voice. "Can't bear it. Her."

One last moment he hesitated, staring at his friend. "Don't let Learmont near her," he said. "She's mad, coming here. You, too, Danny."

Head lowered, he darted out the door, passing a tall, slender figure in midnight blue. "Daniel! I thought I heard you—"

"Larkin," said Daniel. And knew at that moment Nick was right: *Why would she bother with either of us?*

She stepped into the room, smiling. She no longer looked pale but flushed; her hair had slipped from its chignon to fall in a dark haze upon her shoulders. "I couldn't find you," she said.

"Here I am."

She stepped over and took his arm, and together they went into the hallway, walking slowly past paintings and a series of shadowboxes. Downstairs the party roiled on, waves of laughter and bits of music, raised voices, the tinkle of broken glass. But here on the second floor, all was silent, the hall empty.

"Look at that." Larkin stopped, tipped her head toward a pastel-tinted watercolor of a child with butterfly wings perched upon a lightning bolt. The child's face was sly, its long eyes upturned so that they showed neither iris nor pupil. "Isn't that amazing? How could someone know to paint that?"

Daniel shook his head. "I don't know." He stepped closer, looking in vain for the artist's signature.

"I never get tired of them." Larkin gazed at the painting, and Daniel was surprised to see tears in her eyes. "No matter how often I see them . . . I can never keep away. They draw me."

Daniel started to reply, then stopped. A few feet from where they stood, a door opened. A man stepped into the corridor. Slight, dressed in dark trousers and a cable-knit sweater, with black, gray-salted hair falling to his shoulders and a ruddy face, his features saved from boyishness by heavy black brows above deep-set sea-blue eyes. As the door closed behind him, he looked up, startled, at Daniel and Larkin.

"Hello," he said.

Daniel stared at him: was this Learmont? He draped an arm protectively around Larkin, but she barely glanced at the newcomer. The man continued to gaze at them; no, not at them: at Larkin. His expression grew intent, almost disbelieving, until of a sudden he seemed to notice Daniel watching him.

"Remarkable stuff he has, isn't it?" He looked at Daniel and smiled. "Our host."

Daniel's hand tightened around Larkin; he could feel her tense. She pulled away, turning to stare at him in alarm.

"I'll meet you at the car," he said quietly. He smiled for the newcomer's benefit, then gently pushed Larkin toward the step. "Five minutes."

Nodding, she turned and hurried away. The two men watched her go. Daniel straightened, slipping his hand into his pocket. His fingers found the acorn, and he clutched it as he turned to the newcomer.

"I'm Balthazar Warnick," the man said, and held out his hand.

"Daniel Rowlands." Daniel let the acorn slide free. "You're American, too."

"I am. Are you the same Daniel Rowlands who writes for the *Washington Horizon*?"

Daniel smiled stiffly. "Guilty as charged."

"Very happy to meet you." Warnick shook his hand warmly. "I live in the District, too. I enjoy your column. That was a very nice piece you did on Akhenaton last spring."

"Thanks. So you're from D.C.?" He gestured at the wall of paintings. "Are you with the National Gallery? Or the Corcoran?"

"No, nothing like that. I'm an instructor at the University of the Archangels and St. John the Divine."

"Art history?"

"Classical archaeology. My work occasionally intersects with Russell's. Do you know him?"

Daniel hesitated. "No."

"Are you covering this for the *Horizon*?"

"No. I'm here on sabbatical for several months. Working on a book."

"Doesn't your family miss you?"

"I'm not married."

"Ah." Warnick gave him a melancholy smile. "Then you are free to give yourself to research. And it's all research, isn't it? Any bit of knowledge we can obtain, no matter its source, no matter how we go about retrieving it—all fuel for the fire, isn't it? *Fas est et ab hoste doceri.*"

Daniel stiffened. Balthazar Warnick stared at him with an expectant, almost teasing expression on his ruddy face. Daniel stared back. Finally he said, "I think I'd better go."

"Wait." Warnick laid a hand lightly on his shoulder. "Before you do—let me introduce you to our host. Just so you'll know who you're dealing with. Always a good idea, I think."

He began to steer Daniel toward the door.

"I'm sorry, but I told my friend—"

"Oh, she'll wait." Warnick paused, staring up at Daniel with his sea-blue eyes. His expression grew wistful. "They nearly always do. Come—"

And opening the door, he drew Daniel inside.

CHAPTER SIX

Ferdinand Lured by Ariel

At Saint-Rémy, in Provence, in a hospital for the insane, I saw a poor young
artist driven mad by love. With much mystery, he showed me the profile of his
mistress which he had sculpted himself, but in a manner so lacking
in form that the features could be seen by no one but himself.
—*Pierre-Jean David d'Angers,* Les carnets de David d'Angers, *1838*

The train departed Paddington Station promptly *at nine-thirty.
Radborne's third-class ticket gave him a coach that was his
alone, save for an elderly man who blew his nose all the way to
Exeter.

The journey took most of the day. The lemony sunlight that
touched the grimy coach windows in London disappeared by the time
they reached Devizes. The rest of the trip passed in a nickel-colored
blur, rain and smoke smirching the glass, the smell of burning coal
making Radborne feel queasy and light-headed. He had not slept well
the previous night: there had been words with Mrs. Beale when he told
her he was leaving to take a position.

"A lunatic asylum?" She dropped her tatting as though it might soil
her. "Broadmoor?"

"No, I told you, it's in Cornwall. Sarsinmoor, it's called—"

"Sarsinmoor? Well, I have never heard of it. And I have made it a
practice never to let rooms to temperamental individuals—"

"I am taking a position there, Mrs. Beale. I am not a patient."

"—and so I must ask you to vacate your room immediately, Mr. Comstock. And there is to be no question of repayment of your rent or—"

"That will not be necessary," Radborne said hotly. "You are welcome to it. Now, if you will excuse me, I have to pack."

In the third-class coach, he dozed fitfully on a wooden bench, his head pillowed on his velvet jacket and his bags at his feet. By the time they departed Redruth in midafternoon, he gave up hope of getting any sleep. Outside the station he saw women and children waiting for the London-bound train, their barrows full of the late-autumn harvest—broccoli and sprouts and carrots—and tinners with blackened faces and white pits for eyes. The names painted on worm-bitten signposts were incomprehensible: Bowda, Trespettigue, Hendra, Cassacawn, Menkee, Kernick. When he did glimpse a name that he could understand—Death Corner, Catshole Downs—he found no reassurance in it.

The green downs and fields of Somerset had long since given way to a landscape unlike anything he had ever seen, that part of England where warm red sandstone and the granite uplands of Dartmoor surrender to black Devonian slate. Scoured hills bristling with gorse, their peaks etched with strange mounds and ragged lines of upright stones, deep-cleft valleys where black streams trickled through poison-green bog.

There were few trees, fewer buildings. Now and then a narrow road wound between hedges so tall he could have stood on a man's shoulders without seeing over them. He pressed his face against the train's filthy window, fascinated and repelled by the way distant snow-topped mountains metamorphosed into slag heaps so close he might have touched them, then disappeared behind the ruins of ancient settlements. There were gaps like the tinners' empty eyes within crumbling walls of stacked slate and reddish stone. When, after an hour, a conductor passed through the empty coach, Radborne fairly lunged from his seat to stop him.

"Sir! Can you tell me, how long until we reach Sarsinmoor?"

The conductor stared at him blankly. "Where you going, then?"

"Sarsinmoor."

The man shook his head. "Sarsin Moor? Are you sure? No moor here named that."

"It's a place. A . . . a hospital. I was told that the nearest station is Padwithiel."

The conductor brightened. "Ah, Padwithiel—that would be Penrechdroc, we call it. I would say two hours more, if there's no trouble with the track. Two hours," he repeated, pleased, and made his way to the next coach.

Radborne slumped against the wooden seat. He saw nothing but desolation: crags and moorland, granite slabs, a hawk pecking at a sheep's carcass. After a few minutes, he groaned. He picked up his color box and cradled it in his lap. A woman's face moved just within the limits of his vision, hair like smoke, shining flecks of green, a white mouth.

"Go away," he whispered. He shut his eyes, felt a thicket of needles stabbing at his eyelids. "Go away, go away."

For the remainder of the journey, he sat with head bowed and shoulders hunched, his color box on his knees as he tried to shut out the shadows rustling around him.

When he got off the train, the sign at the station read PADWITHIEL. But the conductor had called for Penrechdroc, and the name painted on the side of the tiny station house was Penrechdroc as well. It was dusk now. Radborne stood alone on the platform, staring through the mist in search of Dr. Learmont or a carriage.

There was not another soul to be seen. The village consisted of four ancient cottages with walls of cream-colored stone and gray granite sills, tiny square windows hung with dingy lace. A narrow path wound past the cottages and up a steep black hill, disappearing at its crown into moor and fog.

"God help me," said Radborne, and he shivered. Cold wind carried the smell of burning furze and the sweeter scent of peat fire. He turned and saw another building, set by itself a hundred yards off. Its windows were uncurtained and brightly lit; a painted sign hung above the wide recessed doorway. Radborne hoisted his valise and color box and headed toward it, slowing when he saw the wagons and cart horses that waited on the far side of the building.

Above him the sky had deepened to lavender and indigo. In the dimness he could just make out the inn's signboard—a vivid painting of a grotesque figure with long, slanted eyes and sharp chin, pointed fingers arranged so that it seemed to be holding the very placard it decorated.

COLEMAN GREY, the sign read.

"Mind yerself, there. 'Tis mucky."

Radborne turned to see a man stepping from behind a farm cart. He was compact and dark-haired, his face burned blackish red by sun and wind. He looked at Radborne and nodded, touching his battered black cap. "I'm Kervissey. Yeh'll be wanting a ride to manor?"

Radborne nodded, venturing a smile. "I certainly will be."

"I'll want payment now. Else you can walk."

Radborne hesitated. "All right," he said. He dug into his pocket and counted out a few shillings. This seemed to satisfy the farmer, who strode to a wagon harnessed to a draft horse with hooves the size of casks. Radborne hurried after him. He handed Kervissey his valise, which the farmer unceremoniously tossed into the back of the cart. Radborne winced and clasped his color box tightly.

"I'll keep these up front with me."

"Yeh're riding in back. Get in."

Radborne stared at him in disbelief, but Kervissey only climbed in front and picked up the reins. After a moment Radborne clambered into the back. Kervissey shouted at the draft horse.

"Gas e dhe gerdhes!"

With a lurch they moved forward. Radborne settled himself as best he could on a pile of empty croker sacks, trying to avoid the crusted skin of bird droppings and filthy feathers stuck to the floor. His color box he wedged in a corner behind a wooden crate, then tugged the collar of his greatcoat up around his ears and concentrated on keeping warm.

The cart clattered uphill, leaving the four cottages behind. At the top of the rise, it hied sharply to the left, past a dour Methodist church, its stone walls bleak as a prison. There were a few more houses, which Radborne would have thought deserted were it not for skeins of smoke rising from the chimneys, and a single farmstead where starved-looking sheep cropped yellow grass.

That was all. Around them mist rose in whitish columns, and Penrechdroc disappeared as they started downhill. The horse's plod became a trot. At the bottom of the rise, the mist blew off. Radborne stared out as the moor swept suddenly around them, a vast gray counterpane unrolled from the sky.

"That's Sarsinmoor!" shouted Kervissey. He twisted his head to glare at the swell of gorse-grown hills and treacherous blanket bog, split like a skin where granite tors thrust to the sky. They were miles from the sea, yet Radborne could hear waves beating inside his skull and the skirling cry of lapwings.

"God, what a place," he said.

From bare hills the ruins of abandoned tin mines rose like scaffolding. Ancient hedges crisscrossed fields where nothing dwelled but skylarks and foxes. It was a land that looked as though it had not been occupied but seized: on every hillside Radborne saw what appeared to be relics of strife. Fallen towers, granite beacons, collapsed stone huts, and ransacked burial mounds. All bespoke an ancient, relentless vigilance.

Yet nothing grew here but gorse and gnarled evergreens bowed and broken by the wind from the sea. What on earth could they have been keeping watch for?

Beneath him the croker sacks rustled as he tried to get comfortable. The wind was relentless. He shivered and gazed out at a half-circle of standing stones rising from the heath.

"*Ay!*"

Radborne started as the driver glanced back at him.

"*Kemerough wyth na wra why gasa an vorth noweth rag an vorth goth!* You keep your eyes ahead, Mehster Comstook!"

The farmer banged on the wagon board. Radborne scowled but swiveled until he stared at the hindquarters of the dray horse.

Kervissey spit and shook his head. "Stupid gawk," he said.

The horse clopped on placidly, the farmer grumbled to himself. Somewhere overhead an owl croaked. The wagon splashed through a stream, wooden wheels straining. Radborne sat hunched in the dark and the cold and stared at the back of Kervissey's head. The wind carried the smells of rain and the sea; after a while icy drops began to patter against the dusty sacking. The horse picked its way across open moor and along ancient, deeply grooved lanes that ran between the impenetrable hedges. Within the insubstantial folds of his woolen jacket, Radborne shivered and cursed Dr. Learmont.

Hours passed. Days, maybe. That couldn't be possible, and yet he felt inside an uneasy dream, time a stream he had fallen into, buoyed along by shadows, the wreckage of half-remembered faces. Sometimes he thought he heard voices rising above the rushing of wind. He saw flickers that might have been the sun streaking, meteor-wise, across a sky that was sometimes black, sometimes like an inverted bowl streaked with gold and blue. Unexpectedly he would laugh, then fall silent, shocked by the sound and unable to recall what had torn it from him. Only when he felt the sudden weight of his color box as the wagon rounded a curve did he remember where he was, and why, and when.

Above him the clouds had broken. A half-moon shone just above the horizon, bright as an electrolier. Radborne leaned forward. "How much longer is it?"

"*Is* it? *is* it?' Kervissey replied, mocking him. " 'Tis there, young man! See't? 'Tis the manor house, and there's Doctor waiting for you—"

Radborne stood, rocking back and forth as he tried to keep his balance. "My God," he murmured. "Look at this."

Before him was a vast promontory, ridged with ruined stone walls and separated from the mainland by a narrow land bridge. At its peak stood a house—not an old house, but a gracefully executed four-story manse, built at the early part of the century in the Italianate style, of soft yellow stone and black slate. There were lamps burning in the lower windows, a wedge of yellow light that might have been an open door. Beyond the promontory, and surrounding it some hundreds of feet below, was the sea. Radborne could hear waves thundering against the cliffs and feel them, too—the earth beneath the wagon shuddered with each crash of the tide. He could feel a piercing pain in his ears, as though a skewer had been thrust into his skull.

Kervissey shouted to the horse. *"Gas e dhe gerdhes! Yskynna!"* It began to race up the winding road, the wagon jouncing behind it. Radborne sank back down. The narrow tongue of land leading to the promontory was perhaps thirty feet wide. The passage of horses and carts had beaten the turf down to cracked slate and bare earth. On the far side of this, the promontory seemed an island rising from the dark sea, the manor house a beacon at its height.

Radborne's hands clutched at the pockets of his jacket. He turned to stare northeast and then southwest. In both directions were the same dramatic cliffs, thrusting out into the ocean as far as he could see. Perhaps a half mile to the south, separated by a raging channel that swirled into a whirlpool at its base, reared another spike of black stone surmounted by the ruins of a castle or keep. Radborne could just discern a broken bridge like a dangling thread, the sole remnant of where it had once been connected to the mainland.

"What is that place?" he shouted above the wind.

"Argolkelys!" Kervissey shouted back. "On next headland you'll find what they call Tintagel, though this one's the older. No Christian goes there, don't you think of it! Hold on now—"

Around them the the path fell away into soft green turf and lines of broken slates. Near the manor house, a row of stunted evergreens bent before the wind. The horse slowed its pace, and Kervissey whistled to it softly.

"There now, there now, soon we go home. *Trenos vyttyn, coascar,*" he added, glancing at Radborne.

"What?"

"It's tomorrow morning, lad. Not night anymore. Today—and here you are."

As they drew in front the house, the massive oaken doors opened and Dr. Learmont appeared.

"Mr. Comstock!" he cried as Radborne jumped down from the cart. "How glad I am to see you—come in, come in! I see that you found Kervissey—*mur ras dheugh-why,* Kervissey!"

He nodded at the farmer, then clasped Radborne's hand warmly. "Your baggage arrived safely? And yourself?"

Radborne grinned, in surprise and relief. "Yes—quite safely, thank you! I don't have much, just the one valise, and my paints and—"

He turned to see Kervissey setting his bag and easel upon the granite entryway. "Wait, please, let me—"

Radborne ran back to the cart and retrieved his color box. When he returned, Learmont was counting out a few coins for the farmer. "Many thanks," he said.

"Nos da dheugh why." The farmer yanked at his cap and trudged back to his wagon.

"Nos da dheugh why," replied Dr. Learmont. He was dressed as

when Radborne first saw him, in bright-blue waistcoat and yellow shirt, though his tie was green, not purple. From his waistcoat pocket dangled a silver chain, attached to a pair of long, shining shears. "Good day to you, Kervissey."

Kervissey whistled at his horse; the wagon swung about and clattered off. Radborne watched its silhouette disappear into the shadows receding from the east. "What language was that he spoke?"

"Why, Cornish."

Radborne frowned, thinking of his mother, the few unintelligible verses he could recall her murmuring to him as a child when she sang him to sleep at night. "Are they like the Irish, then? They have their own language?"

"Cornish is more like Welsh. But the last person who spoke Cornish died over a hundred years ago—Dolly Pentreath, and a very old woman she was."

"But . . ." Radborne rubbed his forehead. "Forgive me, I am exhausted. The journey was much longer than I anticipated—"

"Please, by all means come in, come in!"

Learmont darted back through the door. Radborne followed with his color box and easel and finally his valise, thinking it strange that there were no servants around.

He set his bag down inside. The large, airy foyer showed signs of recent renovation, its curving oak stairway and gallery evoking the mode for all things medieval. He could glimpse a dining room at the end of the central corridor, and beyond that a door opening onto the kitchen, something that would have horrified Mrs. Beale—the English middle class had a positively morbid aversion to signs or smells of cooking. Radborne gazed at it all in a sort of stupefied pleasure.

"Are you always awake at this hour?" he asked.

"Why, I was waiting for you." Learmont smiled; his cheeks glowed as though he had been pinched. "And yes, I sometimes receive at odd times—the Great Western locomotives keep an erratic schedule in these parts, and I depend more than I would like upon Kervissey to meet my few visitors in Padwithiel."

Radborne looked back at the open front door. Outside, the dark sky was streaked with viridian, as though someone had scored a knife across the horizon to reveal another sky beneath. The wind had died, but beneath his feet the flagstones quivered like blanket bog.

"We passed another village, back there." Radborne pointed to the mainland. "Closer than Padwithiel."

"Ah, that's Trevenna," said Learmont. "No train there, I'm afraid. A backwater, really, though you might find it interesting. Painters visit sometimes—they think it romantic, because of the ruins. Swinburne has spent time there with Inchbold."

He dug into his pocket and produced a pair of blue conservative spectacles. He put them on, closed the door, then peered down the long corridor.

"Where *is* the girl?" he muttered. "Excuse me."

He stepped over to an Annunciator set into the wall, stabbed at a button. A bell clanged, and he shook his head. "Let's hope she's not gone down for more coal, or we'll be here all morning."

"Do you have no other staff, then?"

"Well, it is always difficult to find reliable attendants. Which is why I was so delighted to make your acquaintance. The fishermen here don't care to labor indoors, and the miners don't care for work in a dark, cold place so reminiscent of the mines."

He gave a barking laugh. "You'll find the folk here very superstitious, Mr. Comstock. The men won't let their women work for me. They never come up here, unless it's to seek better medical advice than they get from the fool who calls himself an apothecary down village. *That* they're willing enough to pay for. I daresay if you visit the public house, you'll hear enough winter's tales about me to fill one of your illustrated magazines."

Radborne smiled. "No, the pub didn't look very welcoming. I was lucky to find your man Kervissey there. Not that he was too happy to oblige me."

"No, he wouldn't be. Ah, here's Breaghan."

Radborne turned to see a figure hurrying toward them. A woman, fair-haired. She wore a faded but well-cut dress of black bombazine; her carriage was erect save for the odd sideways manner in which she held her head, twisted so that she seemed to stare fixedly at the floor. Frayed gloves covered her hands; where the wool had unraveled on one, he could glimpse a finger tinged leaden blue. As she drew beside him, Radborne caught a powerful whiff of chloride of lime and lye soap and an underlying smell of soft rot.

"I'll take your bags, sir." Her voice was an old woman's voice, its soft West Country burr nearly scorched away. Yet her profile showed a girl's features sharpened by toil, her eyes coldly blue as moonlit snow. Radborne watched her lift his valise with no apparent effort; she seemed as strong as Kervissey.

"Put him in the spare room above mine, Breaghan," said Dr. Learmont. "And lay the fire there, if you haven't already."

"Yes, sir."

As she turned, Radborne finally caught a clear glimpse of the rest of her face. He gasped in dismay: her lower jaw had been eaten away to the bone, leaving a ridge of yellowing teeth and ulcerated flesh beneath a frayed cotton bandage.

"I . . . I beg your pardon—" he said, but she was already lugging his valise upstairs. Learmont turned back to Radborne.

"Phosphorous necrosis—'phossy jaw,' they call it," he said. "In the city poor children make matches at home to sell. Breaghan said she produced four gross in a day since she was six years old. The poisonous vapor works its way through their teeth and into the bone. Like lime through flesh."

"God help her! Is there nothing that can be done?"

"Not a bit. Eventually the necrosis spreads to the brain. A terrible thing. I'm glad to be able to give her shelter. She found me in the village one day not long ago—God knows how she came here—and begged for work."

He gestured for Radborne to follow him upstairs. "She does what she can in the way of cooking and tending to the rooms here. I've had no luck finding a chambermaid, so Breaghan is a godsend."

They reached the second-floor landing. Dr. Learmont paused to lean against the balustrade. "She seems capable enough, but you can see why I was pleased to discover you."

Radborne glanced around but saw no sign of patients. The place was sparsely though fashionably furnished—Morris & Company rugs, a worn tapestry, a few rush-seated Sussex chairs—rustic things that suited a gentleman's West Country folly more than a madhouse. "You trust her, then?"

"I do," said Dr. Learmont, but he looked weary as he said it. "The hardest work I take upon myself at any rate. Come."

He started down a wide hallway with oil lamps on the walls, a floor grate from which a thread of warmth expired in a breath of coal smoke. They passed dayrooms, one with a billiards table; the apothecary; a white-painted door with the word REFRACTORY on it.

Then the corridor turned, and Radborne followed Learmont into another wing, older than the first and smelling of lye and lime and chloroform. If it were not for Dr. Learmont's eccentric dress, the glint of shears in his back pocket, Radborne would have imagined himself back at Garrison Asylum. The same clerestory windows, with small panes that would be cheap to replace when broken. The same furnishings, plain deal tables and mismatched chairs, metal buckets tucked into alcoves. Locked doors with small square windows covered by thick wire mesh. There would be patients behind the doors, though he heard no sound but Learmont's footsteps and his own.

"Here we are," said Learmont. "I think Breaghan's made it ready for you."

He opened a door into a small room with a high ceiling and scrubbed wooden floor. Sunlight streamed through the windows, painfully bright, and made the yellow-papered walls shine like brass. There was a wardrobe, a small oak table with washbasin, a chamber pot, a handbell for summoning Breaghan; on the floor a new, luridly colored Axminister rug still smelling strongly of aniline dye; a narrow iron bed with mattresses.

Radborne tried to hide his dismay. Save for the fact that the window was open and had no bars or grille, it was little different from the room a patient might occupy.

"Thank you," he said. He set down his color box and crossed to the window. The light at least was excellent. He leaned out, immediately took a quick step backward.

"Yes," said Dr. Learmont. He joined Radborne, placing his hands upon the sill. "It's rather a shock the first time you see it."

The window looked down upon a sheer cliff. Hundreds of feet below, blue-black water smashed against granite crags. Sunlit mist charged the air an iridescent silver-green.

"The other rooms have grates on them," explained Learmont. "This one did as well, but I thought it made it too dark. For your work."

He indicated Radborne's easel and color box. "Now then, Mr. Comstock. Shall I have Breaghan bring you up something to eat?"

"No thank you. I . . . I think I'd like to rest first. The trip was longer than I thought. Perhaps I could join you for lunch?"

"Of course, of course. A visitor journeying here from London for the first time doesn't realize what a different world it is—a different world. The last aboriginals of Britain lived here—like your red men, driven into the West."

He looked at Radborne. "It's what drew me to form the Folk-Lore Society. We are losing the old ways, Mr. Comstock. Little of that other world remains now. A very few of us would like to do what we can to preserve it.

"But now I must leave you, Mr. Comstock. I have only two patients at the moment, but they both demand my attentions. Please ring for Breaghan if you need anything."

After he left, Radborne closed the door and latched it. He removed his shoes, his overcoat and trousers, and fell into bed. It smelled of horsehair and urine. He turned to face the open window, felt the cold wind on his face. In minutes he was asleep.

He woke suddenly, sitting bolt upright with no idea where he was. The light in the room had deepened; outside, the sky was a hard vitreous blue. Not until he saw his clothes thrown over a chair did he remember. He had come to an asylum in West Cornwall to work.

He ran a hand across his face. He was unshaven, and hot despite the chill sea air. With a groan he stood, and heard a sound above the susurrus of waves and wind.

"*Where is he? Where is he?*" It was a woman's voice, nearly drowned by a man's wordless shout. "*No, Ned, I will not!*"

"*You must!*"

Then there was a third voice, high-pitched, familiar. "*Oh, don't, don't—*"

Before he knew what he was about, Radborne had his cheek pressed against his door, listening.

"*Where is Fancy?*" cried the woman. "*You have not hurt him?*"

"*—don't I say—*"

"*—you doing here?*"

That was the first man's voice, nearly frantic with despair. Quickly Radborne pulled on clothes and shoes and slipped into the hall.

He went only a few steps before finding a stairwell that ascended to where the voices came from. Radborne hurried up, then peered out into a corridor. Just yards away a tall man stood within an open doorframe, his back to Radborne and his arms outstretched as though he were pinioned.

"You *must* let me be alone with her! Now!"

His was the deep, despairing voice—but there was rage in it, too. With a cry he tried to push his way into the room but was stopped.

"You cannot do this, Ned! Learmont will come—you *must* leave her!"

Radborne shrank back. There was the impact of a body shoved against a wall, the muffled sound of a door being forced shut. The first man shouted in anguish; with a shrill whisper, the second man hushed him.

Silence. Radborne heard two pairs of footsteps hastening away from him, through the corridor, then down another flight of stairs. He listened, his heart pounding.

Would Learmont come?

Minutes passed. Radborne took a deep breath and stepped into the hall. He glanced around to make sure he was alone, walked briskly to the door, and opened it.

Immediately warmth engulfed him, a thick, musky odor like a fox's den. His foot nudged something; he looked down and saw a long-handled sable paintbrush that had been snapped in half.

"Who are you?" a voice demanded. "You are not of my people. Tell me!" He lifted his head and froze.

It was the woman on the bridge. She was enveloped within the same cloud of soft grays and blues, though now her clothes were not tatters but liquid folds of heavy Chinese silk, pigeon gray shot with mauve and indigo, the trailing sleeves edged with violet. A crimson scarf was wrapped about her neck, so that for an instant Radborne imagined that her throat had been cut.

"I . . . I beg your pardon. I thought . . . I heard an argument. My name is Radborne Comstock. I have just taken a position here, as . . . as . . ."

The woman stared at him. She was very tall, her legs hidden by the folds of her kimono, her long arms extending from the sleeves so that he could see her wrists, strangely thin and delicate, and her big hands, their ragged nails daubed with red. Her neck was long and columnar, her face heart-shaped, with a pointed chin and smooth white forehead, deep-set dark-green eyes and a wide, delicately curved mouth. She was not young—at least ten years older than Radborne, her mass of loose, flowing hair the color of oak, a deep reddish brown, and falling to her shoulders.

"Have you brought my dog?" The woman gazed at him imploringly, then made a fierce, impatient gesture. "No. I can see you haven't. You are another damned physician."

He could not speak. He had never heard a woman swear or seen a woman with hair unbound. He had painted nude models in van der Ven's studio, but never anyone like this, the room around her ablaze with sun, her hands raised, fingers folded into fists. As he stared, she recoiled slightly, lowering her head so that a spill of dark hair hid her face.

"No," he whispered.

She looked up and stepped toward him. He could smell her, salt and musk and vervain; if he dared extend his hand, he would feel heat radiating from her exposed skin, wrists, throat, cheek, brow. He knew she would not recoil again. Instead she would press her face against his palm; he knew that, he knew that.

"Who are you, then?" she murmured. She pressed her palm against his cheek. He shut his eyes; his lips parted as he forced himself to remain still, still: willing himself to deathly calm so that her touch would be burned upon his skin, her smell. "Radborne?"

He opened his eyes. Her face was inches from his own. He could see that her irises were not pure green but had tiny jagged spokes—peat brown, slate blue, black—radiating from the pupil. Her eyes were wide, not with surprise or fear but a sort of shocked wakefulness.

"Yes." He nodded, conscious of his breath against her cheek. "Radborne Comstock. I'm an artist. A painter. From America," he added in sudden desperation. "I didn't mean to intrude, Miss, Miss . . ."

"*He* calls me Mary. Or May."

"Mary." He hesitated. "Is that your name? Is that what Dr. Learmont calls you?"

"No. He calls me Evienne Upstone."

"Miss Upstone. I . . . I apologize for entering your room. I have just been hired, to—"

He stopped, trying to recall exactly what he had been hired for. Unexpectedly the woman laughed. He flushed, but then he saw that she was not mocking him but seemed delighted. Despite himself he smiled.

"Well, I'm not really certain yet," he said. "I think I'm to assist with a patient here. A painter."

"I am a painter."

"You are?" The woman gave him a look of such scorn he blushed. "Oh. But I thought . . . he said a man. A—"

He stopped again before pronouncing "murderer."

"Jacobus Candell. Yes, he is here," the woman said impatiently. "He is a criminal lunatic. Whereas I . . ."

She turned and with long strides crossed to the back wall. There were windows here, covered by heavy iron grillework, a narrow iron bedstead like his own, and a desk scattered with charcoal pencils, hair pencils, a drawing board. Beside the drawing board was part of a large bird's wing, its pinion feathers the color of porter. An easel held a canvas blotched with every imaginable shade of green: turf, viridis, hellebore, lichen, emeraude, holly. The woman glanced at it and shook her head. "*I* am merely a prisoner."

She stood with her back to him, her hair a dark serpent coiled upon gray silk. From outside came the surge of waves cresting and falling. Radborne stared at her, stricken.

"I'm sorry," he said.

She seemed not to hear, only continued to gaze upon the turmoil of green and gray and blue below. Finally she said, "Did you know there is a country there?"

Radborne ventured a smile. "No." He walked over to her and stared outside. Behind the iron lattice, the window was studded with tiny vortices where grit had been thrown against the glass.

"It is in ruins now." Her voice was almost a whisper. "Long ago a great queen ruled it with her consort. They were very happy, and the queen loved him, but as the ages of the world passed, she grew restless. Someone once had shown her a painting of a place she had never seen. She would see it, and she left in search of it.

"Years upon years she wandered, and saw many things—wonderful things! Places she had not imagined. She saw an owl, and a boy with a net who would catch it, who did capture it, and the owl died. She saw a man in green upon a black horse; she saw many men.

"And though she did not know it, her husband had come in search of her," she went on, her voice rising. "And like her he lost his way, though never so lost as she. Always she was searching for him, and never was he finding her.

"At last she could walk no more: she had come to the end of the world. At the edge of the world, she jumped, and as she fell, flames consumed her. The king called upon the sea to quench the fire, but not even the sea could do so. Only there, see?"

She touched Radborne's arm. "Beneath the water she is burning still. Do you see her?"

He could feel her fingers through his sleeve like hot tongs. "I've never heard that story," he said in a low voice. "It must be very old."

"It is not so old." The woman turned, her eyes too wide and her cheeks white. "I am that queen."

"I don't—"

Behind them came the muted *snick* of a door latch. Radborne turned to see Dr. Learmont. He looked grave; from his hand dangled a large key ring. "Mr. Comstock, would you be so kind as to meet me in my office? Miss Upstone has had enough visitors for one morning, I think."

"Yes, of course. I'm sorry, but I heard—"

Dr. Learmont gave him a look that commanded him to leave. The woman snatched her hand from Radborne and whirled to face Learmont.

"Why will you not give him me? Coward! Coward! You are afraid of me! You are all afraid—"

Dr. Learmont pushed past Radborne. "Leave us, Mr. Comstock! I'll call if I need you."

"Yes—yes, of course."

He turned and stumbled into the hall. The door slammed shut behind him. The woman shouted, words he could not understand. He could hear Dr. Learmont, then Evienne Upstone laughing bitterly.

"Miss Upstone, please—"

"I will not drink it! I refuse—"

"—must take it, Miss Upstone, your welfare depends upon it—"

"—please, no. . . . Where is Fancy?"

Then the sound of scuffling, then silence, then soft weeping.

Radborne leaned against the wall. He touched his cheek and withdrew his hand to see a fingertip streaked bright red.

Blood, he thought, sickened. The madwoman had scratched him.

But when he brought his hand to his face, he smelled linseed oil.

I am a painter.

He looked up. From Evienne Upstone's room, there came no sound. The corridor was flooded with October sunlight, yet he could feel darkness all around, and cold. He recalled the voices of the men he had heard before.

Learmont will come, you must *leave her—*

"Swinburne," he said. He turned and raced downstairs.

He found him at the back of the house, in a long gallery furnished with a few leather armchairs and high windows that faced southwest. In the far corner, a spare red-haired figure stood and stared at the ruined tower on the next headland. Radborne watched him from the doorway, silent. After a minute Swinburne spoke without turning.

"Did you know this is a cursed place?" He was wearing a heavy, dark-green mantle, its hem laced with dried mud and leaf mold. "No innocent babby was ever born here: just bastards and morphodites." He turned suddenly. "Which are you, Mr. Comstock?"

Radborne walked toward him, hands clenched. "Who is the woman? Why is she here?"

"Why is she here? Why is she here?" Swinburne trilled. "Why, because she is a lunatic, sir! Why are *you* here?"

Without warning he feinted at Radborne, then darted to an armchair, sinking into it as though exhausted and clutching his mantle about his shoulders. Radborne stared at him and walked to the window. He gazed out, for the first time noticed a small cottage a few hundred yards from the manor house. Behind him he could hear Swinburne's breathing, high and shallow.

"What business do you have here?" Radborne said at last.

"Why, your welfare," Swinburne said, and tittered.

"Who was the other man with you?"

"Burne-Jones. My friend, once. I have not seen him for many years. I did not expect to see him now. He arrived on the same train as yourself, but in the invalid coach, and had more difficulty finding his way."

"Is she—" Radborne hesitated. "Is she his wife?"

"His wife?" Swinburne's pale eyes widened in astonishment. "Why, no. His wife is Georgie."

"Who was it she called for, then? Another man? Her husband?"

Swinburne looked puzzled, then gave a shrieking whoop. "Fancy! He means Fancy !"

It was a moment before he regained control of himself.

"That is her dog," he said.

He hunched his shoulders, his faded ginger hair caught inside his cloak, and drew his feet up onto the edge of chair. He looked so frail that Radborne felt a pang, to be harrying him like this. But when the little man spoke, his voice was harsh and taunting. "She is Burne-Jones's mistress. His 'muse,' he would say, his 'stunner'—"

He fairly spat the last word. "But she would be a painter, too, you see. She would be an *artist*. Learmont encourages her—he thinks that will bind her to him, but it will never do, never!"

He giggled wildly. Radborne nodded tentatively. "Yes she told me. And I saw that she had an easel, there"—he gestured at the ceiling—"in her room. I was asleep in my own room, but when I woke, I heard voices. I was concerned there might be danger. In America I worked in an asylum. The patients had a little journal that I assisted them with—that is why Dr. Learmont hired me—and my understanding was that I was to serve a similar function at Sarsinmoor. He told me there was a painter here. He wrote to me, offering me a position."

He withdrew Learmont's letter from his breast pocket and held it out to Swinburne, who ignored it. Instead he narrowed his eyes and leaned forward in his chair.

"Are you well, Mr. Comstock?" He tugged his cloak about his shoulders and shivered. "You do not look at all well. It is the chill—the spirit of this damned place. It devours you. You've seen that hag he keeps as a housemaid."

Radborne continued to hold the letter out to him, finally shoved it back into his pocket. "I am very well," he said coldly. "But I would like to know why you have come here, sir. Are you to be a patient?"

Swinburne gave a high-pitched laugh. "Not I!"

"Burne-Jones, then?"

The red-haired man shrank even deeper into his cloak. "Don't be absurd. He came to see *her*. He will not break with her—he refuses to, though his soul is imperiled! Yet they dare not call *him* mad."

"And the woman?"

"She suffers from a moral languor: the air of this world does not agree with her. She was at The Lawn for some months—do you know it? A private ladies' asylum, I recommend a visit—most entertaining."

Swinburne sat up, eyes shining. His hands crept over the edge of his mantle like two white mice. "Learmont found her there and introduced her to Ned. Since then she is his *Mysteriarch;* he says that he cannot work without her, but the thought of her devours him. Everything within this house eats away at something else."

He glanced out the window at the silhouette of the fortress upon the next headland. "*Sublata causu, tollitur effectus.* One must remove the cause for the effect to cease. So Learmont brought her here. He claims that it is for her own well-being: that here she is safe and perhaps may recover from her extremity. I do not think that is his intention for her."

"What is the nature of her illness?"

"Learmont believes that she is inflamed by a sexual nisus."

Radborne looked disgusted. "I would suggest that she is deeply unhappy. She is very beautiful," he added.

" 'The sort of beauty that's called human in hell,' " chanted Swinburne. His beryl eyes glittered. "Such beauty serves as a portal to the Abyss. I would not have her for a thousand pounds."

He paused, seeming to weigh his next question. "Mr. Comstock. Have you not wondered about your employer? He has a highly specialized practice and attends only a very few people. He has been doing so for many years now, in London and Bath. Very discreet, I have had the opportunity to observe him firsthand: we shared a circle in Fitzroy Square—Brown, do you know him? And Monsieur Andrieu, who had such an interesting friend . . . a sort of wild peasant boy, perfectly filthy. Verlaine has just published his poetry in *Lutèce.*"

He sighed and drew a hand across his brow. "No matter. Learmont claims to have inherited this heap, although I don't believe he ever set foot in it until he came here with Candell. I first heard of Learmont from Gabriel, whom he treated for lypemania, a nervous condition."

He broke into another uncontrollable spasm of laughter, rocking back and forth in the armchair. " 'Every physician almost hath his favorite disease!' " Our Dr. Learmont has carefully chosen which maladies he will cure and which he will sustain. He selects those whose honey is distilled from despair and longing, and gorges himself upon it. Oh, he is a greedy creature! Confess, sir—didn't you think it curious to find yourself in the employ of an alienist who specializes in the treatment of melancholy painters?"

Radborne was silent. "It is coincidence," he said at last. "Of course it is coincidence. I told him that I had experience working with the mad—"

"Oooh, *experience!*" squealed Swinburne. He leaped from his chair and paced across the room, stopping in front of the bookshelves. "Our Mr. Comefuck has *experience!*"

His eyes narrowed. "You say you know the tenets of alienism. Are you familiar with the work of Cesare Lombroso?"

"I am not."

"A scientist of the degeneracy of the criminal intellect. His book has not been translated into English, but I have read it in Italian—*Genio e Follia.* Genius and Madness. He is a very great friend of Learmont. They fancy themselves gatekeepers to the mind, and Learmont believes he alone guards the entrance to a portal that only a chosen few may enter."

"You mean Beauty."

Swinburne nodded. "I mean Beauty; I mean Art—these things threaten us, Mr. Cobfinch. Beyond them is a door, and beyond the door is"—he leaned forward in his chair and snapped his fingers—"*what?* Do you know, Mr. Comstock? Have you seen what is there?"

"No."

"*I have.*" Swinburne's voice shook. He stared up at Radborne, his face taut with desperation and longing. "I have seen! Better that I should have died, or disappeared into the desert like Andrieu's boy—

better I had snapped like a thread. And do not doubt that Learmont has seen, too—the gatekeeper whose foot has got stuck in the door! That is how she comes to be here. Tell me, Mr. Confit—do you enjoy watching a cat torment a mouse?"

"No."

"What would you think of a man who gave live mice to his pet, expressly so he could watch her dismember them?"

"I would think he was exceedingly cruel. Or mad."

"Learmont is both. He is like no man I have ever known." Swinburne licked his lips; his gaze darted about the room. "She is his obsession. I do not understand what she is, but I swear to you, Mr. Comstock—you would as well keep a wild jaguar as a house cat! And so he keeps her subdued with his little blue pills and his paregorics. Because he has worked with private patients in their homes, he has avoided the scrutiny of the Commissioners for Lunacy."

"But he can't simply intend to keep her imprisoned here?" Radborne looked appalled. "I will not believe it!"

"It is true."

"But why?"

"Her hungers have become his own. He is obsessed with artists, and their tributes: paintings, poems, songs. But he is not content with Beauty's pearls; he must see how the poor oyster excretes them! He must see the spark of sand that coaxes nacre from the ugly gray shell! More than that: he would see if the pearl itself can create another pearl!

"Think of this, sir: Cygnus deprived of its mate will make the most beautiful sound and then expire. Learmont traps a nixie for Ned to paint, and paint he does—paints and paints and paints, until he is overcome by brain fever and his wife nurses him back to us. I have told you that Miss Upstone possesses a powerful nisus. I believe that Learmont is the biter bit: the master enslaved by his charge. Once she gains power over him, she will free herself. And then . . ."

Swinburne fell silent. Beneath his right eye, a muscle twitched.

Radborne thought he might weep, but the poet only pressed a hand to his forehead. "She will find her way back."

Radborne hesitated. He was fearful of encouraging Swinburne's delusion. It was obvious that the poet's own mind had been turned, by exhaustion or drink, or its denial. "Would that not be a better thing? For her to be among her own people again—her family, her . . ."

He could not bring himself to say "husband." Swinburne raised his head to look at him. His gaze was soft, and for the first time almost kindly. "A better thing? For her, perhaps . . . yes, very well, no doubt it would be. But for us?"

The poet sighed. "I contradict myself, but all art is contradiction. To lose even a small part of the ragged, raging beauty of the world—is that a good thing, Mr. Comstock? Tell me! Because I fear it is not, and yet I know that the toll Beauty exacts of her worshippers is a terrible one. We strive to capture her, imprison her in our poems and our scrawls, but it is we who are maddened. I do not subscribe to Learmont's science: I do not believe that one must be a madman to be a great poet. My own work is the greater now for my own temperance! And yet, and yet . . ."

His voice dropped to a whisper; he stared at the great expanse of windows, the churning sea and cloud-filled sky beyond, but it seemed as though a caul were drawn across his eyes. "I would not see her destroyed."

"Who would destroy her?" asked Radborne. "Learmont?"

"No. Never. But she is not tame. She will never be tame. She dies, as all beauty does, from age or despair or neglect, and she gives birth to herself. And think of this, Mr. Comstock"—he grabbed Radborne's wrist—"what if she should give birth to another? Cygnus stabs her own breast with her beak, lamenting her mate, seeking to feed her young with her own: what if her young thrive? what if her mate hears and comes to claim her?

"Powerful as she is," he said, and his eyes suddenly shone like candles, "what if there should be *two* of them? What if a crack in the world became a chasm? *What if they break through?*"

Radborne gave a small gasp, of laughter and disbelief. "'Break through?' I think it's a damned good thing that Learmont is in charge here—that's what *I* think!"

"You are a child!" shrieked Swinburne, and dropped his hand. "He has brought you here as her plaything!"

"My arrangement with Dr. Learmont is a private one," said Radborne coldly. "I have come here to work, and paint." Without thinking, he glanced upward.

Swinburne made a strangled piping sound and pointed at the ceiling. "You think you have found your muse, eh, boy? Oh, foolish foolish foolish!" he squealed. "'But death is strong and full of blood and fair!' Wait until you see your stunner in a coffin with her hair wrapped around your hand and you must cut it loose! Wait until your bowels are unstrung by grief and you find yourself daubing in shit and blood! Oh, what great work you won't paint *then!*"

Radborne stared, torn between fury and pity as the little man rocked back and forth. Swinburne clasped his head with both hands, blinking furiously. After a moment this seemed to calm him; he loosened his mantle and let it fall from his shoulders, got to his feet and crossed to the wall of bookshelves. "Are you a member of Learmont's Fuck-Lore Society, Mr. Comitas?"

"No."

Swinburne tossed his long hair, pinching his chin between thumb and forefinger. He removed a volume from the shelf, turned to brandish it in Radborne's face. "See! See! This is *my* book, the barefaced thief! She is *always* stealing things."

Radborne expected it to be one of Swinburne's own works. Instead it was a small volume bound in green cloth and stamped with red letters: *Tales and Ancient Drolleries from the Farthest West.*

"They are stories collected by Learmont," said Swinburne. "Inchbold gave it to me as a present, when I first visited him at Tintagel. I found them most interesting. Tennyson confided to me that he did as well."

"I thought Tennyson was dead," snapped Radborne.

"Sarcasm is the devil's weapon." Swinburne flipped through the pages, his eyes bright. "I had forgotten these," he said to himself.

He glanced up at Radborne. "Perhaps you should have this after all." He shut the book and handed it to Radborne.

"Thank you." Radborne opened it to the frontispiece.

Algernon Swinburne, read the signature at the top right corner.

A Collection of Legends, Superstitions, and Lore
Relating to the Cornish People
Collected and Edited by Thomas M. Learmont, F.R.A.
Published by the Greater Outer London Folk-Lore Study Society, 1879

"Thank you." He flashed Swinburne a tight smile and closed the book. "I have a commission to do illustrations back in New York. This might be helpful for me."

Swinburne gave a languid wave. "Do what you will."

Suddenly he raised a finger to his lips. From upstairs Radborne could hear Dr. Learmont's voice and the sound of footsteps. Swinburne looked at him, his pale face flushed. "I cannot stay any longer. My host will be anxious if I am not back before dark."

He hesitated. "You are free to speak of this with Learmont or not: he has no hold over me. He never has."

"You're walking?"

"Of course." Swinburne pulled his mantle back around his shoulders and looked rather prim. "But I would not recommend that you do so—you would lose yourself on the moor. There are bogs that are *filled* with bones, Mr. Comstock."

He made Radborne a curt bow. "It would surprise me if we met again."

"Well." Radborne held up the volume of *Drolleries*. "Many thanks, then, for your book. And I meant to say, before—in the restaurant, I mean—that your poetry was always, I always—"

He felt his ears burn, and shrugged in embarrassment. Swinburne only smiled.

" 'Wert she not born fire, and shalt she not devour?' " he said softly. He reached out a small, thin hand and patted Radborne on the shoulder. "Godspeed you, Mr. Comstock."

In a swirl of green and ginger gray he was gone.

CHAPTER SEVEN

The Higher Pantheism in a Nutshell

The room that Daniel entered with Balthazar Warnick was a wide, welcoming space. Oak bookshelves covered the walls; there were leather armchairs and ottomans, library tables piled with masses of stuff—books, old magazines, curling scrolls of watercolor paper—a rickety library ladder, and a marble fireplace where a small fire burned with a steady, low blue flame.

"Nice place," said Daniel. He looked around admiringly. There seemed to be no wall space unoccupied by books, but they were obscured by paintings, hanging from the shelves or leaning against them. There were even paintings suspended in front of the heavily curtained windows.

"Sorry about the mess, gentlemen."

A man turned from where he stood in front of an oak sideboard, a man wearing a beautifully cut suit with the blue sheen of snow at dusk, his skull defined by a buzz-cut V of silvery hair. His tall frame was nearly skeletal, his face lined yet youthful, with eyes so pale a gray they were almost white, the pupils like holes left by buckshot.

"I don't let the cleaning staff in here anymore—once they threw away a Beth Love I'd just bought. Russell Learmont," he said, and extended a hand to Daniel.

"Daniel Rowlands."

Learmont turned back to the sideboard, where decanters winked ruby and amber in the soft light. "What can I get you, Daniel?"

"Scotch, please. Neat."

"Balthazar?"

Warnick turned his melancholy smile on Learmont and settled into a chair. "The same, Russell. Thank you."

Daniel wandered over to examine a large, unwieldy picture suspended in front of a shelf of books. It depicted a man, tall and black-haired, standing upon the edge of a precipice with a backdrop of flaming sky, a sword in one hand and his helm dangling from the other as he stared into the empty air. A typical Pre-Raphaelite pose and subject, painted on wood, not canvas, yet there was something about the knight's expression that made Daniel feel queasy. The figure looked at once devouring and ravaged, his face a slurry of greenish white and red, more Albert Pinkham Ryder than Edward Burne-Jones. The painting's perspective, too, was skewed. Daniel studied it for a minute before realizing that there were no shadows anywhere.

He frowned. What exactly was the knight looking at, or for? He tried to make out the words on a small brass tag pleached with rust.

HOW THEY WALKED IN

The tag was not set in the middle of the frame, but at the lower right-hand corner, where a jagged metal hinge protruded from it. The hinge was broken. The title was incomplete.

Daniel scrutinized the label, again looked at the painting.

How they walked in—

In what? Who were "they"?

Something poked at his memory, and he felt a sudden sharp thrill of recall.

How they were enchanted. How they were discovered.

He took a step back, trying to take in the entire large canvas.

It was not the work of Burne-Jones. Daniel was certain of that. As he stared, his excitement grew.

Because while this was by another artist, surely the model was the same man who had posed for Tristran in the sketches Larkin had showed him? The same hawkish face, the same deep-set eyes and thin, beautifully curved mouth; the same longing, expressed as devastation rather than desire.

He turned eagerly to the paintings surrounding it, but they were not by the same artist. Most were pencil sketches of a bearded man in a white jacket, a caricature of a Victorian doctor, surrounded by whorls of minuscule handwriting. There were drawings of a bare-breasted woman with wings and a winged animal with the words INORDINATE DRAGON beneath it.

"Andrew Kennedy." Learmont stepped beside him and handed Daniel a glass. "He spent much of the nineteenth century in the Glasgow Royal Asylum."

"Really?" Daniel sipped his scotch. "What was wrong with him?"

" 'Delusional insanity of exaltation.' "

"Meaning?"

"Meaning he believed himself to be some sort of deity, or demiurge, or numinous figure. Not all the time, of course."

"Ah. A part-time demiurge. You don't get benefits."

Learmont smiled. "Nowadays he'd be diagnosed as schizophrenic, or having some kind of bipolar affective disorder."

"Right." Daniel gave Learmont a wry look: this was the guy whose pharmaceutical empire had developed a highly specific antidepressant that, according to a recent article in *Forbes,* now outsold all the older SSRIs combined. "Nowadays you'd put him on Exultan, and he'd have a successful career as a telemarketer."

"Very likely," said Learmont.

Daniel turned to survey the paintings and drawings that surrounded them. "Nowadays you might have trouble filling this room with pictures."

"Oh, you'd be surprised." Learmont glanced to where Balthazar Warnick sat, perusing a stack of books on a low table. "I have a friend who installed an observatory in his office penthouse. Another fellow built a tidal pool."

He began to pace slowly along the wall. "This is my observatory. In here I have a hundred telescopes."

He stopped in front of a small painting crammed with figures vivid as fruit in a glass bowl: citron, emerald, crimson, violet. "And do you know what you see when you look inside one of them?

"A world. Inside every single one of them: a world within the world. Each with its own religion, its own countryside, its own architecture and language, animals and plants and currency and people—kings and queens and gods and devils—"

"And ourselves, mortal men," said Balthazar Warnick from his seat. "Don't get him started, Daniel. I've warned him, he'll need to develop a drug to stop his compulsion for collecting these things."

"I'm not collecting them." Learmont finished his drink, set the glass on a table, and crossed his arms, still gazing at his painting. "I'm conserving them. Protecting them."

"So you say," Balthazar replied. "I wonder if they think the same." He turned back to his books.

Daniel raised an eyebrow. "Do your paintings have opinions on the matter?"

"Of course not." Learmont laughed but gave Warnick a sharp look. "And the artists I deal with these days . . . well, their agents make more than I do."

"But you've been collecting these for a while." Daniel stepped past him to regard a long, cartoonish-looking scroll of brown paper, all balloon-shaped people and dogs and—

"Jesus." He drew back quickly. "That's . . . Jesus . . ."

"He's been institutionalized for some time now," said Learmont. "Most of the charges were dropped, and at any rate there was no way he could stand trial."

"This guy has an *agent?* What, do you troll Bedlam for these people?"

Learmont shrugged. "It's like anything. You go where the talent is."

He turned so that his gaunt profile was cast in shadow, save for the gleam of one silvery eye. After a moment he turned and crossed to join Warnick. "Excuse me," he said to Daniel, and gestured at the sideboard. "Please—help yourself. I've some business to attend to. I'm leaving the country in a few days. A sailing trip, perhaps a month down to the Virgin Islands and then up the coast of America to Maine. I have some business there."

"So I heard."

But Learmont seemed to have already forgotten him. He pulled a chair beside Balthazar Warnick and sat, pointing to a stack of notebooks on the table before them. "I see you found them," he said. "What do you think?"

"I think they're extremely interesting." Balthazar Warnick weighed one of the volumes in his hand, his lips pursed. "But I do wonder. I assume you had them authenticated?"

Daniel went to the sideboard and poured himself another drink, then glanced uneasily at the door. He should leave and find Larkin, get her out of here before Learmont caught up with her.

Though why should she be afraid of Learmont? His gaze fell once more upon the painting of the tormented knight, and he walked over to it, glancing at the others where they sat. They spoke quietly but with no effort at secrecy as Daniel angled himself in front of the painting, listening.

"I brought them to Cottingham," Learmont said. "As you suggested. He's at the new wing now; he took some samples and said the inks are all period. And the books check out. Mid-1880s, standard stock from Frozetting's."

He held up one of the sketchbooks, identical to the others on the low table, all the same slate color, with faded gray labels. Learmont flipped through it, and Daniel could see that the pages were filled with writing and drawings in black ink, with here and there a smudge of color—green, mostly, though there were jots of blackish red.

"Well, I can't argue with that." Warnick picked up another sketchbook and stared at it. "But there's something about them. . . . They just don't *feel* quite right to me."

Learmont frowned. "You don't think they're authentic."

"No. The opposite, actually—they seem *too* real." Warnick glanced at Daniel, who swiftly turned his attention to the canvas in front of him. "Where did you say you got them?"

"County girl, addicted to heroin. She was being treated here in London. I saw them in her room. She said her boyfriend gave them to her."

"Doubtful," said Warnick.

Learmont nodded. "I think she nicked them. Her place was full of things. She tried to sell me some Moche pottery. I told her I'd turn her in to Interpol for fencing cultural treasures. That put her in mind to do business more quietly."

"How much did you pay for these?"

"Two thousand pounds. She wanted ten."

"Do you think she'd talk to me? I'd like to know where they really came from."

Learmont shook his head. "She's gone—off to Tangier or someplace like that. Drug problems."

"Ah. That's too bad." Warnick once again bent over the stack of books. Daniel sidled to the wall and began scanning titles, listening all the while. "Well, I don't know what to say. But I have to ask you, Russell—why are you doing this? After a while this sort of obsession becomes a liability, Russell. It creates an egress."

Warnick set the notebook back down. Russell Learmont picked it up, cradling it protectively for a moment, then replaced it with the others on the table. "The other painting is supposed to arrive tomorrow," he said. He glanced to where Daniel was standing. "I've made special arrangements to have it cleared quickly."

"You'll keep them both here?"

Learmont laughed wryly. "For a bit. Carrying coals to Newcastle, I know: I should just bring this one with me. But I want to see them both together. To see . . ."

He seemed to notice Daniel for the first time and fell silent. Balthazar Warnick looked up as well. His sea-blue eyes held Daniel's for a long moment; then he glanced at the door, put a hand on Learmont's shoulder, and stood.

"Russell, I'm afraid I have to be going." Warnick patted his trouser pockets and frowned slightly. "Oh—my keys. I remember. I gave them to your valet. . . ."

Learmont got to his feet. "You stay here, Balthazar. I need to make a quick call anyway." He looked at Daniel and smiled. "Nice to meet you. Excuse me."

He left the room, leaving the door open behind him. Balthazar Warnick waited until he was gone, then crossed to join Daniel. He said nothing but scanned the books on their shelves, now and then moving aside a painting to get a better look. After a minute he pulled a volume out, then handed it to Daniel.

"This might interest you," he said, and walked away.

Daniel stared at it, a battered volume bound in green cloth. *Tales and Ancient Drolleries from the Farthest West.* Folk tales, he saw when he began flipping through it; there were a few illustrations. At the back, tucked between the marbled endpapers, he found a handwritten note on pale-blue paper.

*Ned's first book which he has disavowed completely. This came to me
from GK at Farringdon, who claims all other copies destroyed. She has
fled again*

    *If she is reunited with ~~erothe hreror borther Iwe~~
fear it is as Lizzie warned me, we are indeed their shades*

       *His life is a watch or a vision
          Between a sleep and a sleep.*

If he returns tremble for us all

Daniel tried to make out the scrawled words: brother? other? He
turned to the frontispiece, where a signature was written in small, neat
cursive.

Algernon Swinburne.

He skimmed a few pages. The verses seemed insipid, the few illustrations crude imitations of Rossetti. He was replacing it on the shelf
when someone slipped behind him and grasped his arm.

"Daniel! I looked all over for you—"

It was Larkin. She'd pulled her hair back into its neat chignon, but
her color was still high, her green-glass eyes too bright. "Things are
winding down. We should think about going." She rubbed her arms.
"Can I borrow your jacket? The air-conditioning was turned up in the
bathroom, I got quite chilled."

"*Your* jacket," Daniel corrected her, and pulled it off. "Here."

He put it over her shoulders, and she smiled, reached to run a finger
down his cheek. "I'm just going to sit by that fire for a minute and get
warm."

"No." He shook his head. "We should go. Let's go. Now."

She looked at him, then shrugged. "All right."

She started slowly for the door, where Balthazar Warnick stood,
watching her impassively. Her hands touched everything she passed—

leather armchairs, bookshelves, a paisley scarf covering a library table—
as though making an accounting of objects in her own room. In her
night-blue dress and velvet jacket, she looked like a stoned refugee from
one of the hippie caravans that toured the English countryside each
summer. Daniel fought the urge to help her, recalling some dim cartoon
voice from his childhood—never touch a sleepwalker, never speak,
never wake her. . . .

She was beside him again. Her fingertips trailed across his cheek;
for an instant she rested her head upon his shoulder.

"Let's go," he murmured.

Daniel took her arm. In the doorway Balthazar Warnick stood and
watched them pass. "Daniel—it was a pleasure meeting you. We should
have lunch sometime, when you get back to D.C."

Warnick's gaze lit upon Larkin. He looked at her, then said, "You
let this gentleman drive, will you?"

She nodded. Balthazar watched them depart, then went inside
Learmont's study, closing the door behind him.

They left the house quickly, passing a few groups of partygoers lingering in the road outside, who gazed at Larkin with bemused curiosity.

"G'night, Duchess!" someone shouted. Larkin seemed not to
hear. Daniel himself was afraid to say anything at all, lest the spell be
broken and Larkin turn and see him as he really was: a gangling,
middle-aged man so obviously out of his depth he was surprised no
one shouted at *him.*

Still, he'd been in this kind of situation before, most memorably a
night with the notorious lead singer of an alt country band, a woman
who had her ex-husband's name branded on her ass. He knew the
kinds of looks he *should* have been getting—that combination of envy,
anger, lust, and sheer disbelief that spelled out *Her? Him?*

And yet no one seemed to notice him. As they approached the

Mini, Daniel turned to stare back at a young man wearing a kilt and a John Travolta T-shirt. He met the boy's eyes, but instead of looking away, the boy squinted, as though trying to see through a smudged glass. His gaze was unbroken. He didn't see Daniel at all.

Larkin touched his hand. "Can you drive?"

"Huh? Oh, yeah, I'm fine."

Larkin handed him the keys, and they got in.

"Go back by Camden Town," she said. "Up past Nick's flat, there's parking there above the Crescent."

He nodded and drove off. He felt neither tired nor hung over; rather, as though he were driving in a dream. Beyond the Mini's wedge of windscreen, the city remained wrapped in April twilight, a tremulous haze of gold and violet clinging to sidewalks, monuments, council flats. Young men and women crowded at every street corner, arms wrapped around each other, their faces wan as rainwater. Daniel rolled the window down, but still the world seemed hushed, save for the odd bit of song or words snatched from the street—*evaginate, survey, willing, dance.* Beside him Larkin sat with the antique red jacket pulled close, the wilted sunflower cupped beneath her chin. Her eyes were only half open. He glanced at her, wanting to part the jacket and take the sunflower in his hands, let its brown-edged petals trace the curve of her breasts and—

"Turn here," she said, and pointed.

For an instant the world went black as they passed beneath a railway bridge.

"And here."

Daniel forced himself to concentrate on negotiating a roundabout. After a minute he asked, "What was the name of Rossetti's wife?"

"Siddal. Elizabeth Siddal."

"Right. Lizzie Siddal. Do you know if she knew Swinburne?"

"Swinburne? Yes, she did—they were extremely close. Why?"

"Well, we were at Cheyne Walk. Just curious, that's all. Were they ever involved—Swinburne and Lizzie?"

"Not that I ever heard. He was a bit of a soft candle with girls, I think. Except for *le vice anglais,* of course." She laughed. "Are you going to research that for your book?"

"You never know." They were in the Crescent directly above Camden Town. He angled the car into a narrow cul-de-sac, looking for a parking space. "She killed herself, didn't she?"

"Yes. Laudanum. 'Death by misadventure.' That's what they called it then, if you were a woman."

"They had a lot of misadventures, didn't they? All those painters."

"There!" Larkin touched his arm, pointing to a space. "Don't all painters have problems? And writers—don't poets have the highest suicide rates in the world?"

"Maybe. Journalists get the highest interest rates, I know that."

They got out. It was very warm now, going on ten o'clock, moist air rising from the nearby canal and crowded High Street below them, the streetlights casting a sepia glow over the tree-lined street.

Larkin stood on the curb and looked down to where the last barrows were being removed from Inverness Street, leaving trails of crushed figs and spoiled blossoms. "Would you mind if we stopped at Nick's first? It's closer than my place, and I have to pee."

"No problem. Where is your place?"

"You'll see."

"Big secret, huh?"

"Shh."

She took his arm, lifting her face to his. The lamplight turned her dark hair to copper-gold. Daniel dipped his head, his mouth grazing her brow. Her skin tasted of salt, and apples; when she touched his chest, he fell back, dizzied.

"Right," he said, and, drawing her to him, began to hurry toward Nick's flat.

Once inside, he was relieved to see there were no messages on the answering machine or ominous bits of paper with Nick's arcane directives concerning unexpected visitors and trash removal. Larkin draped her jacket over a chair; it immediately fell to the floor with a soft thump. She beelined to the fridge and grabbed a bottle of fizzy water, drank half in one long pull and handed the rest to Daniel.

"I'll be right back," she said, and headed down the hall.

"Sure thing." He watched her go, holding the bottle to his forehead. "Shit." He was too old for this by about twenty years, at his most generous reckoning.

Still: " 'Faint heart never won fair lady,' " he said, and began to sing off-key.

"In for a penny, in for a pound—
It's Love that makes the world go round!"

He ran a hand across his unshaven chin and grimaced, finished the water, tossed the plastic bottle into the sink, and turned to the kitchen table. Beneath it lay Larkin's jacket, a pool of crimson and black. He stooped to pick it up, was just turning to drape it back over the chair when he noticed something.

The jacket was heavier than it had been. He held it out and saw a bulge weighing down one side, where the wide pocket hung open. He slipped his hand inside and touched a flat squarish object, thick and with the texture of linen. He pulled it out and let the jacket fall to his feet.

"Oh, no."

It was a sketchbook. Bound in blue-gray boards with a rectangular white label in the center, its edges starting to peel back. Entwined initials were embossed upon the label in gold, with a strong, confident handwriting beneath.

jc
vernoraxia
volume vii
"closer"

"Shit, shit, *shit.*" Daniel looked quickly down the hall where Larkin had gone, then ducked into the guest bedroom.

"I'm just getting changed!" he yelled. He shut the door behind him and leaned against it. "Oh, man . . ."

He recalled the painting in a closet at Paynim House—*A gift of the artist*—and opened the notebook.

The heavy paper stock had grown yellow with age. There was no name on the inside boards. He turned to the first page, a pen-and-ink drawing so microscopically detailed it was a moment before he recognized what it was—a woman's cunt, the black hairs writhing into thorns and tendrils of ivy; tree trunks and tall, straight-stemmed flowers like no plants he had ever seen; tiny, fluttering wrenlike birds and owls, thickets of owls and owl eyes, eyes, eyes everywhere. They were the only things in color: eyes indigo as magpies, green as birch leaves, yellow as primroses. All were focused on what was between the fimbriated tracery at the center of the whorl of flesh and flowers. He drew the book to his face, angling beneath the lamp to get a better look.

But while he could discern faint lines—the suggestion of a horizon, an eyed sun that was an adumbration of the clitoris above it—the images were impossible to keep in focus.

He turned to the next page. It was filled with neat block letters, as though someone were trying to reproduce the precise look of a printed page.

Within her is the world and

"Daniel? You in there?"

He jumped as Larkin rapped softly at the door.

"Right out!" He clapped the book shut, then swiftly and without a sound moved to the cannonball bed where he slept, pulled back the duvet, and slipped the sketchbook under his pillow. He replaced the duvet, grabbed the books on his nightstand—*Passion and Society, London A–Z*, his own notebook—and tossed them onto the bed.

"Sorry!" He swiped his hair back and bounded to open the door. "Just wanted to, to—"

"I thought you were getting changed?"

He looked down at his cambric shirt, damp with sweat. "Right. I'll just—"

"That's okay." She parted his shirt, her fingertips grazing his chest, then leaned forward until he could feel her breath cool against his skin. He groaned softly as her mouth opened and she pressed it against him. Her tongue touched the smooth ridge of his collarbone; he could feel the slightest pressure of her teeth upon his throat. He grasped her waist and pulled her tight against him, but as he did, she withdrew, and his fingers slid across the folds of her dress as though he dipped his hand into a stream.

"Larkin," he whispered, then blinked. The room had grown darker, or no, something had happened to the light. He could still see, could even make out the glimmering halo at the base of his desk lamp, but it had darkened from bright white to a tenebrous brown smear. He turned and saw something moving in the shadows, a firefly shimmer of yellow and green, began to step toward it when abruptly the lamp flared, dazzlingly, and he raised his hands to his eyes. "Larkin?"

"I'm here." She stood by the door, smiling, and raised her hands to him, her face so welcoming and open he thought he might weep with joy. "We should go," she said, and beckoned him to her side. "We should go now, to my place."

Afterward he could not recall leaving the flat, or if he had locked the door behind him. All he knew was that he was outside in the High Street, wearing his own bomber jacket and with his arm around a very tall woman with dark hair unbound, the two of them laughing—at what?

He had no idea. The street was crowded as though it were a holiday. People snaked between buses and cabs and thronged the sidewalks, staring into shop windows, queueing for the cash machines at NatWest and Barclays, shouting at each other in front of the World's End pub. All Camden Town reeked of drink: spilled beer in the streets, beautiful young girls sitting on the curb swilling champagne from the bottle, young men in football jerseys clutching pint cans as they staggered through the outdoor market. Daniel had always felt slightly repelled by this urban bacchanal with its exposed strata of despair—homeless men passed out on the sidewalk with their dogs sprawled beside them, a white-haired woman with yellow-rimmed eyes, teenagers pissing in the alleys, and women with their ubiquitous mobiles, angling for reception on the street corner.

But tonight it all looked different. People smiled at him as he passed. One of the champagne girls leaped to her feet and, laughing, threw her arms around his neck.

"I'm *sooo happy!*" she cried as he grinned and tried gently to disengage himself. "*So* happy."

She stepped away and looked at Larkin, extending a hand helplessly toward her, as though she were on a ship leaving shore.

"Good-bye!" the girl called. "Don't forget us . . ."

"Do you know them?" Daniel asked. They had reached the arched bridge above Regents Canal. Beneath the bridge a tourist narrow boat was moored in Camden Lock, the dark water around it flocked with paper, spent roses, cigarette butts, condoms. People wandered along the canal path with faces shining in the lamplight.

"No." She took his hand and leaned against the bridge. "It just happens. At night, usually, places like this. They think they recognize me."

Daniel touched her hair. "Maybe they do."

"They can't." Her expression grew so sorrowful he thought she might cry, and he moved to put his arms about her. She smiled at him wistfully, for a moment let him cradle her against his chest. "It's always the same."

She turned to look down to where a boy was trying to climb over the guardrail above the lock. "They're always drunk or stoned, coming off a night at the clubs. They see me, and it's always the same. One girl near The Angel, she had a sort of fit—a seizure, it was horrible. Someone called 999, and they took her off in an ambulance. But I didn't know her. I never know any of them."

"Who would think you did?" Daniel shook his head. "I mean, you can't take personal responsibility for some kid OD'ing on Ecstasy or—"

"AW, FUCKIN CUNT!"

They turned to see the boy being yanked back from the guardrail by a policeman. "Or *that,*" said Daniel, and put his arm around her. "Come on, let's go. Which way's your flat?"

"Along the towpath."

"Whither thou goest, I follow."

They walked down the winding sidewalk toward the lock, angling between a bunch of skinheads whose HELLO MY NAME IS badges identified them as part of a tour group from Norwich, and three Japanese girls in translucent pink plastic dresses videotaping each other as they passed around a black cheroot. Larkin nestled against Daniel, her face turned toward his shoulder.

"Which way?"

Larkin said nothing. So he automatically started heading west, toward the zoo. In the near distance loomed the Pirate Club, a small castle built of grimy black brick and concrete; in its shadow, brightly colored narrow boats were moored, giving the canal a sad carnival air.

Larkin stopped him.

"No. That side." She pointed across the canal. "Toward Islington."

They crossed the little footbridge and made their way through the vast outdoor market surrounding Dingwalls. Daniel ducked beneath an awning by a shop selling masks and Caribbean incense. "This place is a nightmare."

More a labyrinth, or millennial souk. In all the years he'd been coming to stay with Nick, he had never learned to navigate this warren of shops and stalls, alleys and clubs and tunnels. Larkin said nothing. Indeed, she hardly appeared to lift her head; instead gently pressed his arm or silently pointed to indicate which way he should go.

At last they came back out onto the towpath, emerging from a long arched tunnel that smelled of piss and gardenias, the cobblestones beneath their feet scattered with waxy white blossoms that glowed softly in the near darkness.

"This way." A stray petal, the misty green of a luna moth's wings, drifted onto the bodice of Larkin's dress as she turned to him. "It's just down here, ten minutes or so. Maybe fifteen. Not long."

"The walk'll do me good. Sober me up."

They passed a few couples heading back toward Camden Town, an old woman walking a brace of standard poodles, a man on a bicycle who sounded his bell as he sped by. To their right was the canal, its surface black enamel beneath a sky so deep a blue it seemed that Larkin's dress had been clipped from it. Now and then a carp rose to kiss hopefully at the air before descending once more. Beside the towpath mulberries grew in profusion, their sweetly rank scent overpowering the smell of ragged white dog roses and diesel drifting down from the street above the embankment. On the far side of the canal were rowhouses, their tiny backyard plots separated by brick walls or neatly trimmed hedges, crumbling stone walls or huge terra-cotta pots filled with geraniums.

"I never knew this was here," Daniel said. "Hey, look at that—"

A woman in a long white dress came running to the edge of the far bank, hair wild about her face. Behind her on a patio a man stood in front of a café table set with candles and wineglasses and a vase full of yellow flowers. The woman shouted after them, words Daniel could not quite make out. Larkin huddled against him.

"Don't stop," she said. When Daniel glanced back, the man had joined the woman and was trying vainly to coax her back to the candlelight. Somewhere a window was flung open and music poured out.

"Where exactly are we?" said Daniel. Every few hundred yards they passed beneath another bridge, its railings broidered with razor wire. Northern Line trains thundered overhead, late weekend traffic crawling toward the M26. Ahead of them the canal curved in and out beneath brick arches. Blackthorn hedges extended toward the water, their white petals falling onto Daniel's upturned face. "It's like the country!"

"It *is* a country," said Larkin, and smiled. Her hand encircled his. "It's just around this last turn here."

Hand in hand they followed the winding path and approached a small footbridge edged with willow trees. As they passed beneath it, Daniel saw a steep stairway leading up to the street. He hesitated and looked expectantly at Larkin. She shook her head and smiled.

"There," she said, pointing. He turned.

"You live on a *narrow boat*?"

"Home sweet home."

"I don't believe it—I've never known anyone who actually lived on one of these!"

"Well, now you do."

And there it was: thirty feet long and seven wide, an old wooden canal boat, low enough that Daniel could have leaned out and rested his elbows atop its roof. It had a long, pointed prow and a tiny crescent step-out aft, where pots of ivy sat, green tendrils trailing into the water. The boat was painted like a Gypsy caravan, blue and green and red, with carved arabesques picked out in flaking gilt, and a row of small round windows, yellow trimmed. Worn lines moored it to iron bollards at the very edge of the towpath. On the prow gilt letters spelled out her name: *Cooksferry Queen*.

"Larkin, this is amazing! *You're* amazing—" Daniel laughed and flung his arms open. "A narrow boat! Can we both fit in it?"

Larkin smiled. "Come see."

She stepped onto the tiny aft deck, bent to find a key hidden beneath a flowerpot, and opened the door. Daniel waited until she stepped inside before following her.

"Wow," he said. "I feel like Alice when she was big."

The space before him was dark and narrow as a closet. Something soft and odorous draped across his cheek, and all unbidden the memory of Sira's garret room flooded him, silk running through his fingers and that sense of infinite impossible darkness, but also the sudden oily taste of burned salmon skin upon his tongue, a pulse of rainbow light. Before he could stammer Larkin's name, the light flickered, then grew steady, and she was revealed standing beneath a kerosene lantern that dangled from the ceiling.

"Be very careful. You're even taller than I am, and—"

"Ouch!"

Too late: Daniel cracked his head on a beam, and sent the lantern swinging. His arm shot out, seeking something to grab on to, and she was there, grasping his hands and drawing them down to his sides.

"Here," she murmured, and pulled him to her. "Daniel . . ."

She kissed him, her mouth sweetly sour; he put his hand upon her cheek, and for an instant it was as though his fingers slipped through

air, the warmth of her flesh enveloping his, and there was nothing between, nothing but that sweet taste against his tongue and an orchard
scent. He whispered her name, dizzy; she stared at him, her green eyes
lambent.

"Don't watch." It was as though she spoke to someone else. She
turned her head slightly, as though tracking something he could not
hear, and he blinked.

Her eyes held no pupil: they were all iris, two fractured stars like exploded bottle glass. Within them coruscating rays seemed to break
apart, then cohere in shifting bands, the color of the sea beneath heavy
cloud, the translucence of new leaves in the sun, black-green, blood-
green, virent. Minute coils of red like wriggling larvae swam through
the green, bursting when they reached the perimeter of each iris, then
dissolving into milky white. He stared, afraid to release his breath, terrified her gaze would return to him.

But she did not seem aware of him at all.

"First fruit, best blossom: nine branches broke to bear me," she
said. A child's voice, clear and very low, as though singing to comfort
herself when left alone in the dark. "Nine branches, best blossom, first
fruit: flesh."

She raised her hand. It momentarily blotted out the lamplight as she
gazed into the shadowy space.

"Be kind and courteous to this gentleman," she said. "He has come
in good faith and of his will."

Daniel tried to speak, but his throat burned. Through his mind
raced every warning word that he had heard about this woman: *She's on
medication, and Nick knows it. She has a history of getting mixed up
with the wrong kind of men. She has boundary issues. . . .*

But before he could move away, she turned back to him and her green
eyes fixed upon his; and they were not terrible at all, but welcoming.

"Stay with me," she whispered. Her cheeks were flushed, her voice
a soft command. "Stay."

"I will," he said, all fear fled. "God, yes, I will."

She drew him to her, her hair a fragrant net across his face, then led him through the tiny passage, the interior of the boat absurdly small, yet somehow it contained all of this, round windows screened with ivy and honeysuckle, drifts of spent apple blossom, lit candles giving off a smell of honey and sun-warmed clover. They came to an alcove, framed with oak planks carved with acorns, oak leaves, rowan berries, within it a bed, wide enough for two. He let her pull him onto the rumpled woven coverlet, dull green, snagged here and there with briars budding white and pink. Her hands around his wrists were strong, insistent, though her touch did not hurt him. As he moved to kneel beside her, his foot bore down upon something small and round upon that broke with a hushed noise.

She did not speak; her lips grazed his throat, his chest. He fumbled at his shirt, but she had already unbuttoned it, his exposed skin cool, then moist, warm where she touched it. Her hands covered his nipples; he would have groaned, but he could not, could make no sound. The sweetness on his lips was honey. It filled his mouth, his nostrils, seeped into his flesh. He thought he would choke, but it was fine as April rain, laving him from throat to chest, then pooling about him on the bed, soaking into the coverlet, dissolving. Everything smelled of it, of her, honey and salt and blossom.

"Come inside," she said.

He tugged his shoes off, socks, trousers. When he dropped them, there was a sound as of dozens of marbles rolling across the floor. Beside the bed a white candle sat on a narrow ledge. Beneath it runnels of melted beeswax streamed down the oak cabinetry. Moths hovered about the flame, their wings blade-shaped, rust red, corn yellow, dusted with gold scales that powdered the air as they flew. They exuded a smell like nail varnish; when they lit upon the wood, their soft-furred legs left minute tracks in their own golden pollen.

"Come inside."

Hc turned. Larkin reclined upon the bed, her hair a russet stream across the pillows. She was naked: what he took for her shadow was the discarded dress: she had no shadow. She still wore the necklace of jet beads and figured gold dragonflies. The candlelight made their wings seem to shiver as in flight.

"Larkin," he whispered.

"Come . . ."

She had small, full breasts, the aureoles dark brown, pansy-shaped, her nipples so deep a red they were almost violet. He cupped them in his palms, and it was as though he held handfuls of apple blossom; when he bent to kiss her, his cock grazed the soft mound between her legs. Her thighs parted; he could feel damp and warmth, his hand moving down the smooth curve of her belly to the inside of one leg. Something stuck to his fingers. He glanced down and saw white petals clinging to his palm, their curled edges already turning brown.

Then her hand cupped his chin and turned his face back to hers; her legs opened wider as she raised her head to kiss him, her teeth bruising his lip; she gently pushed him down until his head was poised between her thighs. She tasted of honeysuckle, sweet bittergreen, and salt. Milky warmth spread beneath his fingers and tongue; when she came, warm liquid seeped not just from her labia and cunt but from the inside of her thighs, like sap sweating from split bark.

As he drew away from her, she cried out very softly; he could not understand what she said, but it was not his name, or any name that he could recognize. He kissed her breasts, her mouth, could feel himself starting to come just as his cock slid inside her. He thrust moaning and came almost immediately, white liquid pearling the dark hair of her pubis and glistening upon the crease of one thigh.

"Larkin . . ."

He laid his head upon her leg. Phantom starbursts from the candle flames pulsed behind his closed eyelids. He stroked her leg, felt the strong band of muscle of her calf, the fine hairs raised by gooseflesh. Something caught between his fingers: he opened his eyes, expecting to see another brown-edged petal or fallen leaf.

It was neither. For an instant he thought he had trapped a moth, then saw pinched between thumb and forefinger a downy feather, fan-shaped, white-tipped and striated with lines of russet, dull orange, umber. He tried to flick it away, but it adhered to his damp skin.

"Look at this," he said, and sat up too fast, his head swimming. He looked over to see Larkin already asleep on her side. He smiled wistfully, then drew the coverlet over her, yawned and scraped the feather onto the wooden ledge where the candle had melted down to a crescent of white and sputtering gold. A moth had been trapped in the cooling wax; as he stared, its fern-shaped antennae twitched frantically, then grew still.

"Sorry, pal." He blew out the flame, lay back beside Larkin, and slept.

And roused, to her pulling him back toward her. He had never known a night so long, hours dropping like water into a well, his fingers and mouth inside her, around her, everywhere, endless. When finally he fell back, exhausted, he could still see her beside him, staring with wide wakeful eyes at the ceiling.

He woke twice more, or thought he did. The first time he lay for some minutes in the darkness, his hand upon Larkin's back. It took him a moment to recall where he was; even then he listened carefully for some outside sound that would lend clarity to this improbable bed, shifting ever so slightly as the current drifted beneath them.

But the night was utterly silent—more silent than he had ever known London to be. No drunks singing, no hum of street-cleaning machinery, no rumbling traffic. Nothing. A pale light filled the room, like moonlight tinged more green than blue. It made the outlines of unknown objects seem even more strange—the high, raised curve of a seat built into the wall; the narrow, tunneled darkness that ran from stern to bow; the splayed fingers of the geraniums on the aft deck, silhouetted against the sky. He sat up and looked out the porthole window directly opposite the bed.

The world outside was green—milky green, a gliding opalescent shimmer, as though he gazed not through air but water. Flickers of emerald appeared, then faded; in the distance a pinpoint of deepest indigo flared and was extinguished, as though someone cupped a giant hand around a sputtering blue flame. Daniel stared, too amazed to feel terror or even to wonder if he were truly awake. Beside him Larkin slept, a strand of hair by her mouth stirring with each breath.

He never knew how long he sat and watched the green world shift and gleam; waves of air, or heat, or some unnameable element erasing, then reshaping it each moment, as the ceaseless passage of waves or the molten explosion of livid matter from the earth's soft heart re-formed a sunless world miles and miles beneath the sea. At one point he heard voices, crackling as with static, then burbling, then growing silent once again. Once something moved directly outside the window, a blurred thing like a great wing or a tree limb thick with leaves.

Then he must have slept again, because he was awakened suddenly, heart-poundingly, by a cry—a long, low wail followed by three deep hoots, like a foghorn.

But it was not a horn. It was an owl, a sound he had never heard before but recognized from countless movies. He looked up to see Larkin sitting bolt upright in bed, staring with wide, terrified eyes at the window.

"It's okay," he said sleepily, and tried to draw her back beside him. His cock was hard again; he leaned over and kissed her neck, her skin salty with dried sweat. "It's just an owl. It probably escaped from the zoo. . . ."

And he was asleep once more, not even desire enough to keep him watchful. When he woke the third time, it was for good. He was alone in bed on a narrow boat in the Regents Canal. Someone had left a window open. Wet willow leaves were strewn across the coverlet and plastered against the walls. Gray, rainy light filled the room. He clutched the blanket to him, shivering, looked around, but saw no sign of Larkin.

"Larkin? Larkin, you there?"

It was not until he swung his feet over the edge of the bed to stand that he saw the floor was covered with acorns: scores of them, some whole, some crushed so that their creamy innards protruded from brown shells, others already starting to sprout, small green fingers plying at the chill morning air, and, drifting among them, a few brown feathers flecked with white.

Part Three

Sketches to Illustrate
the Passions

CHAPTER EIGHT

The Beckoning Fair One

I have wandered in many lands, seeking the lost regions from which my birth into this world exiled me, and the company of creatures such as myself.
—*George Bernard Shaw*

I was in the city when my brother, Simon, called me about the painting, staying in the East Village with Oona, a model-cum-actress I'd met when I was designing the sets for the London run of *St. Elmo's Fire*. We carried on a desultory affair made slightly desperate by her methamphetamine habit and the vespertine light of that long, autumnal year. I liked junkies and addicts, sought them out, in fact: they asked little of me sexually, which was good because my medications killed my libido; they hoarded their deepest emotions and energies for drugs; they didn't look askance at the contents of my medicine cabinet and seldom bothered to raid it. Oona broke up with me that winter, but by the time I went back to the States in March, she'd returned as well.

I was supposed to do sets for the New York run of *St. Elmo*. My years with Red had honed my carpentry skills, and while I never took up drawing again, I was a middling set designer. But backing for the show fell through, and I was left with no job and no place to stay—not for the first time, I should add.

Still, I hung around the tiny storefront theater, doing some preliminary sketches for someone I knew who was trying to mount *The Tem-*

pest. Nights I spent with Oona. She had a sublet on Houston but was afraid of being alone; she seemed happy enough to let me stay for a while. We fucked once or twice for old times' sake, but after a few days managed not to see much of each other. That suited me just fine.

My brother tracked me down at the theater. I refused to carry a cell phone, just like I refused to keep an apartment or any forwarding address. Anyone who really needed to find me knew to track me down through Red, who was the only person I kept in touch with—though I hadn't seen much of him in the last few years and hadn't been back to Aranbega since my mid-twenties. Simon left increasingly angry messages at the theater box office, but it was still three days before I called him.

"How come you didn't tell me you were back?" he demanded. "Where are you staying?"

"With Oona. A great big howdy to you, too, Simon."

"Is she in rehab? Jesus Christ, Val, I hope you're not sleeping with her."

"I'm hanging up, Simon."

"Okay, wait! I'm sorry. Here's the deal: we have to talk."

"So talk."

"Not that kind of talk. Face talk. Business, Val. Family stuff."

I sighed and ran a hand across my chin. "I'm busy, Simon. I—"

"How can you be busy? Listen, I got you a ticket on the four thirty-five shuttle out of La Guardia. You can come back first thing tomorrow—"

"Simon. I can't. It's impossible." Someone started banging on the door; I kicked it, hard enough to splinter the plywood. Whoever was on the other side gasped, then left. "You—"

"Tonight. Dinner. I'll have a car get you at the airport. You can catch the last shuttle back. Or take the train if you don't want to fly. Just get here. And don't bring Oona," he said, and hung up.

I stood in the tiny room, staring at the hole I'd made in the door.

"Goddamn it," I said. I went to find the stage manager, told her I had a family emergency that meant I had to go to D.C. I didn't bother with the E-ticket: when I'd flown out of Heathrow, I was stopped and searched three times, based on my looks and erratic travel history. Instead I arranged for a ticket on the Metroliner. I wasn't supposed to drink with my medication, but I bought a bottle of Jack Daniel's for the trip and split.

Dinner was at a tiny Ethiopian restaurant in a ramshackle house off Logan Circle. Out back was a small garden with two plastic tables and three chairs. The brick walls were overgrown with wisteria, the dense blossoms strewn across the ground like lavender foam. It felt like every place did in those days, at once desolate and precious, the end of another century, not the beginning. There were empty bullet casings scattered among the fallen blossoms, and tattered advertisements for opportunities to improve your English at home.

But the food was good. We were alone, except for a silent young man who brought us injera and tibs and zilzil wat, set on a wooden tray that completely covered the table. The place had no liquor license—for all I knew it had no restaurant license—but Simon had brought two bottles of expensive Médoc. The food was so spicy I could hardly taste the wine, but I drank it anyway, finishing most of a bottle by myself, while my brother sipped abstemiously from his glass.

"So," I said, reaching for the second bottle and a corkscrew, "nice dinner. What the hell am I doing here, Simon?"

My brother mixed a raw egg into a little mound of raw beef, spooned red chili pepper onto it, and began eating with his fingers. "Someone's made an offer on one of Radborne's paintings."

"How much?"

"Four million."

"Jesus." I yanked the cork from the bottle, too hard. Wine arced onto the platter, red chili and raw beef dissolving into a hundred-dollar Médoc. "Four million dollars?"

"Yep."

For the first time all evening, Simon grinned. He was seventeen years older than me, his handsome red face collapsing from drink though he'd managed to keep his muscle tone by working out every day. Just over six feet, he was a good six inches shorter than I was. No one had ever mistaken us for brothers, or even acquaintances. He wore his hair long, like mine, but his was thin and streaked with gray and always smelled slightly rank, from some weird human-placenta-derived shampoo that, ounce for ounce, cost more than cocaine. He wore bespoke suits, slightly shabby, and a ring made from the teeth of a shrunken head he'd bought in Borneo years ago. He looked more like an aging drug lord than a lawyer.

"That's too much money," I said, pouring myself more wine. "Who is it?"

"Guy named Russell Learmont."

"Never heard of him."

"You should have. He's the CEO of Winsoame Pharmaceuticals. Your medicine's probably made him rich. Here."

He handed me a bound sheaf of pages thick as a porterhouse steak. I glanced at the cover.

PROPOSED CONTRACT FOR PURCHASE OF
RADBORNE COMSTOCK'S *ISEULT*
(Detail from *THE LOVE PHILTRE*)

Underneath was the date, Russell Learmont's name, and those of about twelve attorneys.

"Looks like you better get some backup, Simon," I said, and began leafing through it. There was a lot of legal mumbo jumbo and a lot of columns adding up to a lot of money. I looked in disgust at an eight-by-ten of Learmont, a thin, angular-faced Captain of Industry in his late sixties, his teeth bleached blue-white, with the calculated smile and sly eyes of a Preston Sturges con man.

"Christ," I said, and turned the page.

The Love Philtre is thought to be the crowning achievement of Radborne Comstock's career, though it is known only through a few photographs taken in the 1930s during a visit to Radborne's son, Trevor. A break with the earlier, strictly illustrative art that first brought him renown—iconic images of Johnny Appleseed and Paul Bunyan, *The Boys' Own Shakespeare* and *Robin Hood—The Love Philtre* is Comstock's never-completed vision of the classic tale of Tristan and Iseult. A diptych in oils on wood, it depicts the fatal moment when the doomed lovers drink the potion that will forever seal their fate. Darker in tone and subject than Comstock's well-known illustrative work, the painting marks an intriguing moment in American illustration, wedding the photorealist detail of English Pre-Raphaelitism with a late Symbolist sensibility. Comstock's tragic death soon after its completion deprived the American art world of what would almost certainly have been his greatest and most mature body of work. The two paintings constituting the diptych were separated during the 1930s and presumed to have been lost.

   —Reprinted with permission from the catalog for "Days Fair and Foul: A Radborne Comstock Retrospective," Nonesuch Gallery, Boston, 1978

"I don't get it. Who is this guy Learmont?"

"He collects outsider art. Lives in London."

"Do you know him?"

"We've met a few times on the island. He owns a yacht. You've probably seen it—four-master."

"Four-master?"

I looked down at the photograph of my grandfather's painting. The colors had that weird pink tinge you get in old magazine photos—Tristan on the left-hand panel, Iseult on the right, arms upraised so that each held one handle of an ornate silver goblet. One half of the goblet was on each of the panels; the hinges in the center had been made to form part of the goblet, a trompe l'oeil effect. The image was too small for me to get a good look at the painting, but something about the figure of Iseult sent a wave of unease over me.

"Outsider art?" I said. "Radborne isn't *remotely* outsider art."

"You read it. And I'll tell you something else—between you and me, it ain't worth four million either. Maybe two."

"That Parrish only went for four million. And Radborne's not Maxfield Parrish. Or Henry Darger." I handed the contract back to him. "But you forgot one little thing, Simon. We don't actually own *The Love Philtre*."

"We own half of it."

"It says here it was lost."

Simon's grin grew broader. "Red found it. Well, part of it—the woman. In the boathouse, where all that stuff was left when Radborne's boat went down. About a year ago. He was the one mentioned it to Learmont when he was on Aranbega last summer." Simon leaned forward to pour himself more wine. "He has the other half."

"You're kidding? Learmont?"

"Yup. I have no idea how he got it, but he owns it."

Nowadays Radborne would have had an entire medicine cabinet full of Winsoame pharmaceuticals. By the end of his life, his increasingly tenuous connection to reality had frayed, to the point where he was giving away paintings and sketches in lieu of paying tradesmen's bills. Over the years some had made their way back to Goldengrove, returned by generous owners who wanted the works to remain in the family. A few were bought when Simon had funds to afford them; in one memorable instance, two of Radborne's oils showed up at a yard sale in

Cushing, where a family friend bought them for five dollars, then presented them to Simon as a birthday present. Reading about *The Love Philtre* just now, I'd assumed it had ended up in a private collection somewhere, or one of those drab little regional museums displaying Abenaki baskets and minor works by minor American painters like my grandfather.

"I'll tell you, Val, this guy has got a wild hair up his ass over this." Simon reached to stab the color print in my hand. "I'd like to get this over with as soon as possible. I don't need to tell you our portfolio's taken a beating."

"No, you don't need to tell me." I leaned back in my chair, the plastic straining under me. I was bored and tired and ready to leave. "So sell it. What, is there a provision that you need my permission or something? Well, you got it. Now I have to go."

I started to get up, but Simon grabbed my arm. "Wait. Val, listen— I don't need your permission, nothing like that. But I do need a favor."

"Oh. Right."

I stared at him, waiting, was rewarded by the sight of my brother doing his best Innocent Weasel impression. "Nothing major," he said. "Just, Learmont wants this delivered to him in London this week."

"So call FedEx."

"Well, he wants it delivered to him by hand."

"Hire a courier."

"Val." Simon leaned back, smiling. "Look, it's not a big deal. He and I would just both feel a lot better about this if *you* could do it— someone we could trust."

I started to laugh. Simon gave me a thin smile. "All right, he doesn't know you—but this is a no-brainer, Val! Actually, it was Red's idea to send you. Learmont had suggested he do it, but when I talked to Red, he told me to ask you. Learmont has his own Gulfstream; it'll meet you—wherever. New York, you can catch it there. Or here. Whatever you want, as long as it's in the next day or two. The plane brings you to

London, you deliver the painting, he wires the money into the trust. That's it."

"I'm busy, Simon."

He laughed. "Pull the other one, Valentine."

"I just got *back* from London, Simon. Why don't you go?"

"I wish I could. I've got a case coming up on Friday, can't get a deferral."

I shook my head. "Look, this is just too much of a pain in the ass for me right now, okay? I don't need the goddamn money. I've got something lined up—"

"Val, listen to me." Simon took a deep breath. "There's something else. Learmont's offered five million for our half of Aranbega. Goldengrove and the outbuildings, the hundred acres. I told him we don't want to sell right now, but we really have no choice, Val. The taxes are killing us."

"Goddamn it." My hands clenched; I stared down at my feet. "So. You sell to this asshole and Red gets evicted?"

Simon shrugged. "Val, Red's not around much anymore. I don't know where he goes, but he's got his own life. Who can blame him? He doesn't want to stay up there in the middle of nowhere. Do you? Russell Learmont wants to set up a little medieval fiefdom . . . well, let him."

He sighed, smoothed the sparse hair back from his forehead. All of a sudden he looked like photos of our father, exhausted by his pathetic excuse for a life. "Listen, he really wants that painting. I say, let's take the money and run, hold him off for a few years, wait till the market's better, and then sell Goldengrove to him. If he still wants it."

He scooted his chair around the table to sit beside me. "Red's bringing the painting down from the island tomorrow. He'll be at my place around noon. All you have to do is tell me whether you want to fly out of D.C. or New York. I'll call Learmont, and he'll have the plane waiting and all the paperwork. One of his minions will meet you at the airport. You get on the plane, you get off, you get on again. If you want. Stay in London for a while if you feel like it. Crash at Nick Hayward's place; he's living with his girlfriend now. I'll call and tell him you're coming."

I sighed, defeated. "Goddamn you, Simon."

"Great. Thank you, Val. You're a fucking prince."

He stood, pulled out his wallet, and threw a couple of twenties on the table, then looked at me again. "So what do you want to do? Go back to the city and get your stuff?"

I got up, the table nearly toppling as I brushed against it. "There's nothing there I need," I said. I felt in my pocket for my wallet and my meds, picked up my stained suede jacket and pulled it on. "I'll fly out of here. Dulles, whatever. I'll crash at your place tonight. Just tell this guy Learmont I want to fly into Gatwick."

"Gatwick?"

"Yeah." I trudged across the little outdoor garden. "My bike's in storage there. If I'm going over, I'll get it out on the road again."

I looked back at my brother, his puffy, triumphant face, and thought of Goldengrove. I walked over to him, took the portfolio, and tossed it onto the ground, the pages falling among decaying blossoms and broken glass.

"Don't wait up for me, Simon," I said. "I'll get there when Red does."

As it turned out, I never saw Red. I didn't stay at Simon's after all, but a hotel not far from Simon's R Street town house. My brother was waiting at the door when I arrived before five.

"You missed him," said Simon. "He drove all night, got here around two. He ate breakfast and then split. He's got some project he has to finish up this week." He looked slightly remorseful, but more excited: like a kid who'd waited up all night and missed seeing Santa but had a pile of presents to offset the disappointment. "If you'd stayed here, you would've seen him."

"Yeah, but if I stayed here, I would have seen you, too."

Still, I felt bad. It had been a few years since I'd been to Goldengrove to visit Red, and even though we kept in touch by phone, I felt guilty. I stepped inside. "Ah, fuck. Tell him I'll try to get up there later in the summer, okay?"

"You tell him, Val. Christ, you can afford a fucking cell phone. When are you going to stop living like a college student?" He flashed me a cold smile. "Oops—I forgot. You never went to college."

"Where's the painting, Simon?"

I followed him down the hall. My brother had a nice place, furnished with gleanings from Goldengrove, the best of Radborne's paintings and the English Arts and Crafts furniture our grandfather had collected: Lutyens chairs, Vose tiles pried from the fireplace on Aranbega, an original Morris settle. Simon truly loved all this stuff—the happiest I'd ever seen him was after he scored a Harvey Ellis sideboard at Christie's. The sideboard was in the dining room now, and leaning in front of it was a large, flat wooden carton with dovetailed joints. I recognized Red's hand in the craftsmanship and Red's spidery penmanship on the label: "FOR DELIVERY TO RUSSELL T. LEARMONT."

I squatted in front of the crate, examining it. Brass hardware, oiled quartersawn white oak with birch inlays—*it* belonged in a museum. "Did Learmont order this?"

Simon smiled. "No." He was wearing battered jeans and a threadbare Snakefinger T-shirt, hair uncombed and eyes still heavy-lidded with sleep: a vision of my brother that almost made me like him. "You know Red. You'd have to pay him extra to get him to do a bad job."

I hefted the crate: heavy, but not so heavy I couldn't carry it. "So what's the deal? You tell him I wanted Gatwick?"

"Yup. That's no problem. You fly out of Dulles; a car's supposed to pick you up in half an hour." He glanced at his watch. "You want coffee or something to eat?"

"Yeah, sure. Is this thing locked? I'd like to see what it looks like. The painting."

Simon tossed me a key. "Come in when you're finished."

I unlocked the crate. It opened like a set of doors onto packed wood shavings. Momentarily the smell dizzied me: I was back in the boathouse, hunched at my drafting table with green light filtering through the windows while Red planed boards behind me. I carefully pulled away the shavings to reveal a long, broad package encased in bubble wrap. I peeled the tape away with care, standing so I could slide the painting free.

It was a single piece of wood, very wide and heavy. Where would he have found it? The tree must have been immense. I set it down and stepped back to look at it.

It was her. The woman in the room at Halloween: the woman in my drawings. She was floating in the air above a distant, wave-swept sea, her arm extended and her fingers barely touching half of a silver goblet. Her hair was defined by a few thick brushstrokes of crimson and ocher, her face worked in white and umber that had been covered with a thin wash of viridian that still shimmered, vein green. Her eyes were wide and staring, jade green, black: she was staring past where the diptych had been broken. She was staring at—

My breath came fast and ragged. I let my fingers trail down the painting, the barely discernible ridges and declivities where the paint thinned and I could feel the wood grain beneath. Invisible, but it was there, it was there. . . .

"Val? You coming? It's nine."

I said nothing. For another minute I stood, staring, forcing myself to see nothing but a rectangle of colored wood with two broken hinges dangling from one side. There were people in preindustrial countries who when shown a painted image could not see what it represented:

their perception had been honed to recognize patterns in the sky we can't see, but not the *Mona Lisa.*

It was just a painting, and it was not mine. It never had been.

"I'll be right there!" I yelled.

Once again I carefully sealed the painting in its bubble wrap, replaced it in the crate, and padded it with the wood shavings. I closed the doors and locked them, pocketed the key. It tinked softly against something, and for a moment my hand closed around the plastic bottle with my meds. I turned and joined my brother in the kitchen.

We didn't talk much. I had a sudden wild thought to beg him not to sell it, or to steal it myself. But that was crazy; I knew that.

We exchanged gossip about people we knew. I asked if he'd heard from Nick Hayward, whom I'd stayed with a few times while working on shows in London.

"Couldn't reach him. But I left a message on his machine. You still have your key?"

I nodded. When I tried changing the subject to Russell Learmont, my brother just shrugged.

"I don't know much more than you do. He's for real, if that's what you mean. He gave me a hundred-thousand-dollar binder for the painting." I didn't comment on the fact that I seemed to be left out of the loop entirely, except as a go-between. "From what I could find out, he's a legitimate collector of this kind of stuff."

I sipped my coffee. "Yeah, but what kind of stuff is that? I was thinking about it last night, and it just doesn't make sense. If what you were saying is true, that this guy collects outsider stuff. Radborne is way too conventional for that."

I didn't mention what I was thinking: that the painting I'd just seen was nothing like Radborne's other work.

"Who gives a fuck?" said Simon. "Learmont buys this painting, it *becomes* outsider art. Or whatever you want to call it. And think about this, Val." He pulled a stool up to the counter and sat. "After this sale, what happens to everything *else* of Radborne's? What's our portfolio look like then, huh?"

"Simon, nobody is ever going to think Radborne's pictures of Paul Bunyan are outsider art. They were illustrations. I mean, Christ, some of those books are still in print."

"That's not what I'm talking about—I mean those other paintings, the ones at home."

"Home." I finished my coffee and stuck my cup into the sink. "You know, if anyone calls that place 'home,' it should be Red. You paid him, didn't you? For coming down here?"

Simon shrugged. "I gave him gas and toll money. Hey, don't look at me like that! He lives there for free—we could *rent* that place if it weren't for Red."

"Rent to who? Jack Torrance? You really are an asshole, Simon." But I was too distracted to get really pissed off. "Listen, what do you have for cash? I don't want to have to jerk around at the exchange when I get to London."

"Learmont's taking care of it."

That was when the doorbell rang, twenty minutes early. I ran a hand through my hair, still damp from the shower, pulled a wadded-up bandanna out of my pocket and tied it around my head.

Simon made a face. "You know, Val, they're gonna take one look at you and call airport security."

The doorbell rang again. "Coming!" my brother shouted, and hurried out of the room.

I was sorry Simon didn't give me any cash: I'd have liked to see if a few bills would have bought me any negative feedback on Mr. Learmont. Everyone—the driver, the private security guards, the pilot and copilot and steward aboard the Gulfstream—had nothing but smiles when Russell Learmont's name came up.

"He'll treat you right," the driver assured me. "I do this run all the time—pick up his friends from Burning Tree. Mr. Learmont knows everyone."

He smiled. He had beautiful teeth, a Piaget watch, an Armani suit. Red himself would have been impressed by the provisions Learmont had made for his painting—there was enough padding inside that limo to outfit a rubber room. Once the painting was installed, the crate was strapped into a special harness in the rear of the limo. I tossed my knapsack alongside and settled myself in the backseat.

We headed out of town, on through the gray chute of software sprawl that had enveloped the Virginia countryside in the last fifteen years. After a while I asked, "Your employer do this often? Have someone hand-deliver paintings to him?"

The driver nodded. "Oh, sure. A few years ago, he bought an entire building. Some crazy guy in South Dakota, lived in a shack made entirely out of stuff from McDonald's. Styrofoam, a whole wall of little plastic toys of the Hamburglar. Mr. Learmont bought it, had them take it apart. It's stored in a warehouse somewhere now. Guy who built it retired down to Texas."

I thought of Russell Learmont reconstructing a shack made of Big Mac containers on Aranbega. "That's nice," I said.

I stared out the window, trying not to let my mind drift back to the painting strapped behind me. It was just dawn on the last day of April, a late spring that year. Cherry trees and apple trees were still hung with clouds of white and pink. There were wild ducks paddling in streams along the highway. The driver, after asking my permission, put on the radio, and the strains of Schubert lieder filled the car. Something—the music, the growing sunlight, the recent memory of the figure in my grandfather's painting—honed the world to a sharp, fine point that for the first time in years began to pierce the pharmaceutical bubble that surrounded me. I felt joy—not mere contentment or the absence of despair, but joy. As we approached Dulles, the driver called in to let them know we were close to arriving, and while he was talking, I let my hand slide into my pocket. The key to Red's crate was there, the key to Nick Hayward's apartment.

And the bottle containing my pills. I felt it in my fist, a little plastic tube containing mineral salts and mood stabilizers, chemical sutures for a tattered neurology. A few inches from my face, the window was cracked open. Warm wind stirred my hair; the scent of apple blossom. I glanced at the driver, still on his cell phone, let my hand rest for a moment against the top of the window.

Then I opened my fingers and let go. There was a flicker of pink and white above the grass on the median, and already it was gone, already it was somewhere far behind me. Already that was the past. I rolled the window down as far as it would go, breathing in exhaust and apple blossom, and waited to arrive.

CHAPTER NINE

The Entombment

I saw a cloud wrapped with ivy 'round
I saw an oak creep upon the ground
I saw red eyes all of a flaming fire
I saw a house bigger than the moon and higher
I saw the sun at twelve o'clock at night
I saw the man that saw this wondrous sight.
—*Nursery rhyme*

For minutes after Swinburne's departure, Radborne waited, listening for sounds of argument in the asylum's corridor. But there was only near silence, the regular heartbeat of the waves. It was not until he heard the distant echo of a clock chiming eleven that he recalled Learmont's command to meet him in his office. He hurried from the room, slipping Swinburne's book in his pocket.

The manor was as empty and desolate as it had been upon his arrival. Apricot-colored light burnished oaken wainscoting; from the apothecary seeped an attar of potassium bromide and vanilla. He made two futile circuits of the main floor, was just about to admit defeat when he recalled the refractory upstairs. He hurried up the steps and then down a corridor, and yes, beside the refractory was a second door.

"Dr. Learmont?" he called hesitantly, then knocked. The door swung open.

"Ah, you are still here!" Dr. Learmont's face was bright with relief. "I was afraid you had fled."

"No, of course not." Radborne gave a sharp laugh as Learmont grasped his arm and drew him inside. "I was afraid you might be angry at my meddling—though I did not intend to meddle," he added quickly; "there seemed to be some altercation, and I was afraid . . . violence . . ."

"Well, there might have been. I have advised Ned many times not to arrive here without prior arrangement—he has a bad effect upon the unfortunate lady, as I think you now understand."

Radborne nodded, turning. His eyes widened. "What *is* this place?"

Everywhere he looked were paintings. Hanging from every inch of wall, heaped upon the floor, suspended from the vaulted ceiling by chains and wires and pulleys. Landscapes and portraits, broken panels of fresco, tiny squares of wood covered with writing in unknown alphabets, maps of undercities and designs for bridges that spanned entire oceans. Labyrinths constructed of spent lucifers and snips of tin, a life-size human figure made of oakum with acorn eyes. A stuffed owl under glass, its avian head replaced with the wax head of a woman wearing a brittle horsehair wig. A book of thumbnail-size stamps, painstakingly drawn and varicolored, a man-size ball of furry twine. There were pages that seemed to have been torn from illuminated manuscripts, but instead of religious figures, displayed monstrous creatures: a woman's face fixed to the whorled body of a kraken or paramecium, dogs that walked upright like men, a beautiful young girl floating above a ruined tower with a flower in her hand.

Only it was not a flower but a man's sexual organ. The tower was not a tower but another woman's head, with gaping holes for eyes and the top of her scalp broken as though it were a neatly sliced egg.

"What . . . what are they? Who made these?" he asked at last.

"They are mine," Learmont said. "This is my collection—part of it, the things that I love the best. I am compiling them to buttress some findings I have made over years of research and discovery. One day I shall present them all to my superiors. You will find no common work of your countryman John Rogers here, Mr. Comstock. See!"

Eagerly he led Radborne to a large canvas in a plaster frame ornamented with poppies. It depicted a bespectacled man wearing a beetle's carapace and carrying an umbrella; beneath his foot the diminutive figure of a woman could be seen, her tiny legs kicking. The painting's title was *Ready for the Rain.*

"This was given me by the gentleman who painted it. He is like yourself, Mr. Comstock—an illustrator, and a very successful one. Yet melancholia afflicts him so severely that often he cannot be entrusted with his own safety."

Radborne looked around in disbelief. "Do you mean to say that all of these are by your patients?"

"They are all the work of lunatics. And yes, at one time or another many have been in my care."

"But they are extraordinary!"

Radborne crossed to examine a pencil drawing framed under glass, an explosive crosshatch of gears and teeth and blade-edged wheels with a lengthy explication of its proposed use.

Draggonatto for the happy despatch of my enimies

Radborne shook his head, amazed and appalled. "Is this all part of your research, then? Mr. Swinburne mentioned only that you have been conducting an inquiry into madmen who paint."

Dr. Learmont went to a desk that was a veritable forest bed of moldering pages. "It is a part of my research, yes, yes it is. . . ."

He began to rummage through the papers. "Most recently I have been corresponding with other metaphysicians on the subject of monomania. A failure of the will that would appear to be most efficiently treated by moral therapy, yet its sufferers seldom respond to standard measures—galvanism, heliotherapy, iron, and strychnine. You are familiar with Winslow's work?"

He held up a book: *On Softening of the Brain Arising from Anxiety and Undue Mental Exercises and Resulting in Impairment of Mind.*

Radborne nodded. "Yes—Dr. Kingsley gave it to me to read at Garrison."

"You know, then, that according to Winslow a total if temporary cessation of mental exertion should produce deliverance from mania or melancholia. But in my experience it does not! The will to paint or write or compose seems *somehow related to the anxiety itself.* If the activity is forced to cease altogether, the concomitant melancholy grows even more severe, and may lead to dementia or suicide."

Learmont bent over his desk. "Now, where is it? Ah, here!"

He picked up a small pine frame. For a moment he stared at it, then crossed to place it carefully into Radborne's hands.

"Ah," said Radborne. "How interesting."

Inside the frame was a charcoal drawing on cheap, coarse paper. Half was covered with fragmentary penmanship. The other half showed two butterflies, lifelike and well executed. One had its wings outspread; the other was wingless. Radborne tried to decipher the smudged words. "It's in French—'*Rêves fatals.*' Fatal dreams, would that be?" He glanced at Learmont. "Who was he? A man who studied insects? It seems quite innocent."

"His name was Gérard Labrunie, called Gérard de Nerval."

"I am not familiar with him."

"No? Perhaps his work is not to the American taste. He died almost forty years ago, having spent most of his life in a Montmartre hospital run by my colleague Dr. Esprit Branch, and then in the asylum run by Branch's son in Passy. His illness was no secret—he suffered from an extreme form of erotomania and eventually took his own life.

"I spent some time with him in Dr. Branch's hospital. Gérard had tried painting earlier, using crushed blossoms and plant stems to make ink and pigment. Later he was given charcoal and pencils and books to write in. Those results were very striking, as you can see from these."

He indicated a series of drawings grouped together on the wall. All were of women. Or rather, as Radborne saw when he examined them more closely, all were of the same woman. She had large eyes; a smooth, oval face; delicate hands; and long, coiling hair. A pretty face, Radborne thought at first, but as he stared, he began to imagine something disconcerting in her expression: an unnerving intensity, as though she were seeking to burn a hole through a curtained window with her gaze. With a start he recalled the woman on Blackfriars Bridge, and Evienne Upstone.

"Well, he was a fair draftsman," Radborne said at last.

"He was a raving madman, obsessed with a woman who sang on the stage. But he had many friends and was in the care of physicians who encouraged him to write of his delusions."

Dr. Learmont picked up a folio-size book bound in blue leather. "Listen: 'Desiring to make a record of what I have seen, I began to cover the walls of my chamber with a series of frescoes showing what had been revealed to me, and writing within the pages of this notebook the history of what I have learned. One figure was always dominant: that of Aurélia, depicted with the features of a goddess, just as she has always shown herself to me.'

"You see," said Learmont, setting the book down, "that was *his* muse. She inspired his most vital work. He was very fortunate in having friends who visited him and took pleasure from his creation. Very fortunate."

"And you made this part of his therapy—to encourage his delusions? It seems very cruel! His illness is not unusual, you know—a number of my inmates shared these sorts of erotic manias and would write about them. But I couldn't publish them in *The Prism*. I believe Dr. Kingsley kept them in his patient files."

"Nerval's books were *read*, Mr. Comstock. He was a man of genius. His failing was that his visions ultimately maddened him, yet much beauty came of them."

Dr. Learmont picked up another, smaller volume with an engraved cover and handed it to Radborne. "This is the work of a man even more unhappy than Nerval."

Radborne looked at the book.

Les farfadets: Ou tous les demons ne sont pas de l'autre monde,
par
Alexis-Vincent-Charles Berbiguier de Terre-Neuve du Thym

" 'The *farfadets,* or not all demons come from the other world,' " Dr. Learmont translated.

"Farfadets?"

"A close approximation might be 'goblins.' "

Radborne said nothing. Fluid shapes moved across his eyes, the shadow of a man dancing atop a broken wall, gray figures following him through an alley. He made an involuntary gesture, his hand flicking at the air, looked aside to see Learmont staring at him.

"Yes." With an effort Radborne laughed. "Well, *I've* seen a few goblins, in the refractory room at Garrison."

Learmont sighed. "I never treated Monsieur Berbiguier. I wish I had. He spent his life with his *farfadets,* and unhappy company they seem to have been."

"Are they ever not?"

"Oh, yes! I have known a number of men who would not trade their goblins for any amount of gold. Goblins torment them to paint or draw, and we are all the richer for it."

"No matter the cost to their families? Their employers?"

"The world does not lack for earnest men, Mr. Comstock. 'He who has no touch of the muse's madness in his soul, approaches the door believing he will be allowed into the temple by virtue of his Art; but he and his poetry are not admitted: he is nowhere when he enters into rivalry with the madman.' I would not argue with Plato."

Radborne kept himself from an angry retort. He handed the book back to Learmont. "The woman, then? The one you keep upstairs? What purpose is there in encouraging her in her delusions?"

"She is a gifted painter."

"So she claimed. It is an elevated form of derangement, I suppose, for a woman." Radborne hesitated. "She seems to suffer from disappointed affections. Is that correct?"

"It is. She never married and has attached her unreasonable expectations to Burne-Jones. But he is not to be blamed for encouraging her painting."

Radborne looked at Learmont with distaste. "You did."

"You think I am remiss in this matter? Yet I believe—I am *certain*—that it is what keeps her from dying of despair. I assure you, Mr. Comstock, I am a benign jailer! Others would have broken her, or killed her outright, in their efforts to keep her imprisoned. But, like you, I have always found her beautiful."

He stopped. His gaze seemed to turn inward, and his expression grew so anguished that Radborne looked away, embarrassed. "You cannot imagine what it was like to find her—to see such a creature, wandering lost and bewildered in Clerkenwell Green. 'Who breaks a butterfly upon a wheel?'—So yes, I give her paints, and pencils, and canvas, and she draws what she remembers of her life before this. It sustains her, Mr. Radborne. It sustains *me*."

"I would expect the opposite, that it would have driven her to dissolute living. And ultimately it has brought her here, you cannot deny that."

The doctor smiled. " 'Driven her to dissolute living'—has painting done so to you?"

"Of course not," Radborne snapped. "Doesn't her family object?"

"She has none, save a murderous villain who claims to be her husband. She is well quit of him, though of course she will not believe that. She is much better now, I have provided for her from my own estate. In the city she lived for some months at a private home for insane ladies, but Burne-Jones felt that she would benefit from the air in Cornwall, and the solitude. Here . . ."

He walked over to a small easel that held a watercolor painting. "This is something that Miss Upstone produced for me. I think it extremely interesting." He turned to Radborne. "Do you?"

Radborne stared at the canvas, frowning. It held nothing but stabs and smudges of color—yellow, green, black, though mostly green—an utter ruin of celadon and dusky gold.

"It looks as though a child got hold of her paints," he said.

"That's what I thought at first. But see—if you step back from it and stare at this point here." Dr. Learmont jabbed at the canvas with one long finger. "Do you see? There is a figure there, suspended in the darkness."

Radborne scowled but stepped backward, fixing his gaze where Dr. Learmont had indicated. He made out nothing but the same slurry of yellow and green against a brackish ground. Then, as though someone had thrust a telescoping glass before his eye, his vision sharpened.

"Oh!" He flashed a startled glance at Learmont. "Yes! I do see. There's a man there—"

Between folds of color was a columnar figure, two jots of strontium yellow-green marking its eyes. There was little else to indicate that it was anything but meaningless whorls and dabs, green, yellow, black, bister. The figure, such as it was, seemed to float, and even move if Radborne stared at it too long. The masculine form was suggested rather than drawn. What was suggested was grotesque.

"He's . . . it's obscene," said Radborne, flushing. He turned accusingly to Dr. Learmont. "You did not force her to paint this?"

"No. She says it comes to her in a dream. Yet the technique is not dissimilar to what Whistler has done these last few months, don't you think? When he's not mincing about with his fluffy white dog stealing paints. And, Mr. Comstock, come look at this."

Learmont pulled a leather portfolio from a chair and opened it, flipping through the loose pages within. They were all fragments of drawings, with swooping lines signifying arms, legs, torso. Male genitals appeared again and again, along with, perhaps, a man's face: long eyes, black mouth, jagged black lightning in place of hair. Each page was neatly signed and dated, as though the image on it were complete, yet what sane artist would ever think such primitive scrawls could be construed as finished?

"She draws the same things." Learmont held up a sheet that consisted of nothing but vertical bands of black, the edges of the charcoal softened so that the columns appeared to melt in and out of each other. For Radborne the effect was all the more disturbing because it was utterly without meaning. "She really has a remarkable technical facility," Learmont pronounced.

"Where?" Radborne took the portfolio from Dr. Learmont and leafed through the sketches. "I see no evidence of it! This is nothing but scrawls. It's cruel of you to humor her—"

He stopped, his attention caught by a pen-and-ink drawing of a man and a woman in a landscape. The woman was Evienne Upstone. Her dark hair was pinned up, but she wore no hat, only a sleeveless shift that clung to her legs as though wet. Beside her was a tall man, bearded and dark-haired. Burne-Jones? Behind them willow trees sent long banners of leaves streaming above a pond or river. It was a winsome drawing, the faces expressive and attractive. Only the trees held a hint of an underlying disquiet.

"Well, yes, all right," Radborne conceded. "This one is quite good. Is this how she used to draw? Before she became ill?"

"She sketched that for me a week ago."

Radborne handed the portfolio back to him. "So you really are attempting to cure her."

"I am attempting to see the world as she does, a world I saw long ago, when I was much younger. She possesses what Ruskin calls 'the innocence of the eye.' Her bouts of melancholy induce a purity of vision which we have lost."

"But is she then the painter you wrote of, whom you wished me to companion? You said a man."

"I did indeed. Jacobus Candell. I thought after lunch I would take you to meet him. Come now, let's see what Breaghan has prepared for us."

Abruptly he turned and headed for the door. Radborne stared after him in bemusement. He gave a last lingering look at the wilderness of paintings, and followed Learmont into the hall.

Lunch was flabby sprouts and mutton laid out on a side table in a cold room. Radborne was relieved not to see Breaghan in attendance. He felt a small spur of regret, thinking of Swinburne making his way alone across the moor to Trevenna.

"Do your patients ever dine with you?" he asked.

"Miss Upstone does sometimes. Candell never. His deliriums are rare but extremely violent; he also refuses to eat anything that you or I might find palatable—he lives exclusively on eggs and scrumpy."

"Scrumpy?"

"Strong cider. He uses the eggs in creating his temperas and scarcely seems to discern any difference between what he is painting and what he is consuming. I will confide in you, Mr. Comstock. . . ."

The doctor pushed aside his plate. "My hopes were that he, too, might have that innocence of the eye, but I don't think Candell gives a damn for anything but paint and dirt. He is a gentle person, save when the madness overtakes him, but he talks very little. I had thought you might engage him in some social intercourse, you being a fellow painter, and young. You see, he does not recognize himself as an old man. To his own imagining, he is still but twenty-five."

"What was his exact crime?"

"Ah! I forget sometimes you are an American—you have never heard of Jacobus Candell? He was the most promising young painter of his day, admitted into the Academy, beloved of his friends, at the helm of what surely would have been a most remarkable career—*most* remarkable."

Learmont gave a sad laugh. "I tell you this because when you meet him, you will not believe it, unless you have seen his work. Rossetti and his cronies fell under his spell—his *Caliban Freed* was exhibited in '48, but by then he had already gone mad. Early in the year, he visited Egypt—he had a patron, Dr. Langley, who arranged for Cobus to accompany him to the Holy Land and record all that they saw there. It was to be Cobus's *Italienische Reise*.

"Instead it deranged his mind. In his journals he confides that while visiting the Valley of the Tombs of Sestris, he had a vision of the goddess Isis. Tragically, of course, no one saw what he had written in his journals until after the murder.

"Cobus returned to London and resumed his painting, having engaged a young woman named Evelyn Hebblewhite as his model. On the afternoon of October twelfth, he cut her throat with a palette knife, dismembered her, and attempted to hide her corpse in his steamer trunk, along with several bottles of cider and a box of India-rubber erasers. He then departed for the West Country—his intention seems to have been to board a boat for the Isles of Scilly—but he was detained in Penzance and arrested, then brought back to London to stand trial. He was committed to the Criminal Lunatic Department of Bethlem Hospital and remained there for eleven years before I arranged for him to be brought here, at my own expense. He had been given paints at Bethlem but did not have the privacy or freedom to work there. It was my hope that he might resume his work at Sarsinmoor."

"And has he?"

"You may see that for yourself."

"But why was he allowed to leave the hospital? A murderer—"

"They kept him restrained for much of the time," said Learmont. He turned to stare out the window. "A strait-waistcoat combined with electrical therapy and sulphanol would drive the murderous impulses from most people. When I first visited Cobus, he was a scarecrow who could not speak his own name—or recognize it. The psychiaters attending him were themselves living in terrible poverty—a public hospital is not the place to make your fortune in *this* country, Mr. Comstock!

"But his keepers were content with the arrangement I offered them. Mr. Candell has been under my exclusive care since then. He receives the Royal Academy's catalog every year, and many other periodicals, and so has some acquaintance with how the world has turned without him in it. And he has not been without visitors. Rossetti and his brother and sister have all made pilgrimages, and Swinburne, and more recently Burne-Jones. That is why Ned believed this might be an appropriate refuge for Miss Upstone.

"I think, however, that it is now time for Cobus to make the acquaintance of another painter. Will you come with me, Mr. Comstock?"

Radborne looked up, startled, but Dr. Learmont had already left the room. Radborne pushed aside his plate and hurried after him.

"I had dreamed once that I might have many patients here," said Learmont as he walked. "But no one has ever been quartered in the west wing save Mr. Candell. He likes the solitude, and his room affords the most dramatic views of the ruins—something which would overexcite Miss Upstone, I fear. I am hoping to create a more domestic arrangement for her, something suitable for a woman of her sensibility."

They went upstairs, retracing their steps until they entered a narrow hall with walls and floor and ceiling all of stone. The windows were slits hacked in the rock, with neither glass nor drapery to keep out the wind. Radborne shivered; a few feet ahead of him, Dr. Learmont turned. Radborne found him a minute later, fumbling at his waistcoat. There was the scrape of metal against stone. Dr. Learmont pushed open a door.

"Good afternoon, Cobus," he called. "I have brought a visitor for you—you recall that I mentioned a visitor? May I present the American painter Radborne Comstock?"

Radborne followed Dr. Learmont inside. He inhaled the odor of turpentine and blinked. The room was large and held a single immense window, its mullions covered by a grid of iron. It must have cost several times over what Radborne had earned in all his time at Garrison.

"Mr. Comstock," a voice said in a soft Kentish burr. "You are most welcome here."

A figure approached him, a man with a worn, seamed face, wearing an antiquated suit beneath an artist's smock of coarse pale-blue cambric. His gray hair reached to his shoulders, paint-spattered and stuck with twigs, as was his beard. He had very red lips like a girl's, parting in a smile to show grayish teeth. His broad shoulders were stooped, his demeanor that of one who has survived a ravaging illness.

Yet as Radborne gazed into his eyes—the palest blue he had ever seen—all he could think was *He is very handsome for a madman.*

"Cobus, you may remember that Mr. Comstock is visiting from New York City," said Learmont with a smile. "He does not know many people in London, and it was my thought that he might serve you as an apprentice."

Radborne bristled at the term "apprentice," but his reply was cordial.

"I am pleased to meet you," he said. Candell only stared at him, still smiling. His eyes seemed to focus on something just behind the young man. Radborne quickly glanced over his shoulder, but of course there was no one there. Slightly annoyed—had the old man done it on purpose?—Radborne walked into the room, keeping a careful distance from Candell, and began to look around.

"Well, this is impressive." He whistled admiringly. "Who pays for your canvas and wood?"

"Why, Dr. Learmont," said Candell. He smiled again, an expression of ineffable sweetness, and lifted his hand, as though waving to someone far off. "Doesn't he provide for you?"

"Not yet," said Dr. Learmont.

The room was filled with paintings. Not the deranging display of Learmont's office but the familiar hodgepodge of a working studio, canvases primed and unprimed set upon easels or leaning against the wall, tables holding jars full of brushes and heavily crusted palettes, magnifying lenses and boxes of broken charcoals, all of it ripe with the smells of damp canvas, pine oil, solvent, and a faint underlying stench of rotten eggs. On the walls hung finished paintings—a large canvas of a red-haired woman plucking an apple from her breast, a man gazing with stunned recognition at his own shadow, seeing within it the lineaments of a monster. There were portraits, too—a bulbously cheerful man Radborne recognized as Gabriel Rossetti, someone identified as the Supervising Physician of Broadmoor Asylum, and Learmont himself, seated upon a throne of twigs and birch bark and rowan berries.

But in portraits and fantastical paintings alike, the faces had an odd similarity—the eyes unnaturally long and uptilted, the mouths curved in a manner both sensual and cruel. They filled Radborne with a slight disgust, as though he had overturned a log to find an animal's decomposing corpse. He averted his eyes, but the sense remained, blurring into the memory of the woman on Blackfriars Bridge, lingering heat upon his cheek.

"Mind your step, Mr. Comstock," said Learmont.

Radborne looked down as something shattered beneath his foot. "Good Lord," he muttered.

Autumn leaves covered the floor, beech and oak and hawthorn and gorse, with here and there the bristly husk of a beechnut or a heap of acorns like tiny skulls. There were also scores of eggshells. Some seemed to have given up their insides for tempera medium; others had been hard-boiled but only half eaten, adding to the fetor of turpentine and leaf mold. Radborne bent to see what he had stepped on and in disbelief held up the remnants of a glass vial.

"Gold leaf?"

"It is not your fault," said Candell in his soft voice. "I forgot that I put it there."

Radborne shot a glance at Learmont, but the doctor was busy inspecting a small canvas with a magnifying lens.

"You may keep it if you like," Candell added, and patted Radborne on the arm. "This paint, 'It is all fairy gold, boy, and will prove so.'"

Radborne stared at him, then nodded and pocketed the fragments. "Er, yes. Thank you."

He turned and walked to a table near the window, amazed at the array of pigments there—lapis lazuli and viridian, carnelian and *caput mortuum*, ground gems and the crushed remnants of Egyptian mummies, emerald-winged beetles and iridescent blue butterfly wings. An iron cot strewn with leaves and a chewed-up blanket appeared to be the room's only bed.

Candell sidled up beside Radborne. "Do you hear them?"

"Hear them?" Radborne discreetly turned his head. A foul smell came from Candell, rancid oils and spoiled eggs, the unmistakable stink of dead mouse.

"They're not very loud. Listen."

Cobus turned and pointed. For the first time, Radborne saw that the room was full of insects—gnats, which he might have expected, from the filth and litter everywhere, but also myriad scarlet butterflies no bigger than his thumbnail. Candell nudged him, indicating where one battered itself against the window.

"Can you hear it?" he asked.

"Hear it?" Radborne thought he was joking, but a look at the painter's intent face showed he was not. And indeed, when Radborne tilted his head and held his breath, he *could* hear something, the faintest memory of a sound: heavy snow on glass, a falling leaf.

"It is nothing like when they die," whispered Candell.

He went to the corner of the window, gently cupped his hands around the butterfly to capture it, and turned back to Radborne.

"And, of course, that is nothing like when *we* die," the old painter added. "Their conception of mortality is nothing like ours: their lives are so much longer that they have no premonition of what it is to die, to live entire lives with the knowledge that everything must die. For them death is rare and always unexpected. They are utterly without a vocabulary for it. That is why they cannot create art themselves, or recognize what we create. To them we are like paintings. That is why they steal our children and take us as lovers. That is why they collect us."

"Who?" said Radborne. Dread crept over him. "Who are you talking about?"

With a smile Candell took a step toward him, opening his hands just enough that the younger man could glimpse the tiny creature there, its wings brushing against Candell's palms, its antennae black, white-tipped. Without warning, Candell clapped his hands together. There was a pale shimmer in the air about Candell's shirt cuffs, as of chalk dust; then he opened his hands to show a miniature tangle of crushed black and red, a glistening smear of pinkish white.

"They don't make a sound," he said. Radborne watched, repelled, as Candell lifted his hand to his mouth and rubbed it across his lips. "Not a sound," he smiled. "Not ever!"

There was a chiming in Radborne's ears, a sweet belling that grew louder and louder until he realized it was no bell but the sea, waves rising to swell at windows and doors, black and gray and green, waves come to overtake them. The room darkened. Candell's face was a moon before him, beard and hair clouds, yellow flash of teeth. And Radborne saw—he thought he saw—he saw something caught upon the madman's lower lip, something tiny and white and moving, not an insect's leg but a woman's arm.

"Mr. Comstock?"

He blinked. The darkness was gone, the room was filled with light. A few feet from the window, Cobus Candell sat painting, a half-finished oval canvas before him. Radborne looked around, confused and frightened. He touched his throat and felt his hand tremble.

"Where is Dr. Learmont?" he stammered.

Cobus leaned forward, a hair-brush tracing a spiral in the center of the canvas. Without looking up he replied, "He had to go attend upon Miss Upstone. He said he would see you at dinner—didn't you hear him say good-bye?"

"I—no." Radborne shook his head. "I . . . I must have been distracted. Did he—"

"Could you hand me an egg?"

"An egg?"

"At your feet—there, by *Persephone.*"

He looked down. A small canvas was nearly hidden amid the dead leaves beneath the window. Next to the canvas was a dun-colored circlet that could have fit in his palm, a bird's nest. Inside it was a single small egg, tea-colored and speckled with dark brown.

"This?" Radborne picked it up.

"If you please. Thank you," said Candell as Radborne handed it to him. "Chipping sparrow. They like to make their nests of horsehair."

He held the egg up to the light, scrutinizing it. Then he tapped the end of his paintbrush against the egg once, brought the shell to his mouth, sucked at it noisily, and dropped it. At his feet there was a litter of crushed eggshells, along with what looked like dragonflies' wings.

"Doesn't do to have too many of them," said Candell. He began to paint again.

Radborne stood, heart beating much too fast and head pounding as though he had been struck. How long had he been here? When did Learmont leave? Cobus Candell seemed utterly nonplussed, busy with his painting; when Radborne looked outside, the sun had moved westward. He walked over to the window, staring at a ridge of gray cloud above the horizon, as though separated by a knife stroke from the sea. He was afraid to speak to Candell and ashamed of his fear: not of being alone with a madman but that the old man was so calm, so focused upon his work.

"You may look at my paintings if you like," Candell said after several minutes had passed. "That is what most of my visitors do. I don't always care to speak when I am working. I'm sure you must understand."

"Yes—yes, of course."

Radborne turned from the window. He wandered to where a very small canvas rested atop a bookcase crammed with boxes of paintbrushes. The painting showed a banquet, the figures minute but exquisitely detailed, wearing robes and ruffed collars in the manner of Elizabethan courtiers. They were seated around a long table, eating a roasted mouse. They had the same unsettling tilted eyes and cruel mouths that distinguished Candell's other pictures. Still, Radborne admired the old man's technique. None of the figures was bigger than the ball of his thumb, and many of them were smaller. All were rendered in the most extraordinary detail, down to the corselets of minnows' scales and the milkweed down that formed the courtiers' exaggerated collars.

Delectation was written in the lower right corner. JACOBUS CANDELL, BETHLEM HOSPITAL, SEPTEMBER 1863.

Radborne glanced over his shoulder at Cobus, to see if he used a magnifying lens to paint. He did not. The young man turned back to the painting, squinting at what he thought was a split hazelnut. It proved to be a sort of bassinet that held a bawling, red-faced infant so tiny he got a headache trying to bring it into focus.

"How extraordinary!" murmured Radborne. And all done in oils, too! He tried to move even closer, to get a better look, and bumped against the shelf. "Oh, damn."

Jars and brushes rattled, there was a *ting* as something fell to the floor and rolled out of sight. Radborne looked for it but found nothing. In the room behind him, Cobus was completely unconcerned; indeed, he seemed to have forgotten that the young man was there at all. Radborne straightened, his attention caught by one of the brushes on the shelf. He picked it up, his eyes narrowing.

"Sable?" he said aloud in wonder. The long handle was of reddish wood. And the ferrule was . . . gold?

That couldn't be. Radborne held it up to the light. If not gold, then brass plated with gold. The brush hair was long and black, with the faintest frost of white at the tip. When he stroked it against his cheek, it was soft as down.

"It *is* sable!" He glanced at Candell, but the painter remained oblivious. Silently, Radborne poked among the shelves until he found a jar in which other brushes were soaking. He dipped the sable into it, withdrew it, and tapped the ferrule briskly against his index finger. As if by magic, the brush sharpened into a point. He leaned closer to the shelf and drew in the dusty surface, an S so fine it could have been made by a single hair. As he watched, the water dried and the line disappeared.

Radborne whistled softly. Tobolsky sable, too; he'd bet his life on it.

And Tobolsky sable was worth its weight in gold. His own brushes were sabeline—ox-ear hair, dyed white—or squirrel, or camel hair, which was not camel at all but hair from Asiatic ponies. The ferrules on half his brushes had cracked, because they were cheap—a good ferrule was seamless, because the wooden handle absorbed water and cheap seamed metal would split. Radborne had never been able to afford anything better than a single sabeline one-stroke that had some real sable mixed into it. When the nickel-plated ferrule finally broke, he'd repaired it with cotton strips, but it was practically useless now.

And yet a criminal lunatic incarcerated in a Cornish madhouse had thousands of pounds' worth of sable brushes! He glanced once more at Candell, then knelt to see what else he had.

Brushes made of Chinese hog, Hankow he thought; a few Kazan squirrel French quill mops. Varnish brushes, longhaired pointer writers, fan blenders, even a few Oriental brushes. Radborne recognized these because they had no ferrules—the long strands of wolf and pine-marten hair were set directly into their bamboo handles. Save for these, every brush had a gold-plated ferrule, engraved with the painter's entwined initials: *JC.*

Behind him he could hear the steady susurrus of Candell's brush upon canvas. The smell of oils was suddenly so thick it choked him. He covered his mouth with a handkerchief and stumbled to open the door. Candell looked up with mild, pale eyes.

"Are you leaving?"

"No. The fumes are so strong, it's making me a bit ill."

"The poppy-seed oil, I imagine. Or the copal varnish: I was trying it on a corner. Or perhaps you are hungry? There's some eggs. . . ."

"No," said Radborne hastily. "Thank you. It's probably the varnish. I've been spoiled by working *en plein air.*"

Cobus smiled. "I haven't had that luxury in some years."

Radborne flushed, but Candell took no notice, only replaced one brush with another and leaned toward the lower corner of his canvas. "Are you in need of brushes? I saw you inspecting my shelf there."

"No, it's just that there were so many, and . . . well, such *luxury*—"

"Dr. Learmont gives them me. Not even Sir Sloshua ever had so many sables, the hound's prick! And you've seen my pigments!"

Candell laughed, a noise like rusty hinges. "When Rossetti saw my cell, he laughed until he wept—a madman with a treasure-house for a paint box! Mind *you* don't weep, Mr. Comstock. If you do, don't do it in my lapis, ha, ha!"

Radborne managed a weak smile. He stepped over a heap of rags that smelled as though something had nested and then died in them. "But the quality of your work—it's truly remarkable, sir."

He paused in front of another small painting swarming with tiny figures and meticulously detailed vegetation. Its title was *The Wedding-Party*.

"Do you paint from memory?" Radborne asked.

"I have no choice. I have sketchbooks, of course, from my journeys. Recently I have had a model in Miss Upstone."

Radborne felt his throat constrict; he turned back to the shelves and barely kept himself from exclaiming aloud. The shelves sagged beneath hundreds of glass and ceramic jars, holding every imaginable pigment. Common coal, lead white, and hartshorn; *cornu cervium,* that purest black from burned ivory; Cologne earth, precisely what its name implied; Vandyke brown.

And *caput mortuum*—Radborne picked up the container and squinted, trying to read the handwriting on its faded label.

"Oh, that's genuine *caput mortuum,*" said Candell. "Gone out of vogue now—everyone's too squeamish. I gathered that myself when I was in the Valley of Sestris. A dealer in antiquities still had mummies set aside for making pigment. It's very good for rendering dust." He gave another of his croaking laughs. "The color is not from the mummies themselves, you know—it is derived from the asphaltum which they used to embalm the bodies. They mix it with bone ash. Didn't your instructor teach you any of this?"

"No." Radborne replaced the canister, picked up another filled with ground lapis lazuli so pure that it was like a handful of sky. "We worked on brush technique, mostly. And some anatomy, though I'd familiarized myself with that from my medical studies."

"Ah!" Candell set down his brush and beamed. "That is why you are not squeamish! It is a good thing for an artist to have a strong stomach. Some of Rossetti's friends—so fastidious!"

Radborne smiled and continued to investigate the pigments. "It is very difficult to get a good green," Candell went on, picking up his brush again. Radborne had indeed just put his hand upon a shelf of green pigments. "Once you've seen the real thing, you realize how meager our own efforts are. Green bice is good, but copper carbonate is poisonous. Mustn't lick your fingers! Or your brush. *Verd de Vessie,* sap green—that's what I use. I make it myself, from buckthorn berries."

"Rhamnus catharticus," said Radborne. "The cervispina."

Candell looked at him, eyes shining. "Very good!"

"I've studied botany since childhood. I have rather a passion for it."

"Do you? Well, then. You may find much on the moors to interest you, if you keep your eyes open."

Radborne continued with his inventory, marveling. Some of the pigments were so obscure as to be utterly out of fashion; still, they sat side by side with the most common tints and powders. Pure orpiment, the shining gold that could be lightened only with hartshorn; *auripigmentum*—king's yellow—rich and fatally poisonous; all the earths and transparent lakes that Radborne could remember sucking from his watercolor brushes as a child. Mars yellow, *giallolino de Fiandra,* litharge. A tiny vial of saffron, the dried crocus stamens still intact. Zinnober, which Theophrastus said was obtained by shooting arrows at exposed veins of ore in cliff faces. English vermilion and the more precious Chinese. Saturnine red, that dense, toxic powder composed of leads. Rose Madder Lake. English woad. Tyrian purple, *Murex trunculus;* Saxon blue and Haarlem ashes, German azure and ultramarine, *azzurro oltremarino,* the blue from beyond the sea.

"Bremen blue, Milory, verdetta, walrus tusk, Marc black, lac lake . . ."

Like a child reading aloud for the first time, Radborne named each one. Not even Pietro's, where he bought his paints in New York, had so many pigments!

"It is a treasure-house," Radborne said at last. He felt drunk. He wished he could lick his fingers, poison or not: he wanted to spill the pigments onto the filthy studio floor and bathe in them, eat them, stain his body a thousand hues and then dissolve into the stone. "I have never seen such colors! Never."

Candell swiveled on his stool and regarded him thoughtfully, his pale eyes keen. Finally he asked, "Would you like to see what I am working on?"

Unexpectedly Radborne felt his heart lift. "Yes," he said. "I would be honored to see it."

He stepped forward, leaves crunching underfoot, and eased up alongside Cobus's stool. The old painter leaned back to accommodate him.

"Ah," said Radborne.

It was another lapidary oval, less than two feet in height and half that in width, its colors shining as though lacquered. At first it was impossible to determine its subject. Candell had begun painting from the outermost edges in, but in a peculiar spiraling fashion, so that one's eyes tracked around and around, seeking the center.

But there was no center yet—the painting was incomplete, the space in the middle a crosshatch of swirling lines and faintly penciled forms. As in *Delectation,* those figures that already had been painted were maddeningly small. And their sizes varied: there was no relative scale among them whatsoever.

Radborne bent until his nose was an inch from the canvas. From a distance it looked as though a finger hovered at the top—the artist's finger? a giant's?—but from another angle the finger looked more like a tree trunk. Or could it be an arched stone bridge? It was quite extraordinary, the bizarre trompe l'oeil effects this madman cozened from oil and clay; and what in God's name was that? A sort of spiky fungus, thrusting from beneath a pair of legs . . . ?

"Remarkable," he said.

The subject of the painting was a procession, a long skein of figures that began at the bottom of the oval and wound inward, between trees and rocks and hills and streams all luxuriantly overgrown with plants. He recognized harebells and bluebells and foxgloves and various species of fern, but there were others he could not name. Figures peered from the undergrowth; some of these were almost invisible. A few people on horseback wore richly colored clothing, Elizabethan or medieval in style, embroidered robes or stiff farthingales, sky-blue capes, leather boots.

But there was a London policeman in there, too, and several women who were obviously of the street, and two men in deerstalker hats. There was also someone who looked like Jacobus Candell, only much younger, and a man who resembled Dr. Learmont brandishing a pair of shears. And toward the incomplete center of the canvas, there were people dressed unlike anyone Radborne had ever seen—a woman in trousers, men in tight, shining black-and-yellow clothes, another woman in a very short red shift.

"Oh, no," he whispered, frowning. "Oh, look here. . . ."

He blinked, trying to get a clearer view, and began to see that, despite their strange and varied clothing, the figures possessed the same features. At once delicate and sensual, with long slanted eyes and full mouths, high cheekbones, sharp chins; the men feminine and faintly threatening, the women eerily self-composed, eyes half shuttered and lips parted as though about to speak.

All, all were Evienne Upstone.

"They've just come from the wedding night," said Candell. "We are at the very center here—the omphalos, if you will—and all radiates from us. Or will, when the time comes. When Time comes."

Candell stabbed at the canvas. When he withdrew his finger, Radborne saw a slit or crevice in the middle of the painting. A tiny slash of paint, made with a brush tip as fine as a pin, yet its color was the most virent emerald Radborne had ever seen, so vivid it seemed as though a lick of green flame burned through the canvas. Surrounding it was the faintest outline of a door or tunnel, from which all the figures proceeded.

Although he wasn't certain if they *were* proceeding—perhaps they were all going back into the passage? Radborne rubbed his forehead. "I don't know how you don't go blind," he said. "It's all I can do to take it all in."

"But you can't," said Candell. "That's the trick, see? You must try not to see it all at once, or you will go mad."

Radborne forced a smile. "Yes. Of course."

"But you do recognize her? My model . . ."

"Yes," said Radborne, his throat tight. "Yes, I do."

She was seated upon a white horse just outside the tunnel's opening, her hair coiling about her and her piquant face no bigger than a fingerprint. Unfinished as the image was, she was unmistakably the source of all the wild swirl of activity that surrounded her. Like the frozen heart of a waterfall, unmoving yet locked into a simulacrum of Motion itself, beauty and stillness and a sense of numinous release, something about to be revealed, something that would drown them when the torrent was finally freed.

"Yes," said Radborne again. "It is a very fine likeness." There was something else, perched upon her saddle's pommel. "What's that?"

"Her dog." Cobus's hand fell heavily upon his knee; Radborne's gaze followed and saw the inscription in the painting's lower curve.

THE DOG HAS NOT JUMPED DOWN YET

Radborne shook his head. " 'The dog has not jumped down yet?' "

"It can never begin, it can never end; not till then."

"I don't understand," began Radborne, and stopped. Jacobus Candell was staring at him, his pale eyes huge and mouth parted in delight—not just joy, but expectation and complicity.

"Of course you don't," said Candell. "Of course you don't."

Radborne froze. He knew that look, as surely as he knew what happened next. When Candell lifted his hand, Radborne lunged. But before he could touch him the madman seized him by the wrist, twisting it so that Radborne fell, writhing, to his knees.

"You must learn her name!" shouted Candell. "You must learn her name! Swear it! Swear it!"

Radborne struggled, but the madman was too strong. How could an old man be so strong? The tendons in Radborne's wrist strained and popped—his right hand, his painting hand—and he cried out, then gasped. "I swear, oh, Christ, *yes!*—"

"Swear it! You must swear it! You must!"

Radborne shouted wordlessly. He thrashed and flailed, trying to kick at the man standing above him.

"Swear it. You must swear it—"

There was a crack as of wood against rock. With a groan Candell toppled backward.

Dr. Learmont's voice rang out. "Mr. Comstock! The restraint!"

Radborne rolled onto his side, moaning as Learmont yanked him to his feet.

"Take this!" cried the doctor as a tentacled mass of canvas and whalebone slid through Radborne's fingers: a restraining waistcoat. "Get behind!"

Radborne stumbled to where the old man had fallen, Learmont darting behind him. Candell grunted and struck at the doctor, lurching to his feet, but Learmont was already grasping his arm and stabbing at the sleeve with a hypodermic syringe. Radborne thrust the loops of restraint over Candell's head. The old man swiped at it feebly, as though it were a cloud of flies; the mere sight of Learmont seemed to have subdued him.

"Cobus," said Learmont in a loud, even voice. "Cobus, sit down in your chair, please."

The old man stood, dazed and swaying slightly; he stared at Radborne with horror.

"Cobus. Sit down."

With a heavy thump, the old man fell into a chair. Radborne began to pull the restraints around him, but Learmont said, "Stop, Comstock."

Radborne ignored him. "I said stop," Learmont commanded, and put a hand on his shoulder.

"Are you mad, too, then?" Radborne shouted. "He tried to kill me!"

"He's sedated now. I shouldn't have left you alone with him."

"No, you damn well shouldn't!" Radborne pushed at the doctor's hand, grimacing as pain lanced through him. "Christ, he's broken my arm!"

"Help me get him over to his bed. Then I'll see to you."

Radborne swore furiously but obeyed. The old painter was a dead weight, sitting with eyes half closed and mouth slack; when they sought to lift him, he growled, then whimpered softly, then let himself be dragged to the iron bedstead in the corner. Radborne stepped back from him, rubbing his arm as he glanced at Learmont.

"Morphine?"

"And acetic anhydride—tetraethyl morphine. His tolerance for the substance is extraordinary. But let's see to you now."

They left Candell lying on his back in the narrow bed, pale eyes gazing fixedly at the ceiling. Dr. Learmont locked the door behind him, then carefully took Radborne's arm and rolled up his sleeve.

"It's not broken," he said after a moment. "A mild sprain, maybe. I can splint it."

"No." Radborne shook his head angrily. "I can't paint like that."

"Or do much else to assist me."

"To hell with you! You said nothing, you gave me no warning of his temper!"

"You told me you had worked with lunatics before, Mr. Comstock." Learmont slipped his keys back into his pocket. "But no, I shouldn't have left you alone with him. I was distracted, Miss Upstone was so agitated. . . ."

He pressed a hand to his forehead, wincing. "You can see how desperately I need assistance here."

Radborne said nothing. He turned to stare out the grilled window overlooking a barren sweep of hillside that led to the cliff's edge. A whitewashed cottage stood there, bright and toylike in a sudden glint of sun. He thought of Evienne Upstone, her mist of pale reddish hair and luminous green eyes, and felt a sense of loss more terrible than any physical pain. He shut his eyes.

"I'll take the position."

He offered no more, neither speaking nor moving nor opening his eyes. After a minute he heard the doctor say, "Very well," and then Learmont's departing footsteps.

CHAPTER TEN

Contradiction

I love a well-built, circular fortress,
Where a splendid figure disrupts my sleep.
A man famed for his efforts will come there,
The untamed wave booming loud beside it,
Select spot, features blended, bright and fair,
Gleaming bright it rises beside the sea
For a woman who shines upon this year,
Year spent in wild Arfon, in Eryri.
None wins a mantle who looks not at silk:
Never a one might I love more than her.
If she chanced to bless the shaping of song
Every night I would lie beside her.
—Hywel ab Owain Gwynedd, *translated by Joseph P. Clancy*

He remembered everything. That there had been a green world within a woman's eyes; that he had lain with her and heard her cry out at the touch of his mouth; that an owl had called in the night. That order and meaning could be tasted; that desire had a color and the void a sound. That his skin bore the marks of claws; that there were hazelnuts everywhere about him. That they contained each of them a world. That the world beneath him was not earth but water. That everything he knew was wrong. That this world, his world, bounded by steel and grass and poured concrete and bread, a buzzing mobile phone, dried blood, semen, sugar—*that* world was a lie, a scrim, a veil. That he knew nothing, everything. That it was not his world. That he was not he. That she was not a woman.

That she was gone. She was gone. She was gone.

"Larkin?"

He had searched inside the narrow boat. Grinning to himself at first—where could she hide? There was not a door in the place save a thin vinyl folding panel that hid the head; he checked in there, then proceeded to yank open every drawer and cabinet he could find, all the cunning hand-carved built-ins that seemed to multiply as he went from one end of the boat to the other, searching. There seemed to be hundreds of them, drawers within drawers, panels hiding alcoves and engines. How could there be so many? It seemed impossible, yet there they were, holding jugs of water, plastic bags of beans, dried apricots and figs, raisins, shelled almonds, tools. One long, narrow dovetailed drawer held nothing but sea glass still gritty with sand, lavender and green and brown. Another contained a printed edition of a journal by someone named Lady Lewis. A page was marked with a pressed frond, once green, now feathery yellowy.

> . . . returned after walking with Ned Burne-Jones. He was as under a spell, and when we came home at once made a drawing of her from memory; he never altered it, but said it was the head of the mermaid. Often he spoke of her—said he was sure she was a nixie who had come up from the well.

Daniel replaced this and pulled open the next drawer. It was full of photographs, edges crumbling, sepia-toned. A young man on a cliff, his arms around a woman in middy blouse and skirt, her dark hair blown across her face. Two woman standing side by side, wearing identical 1920s-style Japonaise dresses. One had bobbed blond hair; the other wore her dark tresses unbound save for a headband set with a peacock feather. There were scraps of paper scrawled with words:

Lime and limpid green, a second scene
i do think you fit this shoe

A ticket stub from a 13th Floor Elevators concert in Austin in 1969. A videotape of *Chelsea Girls.* A color photo of a beautiful young man with a blond pageboy, wearing a crimson Victorian jacket that was too big for his boyish frame. He sat in a ladder-back chair, staring at a woman who towered above him, her face caught as she turned from the camera so that one had only a misty impression of large eyes and mouth and hair like smoke.

"Jesus." Daniel squinted in disbelief. *Brian Jones?* He started to pocket the photograph, thought better of it, and put it back, then tugged the next drawer open.

It contained seven dolls the size of Daniel's hand, their bodies formed of the bones of animals bound in place with thick red thread. He thought their faces were made of dried fruit—apples, maybe.

But the sweetish smell that pervaded the drawer grew stronger and more disturbing as he removed the dolls. Their faces were identical—eyeless, their mouths indented slits sewn up with green thread. One had a tiny thatch of reddish hair coarse as dried flax.

"Fuck," he whispered, and crammed them back inside the drawer. "Jesus Christ."

He found other things. A model of a castle made entirely of acorn caps. A notebook in which dozens of photographs were pasted, pictures torn from pornographic magazines: pictures of young men, all dark-haired, their eyes rubbed out with an eraser, then drawn in again, crudely, with ballpoint ink. Inside a Ziploc bag, the mummified body of a mouse; at least he thought it was a mouse. There was an unopened prescription bottle of Exultan, a brightly colored box of Exultan samples, also untouched, a large sealed bottle of lithium.

No clothes, though. All her clothes were in Sira's garret.

He shut his eyes.

"Larkin." His voice sounded childlike. He coughed, feeling that he might throw up.

"Larkin," he repeated, louder. "Larkin, where are you?"

He was kneeling on the floor. The boat rocked gently from side to side and made a grating sound when it bumped against the shore. He could hear the sprouting hazelnuts and acorns as they rolled, stirred by the boat's wake. When he looked up, the small windows seemed opaque, a harsh, glittery white. He saw no sign of trees or the brick wall that bordered the towpath, nor of buildings. He saw no trace of color anywhere, no shadows.

"Larkin?"

Horror seized him. The world was gone, the city was gone; he was abandoned, marooned in a rocking shell upon a shadowless sea. He forced himself to stand, went to the door and opened it.

Sunlight blinded him. He shaded his eyes and staggered onto the aft deck. His clothes hung loosely; he felt cold, as though he were still naked. His lips stung. When he drew a hand to his mouth, he felt tiny scabbed blisters, as though he'd been scalded.

"Larkin?"

The world was still there. On the lower limbs of the willow, wasted cellophane wrappers hung like spiderwebs where they had been fetched up by the wind. Behind the embankment early-morning traffic moved slowly in the High Street. A cheerful *brrring brrrring* rang out as a woman on a bicycle sped past, her blond hair rippling behind her. She glanced at Daniel curiously. He looked down and saw that his fly was open, and his shirt protruded from the gap.

"Shit."

He zipped himself up, then drew a hand to his face. The stubble felt greasy, and there seemed to be more of it than warranted by a single day without shaving. He winced, combed his hair with his fingers, and coughed again, covering his mouth. When he glanced at his hand, he saw speckles of blood. He ran his tongue along the roof of his mouth and felt ridges of broken skin. He spit into the canal, ducked back inside, and made his way to the compact galley.

There, amid the detritus he had pulled from the shelves, he found a jar of instant coffee. On the wooden counter was a bottle of still water. He couldn't figure out how to work the tiny gas cooker, so he ended up pouring tepid water over coffee crystals in a dusty glass and drinking the resulting muddy liquor.

This, at last, was suitably disgusting to motivate him to leave. He cleaned up, putting away the stuff he'd left on the counter, then quickly replaced whatever he'd left on the floor, shutting cupboards and bulkheads, making sure the drawer with the horrible handmade dolls was tightly closed. His shoes were on the floor beside the gas cooker. He found his jacket carefully hung on a hook above the fold-down dining table. Had he put it there? He had no memory of doing so. He pulled it on and, without looking back, left the narrow boat.

The gravel-strewn surface of the canal path felt unnervingly solid underfoot. He looked up and down the trail; he was suddenly anxious not to be seen.

There was no one.

But on the other side of the canal, a black-and-white dog raced along the path, so low to the ground it looked patently unreal, like one of those fast-moving painted targets in a shooting range. Even from the far bank, Daniel knew it was the Border collie Fancy.

She has boundary issues.

He spun and began walking hurriedly in the direction opposite that taken by the dog, back to Camden Town.

* * *

It was just past 6:00 A.M. The maze of paths and stalls around Camden
Market had an unfinished look, as though they'd been blocked in by an
artist who'd then lost interest, rows of barrows covered with tarpaulin,
lines of empty pint cans along a brick wall, stray items of clothing—
boot, jockstrap, sequined scarf, a turquoise sock. The handlebars of
an abandoned bicycle rose from the canal. Daniel leaned against a wall
and stared at the black water, trying to fathom what he was feeling. Re-
jection? sexual obsession? a psychotic episode triggered by leaving his
day job?

He shoved his hands into his jacket pocket and felt the smooth nub
of the acorn, snatched his hand back, and searched his other pocket for
his cell phone.

That at least had not changed; maybe what he felt was just hunger
and a very bad hangover. He checked the phone for messages—none—
then wandered up to Camden High Street and into the little bakery beside the newsagent, where he bought a loaf of fresh-baked bread. He
ate it on the street outside. Crumbs hailed around his feet; a barrage of
pigeons immediately appeared, surrounding him in a cloud of gray
and rose pink. He kicked at the birds, shouting as they burst back into
the air.

"Mum, 'e's a bad man," a small boy said as his mother hustled him
along the sidewalk, the two of them glaring at Daniel. He smiled sheepishly, turned to walk toward the corner Starbucks. That was when he
caught a glimpse of himself in the mirror-lined window of a lingerie
shop: a tall, thin man, dark-blond hair a ragged aureole around a
hollow-eyed face, his mouth bruised, and the dusky violet imprint of
three fingers clearly visible upon his neck.

"Oh, my God." He stared at his reflection, shocked, then hastily
began brushing crumbs from the front of his jacket, buttoned his Hen-
ley shirt, and tugged his jacket collar protectively around his neck. He

hurried to buy a large coffee, dousing it with milk so that he could gulp it without scalding his tongue, and went back out onto the street.

Psychotic break, then. Somehow, despite the coffee and the bread, this didn't seem as ludicrous a notion as it might once have. He gazed at the crowds dispersing from the Underground, waiting in line for the bus, filing through the glass doors of Holland and Barnett for vitamins and organic tea. Every woman's face was hers. None of them was Larkin. He felt as though he were being poisoned: horror seeped into him as the realization dawned that he would not find her here, or anywhere.

"Don't," he whispered. "Don't. Go."

He blinked, staring at the sidewalk until the tears receded, then looked across the road to where Nick's building reared above Inverness. A blazing lime-green billboard facing the High Street bore the words MORE THAN ONE PERSON HAS FOUND IT. Above this, the windows of Nick's maisonette glinted as sunlight sifted down through high pale-blue clouds. He couldn't bring himself to return to Nick's flat, couldn't bear the thought of hearing Nick's voice, of hearing him—anyone—speak her name.

"Sorry," a man said as he elbowed past. Daniel saw the man's wristwatch shining above a strip of white skin.

"Ten-thirty," Daniel said aloud. The man glanced back at him, and Daniel shook his head. "Sorry. Sorry."

He began to walk up the street. The day had grown warmer; girls strode into Camden Kitchen wearing tank tops and bicycle shorts. Still Daniel felt chilled and feverish. He shoved his hands into the pockets of his jacket, felt something that was not his cell phone. He drew it out: a business card, which read, "JUDA TRENT . . . PSYCHPOMP@DEMON.CO.UK."

He ducked into the doorway of a shop selling cheap electronics and called her.

"Juda Trent." Her Cockney voice was brisk. "Who's this?"

"Uh . . . Daniel Rowlands. We . . . we met yesterday, do you remember?"

Silence. Then, "God, of course. Where are you?"

"Camden Town. Not Nick's—I'm outside on the High Street. Look, this . . . uh, this, this will sound weird, but—"

"I think you better come over here. I'm in Islington, the very edge of Tufnell Park. Middleton Grove. Caledonia Road's the closest tube, it's about fifteen minutes' walk. Number thirty-seven. I'll be waiting."

It took him nearly an hour. Standing on the Northern Line train, he felt like an escapee from a David Lynch film, his clothes rumpled, his eyes red and aching as though he'd stared into the sun. Whenever he moved, his shirt gaped open and he could smell himself, cunt and burned sugar, an overpowering odor of green apple that made him feel faint and close to tears. He was conscious of people moving away from him; when he got off at Caledonia Road, he saw the couple behind him exchange a look, then start to laugh.

It took him several minutes to orient himself, coming out behind a newsagent and a homeless man selling *The Big Issue*. Daniel walked quickly, his eyes averted, forcing himself not to look at any of the people he passed, rehearsing what he would say to Juda Trent. She was gone: like that. I turned over in bed and—

He began to cry and stopped to lean against a plane tree by the sidewalk. His breath came in gasps; he grabbed the tree trunk and pressed his face against it, the rough bark scoring his forehead. He didn't know how long he stood there, didn't care, just stood and wept, heedless of the looks of disgust or pity thrown by passersby.

"Hey." A voice came at his shoulder. For an instant he thought it was Larkin, and the world flared white and green; then he saw a hand with blue-painted fingernails. "Hey, Daniel. Come on, then. Come with me, lad, it's not far."

She put her arm around him, and he fell against her, ashamed and horrified but unable to stop sobbing. "Oh, God. I'm sorry. I'm sorry. I didn't . . . didn't—"

"Hush, then." She took his chin and gently pushed his face back. "Oh, God, look at you. Fucking hell."

She touched the outer corner of his eye, raw with crying, glanced down at his chest and whistled as she moved his shirt to expose his neck. "Goddamn, Hayward was right. You're a bloody fool. Look what she did to you. Look what she did."

She shook her head. "All right. Can you walk? It's a bit of a ways, but I don't know that I want to be putting you into a cab like this."

"I'm okay." It hurt to talk—the words scraped his throat as though he'd swallowed splintered wood—but just saying it made him feel a bit stronger. "Yes. Let's go."

She lived in a Victorian terrace, four-story houses with neat front gardens and mown lawns, late-model Volvos and Citroëns parked in narrow driveways. Daniel was too exhausted to feel more than mild surprise at how posh her house was, with its well-tended rosebushes and flagged walk, wrought-iron lanterns and security cameras and the polished brass plate with her name on it.

"That's my office there." She led him through a clipped hedge of boxwood to the door. "Like a fucking arsenal, all the cameras, I know. I used to get hassled a lot. Gay bashers, fucking National Front kids. Bothered my clients. Here we are."

Inside, all was spacious and comforting. Big rooms washed with gold late-morning light, the walls a soothing lichen green, thick Kurdistan carpets, old pine harvest tables. Biber violin sonatas played in the background. The very calm made Daniel more anxious.

"This is your place?"

Juda smiled wryly. "I know, hard to believe, innit? Protective coloration."

They went to the kitchen. Daniel slumped into a chair while Juda got water for tea. As the electric kettle heated, she set a plate before him, with a slab of soft white cheese, strawberries, a slice of brown bread studded with bits of hazelnut.

Daniel shook his head. "I can't."

"You must eat something."

"I'll be sick."

"You'll be *very* sick if you don't get something inside you. Believe me, I know what I'm talking about. Here."

She held out the haunch of bread. The smell of roasted hazelnuts made his stomach turn, and he shook his head. "I can't," he whispered. "Please." He knew he sounded ridiculous.

"Eat it." Her tone wasn't pleading but a command. *"Now."*

She handed him the bread. He took a tiny bite, hardly enough to taste it, and immediately began to retch. Juda stood beside him, her hand on his neck. "Swallow it," she said. "Come on."

Somehow he did, forcing himself not to vomit it up again. Juda stroked his neck. "Another. Go."

He ate perhaps half of it, each bite making him double over with nausea. "I can't," he gasped, pushing the plate away. "For Christ's sake."

Juda stared down at him. "It'd be better if you did," she said, and removed the plate. But she seemed to be satisfied. "Now here's some tea—don't worry, it won't make you sick. The point of eating that was to make you feel better, not worse. Do you?"

"No."

He didn't, though his sense of horror began to recede. Certainly it was difficult to retain here, surrounded by the calm strains of violin and theorbo and lute, the red-enameled Aga range and a late David Hockney print beside the outer door.

"Well, you'll just have to take my word for it, then," said Juda. She put a steaming cup in front of him.

Daniel grimaced. "I just bet that's not Earl Grey."

"You're right. It's comfrey and boneset. But it needs to steep a few minutes, so let me have a look at you and see what kind of damage has been done."

He winced as she put her hands on his shoulders and helped him to his feet, then turned him to face her. He stared miserably into her pale eyes; when she pulled his shirt collar from his neck, he looked away. Very gingerly she touched his throat, and Daniel tried not to cry out. "Take your shirt off. I need to see the rest of you."

He obeyed, too sick and exhausted to argue, let his coat and shirt fall to the floor. "Oh, Daniel."

He turned. Within the mirror above the Aga stood a horrible piebald figure, white skin streaked with dull red. Dark bruises were scattered across his chest like lipsticked kisses. His waist looked as though it had been mauled.

"Jesus," he said.

He stared at a smear of red above his rib cage. He wasn't bleeding: the crimson skin was smooth and slightly raised, as though he bore a brand that had healed years before. The perimeter of the wound was pearled with raised bumps like a rash. He turned to catch the light streaming through the broad windows, and saw that the scar formed the perfect image of a hand. He looked at Juda. "What the fuck is it?"

"Wait here."

She left the room and returned a few minutes later with a flannel bathrobe. "Wear this. We'll have to burn that." She looked at the shirt on the floor.

"What?" Daniel felt a spark of indignation.

"Well, clean it, then."

Daniel put the robe on. Judah got a plastic bag, stuffed his shirt inside, then dropped the bag outside the back door. For a minute she remained there, and Daniel watched as she gazed out at the garden with its neat green wedge of lawn, stone statue of a smiling Kuan Yin, an English robin chirping in an apple tree. Everything seemed lovely and precise as a magazine ad—including Juda herself, in beautifully draped trousers, black silk jacket, stark white shirt. Only her blue-nailed hands seemed to belong to someone else.

And yet as he watched, Daniel felt as though blazing light suddenly infused the scene: Shadows crackled and sparked like lightning, then dissolved into the grass like water into parched ground. The robin on its branch was not a bird but part of the tree. The elegantly dressed woman in the doorway was not a woman at all but something else, something—

"See if you can keep that tea down." Juda walked back into the kitchen, motioning for him to sit. "You should be able to now."

"Right." He drew a hand across his eyes and sat. The strange brilliance subsided, along with his nausea. Now he just felt unutterably weary and light-headed. "This is like the worst hangover I ever had," he said, and sipped the tea. "Ugh."

"I could give you some honey."

"That *would* make me throw up." He gulped down most of what was in the cup, pushed it away, and counted silently to ten. "All right, Dr. Trent. Tell me. What happened?"

She pulled a chair beside him, staring at his hands clenched on the table. Very tentatively she began to speak. "Well. First off, she doesn't mean to."

"Doesn't *mean* to? Mean to what? What does she . . . how did she . . . she—"

He yanked at the flannel robe, exposing the livid scars on his chest.

"*That!*" he cried. "Why—*why?* Where did she go? Where is she? *Where?*"

"I don't know. She . . . does this. It's not her intent. She . . ."

Juda rubbed her forehead, her face strained. "How can I explain? She wants you—she wants people, she's drawn to them—"

"Who? You?" Daniel's voice rose wildly. "Did she do this to *you?*"

"No. She can't harm me. But you, people like you. It's what she does to them. When she wants them. When she sleeps with them. If you go with her, if you let her—"

"What's wrong with her, then? Is she sick? Am *I* sick now? How does she . . . what the fuck kind of woman is she . . . ?"

"That's it." Juda Trent lifted her head. Her eyes were wide, calm, not the least reassuring. "She's not a woman. She's not like you, Daniel. Not even like me," and Juda gave a small, bitter laugh. "But she wants you, she's drawn to you—that's *her* sickness, if you can call it that.

"And she poisons you. She doesn't mean to—but when she's . . . when she's aroused, when she wants someone . . . she can't help it. She never remembers afterward. She never remembers from one time to the next. She thinks—when she's with you—she thinks she's with someone else. Someone like herself. That's why her touch burns you."

"But . . . why?"

"Because you are nothing like her, Daniel. You're not who she wants."

"How can you say that?" He couldn't even laugh. It was as though he were listening to someone speak a language he didn't comprehend, Arabic or Mandarin Chinese. "The first time—I mean the first day—the first time I kissed her. This didn't happen. . . ." He touched his lips.

"No. It wouldn't. It's later. When she . . . when she loses control of what she is."

"Where is she now?"

"I don't know. She wanders off, then she comes back. Somehow I always find her."

"And you? Does she do this to you? Does she? Does she burn *you*? Let me see."

He tried to grab her wrist, but Juda pushed him away. "Don't! Daniel—stop! It's because I'm like her."

"A woman? A—"

He stopped, ashamed, and held his head in his hands. "I'm sorry, I'm sorry. God, what's happening to me? I feel like I'm losing my mind."

"You're not losing your mind. Not yet at least." Juda sighed. "Can you tell me what happened last night?"

"No." He wanted to run back into the street and find her; he wanted to punch someone. Instead he took a deep breath, trying to focus on something ordinary, something stolid and mundane.

But there was nothing mundane left in the world. He stared at his fingers splayed upon the table, saw the swirled grain of the wood beneath—a pale, fine-grained wood, ash, but how did he know that?—then furiously clenched his hand and looked away.

The mirror above the stove pulsed with motion. Red-and-blue creatures darted through the air in the garden outside. By the door a silver lozenge held the image of a boy fractured into a hundred parts, poised above a swimming pool. On the table flame-colored tongues unfurled from a gold-whorled globe; insects like emerald sparks flung themselves relentlessly against the windows, striving to gain entry. In another room unseen fingers plucked a lute.

"No," he whispered.

Nothing was ordinary. He saw that now. Everything was fertile and alive, everything. The slate countertops held the coils of imprisoned ammonites; each drop of water that fell into the sink contained a universe. He loosened his belt and undid his trousers, gazed down to see bruises blossoming on his thighs and groin, crimson and lavender and purplish green. Beneath the taut skin of his right hand, rivers coursed. Caught around his wrist was a strand of long dark hair. When he turned toward the sunlit window, the strand of hair glowed copper and green. He brought his hand to his face and let his mouth envelop his wrist, felt flame surge through his mouth to burn his lips.

"Daniel. Stop."

His withdrew his hand, gazed at a scarlet thread of blood welling around his wrist. The strand of hair was gone. He had swallowed it. As he stared at his wrist, an uncontrollable spasm shook him; he bent forward, groaning, and ejaculated against the folds of Juda's borrowed robe.

"Oh, Christ," he moaned, and staggered from the kitchen.

Juda found him in the bathroom fifteen or twenty minutes later. He had showered, and shaved using a plastic woman's razor. The flannel robe he wadded up and stuffed into a hamper. When Juda knocked at the door, he said, "Right there," his voice hoarse as from long disuse.

A moment later he emerged, bare-chested. Without a word she handed him a black linen shirt, and he put it on. The sleeves were too short for him; he rolled them up, leaving the shirt open at the throat, then turned to her and nodded.

"I'm all right now." He felt as though he'd fallen from the top of a house, broken every bone in his body, then reassembled himself: shattered, but somehow alive. "I'd like you to tell me about Larkin."

They went into the living room. Juda gestured for him to sit on the couch. The curtains had been drawn, suffusing the room with twilight. She curled into the corner of the couch, her hair agleam in the near darkness.

"Well, Daniel Rowlands. What do you want me to tell you?"

"The truth. Where is she from?"

"The truth?" She gave him a sideways grin. "You're on sabbatical, Daniel, are you sure the *truth* is what you really want?"

"I seem to have spent the last forty-eight hours making a royal asshole out of myself. I think you better tell me something."

"'Do you think the things people make fools of themselves about are any less real and true than the things they behave sensibly about?' The truth? She's not from here. She escaped into London from somewhere else. She is very dangerous, but she's most dangerous to those who seek her out."

"Like me."

Again that crooked smile. "You're a lucky one, Daniel. Those are just flesh wounds."

She leaned forward to touch the crimson wristlet on his right arm. Pain flared through him; he flinched, and she drew away. "You should have seen some of the others. Not a pretty sight."

"I bet." He sucked his breath in, waited for the throbbing to subside. "Okay. New question. Can I ask why you became a Jungian analyst?"

"Because I was interested in how people like you react under extreme circumstances."

People like me? Daniel wondered, but only said, "You mean when they meet someone like Larkin?"

"Among other things. Such as when they confront a reality they have not been aware of before—say, their own mortality. 'Terror management': how people have adapted to living their brief lives, knowing they will end. There are complex sexual issues. Issues of identity."

"Boundary issues?"

She said nothing, and again Daniel wondered at her choice of words.

How people have adapted to living their brief lives . . . people like you . . .

Not how do *we* live; not people like *us*.

He sat for a minute, then asked, "You said someone was not watchful who should have been. Who was that?"

"Me."

"I don't understand."

"You don't need to."

Daniel smiled. This was like an interview with an unwilling celebrity.

"So what's her real name? 'Larkin'—she told me she made that up. She said she does it all the time. Who is *she* when she's at home?"

"She has a lot of names."

"Yeah? Such as?"

"We don't say them."

Daniel laughed. "What is this, some kind of Jungian cult? I thought all you guys *did* was come up with names!"

Juda shook her head. Her gaze was cold, measuring. "You wouldn't understand it."

"Try me."

"I can't."

"Why not?" This was the wrong tack; he knew that from hostile encounters with more performers than he could remember. But suddenly Daniel felt reckless and angry and even exhilarated, ready to wring a meaning out of the last two days, even if it meant getting himself thrown from this house back into Nick's orbit, even if it meant crawling back to the *Horizon* before his sabbatical was up. "Is this some kind of witness-protection program for the criminally insane? Is she that dangerous?"

He stared challengingly at Juda; she stared back. "Yes. She is that dangerous."

"Then what's her name? Have I ever heard of her?"

Juda said something he couldn't understand, and he shook his head. "What?"

She said it again: Bleth or Beth. Then,

"*She grants humans glories undreamed of.*
Her beauty seduces them, her smile, her eyes,
Her face a flower.
Grant me a song that will seduce all who hear it
Grant me that power
And I will sing only, ever, of you."

Daniel frowned. "What's that from?"

"One of the Homeric hymns." In the subdued light, with her stark silk suit and calm pale eyes, she looked nothing like the scruffy gamine he'd met yesterday, and nothing at all like a boy. Then her mouth parted in a smile without warmth, and once again he was staring at a young man, sly-faced.

> *"If strange things happen where she is*
> *So that men say that graves open*
> *And the dead walk, or that futurity*
> *Becomes a womb, and the unborn are shed—*
> *Such portents are not to be wondered at."*

Daniel's neck prickled. "That's Graves again. Not a primary source."

"*She* is a primary source—that's what I'm trying to tell you." At his scowl Juda shrugged. "I gave you fair warning."

She glanced at her watch. "I have someone coming at one. You can keep that shirt if you want."

She stood, waiting for him to do the same. Daniel remained where he was. What if he were to refuse to leave? What if he were to demand that she find Larkin for him? Juda must know where she'd gone—maybe even somewhere in this house, or in her office, or—

Then he recalled Juda's kindness in seeing him in the first place. He had called *her* after all, a virtual stranger, and she had taken him in, fed him, clothed him. . . .

He had a flash of himself sitting at the kitchen table, coming uncontrollably on her flannel robe, and felt his face go scarlet.

"Thanks," he said, and stood. She walked him to the door. When they reached it, she put a hand upon his shoulder.

"Daniel. Let this be the end of it. With Larkin."

He shook his head. "I can't promise that," he said. "I wish I could—or no, I *don't* wish I could. You're asking me to forget I ever saw her."

"I didn't ask you to do that," said Juda. "You couldn't if you tried. Not now."

Her voice drifted off. She started to open the door, then stopped. "Your book—it's about the Arthurian cycle, is it?"

"Not really. Well, maybe a little, I guess. Mostly it's about Tristan and Iseult, romantic love. I wanted to take up where de Rougemont left off," he said wryly.

Juda gave him her mocking smile. "Maybe you've gained new insights. Most roses have thorns, you know."

She opened the door for him, and Daniel suddenly understood the name she had pronounced before. As he stepped back out into the yellow-glazed afternoon, he turned, placing a hand on the door to keep her from shutting it on him.

"Are there owls in London?" he asked.

She stared at him, silent, but he could see a darker sheen pass across her eyes and hear the quick intake of her breath. Daniel stared back at her and nodded.

"Because there is one now," he said, and left.

CHAPTER ELEVEN

Down to the Wire

Whoever *we reached Dulles, four private* security guards were waiting in front of the hangar for me. I handed over copies of the contract and customs forms and my passport, they removed the crate and whisked it off to the waiting Gulfstream. I was subjected to X rays and the theremin whine of a metal-detection wand before being escorted to the plane.

By the time we finally took off, it was broad daylight. A steward dressed as expensively as the limo driver served me garlic-roasted chicken and haricots verts catered by the Four Seasons in Georgetown, crème brûlée finished off in the Gulfstream's galley. There was an audio-video library, a shelf of books by Joseph Mitchell and William Trevor and Jack Higgins. I could have watched anything I wanted on the wide-screen TV. Instead I knocked off a bottle of St.-Emilion, staring out the window and thinking.

I had last taken my medications the previous morning; I'd forgotten my evening dose. So: a little over twenty-four hours. Enough time to open a crack in my skull and let the light seep back in, but not enough time for me to start tripping off the line.

Was it?

Because I could feel something happening. The rush of wings behind my eyes, that sense of growing out of my body, of the world falling away around me as though I were a tree bursting explosively from the earth. Outside, the cloudless sky deepened to indigo as the day reeled forward. The wings became another heart beating inside mine; I felt an ache, a longing for something I couldn't place, and, for the first time in years, the stirrings of desire.

It was early evening but still bright when we landed at Gatwick. We taxied toward another private hangar, where I went through the security dance again. I watched as a half-dozen guards unloaded the painting; then *Iseult* and I met with more security staff and customs officials, in a security-screening room that looked like the special effects department of a medium-size film company. The security chamber's door opened and a thin woman with blond hair and black rubber ankle boots appeared, flanked by two more guards armed with scary sunglasses and chest holsters. A Winsoame photo ID hung from a chain around her neck.

"Hello, Valentine," the woman said briskly. She opened a leather portfolio, removed a sheaf of papers on a clipboard, and handed them to me. "Janet Keightley. I'm Mr. Learmont's acquisitions manager. Flight all right? Yes? Well, then. If you'll just sign off on this, I'll arrange for the limo to your hotel."

I looked over the papers, a sheet signed by Learmont authorizing her to take the painting. I hesitated, then signed and handed them back to her.

"Thank you." She looked up at me, and I saw her blush slightly. "I'll be happy to give you a ride, if you like. Mr. Learmont's made arrangements for you to stay at Brown's. It's a lovely hotel."

"Will you be there?"

Her blush grew deeper. I toyed with the notion of making a play for her but decided I didn't want to get that close to Learmont.

"I'm not certain what Mr. Learmont has me scheduled for tonight."
She pulled out her cell phone. "Would you like to wait here while I have
my car brought around?"

"No, that's all right—I have something I need to pick up myself." I
pulled out my wallet and fished around till I found the key to the storage locker. "And I don't need the hotel. I'm staying with friends in
Camden Town."

She put her call through, collating the signed pages into another,
smaller portfolio that she gave to me. I looked through it—copies of the
contract for *Iseult,* a sheaf of legal papers. There was also a separate
packet that held any other information I might conceivably need while
in London, along with a calling card, a little plastic wallet containing
fifty quid in five-pound notes, and a prepaid chit for a car service.

"Gee, no toothbrush?" I smiled. "Well, thanks anyway."

"Are you sure you don't want a ride?"

"Uh-huh. That's what I'm getting now—my bike. I used to live in
London. Stored my motorcycle here for when I came back over."

She glanced at my worn leather backpack. "Is that all the luggage
you brought?"

"I travel light. Everything I need is here. Well, almost everything." I
held her gaze until I saw her flush again. "Sure *you* don't want a ride?"

"You're tempting me—but no, I'm sorry." She turned and motioned to the security guards, signaling she was finished. "I just told Mr.
Learmont we were on our way back. He's extremely excited about this
particular painting."

"More so than usual?"

"Well, yes, I believe he is." She glanced at her clipboard again, gave
me a curious look. "You're not by any chance the artist, are you?"

"No. That was my grandfather."

"Ah.

I followed her outside. The Gulfstream had taxied off. A Rolls idled on the tarmac, its back open so that I could glimpse my grandfather's painting cradled in an elaborate leather-and-mesh sling. "Looks like it's traveling in style," I said.

Janet Keightley stuck out her hand. I held it just a little too long, then tipped my head to her. "Sure you won't change your mind?"

She smiled regretfully. "Wish I could. Maybe tomorrow?"

"Maybe."

I waved as the limo bore her and the painting off into the haze of South London.

I had a cigarette, then caught a ride with one of the security guards who was going off duty. He gave me a lift to the storage facility, an anonymous, slightly sinister cluster of buildings on the outskirts of the airport.

"Motorbike, then?" he asked, tossing his uniform jacket into the back of his Citroën. "Triumph?"

"Vincent."

"Really?" He whistled. "What, Black Lightning? Like the song?"

"Black Shadow."

"Fucking hell." He looked at me and shook his head, pulled in front of my rented storage bay, its sheet-metal door throwing waves of heat across the tarmac. "You need a place to keep that, give me a call then, right?" he shouted as he drove off. "I'll take care of 'er for you!"

I walked over to the shed, exultant. I jammed the key into the door, yanked it open, and there she was.

"Oh, baby," I said, dropping my backpack. "Baby, baby. You ready for me?"

Sun poured molten into the shed. I stepped inside, blinking. When I touched the bike's handlebars they felt soft as tar. Gently I wheeled it out and into a lozenge of shade at the side of the building. I locked the bay and turned to my bike.

She was a 1955 Vincent-HRD Black Shadow, one of the last produced before the factory shut down. I'd bought her five years earlier, when I'd briefly gone off my meds after moving to London for a stint—I took the money that should have gone to pay my rent and got the bike, then ended up staying with Simon's friend Nick Hayward. At the time I couldn't explain to anyone why I had to have the bike; a typical manic episode, Simon thought.

But now I knew. Now I remembered: I'd bought her so I'd have her now.

"Miss me, darling?"

I lit another cigarette and went to work. I checked the gearbox, swiping dust and dead bugs from the stands and tire struts, ran a bandanna across the rear suspension with its original cadmium plate—I'd spent months looking for a bike that hadn't been restored with chromium or stainless steel. Last of all I went over the fuel tank, with its triumphant winged Mercury soaring over the words BLACK SHADOW.

I made sure I had enough fuel to get to a gas station, tied the bandanna around my head, and got on, knapsack limp on my back and the Vincent beneath me live and warm as flesh. The engine choked once, then turned over, its roar lost in the thrum of traffic from the motorway. I circled the storage building, leaving a spume of white exhaust, cannoned out onto the road and headed north. The Vincent's oversized speedometer clocked up to 150 mph; I peaked at 90, weaving in and out of the black stream of cars and minicabs roiling around the city like smoke pouring from a crack.

It had been five years, but I still had my key to Nick's flat. I actually hadn't seen Nick himself in years. He was always on tour, or in the studio, or shacked up with a girl somewhere. I figured that this time I'd make a point of thanking him in person.

Traffic was heavy on Tottenham Court Road, so I detoured up to Tufnell Park and drove through Archway to Crouch End. It was a part of the city that always filled me with an almost unbearable nostalgia, mixed with a kind of despair: all those mock Tudors, each with its slip of lawn, pebble-dash walls, plastic flower boxes designed to resemble terra-cotta, plaster garden gnomes with chipped conical hats standing guard over beds of primroses and bluebells homesick for the woods.

It was utterly unlike American suburbia; eerier, the obsessive need for order more desperate, as though there were something dangerous and chaotic to be kept at bay. Like so much of London, it reminded me of something I could no longer recall clearly—a fragment of a dream, some shard of memory pried from me during my months at McLean, lost in the pharmaceutical clouds that had enveloped me since then. It made me ache—a real physical ache, hunger and thirst and desire all bizarrely focused on brick terraces and the sound of birdsong in flowering crabapple trees.

I let the Vincent idle at a stoplight, then turned onto Holloway Road. Traffic was heavy here. Waves of loss and an almost sexual longing made me unsteady on my bike. I decided to stop, parking in front of a pub. It was already packed with people celebrating the end of the week, so I ducked into a grocer's next door and bought an orange squash. I took up most of the shop, nearly knocking over a potted plastic fern as I fumbled for my change. The girl behind the counter stared at the Vincent, threads of exhaust rising from its engine box, then at me.

"You with the Steam Fair, then?"

I gulped down the squash and shook my head. "What's that?"

She pointed at a poster on the door. "Over at Priory Park. You look like them folk. Gypsies." She grinned. "Guess not."

I tossed the empty bottle, waved good-bye, and took off. Half an hour later, I was in Camden Town.

There was a gated alley off Inverness Street where Nick stored trash bins and leftover bits of amplifiers. A drunk had passed out in front of the locked door; I nudged him with my boot.

"Hey. You can't sleep here."

His bleary eyes opened. He started to mouth off, then got a good look at me and quickly stumbled to his feet. "Sorry, squire—din' know there was gentry here," he said, lurching backward into the street and making a clumsy bow. "N'arm done, right? Right?"

"Right." I unlocked the gate, parked the Vincent inside, and locked up again, then started for Nick's flat. I went only a few steps before I stopped.

I had spent a lot of time in London over the years, much of it right here in Camden Town. Getting fucked up, getting laid, doing pickup gigs with bands that'd hire me for my looks, then come after me with knives when I took off with the lead singer's girlfriend. The city— especially this grimy, tourist-infested part of it—lost its charm for me about the same time I put the Vincent into storage outside Gatwick. I'd had a scare over an HIV test, got docked for more VAT than I should have, and lost a job working on a show that went on to Broadway. I'd burned out on London; that's what I thought anyway.

But now, as I stood on the corner of Inverness and the High Street, I felt that same intense, nearly sexual anticipation, a kind of excitement that made me feel like I was nineteen again, looking at a night when I knew I'd score, when I knew I'd end up tangled with some girl, hours and hours to go before the sun came up.

And when it did, I'd just be getting started; it would all be just the beginning of something.

Like now. It was a rush so powerful I could feel the blood stamping at my temples, felt myself grow hard as the hairs on my arms moved in the warm breeze. The smell of green apples wafted from a barrow packing up in Inverness. There was a cluster of girls in front of the Virgin megastore across the street; they stared at me, whispering behind their hands. In front of Nick's flat, a black-and-white dog jumped up on its hind legs and began barking, its pointed muzzle aimed at a sky green with dusk. The windows of old brick buildings blazed like they were on fire. I looked at it all and felt the way I did back when I was a kid, perched on my stool in Red's workshop, staring at the page in front of me with its labyrinth of trees and faces, thinking, *It's mine, it's mine. . . .*

"Fucking hell," I said, and laughed out loud. On the corner of the High Street, a short man with a red hat turned and stared at me. I stared back, grinning, then yelled at him.

"Mine!"

His eyes widened, not in fear but a kind of shocked recognition. He turned and clapped his hands. The black-and-white dog reared back up on its hind legs and began walking toward him, gave a sudden leap, and jumped into the little man's arms.

"Forty minutes!" the man cried. "Forty minutes!"

He turned and ran up the street toward Camden Market.

I stared after him, still laughing, then unlocked and shoved open the door to Nick's flat and strode inside.

Mine, I thought as the metal door boomed shut. *It all belongs to me.*

Not much had changed in Nick's place since I'd last been there. It still smelled of coffee beans and the bitter residue of hashish, old books and the hemp-seed oil Nick used on his hands. One side of the living room was given over to bookshelves and vintage guitars, the other to an antique desk and new digital recording equipment, tiny computers like silvery eggs nested side by side on a long table beneath narrow windows overlooking the High Street. I dropped my knapsack in the kitchen, out of habit checked the back door that opened onto a rooftop patio, replete with bay trees and blue-glazed pots of tropical grass and flowers. Over the last ten years, the flat had been broken into twice, though never while I was staying; prowlers had hopped over from the neighboring rooftop, pried the door open, and made their way into the kitchen before someone called the police. After the second break-in,

Nick had a barred iron security door installed. I made sure the key was still in place, hanging above the doorframe, and briefly considered going outside but decided I was too beat.

Instead I bombed around the kitchen for a few minutes, opening drawers and rifling the stacks of CDs on the table, idly checking Nick's answering machine for messages. Nick's manager, someone in Toronto checking on a club date, and Nick himself, worried-sounding and looking for someone named Daniel.

"Daniel, call me on the mobile. You're a fucking mess. You have to—"
Click.

I switched the machine off, looked around to see if Nick had left his usual List of Important Things—letters to be posted, plants to be watered, names of other visitors who might be dropping by.

But I couldn't find anything. The air felt oddly charged, the way it does before a high wind hits, and there was a faint, pervasive odor—the scent of green apples, so sweetly enticing that I found myself looking to see if Nick had some hidden stash of fruit behind the amps and fax machine.

He didn't. There were drifts of sheet music and disks covering his desk, a digitally enhanced portrait of Nick and a woman with short silvery hair. I finally wandered into the guest room, a small chamber with a single grilled window framing the rooftop garden. The bed was covered with a duvet and matching pillow. Beside the wardrobe a vintage woolen jacket was draped across a table. There were books stacked on the desk, as well as a laptop and PalmPilot. I glanced at the books. An academic journal called *Tristania,* photocopies of Aubrey Beardsley pictures, request forms from the British Library and a bunch of things in library binding: *Lancelot of the Laik and Sir Tristrem; The Saga of Tristram and Isond; Sir Tristrem: A Metrical Romance of the Thirteenth Century* by Thomas of Erceldoune, called the Rhymer.

I set down my glass of water and picked up a battered paperback held together with a rubber band, slid the elastic off, and picked through the pages beneath. Denis de Rougemont, *Love in the Western World*, annotated in four different shades of highlighter.

"Do you know," she says to him, "that I am a sprite?" Eros has taken the guise of Woman, and symbolizes both the other world and the nostalgia which makes us despise earthly joys. But the symbol is ambiguous, since it tends to mingle sexual attraction with *eternal* desire. The Essylt mentioned in sacred legends as being both "an object of contemplation and a mystic vision" stirred up a yearning for what lies beyond embodied forms. Although she was beautiful and desirable for herself, it was her nature to vanish. "The Eternal Feminine leads us away," Goethe said, and "Woman is Man's goal," according to Novalis.

I yawned and dropped the book, loose pages scattering across the desk. I glanced at the bed and wondered if I'd made a mistake not going to Learmont's posh hotel. Nick's guest bed had always been too small for me; right now it looked positively doll-like.

But I was too tired to hassle with anything else. I sat down heavily, the mattress creaking. I took off my boots and T-shirt, dumped them on the floor, and turned off the lamp. Even with the faded curtain drawn, the room buzzed with the electric-blue glow of London night. Voices and snatches of music floated up from the High Street, a monotonous, taunting song chanted by a boy with a thick East End accent.

"Up *and down,* up *and down*
I will lead them up *and down. . . ."*

I shifted, kicking off covers as I tried to get comfortable. At last I settled my head on the pillow and shut my eyes, hoping that exhaustion would do its part.

"Damn it."

Something was under the pillow, something hard. I stuck my hand under it and found a book. I started to toss it onto the floor, then stopped. I reached over and switched the light back on.

"What the fuck . . . ?"

I sat up, heart hammering as I stared at what I held. Even after all those years, my thumb automatically found the cover's frayed edge and slid beneath. The book fell open to where I had last left off drawing in it. A thicket of vines and brambles, a pair of slanted eyes with the irises inked in green, and painstakingly formed words beneath.

He shouted to her that she could not hide from him forever. He would never stop looking for her, no, not in a thousand years! For he is her lord and she is his Queen. She is the world and it is inside her. Vernoraxia would not change no matter how long she remained away from him. There will be no balance until she returns and

I grabbed the side table, desperate for something solid, and felt the wood split beneath my fingers.

"Oh, God," I said. "Oh, God."

It was my notebook, the one I had been working on when my brother shipped me off to McLean. *Ealwearld: Its History,* Volume 7. I stared at the cover, my grandfather's entwined initials above my own swooping adolescent hand, the speckles of ink left by Radborne worked by me into ivy and dogwood blossoms, the faces of birds and women, faceted dragonfly eyes and flowers with the mouths and genitals of men.

jc
vernoraxia
volume vii
"closer"

I let it fall open again and knew just what page would reveal itself—the image of King Herla, maddened by Vernoraxia's flight into the darkness, at his side the great wolfhound poised to leap from a ragged promontory. My mind spiraled back to myself at fourteen, sitting on a rock at Knight's Head and sketching the cliff while Red was clamming on the beach below. As I read now, the cold scent of sea and kelp-strewn mud rose from the page, and the sound of plovers keening on the beach.

My curse is this. Your touch will be madness to anyone but me. You will raven them and they would rather die. I will set my wolfhound here to stand guard and he will not move until you return, nay, though it takes an hundred years. For though you flee we are bound together and Vernoraxia with us, O we are, O Vernoraxia, O my Beloved.

The words began to ripple on the page. I shut my eyes, trembling with rage and loss and the vertiginous feeling that something I had thought irredeemable, something as profound and terrible and final as death, had been miraculously undone. Outside, music rose from the café next door; I could hear the drone of street-cleaning equipment and see flashing yellow lights behind the drapes. I stood and walked unsteadily into the living room, my sketchbook clutched to my chest. I began at the far wall, at first going carefully through the shelves and pulling out books, one by one, then wildly grasping whatever I could find.

"Where are the rest?" I grabbed a dictionary and ripped it open, tearing pages from it as though my books might be nestled inside. "You son of a bitch, what did you do with them? *Where are you?*"

I took books from the shelves and threw them onto the floor, trampling and kicking them aside until the room was white with pages. When the shelf was empty, I stopped, dazed, then knelt among the ruined books. Those that had somehow remained intact I ripped apart, their spines splitting in my hands and covers exploding into fragments of cardboard and pulp.

"Where are you?" I shouted. I picked up *Closer* where it had fallen beside me and cradled it. *"What have you done with her?"*

The phone started to ring. I stood and yanked the base set from the wall and threw it into the hallway. Then I staggered into the kitchen, shreds of paper stuck to my bare chest and blood oozing from a gash on my arm.

"No," I whispered hoarsely. "Fucking Simon. You fucking bastard, where are they? *What did you do with her?"*

It was not until I sank into a chair and stared down at the cover of my sketchbook, the shadowy crescent of a scarlet fingerprint blooming beneath a woman's profile, that I began to cry.

CHAPTER TWELVE

The Rock and Castle of Seclusion

He returned to his room. Breaghan's duties did not seem to include tending him, so Radborne unpacked his own small valise, placing his few items in the wardrobe. Then he set up his easel in a corner with his color box alongside it. He moved slowly, fearful of further injuring his arm, but after an hour or so, the pain eased, and he even managed to move his bed opposite the window, giving him a clear view of the ruined spire on its lonely spine of rock and the dark sky beyond.

Still, even this minor housekeeping exhausted him. When at half past six Breaghan knocked to summon him for dinner, he begged her give his apologies to Dr. Learmont.

"Please tell him I'm unwell—no, thank you, I don't care for any dinner. A good night's sleep, that's what I need."

"Are you certain, sir?"

"Yes, yes, of course—please."

She cocked her head. A sheen clung to her livid blue jaw, so that she seemed to give him a monstrous grin. "I could bring you a tray, sir?"

"No, no, no . . ."

Quickly he shut the door and started to laugh. "A madhouse!" He took off his jacket and was placing it in the wardrobe when he noticed a bulge in one pocket.

Learmont's book, the book Swinburne had shown him. He shut the wardrobe, settled himself on the bed, and began to leaf through the volume.

It was mostly fairy tales, and tales about other rustic supernaturals. Cornish giants, piskies and demons, a section on mermaids and mermen, another on saints. There was an entire chapter devoted to King Arthur, and one on lost cities, another that dealt exclusively with "the virtues of fire." Radborne paged through them thoughtfully, wondering what Swinburne might have found of interest here. Burning feet? The accounts of Sir Tristram, or the drowned city of Lyonesse?

This last reminded him of the story told by Evienne Upstone. He paused, gazing at the window, then flipped to the back of the book. Two loose sheets of cheap blue postal paper were stuck here, folded in half. He smoothed them onto the bed.

They were filled with Swinburne's writing—he checked the hand against the signature at the front of the volume and yes, it was the poet's. Disordered ramblings, of interest to Swinburne or Learmont perhaps, but no one else. Radborne folded the pages together again and stuck them back into the book. He thumbed idly through the volume until an illustration caught him, an etching of a knight and a greyhound.

Queen Eselt, read the title.

A smile washed across Radborne's face: he might do some preliminary sketches from stories in this book. Authentic English folklore, the sort of thing one found sometimes in the ladies' magazines back home. Perhaps he could persuade *Leslie's* to publish one or two of them— certainly Learmont would not object, if some modest financial agreement could be reached. He lay back onto the bed and began to read.

In ancient times a knight lost himself on the moors near Tintagel Head. He and his men wandered for many days, unable to find themselves clear of the mist; but at last a morning dawned when they saw before them a great cleft in the stones. A light came from it, and so the knight bade the others follow him inside. There they found themselves in another country. The sky was green, and the air; even the people had a greenish skin. They brought the knight to meet their Queen, who was named Queen Eselt; and not much time passed before the knight was wed to her.

Then there was much feasting and dancing through the night, but at dawn the knight asked if he could return to his own palace. Queen Eselt consented, giving him many fine gifts. Last of all she gave him a white brachet which sat upon his saddle; but before they left, Queen Eselt warned him that when he and his men returned to the upper world, they were not to dismount before the dog did.

They journeyed back to the upper world. But in his haste one of the men forgot the Queen's warning. He jumped down from his horse and immediately turned to dust, as behind him the others were frozen in their tracks. They remain there to this very day; the dog has not jumped down yet.

The dog has not jumped down yet.
He reread the last line, and then the entire story.
" 'The dog has not jumped down yet,' " he whispered.
What could it mean? He thought of Cobus Candell with his tribute of orpiment and sable and linen, the unfinished painting of a madwoman. *They've just come from the wedding night.*
He remembered a story his mother had read it to him, a story from the book of tales that had been one of his childhood treasures. *Only guess my name and you will be freed.*
Only guess. The image of the woman upstairs expanded within him like a drawn breath, a woman standing before a window filled with quicksilver light, a woman standing at the edge of Blackfriars Bridge. Evienne Upstone and the figure he had glimpsed in a shaft of sun in Southwark.
And yet neither of these was the eidolon he held in memory as though it were a coin clutched in his hand. The curve of her cheek, her

autumn hair lifted by the breeze (there had been no breeze), her mouth pressed against his cheek (it had been her palm, not her mouth), her breasts glimpsed where the bodice of her dress had parted (there had been no parting): all of this was more real than anything in the room around him, more real than the woman pacing in her cell upstairs.

Upstairs.

He could hear her now, walking back and forth, back and forth, as though tracing a path within a labyrinth. He looked up. In the ceiling above him, a tunnel spiraled, the same passage that Jacobus Candell had painted. *The dog has not jumped down yet.* Stone and plaster crumbled to reveal a nautilus with a woman at its heart, her eyes welcoming and mouth parted to pronounce his name. Radborne gasped, then laughed, then began to sing to himself.

> *"I turned and beside me found*
> *The trace of your cheek in my bed. . . ."*

He lay back upon the thin mattress, closed his eyes, and concentrated upon the sound of her footsteps pacing the floor above. Back and forth, back and forth, the sound quickening with his heart and breath. Her skirts moved slowly across the floor, not silk or linen but a swirl of underwater green, fronds parting to reveal white sand like flesh upon the sea floor. If he lifted his hand, he could touch her, a warm curve shaping itself to his palm, softer than Candell's sable, softer than anything. He smelled vetiver, vervain, verdigris; tasted bice metallic as scorched pennies, *mustn't lick your fingers.*

But he did, thrusting one hand into his mouth as the other unbuttoned his trousers, his cock springing free of the knot of cloth and curled warm hair. Above him her steps came more and more rapidly, like a finger tapping glass. He breathed fast and shallow; the room was cold, but he was on fire. His back arched, his mouth twisted to speak her name, but she had no name, only color: *asphodel mignonette malachieteus chartreuse viridis peridot emeraude woodbine vetiver ver-vain. . . .*

When he came, his shout echoed Candell's: *You must learn her name!* And gasping, he rolled over and grabbed at his open sketchbook on the floor, grabbed his pencil and scrawled it there—

Green, he wrote, the letters loping across page after page after page, *Green Green Green Green Green Her name is Green.*

He woke next morning early, honeyed light all around and Radborne ebullient as though he were entering his studio for the first time. He sat up, the chill nestling into his crotch where he had forgotten to button his trousers. He dressed quickly, grabbed his sketchbook, pencils, and overcoat, and ran downstairs.

Dr. Learmont was in the dining room, an empty plate before him and a notebook and bottle of ink. His face was pale, his lanky hair disheveled.

"Mr. Comstock, good day to you. Breaghan will be busy this morning. There is some porridge on the side table there, and coffee and sausages." He bent back over his notebook.

Radborne got himself breakfast and proceeded to eat. Not even Breaghan's lumpy porridge could dampen his spirits. His exhilaration ballooned; he almost laughed out loud, but Learmont's grave expression kept him in check. Radborne could feel a sort of light leaking out from behind his own eyes, spattering the tablecloth with pale emeraude. So he kept his head down, gazing with a furtive smile at his porridge. *Green,* he thought, *the secret is Green.*

After several minutes Dr. Learmont looked up. "I administered another dose to Cobus an hour ago," he said. "When I went with Breaghan to bring him breakfast, I found him still extremely agitated."

Learmont refilled his pen and made a notation in a long column. Radborne nodded without looking up. Eyes, eyes, watch the eyes.

"We often found mercurial blue pills effective," he offered.

"Perhaps," said Learmont, and continued to write.

"A suggestion only," said Radborne. He waited until Learmont turned to reach for something on the table behind him, then shot a look at his notebook.

He expected to see a record of sedatives and dosages. And yes, one side of the book had a recipe scrawled upon it, very badly spelled.

COFF DROPS

2 OZ LODDANUM

1 OZ PARREYGORRIDE

2 OZ ELIXED VITRAL

6 OZ OF HONNEY

2 OZ OF SWEAT NITEN

MICKSSIT AL UPP TOGETHER A TIASONFULL WIN THE COFF IS

BAD

He glanced at the other page.

JACOBUS CANDELL, NOTES FOR THE ELIMINATION OF A
PAINTING BY ITS SUBJECT BY THOMAS LEARMONT

A Fairy Wife Caught	Bethlem Hospital Sept. 1856
Delectation	Bethlem Hosp. April 1874
The Circle at Tintagel	Sarsinmoor Asylum, June 1879
The Wedding Party	Sarsinmoor Asylum, Dec. 1880
The Dog Has Not Jumped Down Yet	Sarsinmoor Asylum, Unfinished

No pharmacopoeia at all, but a record of Candell's paintings. As Dr. Learmont settled himself again, Radborne swiftly turned back to his breakfast. The doctor returned to his notes. After several minutes he spoke.

"Given Cobus's agitated state, Mr. Comstock, I think it best for you not to visit him today." He glanced at Radborne's things near the door. "I see you've brought your sketchbook. You might enjoy walking about the headland, if the weather stays fine. Though I wouldn't recommend going farther into the moor yet—a treacherous place."

"So I've been told." Radborne tapped his spoon against his bowl; then, startled, held the utensil to one side.

He was not imagining it. A flare of green raced around the spoon's bowl, the way alcoholic spirits will burn blue when ignited. His eyes widened; he hurriedly composed himself and looked back at Learmont. "Mr. Candell—is he always so violent?"

"No. In fact he has been almost extraordinarily gentle, here and at Bethlem. I would not have sequestered myself alone with him if that were not so. Only once have I witnessed such a display of temper from him, and that was when he first met with Miss Upstone. I had thought she might model for him—under supervision, of course."

"But she has!" broke in Radborne. "The painting he's working on now—every figure in it is her. Even the men. All of them, every last one!"

"And yet he only met her once, and was most inhospitable." Learmont pushed aside his notebook. "I had hoped he might be cured—he could never be released, of course, but one always hopes for some return to sanity. He seemed to respond so well to the refined morphine solution."

He stared broodingly at the table. "It is very important to me that he continues his painting. What did you think of his work, Mr. Comstock?"

"Well . . . his technique is fine. You said he was at the Academy, so I'd expect that. But he seems drawn to the same subjects. Fairies, I mean."

"That was his bread and butter, before his crime. He could have enjoyed a success as great as Burne-Jones or Millais. You noted all the Shakespearean references?"

"Yes. But the painting he is working on now. It is—it seems the product of a disordered mind. I gather that it was inspired by one of your own stories."

"No. The very opposite. He began work on it at Bethlem years ago. The story I collected from an old woman in Lanteglos. There are literary precedents, of course. Our friend Lady Wilde is attempting to work them into a book of her own."

"What a peculiar coincidence, then. That he painted it." From the corner of his eye, Radborne glimpsed a glaucous shimmer, like the refraction of sunlight on moving water. He swallowed.

"I think I will take your suggestion," he said. "I'm going to explore the headland. That is, if you really don't need me?"

"Not this morning, no." Learmont stood and waited for Radborne to collect his sketchbook, then brightened. "Wait—I do have a thought! I've arranged to move Miss Upstone to the cottage at the tip of the island. That was my other task this morning, and it strikes me that you could look in on her. My colleague Dr. Stansel at Exeter had a pleasant success last year with some ladies he ensconced at the seaside. It's my thought that Miss Upstone's melancholy might be eased if she were exposed to fresh air and sunlight. It is very important that she continue to paint."

"Why?" said Radborne irritably. The flickering green shape was making his head ache. "I would think bed rest and quiet would suit her better. And how can you possibly leave her alone and unsupervised if she's so desperate?"

"Breaghan will stay with her. The poor soul is remarkably devoted to Miss Upstone. But I would be very grateful if you would inquire briefly at the cottage. I've had no chance to visit her myself."

"Yes, all right." Radborne nodded. "I'll make sure I do."

* * *

He felt, leaving the manor house, that he had somehow shed his skin as a snake does, a sudden sloughing off of something as large as himself but scarred, scales falling behind him and the glitter about his eyes exploding into sky. In the courtyard he looked up into a brilliance terrible and minatory, stared down and saw in the furze myriad moving things among twisted spikes of grass and thorny green.

It did not frighten him. On the contrary he laughed, then turned from side to side as if acknowledging others there unseen: making certain that they registered his recognition, that they knew he had not been taken by surprise. He had gone only a few steps before he abruptly dropped to the grass, as though he had taken an arrow in his back. Immediately he sat up, his sketchbook open and his hand fumbling for the pencil in his breast pocket. Then he settled back and began to draw.

He drew the woman on the bridge, the span behind her like a rocket's fiery wake. He had in mind a poem. Not Swinburne but Keats—

. . . her hair she frees;
Unclasps her warmed jewels one by one;
Loosens her fragrant boddice; by degrees
Her rich attire creeps rustling to her knees:
Half-hidden, like a mermaid in sea-weed,
Pensive awhile she dreams awake. . . .

It was not Fair Madeline he drew upon the Eve of St. Agnes but Evienne Upstone. And she was not in a bedroom with her lover hiding inside a cupboard, but floating above Blackfriars Bridge. He sketched quickly, struggling to keep the paper from flapping in the wind; more than once his hasty fingers smudged the page.

At last it was done. For a long time he sat and stared, seeing both the image on the page and the one behind his eyes, and somewhere behind both of them, the woman herself, her eyes like windblown leaves and her smell—grass, salt, crushed green apples.

"Where are you?" he said. He blinked, and small things scattered in the grass. "I'm not blind, you know."

He closed his sketchbook and put away his pencil, stood and began to walk to the cottage.

Once crofters must have lived in it. The deeply recessed windows still held shreds of lace curtain. Broken stalks of daisy and bracken spilled across the granite doorsill. From the chimney rose a white skein of smoke. The turf in front had been recently tilled, and a few late-blooming flowers straggled toward the sunlight, white-petaled, their leaves freckled with earth. Radborne hesitated, then rapped tentatively, his sketchbook tucked beneath his arm. From inside he heard the scrape of a chair. He waited, had just decided to turn away when the door opened.

"Oh—sir—"

It was Breaghan. Her eyes glittered bird-bright as she turned to someone in the room. "Miss, please, it's the new doctor from manor house."

"Yes, yes, please, come in," said Evienne Upstone, and Radborne stepped inside.

She was standing beside a faded green velvet armchair on the far side of the tiny room. Whitewashed walls, exposed beams blackened with smoke above a stone hearth where a peat fire burned. There were homespun rugs on the floor, a table and chairs, a canvas cot that must be Breaghan's, another bed made up with a white coverlet embroidered with poppies. In one corner loomed a painted Welsh cupboard, filled with china and bric-a-brac—teacups, a pottery dog. In front of the window was an easel with a canvas, and beside it the same desk Radborne had last seen in Evienne's room with paints and pencils and brushes and sketchbooks scattered across it.

"You are painting," he said.

She shook her head. "No. I'm still waiting for the canvas to dry—I primed it yesterday, in my other room. Won't you sit, please, Mr.—"

"Comstock," prompted Radborne. "Radborne Comstock."

"Yes. Please."

She gestured at one of the plain chairs. Radborne sat, placing his sketchbook on the table. Evienne Upstone turned to Breaghan.

"Would you make tea for us, Breaghan? And perhaps you might go back to the house and see if there is anything to eat?" She smiled apologetically at Radborne, then sank into the green armchair. "I have just moved into this cottage. I'm afraid I have nothing to offer you."

"That's all right. I've had my breakfast."

"Well, I haven't," Evienne Upstone said, and laughed. Radborne could see that she had grown flushed.

"Dr. Learmont does not arrange for your meals?"

"He does. But I had little appetite this morning. I awoke in the night feeling ill, and Dr. Learmont gave me an injection to help me sleep. My appetite has suffered since I came here. I think it is the wind."

She turned to gaze out the small window. "I cannot sleep at night for hearing it." She glanced at him and smiled. "But perhaps you are not as restless as I am in the night."

Around them Breaghan gathered the tea things. She poured water from a pitcher into a heavy iron kettle and hung it above the peat fire, then began to assemble cups and saucers. Now and then Radborne caught her glancing at him. He straightened in his chair and cleared his throat.

"Well. Dr. Learmont asked me to look in and see that you have settled here satisfactorily. I see that you have."

He stopped. On the other side of the room, Evienne Upstone sat bolt upright, staring at him. The faint glow from the fire gave her eyes a sheen, like beech leaves with the sun behind them; they seemed to have no pupil. Her hair had been pinned up on the nape of her neck in a loose chignon, but as he gazed at her, it all at once unraveled, so that a spray of chestnut brown fell about her shoulders.

Autumn leaves, he thought. His throat grew tight.

"Miss Upstone," he began.

"Look." She continued to gaze at him, a strange blank stare like a child's. Her voice was low. "Breaghan has brought us tea."

"Yes, miss." Breaghan carried the tray to the table. She dipped her knees in a half curtsy, turning her head so that the unravaged side of her face showed a stealthy smile. "I'll go up to the house now and bring your breakfast."

She left the cottage, a waft of cold, clean air filling the room as the door closed after her. Radborne sat, waiting for Evienne Upstone to make a move to pour the tea. She only looked at him and, after a moment, inclined her head toward the table.

"Please," she said, and smiled.

He stood awkwardly. This was women's work, but Miss Upstone seemed to be accustomed to having people wait on her.

"Umm . . . Miss Upstone? Would you like some tea?"

"Yes, please," she replied.

He poured, spilling tea and tea leaves onto the table. Evienne did not seem to care, or notice. There was neither cream nor sugar; the tea itself had a strong bitter smell, like raw almonds. She remained in her chair as he brought the cup and saucer to her. She drank her cupful in one long swallow.

"Oh!" Radborne exclaimed. "Don't! You'll burn yourself!"

"No I won't." A tiny breath of steam escaped her mouth. "It's not that hot. But it doesn't taste very good."

"I'm sorry." He fumbled with his own cup and took a tentative sip. "Ugh! It tastes awful!" He made a face. "I must have done something wrong. When I poured it."

"It doesn't matter." She stood and joined him at the table and poured herself a second cup. "It's warm. That's all that matters."

She drank slowly this time, giving Radborne a complicit smile. He smiled back, relieved, and finished his own cup. When Evienne poured him more, he laughed but drank it.

"Now." She pushed away her cup and saucer and reached for his sketchbook. "May I?"

"Certainly. But you'll have to return the favor. May I?" He pointed to her watercolors on the desk.

"Please do." She gestured languidly. A green flare ran along the veins on the back of her hand, shimmering into bronze between her fingers. The back of his tongue burned and tasted faintly of bice. He recalled Breaghan's sly look, her hand moving between teapot and table.

"The tea," he said in a thick voice. "Poison. She poisoned us."

Evienne looked up from the pages of his sketchbook and smiled. "It's not poison. It's medicine."

"But—" He stopped, struggling for the words. Around him, the room seemed to recede. "But I'm not sick."

"You see things." She held up the drawing of a man with bees streaming from his eyes, a wasp clogging his mouth like a swollen tongue. "So do I."

Her smile widened. "Come," she said, and stood. "Let's walk."

"Is it . . . allowed?"

She took his hand and pressed it to her lips. "No." Her mouth parted, her lips closed over his fingertips. "But come anyway."

She turned and walked away, out the door and into a world of gray and green and silver. Radborne stumbled after her, heart racing. His body shook as though from tetanus, waves of nausea following each tremor. He thought desperately of fetching Dr. Learmont.

But the manor house was impossibly far away. He could barely see it. And now, now it was gone.

"Wait . . . Miss Upstone, please, wait . . . !"

A long way in front of him, a woman strode quickly up a gray hill.

Her dark skirt billowed around her; her long, loose hair was tangled by the wind. He pursued her, calling out for her to turn back, stop, stop.

". . . please, *stop*." He drew up, panting. His nausea had receded, though it took him a moment to catch his breath. "Miss Upstone?"

He was on the open moor. Evienne Upstone was nowhere to be seen. In the distance, perhaps half a mile away, Sarsinmoor's jagged headland bit into the sea, a few gulls wheeling above the manor house. A tiny cottage was silhouetted against the sky. As he watched, a figure crossed the turf and headed toward it. The sun hung low and red upon the horizon.

"Miss Upstone?" he called.

How had he come here?

He could recall nothing. When he licked his lips, they tasted of salt. There was an ashy residue on his tongue. Whatever had been in the tea seemed to have made him sleep, or otherwise lose track of time, so that he was here now with the wind growing bitter and night falling. He ran his hand across his face, feeling a smear of sweat and something sticky.

Blood, he thought. But when he looked at his hand, there was no blood. He glanced at his feet: his shoes were encrusted with mud and sand, a few black strings of seaweed. He bent and pulled the kelp from his soles, then straightened. The figure he had seen heading toward the cottage would have no doubt been Dr. Learmont. Guilt and fear cut through Radborne's daze; for the second time, he had failed in his duties. Quickly he turned and began to walk back toward Sarsinmoor. The wind blew chill from the west, carrying sea wrack and the bacony scent of peat smoke. He shivered uncontrollably, flapping his arms to warm himself. Bracken snapped and crunched where he stepped.

He walked and walked but seemed to come no closer to his destination. The cliffs of Sarsinmoor were much farther off than they looked. He was beginning to feel a slight feverishness; his head seemed to pulse and swell like a flaccid balloon. The relentless wind made his ears ache so that he walked with his hands pressed against them, like a man awakened from a nightmare. His fingers grew numb with cold, and he shoved them into his pockets.

That was when he heard the music.

Someone was playing a pipe. A few high, clear notes, warbling up and down like birdsong. There was no real melody, just the same sweet notes, like a running scale.

But after a few minutes, the notes grew more plangent, even melancholy. Radborne knew of no bird that sang like that.

He stopped, listening, looked about the moor but saw no one. The figure he'd glimpsed on the headland had long since disappeared. At his feet dead grass kept up a steady hissing as the wind flattened it. The light from the failing sun was harsh and without warmth. The shadows that snaked along the ground were black as the withered briars that hung above them. In the near distance, a line of standing stones seemed to hover above yellow gorse.

"Oh, my God," whispered Radborne.

The landscape was suddenly, wretchedly familiar. With a stab of fear, Radborne recalled the drawing Dr. Learmont had shown him— Evienne Upstone's sketch of black columns floating above a wasteland. He began to run toward the promontory, stumbling over rocks and thorn brake.

The piping did not stop. And now he heard voices singing in counterpoint to the rippling notes. The voices were high and without affect and seemed wordless. He looked around but saw no one; yet the music was unmistakable, he was not imagining it. If anything it was louder now. Radborne ran zigzag, hoping to lose his pursuers, but to no avail. The music continued, just behind him. He whirled but saw no one there.

Sarsinmoor was now behind him; he was staring at the village of Trevenna. Was it possible the sound came from there, from a church or schoolyard? It was late afternoon, evening almost. It could be evensong.

Yet the wind was from the west, and the music was all around him, ringing in his ears like a tocsin. It was so loud now he could hear nothing else, not the wind or the sea or his own breath. With a cry Radborne turned and ran toward Sarsinmoor.

He had not gone fifty feet when he saw them. The dog came first, panting as it loped up a long slope to Radborne's left, until they were running side by side. He had never seen a dog so huge—if it stood on its hind legs, it would be taller he was. Its longish hair was black and white. It had a sharp, pointed muzzle; its mouth was open so that it seemed to grin. When it raised its head to gaze at Radborne, he saw huge round eyes with irises the color of water wrung from peat; the whites shone palely brilliant in contrast. It was laughing at him.

Radborne gasped. The creature was so close he could feel its flank against his arm. Then the dog outpaced him, its stride neither quickening nor slowing, its legs slashing through the gorse like shears.

"*Ragresek brathky,*" a voice shouted. Panting, Radborne looked over his shoulder but still saw no one.

The voice came again, so close his ears rang. "*Ragresek brathky!*"

Radborne threw himself to the ground, rolling a few yards downhill. Flints and gorse tore at him before he came to a stop beside a patch of heather, a few blossoms still clinging to it. He turned onto his stomach and lay as flat as he could, staring up at the moor.

Down the slope came a small procession. Four horses pacing one behind the other, gray and white, their sides flecked with flies and burrs. Each bore a rider: three men, one woman. From where he lay, he could not clearly see their faces. Probably they were tinkers. Their clothes were worn and slightly archaic—hoodless capes and heavy leather brogans, pale-gray scarves wrapped 'round and 'round the woman's neck. The men were tall. Their coloring was dark, and they had long dark hair bound back from their foreheads. One had a roughly trimmed beard and mustache. As the horses drew nearer, Radborne got a better glimpse of the woman, also tall and broad-shouldered, with red-brown hair.

Almost he cried her name aloud. Before he could, the horse cantered past, its hooves striking sparks from granite and crushed flint. The three men followed. The smell of them filled the air like smoke. Ripe warmth of horses and unwashed hair, sea salt and oiled leather, and, strongest of all, a sharp green scent like sap.

The odor was so powerful that Radborne winced and rubbed his nose. As he did, the last man turned suddenly and stared at him through the twilight. He raised his hand, pointed at Radborne, and called out in a ringing voice words Radborne could not understand.

With a muffled curse, he pressed himself against the ground. The man drew back the reins of his horse, and, for a terrified moment, Radborne thought he would dismount. Instead the man leaned down from his saddle and grabbed a handful of earth. Ahead of him the others continued, unknowing. Before Radborne could move, the man flung the earth at him.

An explosion of grit and loose soil struck Radborne's face. He shouted with pain, his eyes burning as though doused with turpentine.

"Jesus! Jesus, stop!"

Around him was a flurry as of grouse beating into the air. He wiped desperately at his eyes, yanking his shirt free and rubbing his face until the dirt was gone. When he opened his eyes, the world was smeared with red. After a minute he could see again.

Through slitted eyes he stared back at the moor. Far, far away, on the northwestern horizon, four small figures rose and fell as though borne on the sea. Ahead of them, smaller still, a black speck raced until it was swallowed by the sky. Radborne waited until all were gone from view, then stood.

The sun was a gold sliver barely visible above the black-and-violet rim of sea. Radborne blinked and ran a hand across his forehead. Bits of dirt still clung there; he flicked them away and started toward the top of the rise. He had gotten only a few yards when he saw something on the ground. With a frown he stooped to investigate.

Nestled within a circle of etiolated gray toadstools was a tiny bier made of twigs, its bed woven of dried grass and the stems of beech leaves. It was no longer than his hand. The bottom was covered with brownish tufts of cattail fluff and soft green moss, like a phoebe's nest. On top of it lay another bit of soft brown stuff.

It was a dead bird. Its wingtips were striated with brown and white, its breast speckled with deeper brown. It had a curved gray beak like a thorn, and eyes shuttered by minute gray lids like poppy seeds. When he cupped his palms around it, bird and bier were all but weightless. He picked it up and held it tenderly, wondering what it was, where it had come from. Already he had forgotten the tinkers. He stood, shading his eyes as he gazed into the gold-flecked sky, a haze like smoke blowing from the east, and began to walk back to Sarsinmoor.

CHAPTER THIRTEEN

The Disenchantment of Bottom

never more damaging O Eirena have I encountered you
—Sappho, fragment translated by Ann Carson

He *walked back to Camden Town.* It took Daniel hours, going down every side alley he saw, entering every pub and café and gallery in North Islington, following every auburn-haired woman (or man) until s/he turned and Daniel saw—a dozen times, twenty, a hundred—that it was not her. Too late he thought of what he should have done from the very first and ran panting until he reached the canal path, looking in vain for the narrow boat.

It was nowhere to be seen. But there was the arched bridge, there the willow tree, its fallen leaves forming runic patterns as they drifted on black water. Daniel paused, trying to catch his breath, then ran up to an elderly woman walking her sheltie.

" *Cooksferry Queen,* " he gasped. "It's one of the narrow boats. Do you know where it is?"

"Sorry." She shook her head, concern in her mild eyes. "I've never seen a canal boat here. Little Venice, or there at Camden Lock. You all right, dear? Are you lost?"

"No."

He turned and walked, slowly now, down the towpath toward Camden Town. The blisters on his mouth no longer hurt, though his skin itched as if he had a sunburn starting to peel. At Monarch Wines he stopped, went inside, and bought a bottle of Hill's absinthe, then continued on toward Chalk Farm Road, brown-bagging it.

By the time he neared Nick's flat, the bottle was half empty. His lips no longer hurt; indeed, they seemed amazingly to have healed, the blistered skin smoothed away beneath a sticky, licorice-scented film. There was a buzzing in his ears like a fluorescent bulb. Above him, behind the scrim of late-Victorian buildings and the shining curve of the new Ice Wharf complex, the sky had taken on the satanic emerald glow of vaseline glass.

" 'How lush and lusty it looks,' " he said as a pair of teenage girls stared at him with contempt. " 'How green.' "

"Fucking shitehead," one said, and spit at him as he lurched past.

" 'I think I will carry this island home in my pocket and eat it like an apple,' " he shouted back at them. " 'And sowing the kernels of it in the sea bring forth more islands.' "

He began to run down the High Street, and everywhere people looked at him sideways through cold, white, malignant eyes. "The Beautiful One is here," he said, and doubled over to vomit on the sidewalk. "Oh, fuck."

He was losing it.

He would not lose her.

He couldn't bring himself to go back up to the flat, not yet. He drank some bottled electrolyte solution from Holland and Barrett and felt better. He could hold the image of Larkin Meade's face in his mind for almost a minute now, without being overcome by a desolation so intense it felt like terror. Perversely, the infusion of absinthe focused his mind less on Larkin's physical presence—her voice, the taste of her skin— than upon the question of who she really was.

A fringe artist who'd been collected by Russell Learmont? A fringe person, more likely, but what did that mean? He stood on the High Street and stared up at the sign on Nick's building. His thoughts unspooled the way they did when he was researching a profile of a performer dead too soon or too late, with nothing to go on but the memories of bemused onlookers. *No one ever took him seriously. She always was fine once she got onstage. He told me it was over between them but . . . Who knew she'd be capable of this?* Secondary sources, not completely useless but unreliable, and never as good as—

Of a sudden Juda Trent's words came back to him—*She is a primary source*—and with them the memory of that garbled name.

Not *Beth* or *Bleth;* not English but Welsh.

Blodeuedd.

"Shit." He shoved the absinthe bottle alongside a trash bin.

His notes were in his laptop up in Nick's spare room, along with his reference books, de Rougemont and a Schopenhauer compendium, volumes dealing with the Tristan mythos. Nothing Welsh, though. And it was too late for the British Library.

But Waterstone's was just down the road, and they stayed open till eight.

He hurried down the street and into the bookstore, then downstairs to the section on folklore and world mythology. He scanned the titles until he found what he wanted, stuck between copies of *From Ritual to Romance* and *The Owl Service:* a pocket-size Everyman edition of *The Mabinogion.*

"Right," whispered Daniel.

He flipped through until he came to the Fourth Branch, "Math Son of Mathonwy."

The day Llew went to Caer Dathyl, she was stirring about the court. And she heard the blast of a horn, and after the blast of the horn, lo, a spent stag going by, and dogs and huntsmen after it. "Send a lad," said she, "to learn what the company is." The lad went and asked who they were. "This is Gronw Bebyr, he who is lord of Penllyn," said they. And that the lad told her. And Blodeuedd looked on Gronw, and the moment she looked there was no part of her that was not filled with love of him. . . .

With her lover she murdered her husband, Llew, but Gwydion found Llew's decaying corpse and brought his bones to life, then changed Blodeuedd into a bird. Blodeuedd, Flowers, became Blodeuwedd, Flower-Face: the owl.

"Hoot," said someone beside Daniel. It was Nick. "You win the prize."

Daniel stared at him coldly.

"I saw you through the window. I was looking for you, Daniel. I was worried."

"Yeah? You should've been worried two nights ago at Sira's."

"I know, I know." Nick stared at his hands, raw lines scabbed with blood. "Look, I don't know how many times I can say this, but I'm sorry, Danny, I'm fucking sorrier than I have ever been about almost anything."

"Why did you do it, then?" Daniel said. "Why? You were my *friend*. . . ."

"I know." Daniel looked over to see his friend's topaz eyes dark with pain. "Come on, lad, let's go."

Daniel hesitated, then slid the book back on the shelf. Nick looked Daniel up and down, and his expression softened. "You stayed with her. Oh, Danny."

"I need to find her. Do you have her phone number? Or—"

"Danny. She's gone." He pointed at Daniel's bruised throat. "That's as good as it gets, lad. Let her go." He glanced at the bookshelf, then murmured, " 'We make her owls but she wants to be flowers.' Or is it the other way around? You remember," he said, and pointed at *The Owl Service*. "Although I don't think our Larkin wants to be owls *or* flowers."

"What does she want, then?"

"She wants to go home." Nick shook his head sadly. "She wants to be whole. You and me, Danny? We're the things her wings touch when she flies by. She will never come back to us. Not ever."

They started upstairs. For a minute Daniel said nothing. Then, "You saw her a second time. Sira told me. In Prague."

Nick hurried ahead of him, out onto the street. "I did. And it almost killed me. *She* almost killed me."

"Do you mean she tried to murder you?"

"I mean she can't touch us without destroying us. It's like lightning striking twice. That's when I started putting it all together."

"How?"

"Because she wasn't the same person. I thought she was, I wanted her to be—but she wasn't. She was dead, Danny." Nick's voice faltered; he stared straight ahead, his eyes unfocused. "Rob told me. A fire in her flat in Lambeth. I'd forgotten about her by then; or no, not forgotten, just put her away. Refused to think of her. A triumph, when a day finally went by and I realized I hadn't thought of her at all.

"I was in Prague, just kicking around. A few gigs, and I decided to stay on for a bit. I saw her in a café. It was her—I knew it was her soon as I laid eyes on her—but she was different. I mean, she *looked* different, but I knew. I could tell. And when I went with her . . ."

He shuddered, turned and held his hand out so Daniel could see it shaking uncontrollably. "Like that. *She wasn't dead.* Whatever the fuck she was, whatever she is—she's not like us, Danny."

He looked up. Daniel swallowed. "Then . . . why? why did you . . ."

His voice died, and Nick nodded. "Same reason you are.

"The first time was different. We'd met, and I . . . I started seeing her. She had some songs—ballads, twelfth-, thirteenth-century trouba-dour stuff. Amazing material, I have no idea how she came by it. Just about crumbled in my hands. It was only after she left that I started writing anything worthwhile. I did the first drafts of *Human Bomb* back then."

"Troubadours?"

"I guess that's your territory with Tristan, right?"

"And she had actual manuscripts? These ballads?"

"Yeah. But they're gone now. I mean, if you wanted to use them for your book. They really did just crumble one day. I was thinking of giving them to the BM or something; it seemed kind of criminal for a nob like me to have them. But after she left, they just sort of fell to bits. Like me," he added. "And you.

"She had all kinds of things, Danny. An absolutely beautiful, absolutely perfect manuscript of some ancient Irish poem—like something from the Book of fucking Kells, it was. Not the kind of thing you keep in a doss in Lambeth."

"How'd she get them?"

"She always told me people gave them to her—or no, what she used to say was that they belonged to her. She said someone had stolen all her things, and she had just a few of them left. All these precious books and manuscripts. Drawings, too. Paintings."

Daniel rubbed his arms, his flesh prickling. "Is she . . . do you think she's some kind of kleptomaniac?"

"She'd have to be a goddamn brilliant one to get all this stuff and keep hold of it. A regular master thief. No. I think it's more like what I said, people gave her things. Like tribute." He bared his teeth in a smile. "Like me: all those songs on *Human Bomb* were dedicated to her."

"I never knew that till Sira told me."

"How would you? Never said so in the liner notes, but they were. Fucking off my nut, I was, too. Best songs I ever wrote, don't think I don't know that. There were other songs, stuff I recorded but never got released."

"I never knew any of this. What are they like?"

"Oh, you know. Ballads. 'Songs in the style of.' That manuscript she had, the Irish one—I don't know if she nicked it or what, but it was incredible. You know the Yellow Book of Lecan?"

Daniel shook his head.

"It's like the Book of the Dun Cow. Old Irish sagas and poems. There's a famous Irish story called 'The Wooing of Etain'—what's-her-name did a version of, Lady Gregory. The other one, too—Oscar's ma. Lady Wilde. This is the kind of stuff you know if you're the Dread Legendary Folksinger. But for all these thousand years there were just fragments, until a full version was discovered up in Cheltenham, back in the 1930s, tucked in with the Yellow Book of Lecan.

"But see this, Danny—our girl, our Larkin, *she* had a copy of it! Gorgeous illuminated manuscript . . . like a dream, it was. I could not fucking believe it. To hold that in my hands, the entire story—like *that*—it was incredible. One of the greatest moments of my life."

"Could you read it? Wasn't it in Gaelic?"

"Oh, it was in Irish, all right. And no, I can't. But *she* could. Even considering the fact that it was hard to figure out where the letters ended and the pictures began—she could read it. Like the funnies, Danny."

He stared at Daniel, his eyes glistening. "Ha, ha."

"Ha, ha," said Daniel, and looked away.

They had reached the corner by the World's End. The traffic light was red. Daniel stood, mulling over all Nick had told him. "What's the story about?" he said at last. "Who's Etain?"

"The second wife of Midhir; one of the de Danaan. Midhir's other wife was jealous of her, so she turned Etain into a butterfly, then sent a storm to blow her out of Tir Na Nog and into the land of men. Etain fluttered about wretchedly for seven years; then she fell into a cup of wine and was swallowed by another queen. Nine months later this woman gave birth to a second Etain, just as beautiful as the first, and when this Etain grew up, she was wed to a mortal king. It ends with

Etain's mortal husband so raving mad he declares war on the Tuatha de Danaan and nearly destroys all of Tir Na Nog. So now even the Land of the Blest has been laid waste, and for what? A *girl*, Danny. The moral of the story is, she ain't worth it, Danny. How could she be worth it?"

Daniel looked across the street. The light had changed several times, and they still hadn't moved. "If Larkin was here right now," he said slowly, "I mean right this minute—if she was to walk up to you right now and stand here in the street with me right next to you and ask you to—would you go with her?"

"In a heartbeat."

The light flashed green; they walked. As they stepped onto the opposite curb, Nick began to sing in a low voice.

> " *'Tis she that was sung of in the Land*
> *'Tis she that strives to find the King*
> *'Tis she who is the woman who comes to him*
> *And she is our Etain afterwards.* "

Daniel gave him a wistful smile. "Is that one of the songs you wrote for her?"

"No. That's from the manuscript. It's gone now," Nick said sadly. "Turned to dust in my hands, like that."

He looked up, his expression tormented, and gestured helplessly. "Like everything she gave me. All I had left was what was in here."

He tapped his head, then made a face. "And the scars, too, of course. *Don't say I never gave you nuffink, Nicky!*" he cried in a shrill voice, and laughed. "Ah, well. Probably best thing that ever happened to me. I did *Human Bomb* and met Sira and lived happily ever after. End of story."

Wrong, thought Daniel as they approached the corner of Inverness, but he said nothing.

* * *

"You don't mind if I come up with you?" asked Nick as he unlocked the door to the flat. "Sira needed some CDs, and I keep my stockpile here."

"It's your place." Daniel stood behind his friend, shivering in the early-evening breeze. "God, I just want to lie down and sleep. For, like, a week."

"Best thing for you," said Nick. He pushed the door open and waved Daniel inside. "A nap and a poke, that's what my mother used to say."

"Nick, I knew your mother. She would never say that."

"Maybe it was Dad, then."

They walked upstairs. Daniel felt his heart lift slightly as the familiar smells of coffee and hash and Indian spices enveloped him. If he looked at it objectively . . . well, Larkin had been only a one-night stand. He hadn't done something like that in twenty years; hadn't actually *felt* like that for much longer, crazed with longing and the sense that sex could somehow open a door to a fantastic world that would explode this one into gray shrapnel.

It was a relief, really, to have it behind him. They reached the landing where Nick's bicycle helmet and assorted rain gear hung, turned and walked into the kitchen.

And stopped.

"Hello, Nick." A deep voice boomed through the flat. "It's me. Val. Val Comstock?"

Daniel looked up. In the middle of the kitchen stood one of the biggest men he had ever seen off a regulation basketball court. Easily more than six and a half feet tall, broad-shouldered and . . . well, *huge*—with a filthy red bandanna around his forehead and lank black hair falling to his shoulders, deep-set eyes and hawkish nose, close-trimmed beard and mustache that gave more definition to his chiseled features. He was much younger than either of them—Daniel pegged him at thirty. But his stained SHOCKHEADED PETER T-shirt, baggy corduroys and clunky black boots, frayed leather braid around his neck and silver earrings made him look even younger than that.

"Nick? Remember me?" Val said. He was so ridiculously larger than life that Daniel almost laughed. Then the young man's gaze fell upon him, and Daniel froze.

Larkin, he thought, and fought a wave of panic. *Jesus, he looks like Larkin.*

"Val?" Nick laughed in amazement. "Little Val?"

"That would be me."

Nick danced across the room. "Christ, lad, they been putting steroids in your beer? It's good to see you!"

They shook hands. "My fuckwit brother didn't call, then?" said Val. "He was supposed to let you know I was coming. I still have the key."

He held it up, a thread of brass in his huge hand. "But if there's a problem, I'll just crash at a hotel—"

"No, of course not, no problem at all!" said Nick. "I mean, as long as you can fit in here."

Val smiled and looked at Daniel. "I'm Val Comstock," he said, his hand reaching out past Nick's head.

"Daniel Rowlands."

"Hey, you're American." Val grinned. "Me, too."

Daniel smiled wanly. "Yup." He wondered where, in fact, this overgrown kid would fit. The security door leading onto the rooftop patio was open; maybe he could sleep out there. He looked back at Val and felt the pinch of envy. "I'm staying here at Nick's for a few months, researching a book. I'm a writer—a journalist, with the *Washington Horizon.*"

Val nodded. His eyes met Daniel's—hazel eyes, mingled green and amber—and flickered challengingly: *Oh, yeah?*

But all Val said was, "I'm just making a delivery. One of my grand-father's paintings. This is all Simon's doing, of course. My asshole lawyer brother. He negotiated some deal, and as usual I have to be the bagman."

Nick peeled off his anorak and went to the fridge. "How long you staying, then? Beer?"

"Yeah, sure," rumbled Val, and Nick handed him a bottle. "I dunno. I'm feeling kind of restless. Might just hang around for a while."

Nick nodded. "Beer, Danny?"

"No thanks."

Daniel glanced into the living room and saw that one of the book-shelves was empty. Under it stood two big black trash bags, filled.

Val's gaze followed his; he shrugged, then said, "Oh, yeah. Nick. I kind of made a mess in there. I'll reimburse you for it—but there's something I need to ask you about."

His rumbling voice dropped almost to a whisper. There was some soft, implicit threat in it, a sense of someone being reasonable who maybe hadn't had a lot of practice. Uneasy, Daniel glanced again at the living room, and this time noticed bits of torn paper on the floor be-neath the windows, the ripped cover of a paperback.

"Actually," Val went on, "probably the person I really need to talk to is Simon. 'Cause this sketchbook of mine that, like, disappeared when I was fifteen? I found it here. Just now. But—"

From downstairs came the squawk of the doorbell. Nick started for the hall but stopped at the *boom* of the outer door banging shut.

"That'll be Sira," he said as a voice rang from the stairs.

"Nick? You here?"

Daniel turned. It was Larkin.

"Why, look who's here," said Nick. He had gone pale as paper. "She's a rainbow."

She was wearing faded, much-patched jeans, a tunic of worn tie-dyed velvet, green and red and blue and yellow. Her hair was loose around her shoulders, strands of gray and auburn tangling in the fringe of a long turquoise scarf. The getup should have been ludicrous, but, gazing at her, Daniel felt his heart constrict painfully as he lifted a hand to greet her.

"Oh, hello there, Daniel." She smiled blankly, not exactly as though nothing had happened between them but as if it had all been decades ago. "I forgot you were staying here. I was just stopping by, I think I left my coat the other night."

"*Last* night," Daniel started to say. But then she turned from him, and the words stuck in his throat.

Once, years before, he had been hiking alone in the Moab wilderness in Utah, when in the distant glass-blue sky he had seen two small prop planes collide. His horror had mingled with astonishment. How was it that in all that vast open space the planes had managed to find each other? His amazement was compounded when he later read that, elsewhere in the desert, another hiker had been killed by the falling wreckage.

"Maybe the really incredible thing is that it wasn't you," his girlfriend said when he finally told her about it. "Maybe you were lucky, seeing it happen."

Seeing it happen.

On the other side of the kitchen, Val Comstock was staring at Larkin, but she hadn't really registered him yet. She was looking at Nick, her lips parted and her face tilted to one side, as though she were trying to figure out what was going on here, what she had wandered into. A surprise party? An argument?

"Um . . . ?" she said, turning.

And saw Val.

A shimmering instant, the moment between when a crystal glass is struck and when it cracks. Daniel's hand grasped the corner of the kitchen table; Nick stood with his beer, mouth open to speak. Separated by the table, Larkin and Valentine Comstock stared at each, Larkin in her outdated Gypsy glory, Val with his dirty red bandanna and sweat-stained jeans and T-shirt. In the back of his throat, Daniel tasted bile, bitter green suddenly flooded by the taste of scorched fish. There was a scent of apple blossom and the sea. Somewhere a dog barked. Very slowly and without looking away from Larkin, Val reached to set his beer on the table, his hazel eyes wide and wondering as a sleepwalker's.

Enchantment.

Daniel saw the pen-and-ink figures of conjoined lovers in a field of endless green and white, felt Larkin's hand upon his face and taloned fingers clawing at his breast.

Discovery.

"I know you," murmured Val. Gazing at him, Larkin nodded silently.

"Yes," she said, and Daniel felt a door close upon him forever.

Recognition.

CHAPTER FOURTEEN

The Triumph of Time

I AM that which began;
Out of me the years roll;
Out of me God and man;
I am equal and whole;
God changes, and man, and the form of them bodily; I am the soul.
—*Algernon Charles Swinburne, "Hertha"*

It was not dusk but dawn, not dawn but night, not sun rising or setting but flame. The world was on fire; no, not the world, he saw as he began to run, not the world but Sarsinmoor.

"Evienne!"

He raced across the narrow land bridge, all the air roaring. Heat surrounded him like a wall crashing down; he was trapped inside a vast athanor, flame and smoke and tiny black things soaring everywhere, beneath him the ground rippling and gorse crackling like flesh upon a spit. He shouted and beat futilely at the air, running with his head bowed against waves of crimson and black and blinding white. "Evienne!"

The manor house was ablaze. But when he reached the courtyard, he saw that only the front of the building had been consumed, and its lower story—the old wing to the back was intact, and while flames beat at the upper floors, they had not yet reached them. He paused, coughing and struggling to catch his breath. On the cobbles a safe distance from the building, paintings and boxes and wooden crates were strewn, hundreds of them.

"Comstock!"

He looked up to see Learmont staggering from one of the side doors, dragging a huge canvas.

"Help me," the doctor gasped, nearly falling as he wrestled the painting to the ground. "Must save them . . ."

"Where is she?" cried Radborne. He grabbed the painting from Learmont and thrust it aside. "Is she inside? *Where is she?*"

"She?" Learmont looked at him dumbfounded, then gave a gasping laugh. "*She* is gone! Torched her nest and fled!"

He turned and began to run back toward the house. "Surely Kervissey will have seen the flames in Padwithiel— help me get the rest of them!"

"The paintings?" Radborne grabbed at him. "Are you mad? What about Candell—is he safe? Where is he?"

"His work is there!" Learmont shouted, pointing to the piles of canvas and crates, then pushed Radborne from him. "I freed him—he has gone to her!"

With a groan he turned and ran back inside.

"Gone?" cried Radborne. "Evienne!"

He tore off his jacket, covered his face with it, and ran. The stench of burning gorse was everywhere; above him glass and stones exploded from the heat and rained down. He ran behind the manor house, where scattered heaps of fallen wreckage blazed, drew to a halt, panting, and peered through the smoke to the cottage.

It seemed to be intact, though runnels of fire spat and tore through bindweed and thorns at his feet. "Evienne! Breaghan!"

He raced to the door and yanked it open. Inside, all was as he had left it just hours before—the teacups still on the plain deal table, Evienne's watercolor on the easel, a thread of ash clinging to the spent peat fire. Of Evienne Upstone there was no sign, nor Breaghan.

"You'll not find her here, Mr. Comstock," a voice said. Radborne whirled. "And she'll not find you either. She's got from you what she needed, and she's gone, gone."

In the doorway stood Jacobus Candell. He wore his paint-spattered smock but was barefoot; his hands were cut and bleeding, as were his feet. He stank of turpentine and linseed oil. "The doctor set me free to help him. I told him that I have left you my things, Mr. Comstock. The lapis lazuli is pure, and I have already told you about the *caput mortuum*. I trust you can prime your own canvas. I have done with painting for a while, I think."

"Cobus." Radborne strode over to him. "Cobus. Is she . . . have you hurt her? I swear to God I will kill you if she's been harmed!"

Candell's pale blue eyes shone. "Harmed?" He began to laugh. "I would not *harm* her, Mr. Comstock—could you harm the sea? Could you harm *this*—"

He turned and ran back outside, darting clumsily back and forth until he came to a blazing patch of gorse. Then Radborne had hold of him, pulling him away roughly. "Stop it! Tell me where she's gone— *where is she?*"

Candell did not struggle to escape. He gazed at Radborne with that ineffably sweet smile, then lifted a sticky red hand to touch his cheek. "You won't find her, lad. Nor the other. The midwife."

"What are you talking about?"

"The deformed woman. That is all they wanted of you—to beget a child."

"A child?" Radborne fought for breath, squeezed his eyes shut. He saw the tiny bier in the grass, the body of the wren inside it, a woman lying on the moor beside him, then a woman in the distance astride a horse. "I . . . I lay with no woman."

Candell laughed softly. "That is true. But you straddled her all the same, and your spunk is as good as any man's. She's gone to lay her egg in another's nest now, sir—you won't find her."

He dug his hand into the pocket of his filthy smock and withdrew a speckled egg, held it up for a moment, then crushed it between his fingers. "Chipping sparrow," he said regretfully. "Not hers. The midwife took it—put it in a box, she'll keep it for a hundred years if she has to. You'll never see your son, sir. Not that'd you recognize him if you did."

He shoved his fingers into his mouth, sucking them noisily. With a shout of rage, Radborne drew back his hand to strike him. As he did, he saw Candell's eyes widen, staring past him, past the cottage, toward the cliffs.

"Oh, wonder!" the painter cried, and, trembling, fell to his knees. "Oh, but see . . ."

Radborne turned.

At the edge of the cliff, two pillars of flame reared into the air, ten feet, twenty, a thousand. They rippled and flared like auroras of emerald and ice and jade, coruscating green and black, as slowly and inexorably they pulsed up and down, like infernal pistons. Radborne screamed, seeking to shade his eyes, but nothing could keep that terrible light from him, or its sound: it ignited his very brain, searing skull tongue teeth eyes, until all he could see was radiance, a horror of incandescent emerald that clamored like a gong, giving off endless echoes. He stumbled backward and fell, rolled onto his stomach, then got to his feet, staggering as he ran.

"WONDER!" a voice shouted. Hands grabbed him. Radborne pushed them away frantically, had a glimpse of a dark form suddenly thrusting through the brilliance. "WONDER!"

"*Cobus, no!*"

At the edge of the cliff stood Jacobus Candell, holding at arm's length a blazing branch of gorse. At his feet a small form furiously dashed, jumping and snapping at his hand. As Radborne watched, the blaze flickered, then leaped, touching the hem of Candell's smock.

There was an explosive whiff of turpentine, and Radborne stared in horror as Candell erupted into flame.

"*Cobus! No*—"

The figure raised its arms, reaching toward the shining heavens. "*Wonder!*" it screamed.

There came an instant where it was all one thing: man and light, green and black, night and day. Then with a sound like an exploding cannon, the radiance was gone. Radborne stood beneath a night sky, Sarsinmoor ablaze behind him and someone shouting his name.

"Comstock! Comstock, you meddling *shite*!"

Someone grabbed him by the arm. "Swinburne," Radborne whispered, and coughed convulsively. "Swin—"

"He's here!" the poet shouted. "Quick!"

Another figure appeared in the fire-streaked darkness, a coachman clutching a lantern. "Kervissey's got t' doctor!" he shouted. "Bring 'im to the coach, sir!"

"Can you walk?" Swinburne cried, pulling Radborne to him. "Come, I'll bear you as much as I can."

They stumbled through flame-licked gorse, smoke swirling around them and the manor house bellowing with flame. Radborne was nearly deafened; tears of agony and terror streamed down his face as Swinburne drew him to the narrow spit of land that bridged the gap between Sarsinmoor and the headland. Halfway across it a wagon lumbered away from them, piled high with crates and canvases. Radborne recognized Kervissey's dour head beneath its cap, and a taller, sparer figure, standing to gaze back at the fiery ruins.

"Learmont." Radborne mouthed the name through scorched lips.

"Here, Mr. Comstock." They had reached a coach in the courtyard, its blinkered horses snorting and shrieking as a groom struggled to keep them still. Swinburne stepped aside as the coachman pulled the door open. "This is Inchbold's man. He'll bring us to Trevenna."

"Trevenna." Radborne clambered into the coach, then turned empty, maddened eyes upon the little man beside him. The coach door slammed shut. The coachman shouted and the horses lunged across the courtyard, away from the blaze. "You . . . how did you . . . ?"

Swinburne gasped and settled back against the seat. He ran a hand through his wild ginger hair, then looked at Radborne. "My conscience would not let me rest. Thinking of you here, alone with them. . . ."

He grasped Radborne's large hand tightly in his own small one.

"One who is not, we see: but one whom we see not, is.

"Gabriel, my sad bad glad mad brother—I could not save him, nor Lizzie, nor poor damned Ned. But you . . ."

The poet's eyes narrowed. As the coach clattered across the moor, the ruins of Sarsinmoor behind them, he gave his shrill peacock laugh.

"You, Mr. Cuntwit, Fancy's fool and an American to boot—you have made a hero of me at last!"

CHAPTER FIFTEEN

The Dog Jumps Down

If Love dwelt not in Trouble, it could have Nothing to love. . . . Neither could
any one know what Love is, if there were no Hatred; or what Friendship is,
if there were no Foe to contend with. Or in one Word, for Love to be known
It must have Something which It might Love, and where Its Virtue and Power may be
manifested, by working our Deliverance to the Beloved from all Pain and Trouble.
—*Jakob Böhme*

I n *Nick's flat a cell phone* rang. Val and Larkin didn't notice as, light as
a fox, Nick was across the room to answer it.

Daniel did not stir. Only he had known that the phone would
ring; only he had known that Val would move as though underwater to
pick up his beer from the table; only he had seen the pair of interlocking
circles left upon the unpolished wood surface by the sweating bottle.

"Wait," Daniel said.

But he didn't really speak, just watched silently as Val held out his
hand to Larkin, then cocked his head toward the door that led onto the
rooftop. Larkin smiled. She lifted a hand as though waving good-bye or
hello and followed Val outside.

"That was Juda," said Nick. He looked around uneasily. "Checking
up on you. I told her you seemed to be convalescing, but she's on her
way over to see for herself. Daniel?"

Daniel said nothing. He was staring out the narrow window above
the sink, glass framing the green world outside: glossy jade branches of

bay trees in terra-cotta pots and arching fronds of cordiline, three young white birches with silvery leaves like coins spinning in the evening breeze; banks of anemones, a lattice of blooming passionflower. Sira tended it, and a gardener who came once a month. Now two tall figures were silhouetted against the brick wall of the building next door, each with a rain-colored aura, misty green and bluish gray: they were leaning toward each other to form a sort of arch through which the white petals of anemones fluttered mothlike.

"Daniel?" Nick touched his shoulder. Daniel did not move. "Leave, her, Danny. Come have a drink. Sit and have a beer."

From the rooftop came the hushed sound of Larkin's laughter. This time when Nick's hand touched his shoulder, it remained there. Daniel turned away.

"I'll just have some water." He sat and cradled his head in his hands. "I've had too much to drink the last couple of days. Maybe I should go back to D.C."

"Don't be rash, now," said Nick kindly. "You're just out of practice"; and he gave his friend a liter of sparkling water and a glass. "You know Juda's a doctor. She could prescribe something for you. To help you sleep."

"I don't need help sleeping."

"Something to make you feel better, then. Just for the short term. Until you get on your feet again."

"I don't need to get on my goddamn feet." Daniel stared rigidly at the table in front of him. The moisture left by Val's beer bottle had dried, but the imprint of two linked circles remained. His fist smashed the rough surface, rubbing at it until friction made his hand burn with pain. When he lifted his hand, the circles were untouched.

"Danny," Nick said. "Listen to me. Juda knows—"

"Knows *what?* Christ, I don't even know if Juda's a guy or a girl. Do you?"

Nick took a sip of his beer. "Both, I think."

"Both?"

"Well, yeah. You know. She walks like a woman but talks like a man? Hermaphroditic."

"You mean, a transsexual?"

"No. She was born that way. I guess. I mean, assuming she was born."

The doorbell buzzed again. There was the squeak of keys in the lock, followed by the thud of the door slamming shut and Juda's brash voice echoing up the stair.

"Nick? You still here?" She halted in the doorway, pale eyes fixed on Daniel. He looked at her but said nothing, and she came inside to join them. "Hello, Daniel."

He nodded. She had changed into loose cornflower-blue trousers, a thin T-shirt that made her bare arms look as frail and insubstantial as a child's. In the light her unruly shock of hair glowed orange. She stared at him; as he stared back, he noticed that not just her nails but her fingers were the same color as her pants.

"I'm here," he said. "I'm fine. Just ducky. You can leave now."

"Everyone's here." Nick tugged at one gold earring. "You. Daniel." He thrust his chin in the direction of the door that led to the rooftop. "Her."

Juda looked quickly out the window. "Larkin, you mean? You should have told me." She darted to the sink and peered out. "Who's that with . . ."

Her voice died. Daniel turned to see her staring into the garden. Her expression was rapt, torn between disbelief and fear and a joy so profound it scared him.

"*Shit.*" She began to climb on top of the sink, hands splayed against the window frame. "Nick! Who is that with Larkin?"

"That's Val Comstock. Little brother of a guy I used to buy coke from a long time ago. He stayed here for a bit, oh, I guess it's been five or six years now. Why? D'you know him?"

"That's not anybody's little brother." Juda shook her head. "Fucking hell . . ."

Daniel hurried to her side. "Who is he, then?"

"Someone I knew a long, long time ago."

"Yeah?" He peered out the window, squinting. The two figures had disappeared behind the veil of birch leaves. "Like, in prison, maybe? Rehab?" He looked at Nick, scowling. "He looks like a goddamn barbarian."

"Val's not a bad kid. Used to do some kind of theater work. For a while he fronted a band up near Finchley Park. You might like him."

"I doubt it."

All three of them were in front of the sink now, jostling to get a view outside. Laughter wafted up from the café next door, the stuttering beat of electronica. Daniel could just make out the pair behind the lattice of vines, green-black shapes that seemed to swell and shrink like shadows on moving water.

"I don't like him," Daniel announced. "I don't trust him."

"Christ, Dan, he's just a kid," said Nick. "Smarter than he looks, too."

"Right. Conan the Grammarian." Daniel started for the door. "I'm going to—"

A furious burst of sound echoed through the kitchen. Daniel stopped and stared out onto the roof. The noise came again, loud and frenzied.

A dog barking.

"That's Fancy!" Juda cried. She pushed Daniel aside and ran out onto the patio. "Fancy!"

Daniel ran after her.

"Fancy !"

On the low parapet that overlooked Inverness stood the Border collie. Every hair on his body seemed to be raised, so that he looked twice as big as when Daniel had last seen him. His muzzle pointed straight down into the street, and he was poised to leap, his front paws scrabbling at the edge of the brick ledge.

"Fancy, no!"

The volley of barking gave way to a low, anxious whine. Daniel looked around desperately. There was no sign of Larkin or Val Comstock.

"Fancy—here, boy!" Nick ran toward the parapet, Juda at his heels. The dog glanced back at them, its eerie, mismatched eyes shining. Then it turned, crouched down upon the ledge, and jumped.

"No!"

Juda shouted, a high wail that drowned out the throb of traffic. Daniel raced to the edge of the parapet and stared down. In the street below them, the black-and-white collie darted through the crowd, barking madly as people moved away, startled.

"Fancy!" Juda shouted, leaning over the wall. "Fancy, wait!"

At the corner of Inverness Street and the High Street, a massive figure stood holding the upright handles of a motorcycle, chrome and beetle black. A woman with long auburn hair eased herself onto the seat behind him as the dog leaped and snapped at her feet.

"Larkin!" Daniel started to scramble onto the parapet. "Larkin, don't!"

"You fucking daft?" Nick shouted, yanking him down. "Danny, stop!"

"God, I don't *believe* it!" Daniel shouted, feeling as though he'd been run through with a knife. "What the . . . how the hell did she get *down* there?"

A sudden roar from the street. Smoke billowed from the motorcycle. A group of teenagers screamed and cursed in delight as the bike lunged forward into traffic, heading north on the High Street. Behind it raced the Border collie, its belly skimming the ground as it ran. From the rooftop Daniel and Nick and Juda stared down like onlookers at a train wreck.

"He's done it, then," Juda whispered. "All this time, he's finally done it."

"We better go after the dog," said Nick. "That's a Vincent HRD, that bike. Black Shadow. I remember when he bought it."

"Black Shadow? Black Shadow?" Daniel turned to him, fist raised. *"How did he get in? You—"*

Juda grabbed his hand. "Stop it, Daniel! He's right—I have to get the dog. He'll lead me to her. To them."

"I'm going with you," said Daniel.

Juda started to protest, then stopped.

"Me, too," Nick said.

She hurried back inside. Nick quickly locked the back door. Juda was already running downstairs. Daniel started after her, then stopped. He glanced at the living room with its denuded bookshelf and torn pages littering the floor.

"Son of a bitch," he said.

He ran into the guest room. His books had been moved, the battered copy of *Love in the Western World* plucked from its rubber band so that loose pages were everywhere. He turned to his bed, yanked back the sheets and blankets, looking for the notebook he'd placed there the night before.

"Damn it—it's gone!"

"Daniel!" Nick's urgent voice came from downstairs. "C'mon now!"

Daniel kicked at a pillow, grabbed his satchel and leather jacket, and ran downstairs.

"Juda's gone ahead to get the car," Nick said as Daniel ran up alongside him in Inverness Street. "Freak thing, wannit? That dog landing in one piece?"

"Freak thing is how the goddamn dog got there in the first place.

You think of that, Hayward? How did that dog get on the roof? Did it fly there? And this guy Comstock? His brother's a drug dealer, and you give him a key to the flat? Are you nuts?"

Nick shrugged deeper into his anorak. "Did he rip you off?"

"A notebook of mine is missing. Not to mention a lot of *your* books appear to have been destroyed."

"I never had a problem with him before," Nick said plaintively. "His brother had him put in hospital for a while, but he seemed to be okay."

"'In hospital'? What do you mean? What kind of hospital?"

"Look, I don't even know them that well, Danny. The boy had some problems when he was a kid. He bashed up Simon—the older brother— beat him with a plank or something. Messed 'im up pretty bad. They put him in some sort of place. But you know, I've wanted to take a bat to Simon myself a few times—"

"Nick! What *sort* of place?"

Nick shrugged. "I think a sort of mental hospital."

"A *nuthouse?* You let this guy into the flat where *I am living* and—"

"Jesus, Dan, it was fucking years ago!"

"Yeah? Well, now he's taken off with Larkin, and that was fucking *minutes* ago!"

At the corner of Inverness Street and Gloucester Crescent, a black Mercedes pulled up and honked. Juda leaned out the window. "Nick! Daniel! Move it!"

Nick jumped in back. Daniel slid in beside Juda. The car was done up in leather and walnut; it smelled of Gitanes and coffee.

"Nice car," said Nick. "Do you have a GPS to follow the dog?"

"It's rented. He went north up toward Kentish Town." The car roared into Parkway, then headed for the Kentish Town Road. "Don't worry, I can find him."

"What about Val Comstock?" demanded Daniel. "Nick says he was institutionalized for trying to kill his brother. Is he one of your patients, too?"

"No, he's not one of my patients."

"But you knew him, right? You *knew*—"

"Daniel." Juda's voice rose dangerously. "Listen to me. I don't know Val, but I—how can I put this so it makes sense to you? I *recognize* him."

"You mean, because he's crazy?" Daniel stared out at traffic signals, bus stops, club queues, all flickering past like a deck of cards tossed into the air. "And . . . and . . ."

He clenched his fist and struck his thigh, trying to keep from grabbing the wheel from her and slamming the car into a wall.

"Why are we doing this?" he cried. "We're chasing this dog—which I don't see anywhere, do you?—and Larkin and some berserker I have never seen before in my life—*why?* Because I'm willing to believe that *I'm* crazy, and I've known about Nick for a long time now—but, Dr. Trent, you . . ."

He pounded the glove box. "You're driving a nice car! You have a house, and clients, and expensive clothes—why are you doing this, Dr. Trent? *Who is Larkin Meade?*"

"There!" Nick shouted from the backseat. He leaned out the window, pointing. "Fancy! Come here, Fancy!"

The car swerved across the traffic lane and into a side street. Daniel could just make out a black-and-white shimmer in the smudged wash of brick and asphalt in front of them. They followed the dog along the street, winding up and past a row of old one-story warehouses, until the road once once more joined a major thoroughfare. The Border collie arrowed off to the left, skirting the curb, and raced on, three or four car lengths ahead of them. Daniel could see its muzzle bared in a long white-toothed grin, its legs moving tirelessly.

"There!" cried Nick. "He's gone up there!"

"Where are we?" said Daniel. The roads they'd been following had slowly risen higher and higher, so that he glimpsed jagged vistas of the city all around them: rows of terraced council housing, a shimmer of glass and steel atop a hill, far-off sweeps of green and brown.

"Waterlow Park," said Juda. "He's heading toward Muswell Hill."

The Mercedes moved swiftly through the traffic, veering onto side roads whenever Juda or Nick sighted the dog running like a mechanical hare in a greyhound course. Daniel was hardly aware of it. He kept seeing those two tall figures moving toward each other through the leaves until they formed a single entity flaring into emerald light.

"Ally Pally?" wondered Nick. "D'you think that's where they're headed?"

"I don't know," said Juda. "He'll go until he finds someplace he recognizes, or she will."

The car stopped at a light beside a fish-and-chips shop; the smell struck Daniel like a hammer blow, a curled rainbow tail and fire searing his fingers. The light changed, the car lunged forward. Another ghostly city took shape around him—no, not another city, this one, though it was as if he saw it for the first time. There were the pubs, the cobblestone streets; soft brown London brick and crumbling warehouses, the spire of a stone church, a gray schoolyard behind tall iron gates. The Highgate tube station, locals named the Archway and Clissold Arms. Old men with heads bent over glasses at a mahogany bar and back rooms full of boys in Arsenal shirts. Two gangly young men shouted, then pummeled each other, reeling across the sidewalk while music echoed from a jukebox.

"Hey!" said Daniel. "Isn't that . . . that's—"

The boys tumbled head over heels as a black-and-white dog raced past and they flickered and disappeared, like a television screen fizzing into snow.

"There!" shouted Nick. "There they are!"

He jabbed at the windshield, pointing to where the motorcycle stood idling at a light. Beside it the Border collie danced and barked.

Juda swore, wheeling the car so it went up onto the curb. Before it came to a full stop, Daniel had lunged into the street.

"Daniel, *no!*"

He ignored Juda's cry and started running. "Larkin!"

She was only a few yards away, seated on the back of the bike. "Larkin!" he shouted. "Larkin, wait!"

She turned. For an instant he saw her clearly, her mouth half parted as to speak, her brow furrowed.

"Larkin," he gasped, close enough to touch her. "Larkin . . ."

She did not see him. She did not stare past him but through him: he was a trick of the light, casting no shadow. He was invisible.

"Larkin." He couldn't hear himself. How could he, when he didn't exist? *Larkin.*

The light changed. The woman nestled her head against the shoulder of the man in front of her, and in a roar of exhaust, the bike shot off.

Daniel shouted. Something flung itself against him, and he stumbled. When he looked up, the motorcycle was gone.

"Fancy! Stay there, that's it!"

Beside him Juda Trent ran up and grabbed the dog. Fancy yelped frantically as she slipped collar and leash over its head.

"There," said Juda. She laid a hand on the dog's head, and it quieted. "That's my sweet, that's my Fancy. . . ."

Daniel stared numbly at the street. Fancy strained at the leash; Juda spoke to him sharply, and the dog sat.

"Come on!" Daniel cried impatiently. "We'll lose them!"

Juda shook her head. "He found it. The Edgware Road—the old Roman way. It will take them to the motorway west." She turned and headed to her car.

"You're not going without me!" Daniel yelled.

"Suit yourself."

They got in. Juda stared impassively at Nick still in the backseat. He shook his head.

"No." Nick opened the door and climbed out. "Not me."

Juda backed the car off the sidewalk. Nick stood, watching. As the car waited for the light to change, he called anxiously to Daniel in the front seat.

"Whyn't you come back with me, Danny? Come on. . . ."

"No. I'm going after her."

The car began to move. Nick waved his hand in farewell. Juda stared straight ahead as Daniel watched his friend recede into the distance.

"You shouldn't come," Juda said at last. "But I'm not going to waste time arguing."

"Where're we going?"

"The West Country. Cornwall. Sleep, if you can."

They took the North Circular out of the city, west and south through suburban and industrial wastelands until they reached the M4. Near Slough they stopped for gas.

"Do you want me to drive?" Daniel asked. He felt dangerously wired, his nerve ends buzzing and spitting with a sense memory of student amphetamine binges. "You must be exhausted."

She said nothing, just swung the car back onto the roadway. It was past eight o'clock, yet the sky looked high and misty blue as a seaside morning, the sun a dazzling yellow lake upon the western horizon. Daniel glanced back to see Fancy sprawled across the seat, long, rose-pink tongue dangling, one eye clear and calm as twilight, the other glittering gold. He turned to look at Juda.

Strands of damp hair clung to her forehead. She gripped the steering wheel so hard that the bones of her hand stood out like tines. The bluish pallor that saturated her nails and fingertips had spread—her hands had an unmistakable glaucous sheen, like the dusty bloom on wild grapes.

"You should try to sleep," she said. Her face was taut but calm. "I'll wake you if I need a break."

He thought it would be impossible to sleep, but soon he succumbed to the potent drone of the car engine, the monotonous flicker of council estates and shabby mock Tudors, now and then the hierarchic expanse of a stately home like a childhood dream rising from the long gray hangover of suburban England. He slept through Bristol, where they turned onto the M5 and began heading south, past Taunton, past Exeter, finally woke to night and the smell of moist green things and Fancy's cold nose burrowing into his neck.

He yawned, pushing the dog into the backseat. "Where are we?"

"We're in Cornwall now. We crossed the Tamar hours ago. Have you been to the West?"

"No. Never been out of London."

"Shame you can't see it. But it's there. . . ."

She rolled down her window and let her hand trail into the night. A pungent odor filled the car, cow manure and fresh-cut hay, also a grassy, honeyed smell that made his mouth water.

"Gorse," Juda said. "And heather. There's other things, too, flowers, but I don't know what you call them. We're crossing Bodmin Moor now. No one knows these roads unless they live here."

"How do you know it, then?"

"I have a little house on the north coast, near a place called Padwithiel. Just a cottage."

Daniel looked outside. Above them the night sky was the deep iridescent green of a mallard's head. It seemed to reflect the lights of some great city, so bright he could read the few road signs they passed.

But there was no city here. He gazed out at the black tors and barren hills and had the unmistakable, disturbing sense of being watched, of having wandered into a place where he was not welcome.

"We'll cut back to the coast now," Juda said after some time. "Look."

In the distance stretched a vast darkness—the sea. Silvery light shimmered across a shifting expanse of black and lunar green; he could hear the rhythmic roar of waves, like the breathing of a sleeping giant. He held his hand out the window, brought it tentatively to his mouth, and tasted salt.

"Land's end," said Juda. "Actually, Lands End is south of here—fucking Thatcherites turned it into a carpark. But this'll give you an idea of what it was like. What it is . . ."

She pulled the car off the road, onto turf starred with tiny white flowers. "Here," she said. She hopped out, Fancy jumping down at her side. "Look."

He followed her, walking across short, springy grass until Juda grasped his arm. "Be careful," she said, and pointed. "See that?"

He drew up, aghast.

A few feet in front of them, the world ended. They were at the brink of a sea cliff hundreds of feet above a roiling swath of waves. Far below was a crescent-shaped beach, flanked by wave-gouged granite pillars and a seemingly endless line of cliffs, dramatically undercut by the relentless pounding of the ocean, their crowns of heather and gorse as insubstantial as sea foam.

"A couple of hikers go off every year," said Juda. She stood with her back to him beneath the eerie green sky, the black-and-white dog sitting watchful at her feet. "Sometimes they just have to leave the bodies—can't get a rescue squad down, and if a storm comes up, it's too dangerous to bring in a helicopter."

Daniel turned to look at the countryside behind them. There was the road, gray and winding for a few hundred yards before it disappeared. Beyond the road a steep hill sloped upward, gorse-grown, with scattered cairns and a line of standing stones, dark and ominous. At the very top of the hill stood a tower of stone, its base littered with fragments of broken rock and the remains of a wall. "What's that?" he asked.

"It's a beacon. A watchtower. They're all along the coast."

"But what are they for?" said Daniel. "There's nothing here."

"They keep watch." Juda drew alongside him, chucking softly to the dog. "People have been here for thousands of years—digging for tin, mostly, but gold and silver, too. Tourmaline. There's disused mines all over the West, and some still active. In the early days, they just dug trenches in the ground and looked for metals. They made beautiful things, the people who lived here."

She bent to pluck a blade-shaped leaf and handed it to him, so he could see the white flower blossoming from its base. "Asphodels. This is when they bloom. May Day."

"But the towers—what were they watching for?"

"Raiders. And us." She turned to stare at the ocean. "We were not invaders or conquerors. All that they knew was that we were unlike them. They didn't know we found them beautiful. They didn't know that we found this"—her arm swept out to indicate sea, cliffs, ruined towers, and standing stones, all the night-glimmering world around them—"all this, all this, beautiful. . . ."

Her pale eyes glittered, and her face shone with a joy like grief. "What was the name of your book? Nick told me, while we were waiting for you at Learmont's."

Daniel stared at the flower in his hand. He could hear the pounding of the sea, a faint throb in the earth beneath his feet. He let the blossom fall, to disappear amid the tangle of bracken and heather.

"*Mortal Love,*" he said.

"Mortal love," repeated Juda softly. "That's what draws us. Your taste, how fast you move and how soon you die . . . we see how with every moment you quicken with your own death and it is so beautiful— it moves us, it captivates us—"

She took a step toward him and he flinched, but Juda only shook her head, saying nothing, then reached for his face and very gently laid her fingers upon his cheek. The warmth of her flesh seeped into his

own, and for an instant there was no membrane of skin or bone between them, nothing between them at all, only a sweetness that he could
somehow feel rather than taste, a slow, thick pulsing inside her veins,
the flash of his own blood within her fingertips, and then her lips upon
his forehead, her breath warm upon his brow.

"What you feel for her, Daniel," she whispered, and her hands
rested upon his shoulders, light as leaves falling. "That desire for something hopeless, for what is already gone, for what can never be yours—
we, too, know that. Every time we touch you, we taste your mortality. It
is the closest we come to understanding what it is like for you: to live
knowing that you will die."

"But . . . you said that you die here as well—you said you become
trapped—"

She nodded. "We do. But it's not the same. You burn, somehow,
even after you die. We just go out, like a flame. And we leave nothing behind, no paintings, no books, no songs, no monuments. We don't understand them, but we love them, your making of them. And that is
what she desires. Seeing herself transmuted into all those things. She
craves that. She tries to make it happen. So that when she at last goes
out, something of her will remain here."

She gestured past the sea cliffs to the shifting dark. "There, nothing
ever changes. No one ages, everything is the same. Only your people
leave a mark upon the world. Like the sea, the way it shapes the rocks
over time? That's what you have done. That is what she wants: to be
changed, to bear the marks of time that you leave upon her. She herself
has tried to do as you do, to leave something permanent behind. She
does not understand that it scars you. She doesn't understand that it
can kill you. She never remembers that for you, for all of us, it cannot
last. Mortal love . . ."

She fell silent and laid her hand upon Fancy's head. Daniel looked
down to see the dog staring at him with prescient eyes, gold and gray-
blue.

"You don't believe me," Juda said.

"I don't believe in anything." Daniel looked away. "Or no, that's not it. I believe in everything now."

He drew a hand to his face. Exhaustion had almost driven Larkin from his head. Now she was back inside him, a pressure behind his eyes, his skull. "I can't live without her. Juda, I will die."

"Daniel, don't you understand? *She can't stay.* She doesn't belong here. She doesn't belong with you. None of us do. We have the chance tonight to return, all of us—"

"All of who?!" he cried. The dog gave a warning bark. "Val? She doesn't even know him! She—"

"Daniel, listen to me! You're wrong. They've known each other . . . forever. They quarreled, is all. She ran off and became trapped here. And her being here changes this place—both places, your world, ours. Our worlds suffer. We diminish. She has all but forgotten who she was, what she is—but I have not."

She lifted her head. Her skin had a twilit gleam, the same foxglove glow he had seen on Larkin's face—when?

All the ages he had known her could be measured in hours only.

"Daniel," said Juda. "Daniel, see me."

She raised her arm. A flare of blue-green ran down it: beneath the skin were spikes of emerald lightning, forearm, fingers all aflame, and, where her heart should have been, a trembling green-black shadow like branching dendrites, neurons, a tree.

"Who are you?" he whispered.

"Give me your hand." She was neither man nor woman but a thing that moved in light. "I will make amends, Daniel. You'll forget her, it will be better. You can go home."

"No . . ."

He backed away, shading his eyes so he wouldn't see her, that slim figure flickering green and black against the night sky. "Let me come with you! Juda, please! I swear, just let me see her again—let me talk to her, I can help her, she knows me, she—"

"*No!*" For an instant the flare of emerald nearly blinded him. Juda seemed immense, a tower of green flame rising from the hillside, streams of shadow racing toward the sea cliff. "You will *not*—"

Daniel cringed, yet even as he raised his arms, the violent blaze of green faded. He blinked, phantom bursts of gold and black flickering across his vision, but beside him there was only a slender young man, his tousled blond hair damp with sweat.

"Juda?" said Daniel.

The boy lifted his head, and yes, it was Juda, her skin moon-pale and sickly. She bent and retched, hugging her arms to her thin chest, then straightened, her entire body trembling.

"I couldn't have hurt you, Daniel." Her voice was barely a whisper. "I no longer have any real power here. We have so little time. . . ."

She coughed, then weakly snapped her fingers. Fancy dashed back through the bracken, panting. From somewhere high upon the hillside came the querulous cry of a tawny owl.

"You're a fucking fool, lad," Juda said. "She'll drive you mad, whether you have her or no. And you won't have her, Daniel."

She turned and headed for the car. He stared after her, surrounded by the smell of crushed fern and the memory of Larkin beneath him, the scent of apple blossom, feathers brushing his cheek, Juda's mouth upon his brow.

"I will!" he shouted, and followed her.

In the car he fought to keep anguish from overwhelming the memory of what he'd seen. Could the world really be as Juda said, permeable and malleable, combustible as dry grass, vulnerable to the smallest spark, then dangerous, even fatal?

Could *he* be like that?

Just days ago the notion would have been so absurd that he would never have considered giving voice to it. Now he could think of nothing else. The world had blown up in his hand, in his head, like a bottle rocket with a defective fuse. And here he was as he always had been, taking notes in the front seat, the detached outsider, the critic watching the show.

Yet he was no longer detached. Somehow—and this was the most incredible and terrifying thing of all—somehow, without wanting to or even knowing it had happened, *he* had become part of the show. And it was as he had always feared it would be: he had let his guard down just once, just for a few hours, and the entire universe had come crashing down around him.

"Shit," he said.

He still had his wallet, plenty of cash, and a half-dozen credit cards; he could get out and start walking, and eventually he would come to a place where he could sleep for what remained of the night. In the morning he could take a cab to Penzance and hop the railway back to London. He'd find another flat; he'd finish his book, return to D.C., and await a modest success as a first-time author even as he resumed his work at the *Horizon*.

None of this would ever have happened. His friendship with Nick would be pretty much as it always had been; Larkin Meade would be a woman he'd spent a hazy night with once in a narrow boat moored on the Regents Canal. He would call Balthazar Warnick and meet him for lunch, and they would talk about Daniel's book and the pleasantly dull details of university life. The world would be as it ever was, as it really was. And so would he.

They continued on down the coast. Juda said nothing, only stared at the road before them as it wound through a tiny village, a cluster of farms, and a pub, past a worn wooden sign that read PADWITHIEL. On one side stretched the endless moor, on the other the line of sea cliffs.

Perhaps a mile distant, a rugged promontory extended from the headland. A narrow ridge of stone connected it to the coast, a natural bridge. On the point Daniel could just discern a ruined building.

"What's that?" He sat up. "Is it Tintagel?"

"No. Tintagel's that way."

She pointed farther south and west, to where another spar of land rose from the Atlantic. "That's Sarsinmoor—what's left of it anyway. One of your insane asylums. Like Broadmoor, or Bedlam. It was destroyed by a fire in the nineteenth century."

The car made a sharp turn down a long, deeply rutted lane. "This isn't a four-star B&B," Juda warned. "There's a couch in the front room; you can sleep there. I was going to give you the bedroom, but I think I'm going to claim it. I . . . I'm not very well."

She shivered, hunched over the steering column. For the first time, Daniel pitied her—or him; whatever Juda was. She looked ravaged, her eyes sunken, her hands a dark, dank blue. The awful thought came to him that what he had seen of Juda over the last few days was just a kind of disguise, Juda passing for whatever she thought humans looked like.

In which case, Larkin . . .

"Here," whispered Juda. The car shuddered to a stop in front of a cottage. A single, wind-harrowed oak stood somber as a gallows where the drive ended. "We're here."

She stumbled out and walked unsteadily toward the door. The cottage was set into a small declivity, like a stone tossed into a bowl; it was built of weathered granite, with a slated roof and shallow eaves, small recessed windows, a rotting rain barrel at one corner. Everything was overgrown, seemingly abandoned. By the front door were lengths of old iron pipe and plastic bags overflowing with moldering plasterboard and insulation.

"I've had the plumbing updated." Juda unlocked the door and pushed it open. "It's a mess, sorry."

He followed her in. A single, sparely furnished room, just a sofa and two armchairs with faded chintz upholstery, flagstone floors, a step down to a tiny kitchenette, two steps into a narrow hallway. "Bathroom's there," said Juda. "My room's there. Couch is there. I have to sleep or I'll be ill. Don't try to leave."

She stared at him, her eyes feverishly bright. "People get lost at their own doorsteps here on the moor. Mist comes up, you'll disappear forever."

She ran a hand across her face, and he could see her fingers trembling. "I should never have let you come."

"Where are they?"

She shook her head. "No, Daniel. Stay inside. It's not safe for you out there. Not now, not tonight." She turned and started for the bedroom. "You can take the car back tomorrow."

"Me? What about you?" he demanded. "What about *them?*"

She went into the bedroom, closing the door after her. Daniel strode angrily toward the front door. The dog Fancy sat there. Its tail waved slightly and it whined, but when he reached for the knob, it got to its feet, growling.

"Right," said Daniel.

He turned angrily and looked for another way out.

There was none. He saw a shallow fireplace filled with ash and charred turfs, an electric heater, a chair piled with camphor-smelling crocheted afghans. He went into the tiny kitchenette, grimacing, and tried to recall when he'd last eaten. Bread the previous morning, he thought, and absinthe. He wasn't hungry—on the contrary, he felt wired, edgy to the point of mania—but he looked around till he found a tin of Cornish gingerbread, stale, but he ate it anyway. He put some water in a bowl for Fancy, then wandered back into the living room.

"Here," he said, setting the bowl down beside the dog. "Not that you deserve it. I should have let them shoot you."

His watch read nearly 4:00 A.M. Already the sky was growing pale, the green spring night draining into ultramarine and citron yellow, luminous as the streaked curve of an abalone shell. He peered out a window, could barely make out Juda's car through yellow-green mist. The lone oak was shrouded as with cobwebs. He turned and started to pace across the small room, his hand slipping into his pocket and closing around the little talisman he still bore: the acorn. He thought of Larkin as he had first seen her in the room at Sira's flat, thought of her staring through him, her arms tight around that tall figure on the motorcycle.

Valentine Comstock.

Daniel's stomach clenched. He stopped, made a fist, and slammed it hard against the wall.

"Shit."

The pain was intense and satisfying. He bashed his hand again, and again, until his arm ached. When he finally stopped, he looked across the room to see Fancy watching him, head cocked and mismatched eyes narrowed.

"Just a little taste," said Daniel. "Just a fucking hint."

The dog's ears sleeked back against its skull. It growled as Daniel stared at it. Fancy stared back unblinking and continued to growl, a low sound that ran into the thrum of waves against the nearby cliffs.

She hadn't seen him. She hadn't seen him at all. And yet only minutes had passed—seconds—before she'd fled with Comstock. Daniel stood in the middle of the room, breathing hard.

She doesn't belong here. She doesn't belong with you.

"Yes she does," he said under his breath. "She does. She will."

He didn't know how long he stood there, talking to himself, or maybe he was only thinking. He didn't know, he didn't care. Only when he looked up again, the windows gleamed more brightly, a clear pale yellow veined with new green, like crocuses.

It was dawn.

He shook his head, then drew a long breath, to see if that changed anything. No. He stared at his hands. He felt strong; he extended his arms and felt the muscles tighten, flexed his fingers, then relaxed, and looked at the front door.

The dog Fancy sat staring at him. Its eyes caught a shaft of light and glowed, no longer blue and gold but a radiant emerald green.

"Fancy," he whispered.

The dog scrambled to its feet. It turned and pawed at the door, whining.

"Fancy."

He looked back at the door to Juda's room. It was still closed. Silently he crossed to the front door, wary lest the dog turn on him.

It did not. It remained where it was, ears canted upright, tail straight behind it, jaws closed tight as it moaned softly and gazed at the door. He reached for the knob, hesitating before he grasped it and turned. The dog whined louder as he cracked the door open.

Her scent overwhelmed him. Apple blossom, green apple, a smell of the sea that was not the sea he knew.

Closer, the stolen notebook had read.

They were very near.

"Fancy," he said softly. "Here, Fancy. Smell them?"

He slipped outside, the dog crowding after him. "That's it, Fancy— take me to her."

With a low bark, the dog arrowed out into the dawn. He started after it, then stopped and ran to the pile of trash by the door. He grabbed a length of iron pipe and hefted it—heavy as a club and longer than his arm. It whistled as he slashed at the air; then, clutching it to him, he turned and ran after the dog.

A wind had risen from the sea. Mist whirled and lifted around him. He could see as clearly as though it were broad daylight.

There was the main road, there the downward slope that led to Sarsinmoor, there a sky the color of sunshot rain, there the shining sea.

And there was the dog. It stood at the edge of the road, looking back at him as he ran, and fairly somersaulted with excitement. He was near enough now that he could see its entire body shudder, as with a yelp it turned and, faster than he could have dreamed, raced across the road and on down the stretch of heath toward Sarsinmoor.

"Fancy, wait!"

He ran, his legs whipped by gorse and blackthorn. The iron pipe burned his hand as though aflame. Ahead of him the collie ran so fast it seemed to skim like a seabird above the moor. Daniel followed it down the hillside without stopping, until he reached the narrow spit of rock and turf that connected the promontory to the headland. He shoved the pipe into the ground and leaned on it, gasping.

Fancy was already a speck on the far side. Daniel watched as the dog angled off toward the ruins of the building. He could just make out the silhouette of a motorcycle, black beneath one tumbled wall.

"Fancy! Wait!"

But he knew it didn't matter now. He didn't need the dog. As he straightened, the wind came up from the sea, fresh and warm, so thick with the smell of apple blossom that he was dizzied and had to cover his mouth and nose until the faintness passed.

"Larkin." He grabbed the length of pipe and began to walk across the causeway. "Larkin, wait."

He did not look to either side. Far, far below he could feel the sea; droplets of spray dashed him as the spar of land beneath his feet shuddered. Ahead a gray-green veil clung to turf and stone, rising to engulf him, then falling away as he cleaved it, parrying the air with the iron pipe, and walked through. Only when he reached the other side did he stop, his breath coming fast as he stared at what was before him.

Once it must have been a marvel, beautiful as one of those stately homes he'd glimpsed from Juda's car: the other England that haunted this one, the realm he had dreamed of for as long as he could remember. Waterloo Sunset, Shangri-la, Logres—the world Nick had mocked him for falling in love with, the world Nick had always known was really there, the world Daniel had believed was forever denied to him, a place where he had no more right to be than the moon.

But he was there now. He gazed at the wrecked beams and joists of Sarsinmoor, and it was as though he had known it all his life, stones dark with soot and the blackened marks of flame, charred timbers and fragments of glass like eyes, a porcelain sign dangling from a split beam, its surface crazed, but he could still read the black letters.

DINING ROOM, APOTHECARY, KITCHEN, SCULLERY, REFRACTORY

As in a dream, he walked through it, the wreckage of Sarsinmoor. Everything was overgrown with tall yellow grass, green-tufted heathers, and long, delicate running vines with fragile white blossoms that loosed a breath of lavender and smoke when he touched them. He stepped over collapsed walls and through charred openings that had once been windows, picked his way among cracked stones and thickets of greenery, using his pipe now as a cane, now as a sword, hacking through vines and crumbling mortar. Now and then he recognized some remnant of Victorian life—a metal bucket, a blackened sarcophagus that had been a bathtub. Of the dog Fancy, he saw no sign.

But as he approached the far side of the ruin, Daniel came across what appeared to be far more ancient relics. Walls formed of compressed slates, a medieval arch opening onto a tumbled landscape of turf-grown stones and trees, the remains of a small cottage overlooking the sea. The scent of apple blossom was so strong it choked him, and for several minutes he stood motionless beneath the arch, one hand resting upon the sharp slates, the other clutching the iron pipe to his chest. He could feel something pushing at him, a weight like water rushing down, denying him entry.

"I will come!" he shouted. "Tell them I have come!"

He came through.

Before him was a vale of apple trees in bloom. Light filtered through white blossoms and pale leaves, light the color of tourmaline and shallow water, greenstone and beryl and new-grown ivy. He shut his eyes and stepped forward, feeling his way, the earth soft beneath his feet, until blossoms brushed against his cheeks and he felt the gentle touch of branches grazing his brow. The smell of apple blossom no longer sickened him; indeed, he no longer breathed it at all but felt it move softly in and out and through his very being, like wind in a room where all the casements have suddenly been flung open. He raised the hand holding the iron pipe, but the pipe was gone: he held a slender branch, curled leaves like fingers grasping his. He opened his eyes and lifted his face to the trees, white and pink and pale green spattering his cheeks like rain. He opened his mouth to taste honey and green fruit and the sweet cooked flesh of salmon, the sugared bite of wormwood, bittersweet and healing.

Here, someone called him. *Here!*

It was not a person, but Fancy's low urgent bark. Daniel lowered his head and saw the collie, almost hidden within a soft thicket of grass and green ferns. It stared at him with eyes no longer warning but alert and sharp with delight as a child's.

Here! it barked again, and Daniel went to see what it guarded.

"Larkin," he whispered.

They were asleep upon the ground, nestled within a bed of clover and woodbine and fallen apple blossom, both taller than he had remembered, taller than anyone he had ever seen, their long white limbs entwined and their dark hair twisted together as ivy enwraps the tree. Almost they might have been twins, or one form faced into a mirror: the same high, wide brow; the same strong mouth and columnar neck; long-fingered hands with fingers linked, breast pressed to breast and faces slightly upturned so that they shone in the first spark of morning, gold and green and white. A needle could not have slipped between them, nor a sword; and where their flesh met beneath their hollowed throats, he could see a single strong pulse, like the measured fall of water into a still pool.

They have one heart, he thought, and looked away, amazed and shamed, his own heart breaking inside him.

Above him the apple trees stirred. The sky beyond them was clear and bright, though the sun had not yet showed above the horizon. He could hear the dog Fancy breathing and a twitter of birdsong. He lifted his hand to brush the hair from his face, looked down and saw something in the grass at his feet—a notebook, its cover stained with dew.

Closer.

He picked it up, opened it, and slowly began to turn the pages. Hundreds of pen-and-ink drawings, unbearably beautiful and strange—women with blossoms for breasts and eyes, birds that became men, an army of butterflies brandishing rapiers and javelins against a doctor wielding an immense hypodermic needle. A boy in a straitjacket, grinning as tiny winged creatures issued from his mouth and ears and nostrils, each minute figure as painstakingly drafted as an architectural drawing, each one lovely as the apple blossoms nodding overhead.

All, all were Larkin Meade.

Within her is the world. A time there was when Vernoraxia was lost to us and with her all our hope. A girl green as elderflower. You make her owls when she wants to be flowers. I am that queen.

He reached the last page. It showed a woman, a crown of vines and flowers upon her brow, standing alone within a grove of winter trees. Her face was so rent with grief that for a moment Daniel closed his eyes and looked away. Then he turned back and read the final words.

I have wonyd ten wynters and more
In wyldernes wyth mekyll sore,
And have won my quen awey,
Owte of the land of fary. . . .

Kyng Orfew. Daniel knew it from his grad-school days. But what kind of teenage boy would quote from a twelfth-century Breton lay?

The quen was awey twight,
And wyth the feyry awey i-nome:
Ther was cry, wepyng, and wo;
The kyng unto hys chamber yede tho,
And oft he knelyd onne the ston,
And made grete sorow for sche was gon,
That ne hys lyve was i-spent.

I am that queen.

He closed the sketchbook. One last minute he gazed at her where she lay sleeping. He knew—absolutely, irrevocably, hopelessly—that he would never again look upon anything so beautiful, anyone he would desire like this, to the point of madness, mayhem. *It destroys you, yet she would die of it: mortal love.* Then, stepping carefully among the sweet crushed bracken and trailing woodbine, he leaned down to place the book between the lovers. It rested in the dark fissure between Larkin's breast and Val's, and as Daniel drew back, he heard her make a soft sound deep in her throat, then saw her smile as her hand moved to cup her lover's cheek.

Quickly Daniel turned away. He had just started to walk from the grove—blindly, his breath a stone in his throat—when someone grasped his arm. He pulled up short, ready to strike whoever was there, and saw that it was Juda Trent.

"You didn't wait." She was white, her face racked by fear. Then she stared past him to where the lovers lay side by side beneath the trees. Her expression changed to disbelief, and Daniel knew that her fear had not been for him. *"Oh . . ."*

She darted past him, flinging herself down to kneel beside them with her hands held out protectively. Beside her the Border collie stood guard, tail wagging wildly though it made no sound, and as Daniel watched, he saw Juda's spare form fill with light like water, until, like the other two, she shone, tall and beautiful and unsparing. She was no more a woman now than he was, nor a man, yet still he could see something of Juda Trent flickering within that form, like the small blue heart of a flame.

"They are safe," she whispered. Her gaze met Daniel's, and he saw that her eyes brimmed. "Daniel Rowlands. Thank you."

He said nothing, just shook his head. Juda got to her feet again and stepped to his side, looming above him like a tree. Heat radiated from her as from a furnace. He forced himself to remain still, not to flee. When she touched his brow, a small gasp escaped him, though he continued to stare fiercely at the ferns and flowers clustered around his feet. For a long time, he didn't speak. When finally he did, his voice was low but steady.

"'Lord, this question would I ask—which was the most fair and generous, as thinketh you?'"

"You, Daniel," Juda said softly. "You were."

He nodded, and at last he raised his head.

"Thank you." He glanced to where the sleeping queen and her consort lay. As though she heard him, the woman stirred, lifting her head and staring dazed at the sweep of green and white above. She gave a small exhalation of relief at the glowing form beside her, and bent to kiss his brow.

And as she did, her gaze fell upon Daniel, watching from a few feet away. For an instant he thought she did not see him. Then, "Daniel," she whispered.

He nodded. At her side the sleeping king yawned and blinked, but she had already gotten to her feet and in two long steps was at Daniel's side.

"I thought I dreamed you," she said, gazing down at him. He still could not speak, for mingled grief and joy. That she had remembered. That somehow he, too, was real. "But . . . ?" She looked confused.

He shook his head and, for the first time, smiled. "No. I mean, I don't think so."

He laughed wryly, looking at the vale of blossoming trees, the dark-green ridge that marked the cliff edge, sea and sky melding into a single scrolled scape, shining, verdant, a flare of blinding emerald-white in the center of the eastern horizon like a tear in the world. His breath quickened, and he looked away, to where Juda stood beckoning at the other figure just rising from the green earth.

"We must go," Juda said. She crossed to Daniel, the dog Fancy at her feet. It alone remained unchanged, except for its eyes, green and gold now and laughing as a boy's. "Daniel. Do you remember what I told you last night? I can make amends. . . ."

Her outstretched hand reached for his face, but he turned aside.

"No! No," he said, no longer caring that he wept. "That would be . . . that would be worse."

Juda stared at him. "Very well," she said. Then, her face ablaze, she turned to the others. "It is done, then! My lord—"

The figure that had been Val stared at Daniel kindly. He seemed scarcely less feckless than when Daniel had first seen him, but then he smiled, with an expression so rapturous and knowing that Daniel could only laugh and raise his hands in defeat.

"Go!" Daniel said. Fancy barked, the sound echoing from the cliff like horns blowing, and Daniel waved good-bye to him, too.

The three turned and started for the cliff. Suddenly Daniel cried after them.

"Wait!"

He thrust his hand into his pocket and withdrew the acorn. "This!" he said, running up to the woman. She stared down at him as he held it to her. He swallowed, his mouth turned to sand, and said, "This—the acorn. It's yours. It must mean something to you. I mean, I saw you, and . . ."

She looked at him, then at the acorn, as though struggling to recall what it was. Then she smiled.

"Oh, no," she said. She extended her hand, her fingers unfurling like a leaf. "It belongs here. It is just that I always found them so beautiful and strange. Like everything here. That they are so small and so quickly grow."

She closed her hand around his, and for a moment his entire being rang like a bell. "It would not thrive if I were to take it. Keep it," she said. "Make it grow."

He could say nothing, just, at last, "Larkin . . ."

She smiled, as though recalling a childhood name. One final moment she gazed at him. Then she turned and joined the others waiting for her.

A voice like thunder rolled across the grass. "You can keep the motorcycle," it said. "The key's in the lock."

Daniel nodded. He drew the acorn to his lips, shut his eyes against hot tears, and kissed the smooth small bole. From the near distance came a volley of furious barking, ecstatic shouts of amazement, joy, welcome; crashing waves and, faint and far-off as traffic on the M-1, the sound of horns.

"Don't go!" he cried, and opened his eyes.

The world had turned to gold. There was no line of demarcation between land's end and sky and sea. Before him a city hung in the air, spires and pennons and a whirl of birds, blue and gold and silver, green leaves and the endless flash of things that flew and dove and sang. The world he knew rolled back like a wave from sand, the world was revealed: one blazing instant like a flash of flame, and he could see it all, both of them, all.

"Larkin!" he shouted. *"Larkin!"*

And it was gone. Before him the sun rose from the dark roil that was the Atlantic, bands of green and yellow striping the sea cliffs. He stood upon a small rise, alone. Behind him was the ruins of a cottage, the wreckage of a manor house. It was morning. The air felt cool and sweet; there was a smell of rain, heavy clouds upon the horizon that boded a storm later. At the farthest reaches of his vision, on the sea beyond the black spars of Tintagel's headland, he saw the white flash of a four-masted schooner under way. No apple trees, no blossoming vale.

Only, tucked into a patch of bracken as within a wren's nest, a sketchbook with faded green binding and carefully inked letters.

And, held so tightly in his hand that he bore its mark for many days, a brown-and-green weight like a living jewel.

An acorn.

Part Four

The Order of Release

CHAPTER SIXTEEN

The Order of Release

THE GUARDIAN
June 11

TYCOON PHILANTHROPIST FEARED LOST AT SEA

Billionaire philanthropist Russell Thomas Learmont, who re-tired earlier this year as CEO of Winsoame Pharmaceuticals, has been reported missing and is feared lost at sea off the coast of Aranbega Island, Maine. Learmont, former head of the world's largest pharmaceutical corporation and an experi-enced sailor, departed Hastings on May 1 aboard his 75-foot four-masted yacht Tinker's Dame. Lawrence Feld, a spokes-man for Winsoame, reported that yesterday afternoon contact with the Tinker's Dame was abruptly disrupted, less than two hours after the yacht departed Cushing and shortly before it was due to arrive at Aranbega Harbor. Fishermen aboard a small boat off Vinalhaven Island reported receiving a distress call shortly after four p.m., but rescue efforts were hindered by high seas and savage gales clocked at more than 73 miles per hour. Learmont was traveling with a crew of six, including celebrity chef Gustav Parnell. The United States Coast Guard has begun search-and-recovery efforts, but hopes of finding survivors are slim.

THE GUARDIAN

September 17

The British art world rejoiced today when it was announced that the collection of the late Russell T. Learmont, philanthropist and owner of the world's largest collection of art brut and so-called outsider art, has been left to the Tate Gallery. In addition to the collection, which consists of some five hundred paintings, sculptures, notebooks, and drawings dating back to the seventeenth century, Learmont left a gift in excess of £50 million, to be held in trust by the Tate in perpetuity for the establishment of a gallery to house the permanent collection.

"We are just ecstatic about the whole thing," Tate spokesman Garrett Swann said in a public statement. Plans for the gallery are already under way, with construction slated to begin sometime late in July. In the meantime, selections from the collection will be on display at the Tate Modern, beginning later this autumn.

TATE ART NOTES

7 November

The much-anticipated opening of "Eros and Pan: Selections from the Russell T. Learmont Collection" will take place on Saturday, 3 December, with a private reception for Tate Supporters following a lecture by Professor Balthazar Warnick of the University of the Archangels and St. John the Divine. Warnick, a longtime friend of Learmont's and trustee of the Learmont Collection, will speak on the origins of Learmont's collection in that of the philanthropist's grandfather, the eminent Victorian physician Thomas Learmont.

A highlight of "Eros and Pan" will be the first public viewing of a symbolically charged nude pen-and-ink drawing by the hitherto unknown artist Evienne Upstone, believed to be a patient of Dr. Learmont. Upstone's drawing was recently discovered beneath Radborne Comstock's painting *Iseult* during the course of its restoration by the Tate staff. Her work, titled *Nisus* by the curator who discovered it, is considered remarkable in both the frankness of its subject matter and the fact that Tate researchers have been unable to find any record of the artist, who is believed to have died in the same asylum fire that killed the Victorian "mad painter" Jacobus Candell in 1883.

There will be a fee for this special exhibition.

CHAPTER SEVENTEEN

The Masterstroke

Hold beauty.
—*Anne Carson, "The Beauty of the Husband"*

Early in December, Daniel visited the Learmont exhibit at the Tate Modern. There were a number of works by self-taught artists of the last two centuries: notebooks and sketches, maps of imaginary places, architectural drawings, quite a few unsettling sculptures, two works by the Victorian fairy painter Jacobus Candell, and several paintings by Radborne Comstock, including the diptych *The Love Philtre (Tristan and Iseult)* one-half of which Daniel recognized from Learmont's study.

The already notorious drawings by Evienne Upstone hung on the opposite wall—pen-and-inks with colorwash. A card identified the largest one as *Nisus.* There was little known of the drawings or their creator, but Daniel had read that the Tate had hopes of discovering more about her in the trove of material left by Russell Learmont. Daniel had his own suspicions, especially after viewing Radborne Comstock's tragic and haunting *Iseult.*

Comstock's work, sadly, looked pallid and relentlessly mundane in comparison to Upstone's. *Nisus* had odd visual echoes of artists as disparate as Mark Rothko and Odilon Redon, Gustave Moreau and

Willem de Kooning. It was at once abstract and sexually suggestive—almost pornographic, Daniel thought with sad amusement. There were long explanatory notes beside each drawing, and he waited patiently until he could read those for *Nisus,* compiled by the noted feminist scholar and self-styled agitator Charlotte Moylan.

One of the only erotic male nudes by a Victorian woman artist, and certainly the only one to so blatantly engage the viewer in the highly sexualized, masculine-claimed dynamic prevalent from that age to our own, *Nisus* is a superb example of . . .

"She tends to come on a bit strong," said a voice beside Daniel. "Charlotte Moylan, I mean. She was a student of mine, some years ago. At the Divine. She must be about your age, I imagine."

Daniel turned. To his delight he saw the slender figure of Balthazar Warnick, elegantly clad in a charcoal-gray suit and bespoke shirt that matched his sea-blue eyes. "Professor Warnick! I thought you were back in D.C.!"

They shook hands, Warnick giving his melancholy smile as he glanced at the framed drawing. "I was. I came over a few weeks ago for the opening—I'm on the board of the foundation Russell set up for his collection. We have a trustees' meeting shortly, but I wanted to take another look at this."

They edged toward the center of the room to observe the crowds, small ones for Comstock's diptych, larger ones in front of *Nisus.*

"It really is incredible," said Daniel. He watched a group of American tourists gathering to read Charlotte Moylan's printed exegesis, all middle-aged women wearing T-shirts emblazoned NUNS ON THE RUN. "You know, that public perception about an artist could change so quickly, I mean literally overnight."

"Well, quickly, maybe," agreed Dr. Warnick. "But not convulsively.

I think that perhaps these big changes happen more like the way the body heals itself, when we sleep and dream. Who's to say that the world doesn't dream sometimes, too?"

"I guess." Daniel glanced curiously at Warnick, but the elegant figure only watched, smiling slightly, as the Nuns on the Run pointed at Upstone's drawing. "It's still weird, though."

Warnick turned, gesturing at the door. "Shall we?"

They strolled into the corridor. "What about you, Daniel?" asked Professor Warnick. "Last time we talked, you were on sabbatical. You were writing a book, weren't you? Did you finish it?"

Daniel shook his head. "No. It's strange, but I guess I just kind of burned out on that idea—the nonfiction one, I mean. But I've been thinking a lot lately about doing something completely different."

"Which is?"

"A novel. I applied for an extended leave of absence from the *Horizon*—they're not happy about it, but I can continue to do freelance writing from here. 'Rowlands's London Journal,' that kind of thing. And I can always just cash in an IRA if I have to.

"So I'm staying with my friend Nick Hayward, kind of kicking these ideas around. I have all these notes from the book I *was* working on, and . . . well, some other stuff that came to me over the last few months. I thought I might try to work them into something completely different—different for me, I mean. So. A novel."

"A novel." Professor Warnick looked up and gave him that enigmatic smile. "Do you have a title?"

"I do. *Mortal Love.* That's the title my other book was going to have."

"Have you told your publisher about this sudden change of heart?"

"Not yet. I figure I'll just hand them the finished manuscript and start running."

Balthazar laughed. "Well, if you need any help when the time comes, give me a call. I might be able to put you in touch with some people."

He paused and glanced back at the gallery they'd just left. "Do you know Charlotte Moylan's work?"

"Moylan?" Daniel shrugged. "Just the crazed Feminist Avenger stuff."

"I should introduce you to her. She's more interesting than you might think."

Daniel shook his head. "No more interesting women," he said. "Not till this book is done at least."

They went outside, where the blue-violet light of early evening streamed across the Thames, glinting off warehouses and the dome of St. Paul's, barely visible behind skyscrapers, the London Eye, and the arching web of the Millennium Bridge. Daniel was headed for where he'd left his motorcycle in the carpark, Warnick a few blocks north to Vinopolis for his meeting

"I would invite you along, but . . . well, trustees," Warnick said apologetically. "Russell left an incredible amount of work for us to do. Some of it I'd rather *not* do, but . . ."

He smiled his melancholy smile, then extended his hand. "Duty calls. Glad I ran into you, Daniel. Good luck with the novel. And please—call me when you get back to D.C."

Daniel shook his hand and smiled. "I'll do that. Thanks."

He stood and watched as Professor Warnick walked along the Embankment, a deceptively small man in a deceptively large city, until he disappeared into the London twilight.

It was well past 2:00 A.M. when Nick arrived home that night, laughing raucously as he shouted farewell to someone in the High Street, then banging his way upstairs.

"Danny boy!" he cried, and stormed into the kitchen. "Wakey-wakey! You wouldn't fucking believe who showed up after the gig, fucking—"

He stopped. All the lights were on. Music blared from the stereo—an electroclash version of the "Liebestod," and why in God's name would Daniel be listening to *that?* At the kitchen table, Daniel's gangly form was hunched over his laptop. Stacks of books and papers and notebooks were piled about him, coffee mugs, several empty bottles of fizzy water and a nearly full one of absinthe, the remains of dinner from Parkway Pizzeria.

"What the fuck is this?" demanded Nick.

"Shut up," said Daniel, and scowled at the computer screen. At his elbow were stacks of books and CDs—*Collected Poems* by Laura Riding, *Folklore of the British Isles,* Val Comstock's sketchbook, *Astral Weeks* and Nick's own *Sleeping with the Heroine,* along with a postcard from the Tate Gift Shop. "Not a single word from you now, Hayward."

Daniel glanced at the postcard—a reproduction of Radborne Comstock's diptych *The Love Philtre.* After a moment he looked up and flashed a beatific grin at his oldest friend.

"For God's sake, Nick," he said. "Can't you see I'm working?"